My Thomas

A NOVEL OF
MARTHA JEFFERSON'S LIFE

ROBERTA GRIMES

Ŧ

PUBLISHED BY DOUBLEDAY
a division of
Bantam Doubleday Dell Publishing Group, Inc.
666 Fifth Avenue, New York, New York 10103

DOUBLEDAY and the portrayal of an anchor
with a dolphin are trademarks of Doubleday,
a division of Bantam Doubleday Dell Publishing Group, Inc.

Book Design and illustrations by Cathy Braffet

Family Tree and Map by Patrice Fodero

This novel is a work of historical fiction. Names, characters, places, and incidents relating to nonhistorical figures are either the product of the author's imagination or are used fictitiously. Any resemblance of such nonhistorical incidents, places, or figures to actual events, locales, or persons, living or dead, is entirely coincidental.

Library of Congress Cataloging-in-Publication Data

Grimes, Roberta.
My Thomas : a novel of Martha Jefferson's life / by Roberta Grimes. —1st ed.
p.   cm.
1. Jefferson, Martha, 1748–1782—Fiction.   2. Jefferson, Thomas, 1743–1826—
Fiction.   3. United States—History—Revolution, 1775–1783—Fiction.   4. United
States—History—Colonial period, ca. 1600–1775—Fiction.   I. Title.
PS3557.R489983M9   1993
813'.54—dc20   92-14825
                                                                   CIP

ISBN 0-385-42399-3

Copyright © 1993 by Roberta Grimes

All Rights Reserved
Printed in the United States of America
January 1993

1   3   5   7   9   10   8   6   4   2

First Edition

For Oliver Christensen, my father and friend,
who didn't quite live to see this book in print.
He was a proud man full of grand ideas. I think
he and Thomas would have liked one another.

The Jefferson Family

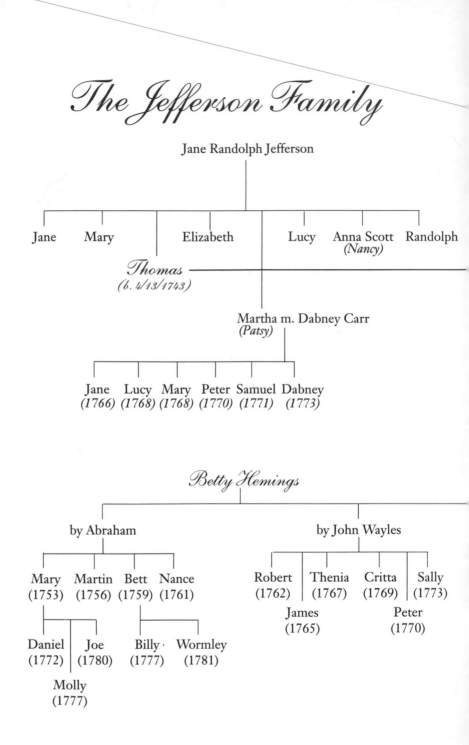

Jane Randolph Jefferson

Jane   Mary   Elizabeth   Lucy   Anna Scott   Randolph
                                    (Nancy)

Thomas
(b. 4/13/1743)

Martha m. Dabney Carr
(Patsy)

Jane   Lucy   Mary   Peter   Samuel   Dabney
(1766) (1768) (1768) (1770) (1771) (1773)

Betty Hemings

by Abraham   by John Wayles

Mary   Martin   Bett   Nance   Robert   Thenia   Critta   Sally
(1753) (1756) (1759) (1761)   (1762)   (1767)   (1769) (1773)
                                             James   Peter
                                             (1765)   (1770)

Daniel   Joe   Billy · Wormley
(1772) (1780)   (1777)   (1781)

Molly
(1777)

Includes only people mentioned in *My Thomas*.

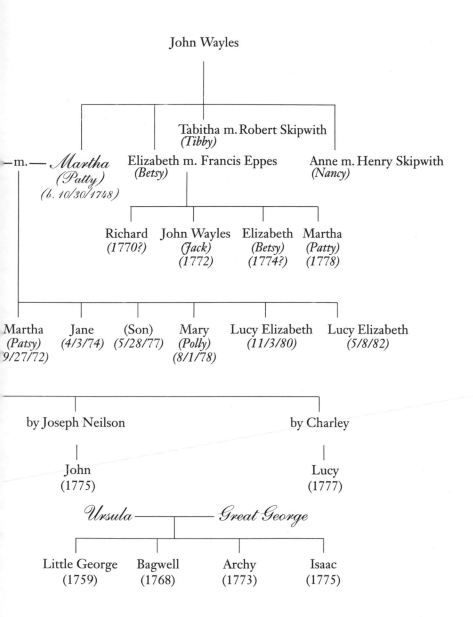

John Wayles

Tabitha m. Robert Skipwith
(Tibby)

—m.— *Martha*   Elizabeth m. Francis Eppes   Anne m. Henry Skipwith
(Patty)   *(Betsy)*   *(Nancy)*
(b. 10/30/1748)

Richard   John Wayles   Elizabeth   Martha
(1770?)   *(Jack)*   *(Betsy)*   *(Patty)*
(1772)   *(1774?)*   *(1778)*

Martha   Jane   (Son)   Mary   Lucy Elizabeth   Lucy Elizabeth
(Patty)   *(4/3/74)*   *(5/28/77)*   *(Polly)*   *(11/3/80)*   *(5/8/82)*
9/27/72)   *(8/1/78)*

by Joseph Neilson   by Charley

John   Lucy
(1775)   *(1777)*

Ursula ——————— *Great George*

Little George   Bagwell   Archy   Isaac
(1759)   *(1768)*   *(1773)*   *(1775)*

Martha Jefferson's Virginia

Maury River

▲ *Charlottesville*

Monticello ● ● Shadwell

Rivanna River

Spring Forest

Elk Hill

James River

Elk Island

Fine Creek

Hors du Monde ●

Poplar Forest ●

Appomattox River

N

W   E

S

● Plantation
▲ Town

kahoe

▲ *Richmond*

Chickahominy River

r

nchester

Berkeley
Westover

Bermuda
Hundred

Shirley

The Forest

▲ *Petersburg*

Williamsburg
▲
Jamestown ▲*York*

*Chesapeake
Bay*

Newport News ▲*Hampton*

▲*Norfolk*
▲
Portsmouth

ACKNOWLEDGMENTS

THE THOMAS JEFFERSON MEMORIAL FOUNDATION WAS remarkably helpful to an unknown writer who presumed to tell this very private story. Lucia C. Stanton, its director of research, answered for me many dozens of questions, some of which were so odd and obscure that they must have required a great deal of work.

Alf J. Mapp, Jr.'s wonderful two-volume biography of Jefferson makes Thomas live again for the reader as he must have seemed to those he loved. Alf encouraged me to write *My Thomas* and answered my questions along the way; then when it was complete he read portions of the manuscript and made a number of helpful suggestions.

For their time freely given, and for their friendship, I am deeply grateful.

AUTHOR'S PREFACE

*T*HOMAS JEFFERSON IS ONE OF OUR GREATEST HEROES. We owe him an incomparable debt, yet few of us know him as anything more than a dusty part of our distant past. For this he has only himself to blame. Always intensely private, he allowed no public examination of his personal life, and of that part of his life which he held the most private he tried to destroy every bit of evidence. Jefferson described his marriage as "ten years [of] unchequered happiness," yet without hard evidence most biographers have paid little attention to his marriage. This has distorted our understanding of Jefferson and made really knowing the man more difficult. By putting a living wife into the void of his marriage I hope to begin to correct this distortion and let readers come to know Thomas Jefferson as only his wife ever could have known him.

Jefferson destroyed Martha's journals and letters, but a surprising amount of evidence remains in the unswept corners and cracks of his life; we can come to know her pretty well. Although presented as a novel, this book is meant to be accurate in its depiction of Thomas and Martha. If her journal had survived, I believe that this is pretty much the way it would have read.

My Thomas

FOREWORD

Sarah Eston Hemings
August 14, 1946

MY GRANDMOTHER BELONGED TO THOMAS JEFFERson. That is my little claim to fame. She said she was something more than his slave, she claimed he was the father of her children, but you can't blame her much when you think about the kind of life she must have led. For a long time I thought her little lie was only a harmless grab at glory, but then I read this book that you are holding open in your hand.

I expected to carry my secrets with me wherever I am going, up or down, but I find myself now eighty-nine. At eighty-nine you finally get some distance. At eighty-nine you care a whole lot less for the feelings of people a hundred years dead and what you care about, if you care about anything, is neatness. Leaving the place a little neater.

You ought to be told I never passed the eighth grade, but I taught a school for thirty years and I worked as librarian thirty more. In Wisconsin in the seventies they let you teach if you were single and able to control the boys, and I moved to the library in 1900 when they tried to make me get a certificate. So I know words, and since I know words I was able to teach myself the rest. I spent sixty years drumming that fact into children and not a tenth of them took my advice, so the rest of them lived and died plain stupid. At eighty-nine I've even stopped caring about that.

This book that follows is a lady's journal. I had it from my mother when she died in '16 and she had it from my father, who died in 1860 when I was only four. He had it in turn from his mother, Sally. He was the youngest of her children. Sally Hemings had it down from Tom, who took it from the dying hand of the lady, and that was in 1782. So you see, the time is short and the hands are few.

I never cared much for Thomas Jefferson. Never mind the fact I can claim a connection. My father was a slave of his, but my father was only one-eighth black and late in his life he chose to live white. Until this minute I myself was white, so now I am telling my first secret. It tickles me to say it. I live in a home here that won't take colored but nobody will see this until I am dead, and I laugh to think of them coming in here after the fact and fumigating my room. That thought does give me the greatest pleasure.

So I have this journal down from my mother. She gave it to me and told me its story and she told me to pass it to my own daughter, even though she knew I was sixty years old and never married in my life. She was addled, poor soul. She lost her mind while I have lost my body, and I assure you hers was the greater loss. So I had this book but I tucked it away for six or seven years. It was my mother's and the sight of it pained me with all the whole baggage of pain I feel in dealing with your dead mother when both of you should have done things different but now it is very much too late. They broke my leg. Broken bones to me now are like a bump on elbow since my bones are so brittle with age and decay, but my first break was my first laying up, I needed something to do then I thought of my mother's old tattered leather-bound book the pages falling out and the folded letters stuck in here and there.

That first time through it was hard to read, Mrs. Jefferson used the old f-for-s and her spelling was peculiar, and her punctuation was only periods at the ends of run-on sentences that linked several natural paragraphs. I could see her dipping, dipping and writing, then lifting her head to think of a period. Charming, but very hard to read.

I learned enough, though, to want to know more. There was an old claim, after all, that Thomas Jefferson was my

FOREWORD

Sarah Eston Hemings
August 14, 1946

$\mathcal{M}$Y GRANDMOTHER BELONGED TO THOMAS JEFFER-
son. That is my little claim to fame. She said she was something
more than his slave, she claimed he was the father of her children,
but you can't blame her much when you think about the kind of life
she must have led. For a long time I thought her little lie was only a
harmless grab at glory, but then I read this book that you are holding open in your hand.

I expected to carry my secrets with me wherever I am going, up
or down, but I find myself now eighty-nine. At eighty-nine you
finally get some distance. At eighty-nine you care a whole lot less
for the feelings of people a hundred years dead and what you care
about, if you care about anything, is neatness. Leaving the place a
little neater.

You ought to be told I never passed the eighth grade, but I
taught a school for thirty years and I worked as librarian thirty
more. In Wisconsin in the seventies they let you teach if you were
single and able to control the boys, and I moved to the library in
1900 when they tried to make me get a certificate. So I know
words, and since I know words I was able to teach myself the rest. I

spent sixty years drumming that fact into children and not a tenth of them took my advice, so the rest of them lived and died plain stupid. At eighty-nine I've even stopped caring about that.

This book that follows is a lady's journal. I had it from my mother when she died in '16 and she had it from my father, who died in 1860 when I was only four. He had it in turn from his mother, Sally. He was the youngest of her children. Sally Hemings had it down from Betty, who took it from the dying hand of the lady, and that was in 1782. So you see, the time is short and the hands are few.

I never cared much for Thomas Jefferson. Never mind the fact I can claim a connection. My father was a slave of his, but my father was only one-eighth black and late in his life he chose to live white. Until this minute I myself was white, so now I am telling my first secret. It tickles me to say it. I live in a home here that won't take colored but nobody will see this until I am dead, and I laugh to think of them coming in here after the fact and fumigating my room. That thought does give me the greatest pleasure.

So I have this journal down from my mother. She gave it to me and told me its story and she told me to pass it to my own daughter, even though she knew I was sixty years old and never married in my life. She was addled, poor soul. She lost her mind while I have lost my body, and I assure you hers was the greater loss. So I had this book but I tucked it away for six or seven years. It was my mother's, and the sight of it pained me with all the whole baggage of pain you feel in dealing with your dead mother when both of you should have done things different but now it is very much too late. Then I broke my leg. Broken bones to me now are like a bump on the elbow since my bones are so brittle with age and decay, but that first break was my first laying-up. I needed something to do. So then I thought of my mother's old tattered leatherbound book with the pages falling out and the folded letters stuck in batches here and there.

That first time through it was hard to read. Mrs. Jefferson used the old *f*-for-*s* and her spelling was peculiar, and her punctuation was only periods at the ends of run-on sentences that often combined several natural paragraphs. I could see her dipping and writing, dipping and writing, then lifting her head to think and adding a period. Charming, but very hard to read.

I learned enough, though, to want to know more. I had that old claim, after all, that Thomas Jefferson was my grandfather, and while I knew the truth of it I felt a little taken with the claim. My mother told me so many times that Sally Hemings lied about her children's father that when I found the story in a history book I developed a little contrary belief. While my mother lay dying I even told her I believed the story and I always had. But then I spent twenty years in a study of Jefferson. By now I know as much about him as anybody else alive, and more, because I have read this journal. For a time that seemed to be enough, but perhaps in the end I am not above my taking my little grab at glory. Nobody will remember a dead old lady who might or might not have been Thomas Jefferson's granddaughter, but they will sure enough remember the dead old lady who published Martha Jefferson's journal.

Before you read further I should say one thing. Don't judge these people by today. They didn't know what the next hour would bring so they had no thought of the far future, the growth of the nation nor the Civil War nor the two world wars nor any of it. History is forward. Read this book looking forward. Forget about everything that happened after October of 1770 and you'll start it out in the right frame of mind.

There is an irony in the fact they didn't know the future. Martha died too young. At the time of her death Thomas Jefferson was disgraced and she didn't see how he could redeem himself, nor did he. All he knew was that the end of her life felt to him like the end of his own, so when Martha died he lost his mind and he stayed right out of his mind for months. This was hard for the other founding fathers to accept, this grief a man could hold for a woman at a time when men buried two or three wives and they were busy with more important things. But the most important thing to Thomas Jefferson was Martha. He never in his life got over her death, and in the end he even burned her papers and all their letters to one another. Historians say he was protecting his love letters, but it was more that he was protecting his wife. The things he loved best about Martha were quirks he thought nobody else would understand, and he couldn't bear the thought of any but the most forgiving eyes on her. So before he died he burned her letters. She outfoxed him, though. She saved her journal.

I have helped her out a little with this. I fixed the spelling and punctuation and changed a few words to make a better sense of it. She would have wanted that. I think she's glad of my help.

So am I doing this for me? Am I doing it for neatness? Maybe I am doing it a little for my father, whose face I think I can just remember. He would have wanted to see the truth get out now that his mother and his wife are dead so there is nobody living to be hurt by it.

He had an odd life, did Eston Hemings. He was freed by Jefferson's will in 1829 and he moved out to Ohio, where he married colored and began a family. Then in the 1850s southerners were coming to take up the colored and enslave them again so he moved on to Wisconsin. He took the name of Jefferson and passed for white in case the raiders might get that far but my mother always knew the truth of it.

My mother was working as his nurse when she took up with my father. She was still in her teens, all his children were older, and in fact they told his wife his son Wayles was my father so she wouldn't make a fuss. My father was sickly so my mother would tend him and he told her all his slavery stories. Then before he died he gave her this journal. My mother swore he loved her, but late in my life I have come to believe he took up with her to copy the gentlemen he saw in his youth who were always taking up with their teenage slaves. I don't judge him for that. I only see its truth. After his death my mother took the name of Hemings since his other family wasn't using it. She worked for board until I was twelve and after that I wouldn't let her work. I thought I was taking my father's place.

So maybe I am doing this a little for him, setting all the lies to right. But mostly I am doing it for Martha. This is what she wanted most, this chance to come out and defend her husband. Just the fact that he turned out not to need defending shouldn't take away her little grab at glory.

The big-shot biographers have always thought that Martha was nothing in Jefferson's life. He had all the usual things he needed, a horse, a desk, a wife, like that, and the wife not for long. How could she matter? But the joke is on them. She was everything.

THE FOREST OCTOBER 7, 1770

$\mathcal{I}$ begin to keep this journal at the suggestion of a gentleman who fears I shall lose my life unless I write it down. I think this a peculiar fear, and said so to the gentleman, whereupon he took from his pocket-book a worn Virginia Almanack and said, "For example, I can tell you where I was on Wednesday last."

I looked, and found that on Wednesday last he had paid 45 shillings to Harry Mullins and settled his accounts with Speirs and Ford and paid two shillings for an entertainment at Byrd's Ordinary. And he thought this important! Gentlemen ever think upon money and other such too abstract things, and they lose thereby the joy of the moment. I thought he could live better without his book.

"Your third of October is gone," he said. "Mine I shall recall in some detail forever."

"Mr. Jefferson, on Wednesday last I rendered a kettle of fat for soap and stuffed the sausages you ate this day and turned beds, I think, to prepare for the ball and rocked my son for the pain in his ears. What might I want to remember of that?"

I had spoken in jest, for I knew not the sensitive nature of this gentleman. He felt reproved. His face went starkly pale and his cheeks grew pink by the fire's light. I had a terrible thought of the air between us stiff as glass. "But you are right, sir!" I put my hand on his sleeve, the gray brocade I had thought so fine when first I saw it at the ball that night. "I know you are right. Indeed you are right. But some lives are better recorded than others."

"Mrs. Skelton." His voice was gone as stark as his face. This dance of words at first acquaintance is a very careful minuet, and there I had all in a clumsy moment trod very hard upon his toe.

I opened my fan, for my cheeks were heating. I had made myself believe all evening that I only entertained my Pappa's guest, yet my own dismay made me know that I most greatly desired Mr. Jefferson's friendship. This I must not do, for I had resolved that I would not remarry. So my warm delight in Mr. Jefferson's company, as if he shed a radiance into the room, served for nothing at all. It only rose to flame upon my face. I thought to flirt, for flirting is my certain defense against any greater intimacy. Flirting charms a gentleman while it puts him away; it lets the lady lead. I lowered my eyes and fluttered my fan and said the first artful thing that came into my mind.

"Indeed you are right. All we may ever keep of each precious day is its memory. So in memory of this evening, sir, I vow to begin to keep a journal. But I shall not record in it shillings spent nor featherbeds turned nor hog-fat rendered. What I shall record will be all that matters. Emotions, Mr. Jefferson. I shall write what I feel."

Then I lowered my fan and smiled at him, and I saw in his face such a play of emotions that I nearly laughed aloud. He was charmed and distracted and surprised out of words. "You may read it, Mr. Jefferson," I boldly said, and then it was my turn to feel abashed. There is a brazenness to flirting that gave me not a care when I was young, but at twenty-two I feel the shame of it. "That is, you might read some part of it," I corrected myself from behind my fan.

Mr. Jefferson is such a kindly soul that my discomfiture made him forget his own. "I should like that very much," he said with the warmth of our earlier conversation. "You shall read my shillings and pence and I shall read the gentle thoughts of your soul. I should like that very well indeed."

That moment recorded and read again, I come to the conclusion that this my emotional journal might serve very well. I proposed it in play, yet the thought compelled me, so today I have begged of my Pappa this blank-book meant for his legal cases. He had it from a binder who wanted his trade but he never bought its fellows, so he gave it me now with all the ease of any valueless gift. So many white pages! The fluttering bulk of them thrills and dismays me out of mind, for journal-keeping in a book so fine seems a duty near to sacred. Shall I search for adventures to feed my journal? Shall I move my thoughts onto a higher plane?

It seems amazing what I can recall when I sit with my journal to write it down. I have written my conversation with Mr. Jefferson as the cat heard it dozing upon the hearth, near all of the words and perfected by the fact that I have thought them through a second time. I fear I did not say, "I shall write what I feel," but I said instead, "I shall write what I think." Yet now I prefer my second version so I shall let my journal believe it true. And I make a further discovery of journal-keeping. A few words written may stand for many. Comes again to my mind as if I see it fresh the whole of the ball that went before, so I feel the very chill of the ballroom that thickens like ice within my bones. I hear the fiddle tune to the harpsichord and the rustle of gowns and murmur of talk as Pappa nods and the fiddler begins "Les Petites Demoiselles" so merrily.

I had that first minuet with my Pappa. We always open the ball together. He is a gouty dancer most tender of feet who dances in the fashion of twenty years past, while I dance in the very latest fashion, which is greatly fancy of step and gesture. We look, we are told, quite comical, and I smile unto laughter, and so does he.

When Pappa had danced to the end of his wind I had reels and country-dances with some few gentlemen who claim that right at every ball and will not be disheartened. I dance once with each and fly to the next with what must seem an excess of gaiety but is nothing more than a wish to be free of them. So I gaily danced with my usual spirit, freeing myself from my chain of beaux, and as I danced I noticed Mr. Jefferson standing tall and quiet by the parlor-door. I had gained my first sight of him only that morning and had my introduction at dinner-time, yet the sight of him was so pleasing to me that I felt from the first a discomfiting connection. I feared that he thoroughly knew my mind, my rejection of my suitors and my liking for him, so I danced along faster and averted my face that he not read my thoughts within it. After I had flown from my last failed beau, I took my turn at the harpsichord. This I played on heartily until I had a thought of eyes upon me and I found Mr. Jefferson standing beside me wearing a look most warm and kind. I dropped every finger onto the keys. I recovered, but then all the dancers were off so I hastened the measure to catch them up.

"Will you dance again, Mrs. Skelton?"

My cheeks were heating despite the cold. All my art in casting suitors aside seemed of a sudden mere artifice, for never had I met a gentleman since Bathurst's death these two years gone who had seemed to me aught but dim and foolish. To cast aside a beau who seemed warm and wise and who looked at me as if he had determined to love me required a more practiced skill than I possessed. "Forgive me, sir. I must play on. Now I am behind the fiddler. Please do excuse me." This and other such-like things I said when I could say words out between the notes.

"Here is your sister, Mrs. Skelton."

Pappa was nursing his gout by the fireplace while he plotted out matches for his daughters. Tibby is but sixteen, so he pulled her from the dance and bid her replace me at the harpsichord when he saw that his eldest had set her hook into a splendid fish. I had a thought to say the like to Mr. Jefferson; there was such humor in it that he surely must laugh. But I said nothing. I only put my hand on his fingers and curtsied deeply for his bow, and we whirled into the country-dance.

After that first dance came other dances. We had a heating spirited reel and a country-dance of the handkerchiefs. Mr. Jefferson dances along most fine, light on his feet despite his height and very loose of limb; there is a happy intensity to all he does, so he bows more deeply and steps more distinctly and speaks and listens with more attention than any other gentleman. Soon we were conversing in the intervals between the tunes, but it was only when the jigs began that I found a reason to slip away. I thought him too shy and dignified to want me to chase him around the room as some of the other ladies were chasing, to the great hilarity of all the gentlemen. I stood on toes and said to him, "I am warmed too much for the chill of this room. Will you retreat with me to the parlor fire?"

We were alone in the parlor. We sat on the chairs. I tipped the firescreen to shade my face. We talked, I recall, of a mare he hopes to send to Partner, the English stallion from which we have just had a very promising filly. We talked of apples next, and then he told me he is building his home-farm on the top of a mountain. His servants have leveled the highest height, and there he has built what he assures me is a most unpretentious temporary cottage where he plans, nevertheless, to be living this winter. From there we went to talking of the swift passage of time, and from that exchange arose his thought that I should keep a journal.

So our Friday evening was happily spent. Less promising had been our morning meeting. This being late of a rainy Sunday with

Jack asleep and his ears at peace and an hour to come before candle-time, I shall tell what I can of the rest of that day. And since this venture of journal-keeping seems much like making a new acquaintance, I commence by recording my history.

My Pappa is a practical man. When he saw that Providence had blessed him with four daughters to be given in marriage and a home-farm near to Williamsburg, he built to the eastern end of his house a ballroom larger than the house itself. It is, I confess, hardly more than a barn, for which it often serves in summer, and the smell of curing tobacco fills it even at the moment of minuet. But it serves very well its intended purpose. Pappa offers his balls each year at the spring and fall sittings of the Burgesses, and whether or not these balls were the cause he has disposed of two daughters out of four. That his first has come back seems to him no more than a passing inconvenience.

It is Pappa's keenest wish that I should remarry and my own keenest wish that I should not. To be an aged spinster is a shameful thing, but I am no spinster; I was married at eighteen and widowed at nineteen and my little son Jack is nearly three. I cannot face again all the trials of marriage, yet I find a pang in putting it by for its promise of love and nurturance which persists even though I found the promise hollow. My Pappa's resolve that I must remarry has strengthened my own that I shall not, for I needs must cultivate a solid will if ever I am to prevail against him.

I feel now but a more ardent version of my first reluctance to be a bride. Bathurst was the brother-in-law of Pappa's third wife. I had known him since the age of twelve and played with him at cards and pebble-games and ridden out on our pair of grays we had raised from foals to pull our chaise. Ever he swore that I would be his wife. This promise of Bathurst's was a comfort to me at the callow age of twelve. Yet when I was fifteen my Pappa began to give his balls that he might marry his daughters, so then I had my three years as a belle. Then did I dance! Then did I flirt! At seventeen I had four loving suitors all paying their addresses to me at once, and more beyond them, a whole garden of beaux where I might stroll and flirt for my own pleasure.

I had no wish to pluck one flower when I might enjoy the garden. Yet Betsy grew fast behind me in age and she fell much in love with Francis Eppes, so Pappa commanded me to choose a husband that I not obstruct my sister. Francis is the nephew of my dear dead mother and Bathurst was related to Pappa's third wife, which symmetry so pleased my fond Pappa that I accepted Bathurst. It seems foolish that I chose my husband primarily upon my Pappa's whim, yet I sit here now and truly that seems to have been my strongest reason. I had a thought that gentlemen were much alike so it really mattered little.

My Bathurst was bold and dark of look and grim of the habitual set of his mouth, yet pleasant enough, had the petulance he showed before his wedding-day been the worst that I would see of him. But it was the best. What had been boyish sulking swelled after marriage into genuine rage, and his determination to have his will, which had been the cause of childhood bickering, became after marriage an iron rule. I shall not again place myself and child beneath the control of a gentleman who may delight before marriage in order to woo but will turn once we are wed into a tyrant-king.

Still it seems an adventure, this widowhood, if I may but see it in that light. A widow controls her own property and holds her own children and chooses where ever she will make her abode, which seems a very garden of decisions. I know no other unmarried widow. Most are wed again before the grass grows upon their husbands' graves, which is a sorry pity since to marry or not is near the only choice that a woman may make and the making of it in the negative gives her rights that she may earn in no other way.

So on Friday morning I did not dress like a lady expecting beaux for a ball. I was only very plainly attired in jumps with a bedgown and apron over. I spent that morning with Betty and Ondine and Suck preparing dinner for sixty people, which history said was the number we might expect to arrive by three o'clock. Jack's ears were bothering him less that day, but he wanted to stay close by to me so Betty's daughter was coddling him on a corner of the kitchen floor.

"He is fussing, mistress!" she called to me. She is eleven years old and a child of no patience. I put her aside while I worked with Ondine at stuffing the quails that would wear to the table their own heads and feathers returned to them and set upon nests of their own pickled eggs.

Bett called again. I could hear Jack fussing the angry sound he makes when the pain is rising. I left Ondine to finish the quails and I said to Betty, "He might have laudanum. It will vex my Pappa if he spoils this day." That is why we were passing through the kitchen doorway at the moment when Mr. Dalrymple's carriage rumbled into the kitchen-yard.

This gentleman is Pappa's choice for me. His late first wife was a Carter cousin and he has hundreds of pounds a year from England, but he is a callous gentleman who cares too much for the show he makes. The thought of Mr. Dalrymple once alarmed me with the worry that I might be compelled to accept him, but now with my firm resolve not to wed I find in his pomposity much high humor. Courtship being what it is, with ladies meant to feign a lack of interest, I have been unable to persuade him that I am not merely being coy. I had worn work-clothes to discourage him, so I was glad to see his carriage coming and vastly amused when his postilion directed his horses behind the house into the kitchen-yard.

Mr. Dalrymple travels like the Governor himself in a carriage of dark green trimmed in red. He had standing at the back of it four footmen in varied livery so I knew he carried other gentlemen within. His custom when he traveled was to carry the most honorable gentlemen he could find, and since the day promised rain he had found three companions willing to bear him for the sake of the ride.

My suitor had a new postilion. His former boy had run away, and I knew from Pappa he had bought a new Negro who had been in country for barely a year and was hardly past his sickness. He bought him, I could see, for the show he made, so fine and black on the blacker horse, and for the savings in cost. But I know he rued the savings when his new postilion knew no better than to drive a carriage full of noble gentlemen right around the house into the kitchen-yard. "Idiot! Fool!" Mr. Dalrymple called, and he bounded out the door of his carriage. He pulled the poor boy off the near leader and seized from his hand the postilion's whip, and he began to beat him about the head while the boy but trembled and made a sound that was very like Jack's painful fussing.

I reached for my son to protect him from the sight but Betty had him first. She caught him up with his face in her bosom before we confronted that scene again. The other gentlemen were descending. I could see they were as vexed as we, and as helpless as we to intervene. While it is not polite to beat one's slave, it is less polite to grab the whip and belabor the gentleman in his turn.

That was when I noticed Mr. Jefferson. I guessed at once who he was. My Pappa had described for me this tall young lawyer from Albemarle who went Burgess at only twenty-six and is kin to the Randolphs and heir to a respectable acreage far to the west beyond Richmond. I had thought Mr. Jefferson must be another of my Pappa's unfortunate marital candidates, which misapprehension made yet more confounding my first complete sight of him.

He seemed to me remarkably tall, the tallest man that I had ever seen, with a strong nose and chin and a look about him of sweet good humor and gentle wit. His hair was red-brown, less ruddy than mine, but I thought our coloring much the same. He wore an unadorned brown coat and a plain black ribbon on his queue. His hair above his ears was not even curled, but it played unruly on the moistening wind. I liked that lack of wig or powder. I liked the long calm look of him as he stepped down out of the carriage door. And I liked what came next. Mr. Jefferson looked at me with my child and my maid standing helpless at the kitchen door, and as he looked, he stumbled. I would have thought him the most ungraceful of men had his stumble not been deliberate, but I saw how with care he contrived to place himself directly beneath the whip.

"Pardon me, sir!" He caught Mr. Dalrymple's hands as if he meant to right himself. He put an arm about the gentleman's shoulders, standing as he did so far above him that he seemed to be a father instructing his son. I listened as we passed, and I heard Mr. Jefferson commending Mr. Dalrymple on the wisdom of his new postilion in having chosen the kitchen road for its deeper ruts and more obvious use. "The boy is learning quickly, Henry," I heard him say while he contrived to limp. "All he wants is a little instruction in custom."

That moment in the kitchen-yard changed all my plans for the afternoon. While Bett rocked Jack in my chamber-corner until the laudanum had its effect, Betty and I must find something splendid for me to wear to the ball. I had planned a brown sack-back trimmed in black to further discourage Mr. Dalrymple, but the thought of that gown and Mr. Jefferson together was a juxtaposition not to be borne.

"Your Pappa will believe you seek a beau, mistress," Betty said as she searched with me through the press where I had folded away all my gaudy gowns at my husband's death. "If you dress yourself gaily he will think you past mourning."

"I will not marry again. You may count on that."

"Then make yourself less pretty, mistress."

Betty has all of a slave-woman's wisdom. She declares that her fortune and her bane is her face. And she is right, I know, for a gaudy gown is like a sign upon the bosom begging the attention of gentlemen who might be in the way of a wife. That I did not want, but I only wished to show good Mr. Jefferson how grandly I am able to dress when ever I might choose to dress. "I only refuse to be wasteful," I said for feeble explanation. "It seems a sorry pity to waste these gowns."

My poor dear mother died in childbed only days after I was born so forever she will be for me twenty years old, as she is in the miniature my Pappa gave me when I was near about the age of four. As a child I found comfort in her face when my step-mother ever upbraided me, styling me most ugly and slothful and making me a servant to her own children. My miniature not two inches long seemed greater to me than the living lady. As I grew, my mother remained twenty years old, now older sister, now equal friend, until now she comes to be my junior. I protect and comfort her in my turn.

Her miniature shows a lovely beauty, although my Pappa swears it is a pallid likeness. She had red hair which was prone to curl and a tiny, fine-boned, wistful face and a look she must have struggled for, as if she did no work at all but she sat on a cushion and smiled all the day. I have had some of her gowns made over for me, and what I searched for with Betty was a green brocade with side-hoops and many gold lace roses. I thought it might go very well with the yellow stomacher and petticoat my sister Tibby had given to me when she passed my own height at the age of twelve.

"Will Tibby's quilted petticoat move, Betty? Think you it might do well for dancing?"

"Will you look at that gentleman!" she said, sounding vexed. "How are those poor boys ever going to grow up?"

Betty was at the window looking out at the boys gathering cider-apples in the orchard. I went to the window and saw Mr. Jefferson standing in a crowd of the slaves and two of Betty's sons among them, showing the boys how to throw an apple to knock other apples out of the trees.

"Mr. Stevens is going to switch them for sure, he sees them doing a thing like that!" But Betty could not call to Mr. Jefferson. I could not call to Mr. Jefferson. Even our overseer, Mr. Stevens, had not the position to reprimand a Burgess for throwing apples.

Mr. Jefferson told me when we talked that evening that the gentlemen were then at their cards and their pipes, and since he neither smoked nor gambled and he meant to plant apples in the spring he had gone out to see what varieties we had and how they were doing in our ground. When I told him that our overseer would not approve of throwing apples, he said it had been an experiment. He had asked Martin Hemings if throwing would work, and since Martin had not known the answer Mr. Jefferson had determined to find out.

I needed two gowns, a simpler one for dinner and a gaudier one to wear to the ball. The green, when we found it, was wrong with the yellow, so for the ball I chose my sister Betsy's apricot lustring which might well never fit her again. Betsy is very great with child, and she has put on such a layer of flesh that even her stays are unlikely to help her. For the dinner I chose a gay pink chintz with a white linen petticoat embroidered in many-colored flowers.

The dinner table for sixty people had been set upon trestles on the ballroom floor and spread with a length of homespun linen and laden with the fruits of our three days of work, our quails and sausages and squash-corn salads and kidney-mutton savories and sweet-potato biscuits and our cheese-cakes and moonshines and orange pies.

Some ladies in attendance wore homespun, too. This seems to be a coming fashion, what with the nonimportation resolutions imposed upon us by the Association. The King has resolved to tax our imports to pay for business of his own, and this affront has so heated Virginia that gentlemen have been pleased to ban the import of nearly every thing. When Governor Botetourt gave a holiday ball every lady there was in a homespun gown. For me, however, this banning of imports is taking a switch to one's own head. If gentlemen had to spin and weave, they would show a greater respect for cloth.

There was such excitement on the air! I could not help but feel it, too, even though I was grim to resist for fear that it might charm me into making one gentleman more important than the rest. My custom is to play the harpsichord as a reason for avoiding most of the dance, and I generally play it even at dinner, before and after I have my bite. Mr. Burwell's William is a fair hand at the fiddle so we play together, he and I. We did this while the company gathered, choosing a light Italian tune, which I played while William improvised a sprightly gay accompaniment.

Betty is training Bett to be my maid because Ondine has slow rheumatism. More and more, Betty is compelled to assume control of the house. Even though she is breeding again and only weeks from childbed she oversaw the dinner serving, using for waiters mostly her children. Martin and Bob came in from the orchard, and Mary, Betty's oldest, whose mind is willful, and even little Jim. Nance came in to see the dinner with baby Critta on her hip, and this occasioned one awful moment which makes me shudder even now.

My Pappa has married and buried three wives. The last of them lived for barely a year. That he turned from marriage after that was a thing that did not surprise me at all, but that Betty's children began to come paler a year or two after his last wife's death was a phenomenon I did not understand until after my own marriage. Our Betty's father was a sailor named Hemings who left her complexion rather pale. Her oldest children are tall and dark, but Bob and Jim are bright mulattoes with heads of molasses-colored hair. Baby Critta is a gray-eyed towhead. In the arms of her own dark sister, Nance, she looked as white as any child.

"John!" one of the gentlemen called to Pappa from partway down the table. "John! Is this a grandchild? Who is this?" Since he knew that a baby at a ball wearing nothing but a threadbare blanket could never be a child of the family, he said this only to tease my Pappa.

"No," Pappa said. "She is a servant's child."

Pappa seemed amused by this interplay, but I felt knotted-up with rage. That every lady cast her eyes demurely and every gentleman thought it a jest was a fact I had more reason to rue than any other person there. I grimly looked the length of the table and found Mr. Jefferson sitting in what looked to be a mortified silence. I liked him still better for his stricken face. I resolved at that moment to make his further acquaintance.

But now it is long past candle-time. Jack is waking from his nap and fussing for milk and bread for supper. And I am tired, but I find that writing all of this down has eased my mind. I am going to like journal-keeping very well.

THE FOREST OCTOBER 20, 1770

𝒫appa has returned this night from Williamsburg with news that drives me back to my journal. I shall think of this more calmly if I write it down. How shall I begin? My hand is shaking.

Pappa's chaise returned near eight o'clock, he having dined at Charles City Court-House with other lawyers who were passing there. He was not expected this week at all, so the step of his boot within the hall set my slipper so quick upon the stairs that the rush of the air blew out my candle. Betty was quicker to greet my Pappa, since she lives with her youngest off the dining-room in a chamber which was a storage-cellar. She held her candle that he might doff his greatcoat and see to hang his hat on its peg, and they spoke in low tones as ever they converse, like people so long and so placidly wed that they near avoid a need to speak at all.

"I stay just the night."

"The fire is banked."

"Something cold, then."

"Does your sore improve?"

"Well enough."

"Then sit thee down."

We took cloaks and went out to the kitchen to find the fire abated to orange embers just bright enough for the smallest kettle. I set the kettle among the coals and shaved my Pappa's chocolate while Betty carved his ham and hunted up the remnant of the dinner-pudding. We worked in silence and a darkness made blacker by that orange ineffectual glow of the fire. I had it in my mind to remark that I am glad of the kindness Betty shows to my Pappa so he need not be alone in the world and yet he need not wed. I had found a comfort in witnessing their moment of greeting one another in the hall. I would have spoken, but my thought was too close to a topic which never may be opened between us. I may not consider them in my Pappa's chamber. Yet ever the thought comes to my mind to imagine them there as they are by day, he careful of her in respect of her temper and she efficient at serving him.

We set out his food in the dining-room. He paced while we laid it and he ate most restless, sitting, but then having a thought of a book or some order he had meant to give to his coachman so he must stand again upon some errand. I knew that something was troubling him and pleasing him in equal measure. Betty and I exchanged many glances before he stood for a final time and said that he must have a word with me.

We went up to my chamber. I set the candle on my clothespress, far enough from Jack's small bed that it would not awaken him. My Pappa stepped to look at my son, then he came back to pace at the edge of the light. It was warm in my chamber by grace of the fire. He removed his coat and threw it on my bed. "I had dinner and conversation with a friend of ours on Thursday last," he said to me. "A friend of mine and, I am pleased to say, a friend of yours."

I said nothing. I picked at a petticoat-thread while my Pappa wound himself up into words.

"Mr. Jefferson is very well considered. He has been frank with me about his fortune, and I am pleased to say it approaches your own. He will make a good living as a lawyer, I think, and he is a Burgess at twenty-seven. He has the confidence of prominent men. You could do, my dear Patty, a great deal worse."

"I will not marry, Pappa."

"He was charmed when he met you at the ball. I am pleased to hear that you let yourself be charming," my Pappa said with a sidelong glance.

"But I will not marry."

"Of course you shall marry!"

My Pappa is a gentleman not very tall and he will not wear a wig although his hair grows thin, but he has a seething spirit which makes him seem to be always about to lose himself in either anger or laughter, in some strong emotion. He contains his laughter in the presence of ladies, and when his temper rises beyond his will I have seen him strike a fence with his riding-whip that he not commit a violence upon a slave. I try to avoid provoking an anger which he must then labor to overcome, so I had ever let him believe that I only awaited my proper suitor. That I could no longer do. My thought of Mr. Jefferson would not support from me the most benign dissembling. "I will not marry," I said most gently. "Whether I shall marry is my own choice."

"What nonsense! Every female marries!"

"Then here is a new thing under the sun." I was of a sudden near to tears, and feeling this weakness greatly vexed me. However much I say that there can be no shame in an unmarried widow, indeed there is shame enough that we both feel it. Why does no man marry John Wayles's daughter? And she even an heiress? Can she not buy a husband? Oh, I do feel it! And I rue it! Why should this which is my only life be so constrained by the minds of people who have no care at all for me? I said, "There is no man I want for husband, Pappa. I truly have no wish to marry."

"You have no wish? No wish? But this is your life! This is not some lady's-play!"

Here Jack cried a sound from out of his sleep which made us both wince for my Pappa's loud anger. Pappa seized my riding-whip from off my press and near upset the candle.

"I do not like marriage." To my shame tears began, but I kept them within my eyes by an effort of will.

"You must marry! You are just twenty-two!"

"Decency required me to marry the first time, but a widow has the right to mourn forever."

"You do not mourn!"

This is largely true, but ungentlemanly indeed for him to remark.

I knew that my Pappa would not apprehend my female reluctance to trust in marriage, his strength being such that my fears born of weakness would be as foreign to him as the Man of the Moon. He would understand nothing, so from my desperation I gave to him a reason close to his own heart. "I will keep my own money, Pappa. While I do not marry what Bathurst left is in my control, but if I marry my husband will take it from me."

"That is no reason to deny yourself a marriage!"

Gentlemen ever think upon money. I had thought this a reason any man would understand, so for Pappa to pass it off as nothing felt like a blow against my breast. For I never could give him my other reasons. Oh, devoutly do I have reasons! They tumble in my mind on every night so I cannot sleep for their commotion.

I never could say how the mother of my sisters used to pinch my face and shame me for being less to her than the children of her own body. I suffered under that lady for my whole childhood, and suffered the more because I never dared complain of her to my Pappa. And how could I tell Pappa about Bathurst's Lovey? Every gentleman, it seems, has a maid to his bed, and my Bathurst had a mulatto maid who bore him a pale child when our own babe was only six months old. I never could share with my Pappa my reasons. The perpetrators were dead souls dear to him. Hearing of their transgressions would greatly distress him or, worse yet, it would prompt him to defend them and belittle my pains. So I never could tell my Pappa my reasons. But I knew with every fiber of my soul that my baby would never suffer a step-father and I would never suffer another Lovey.

"Mr. Jefferson has asked if he might pay you his addresses. I have given him my consent."

"He may address me if he will! I will never marry, and if the gentleman asks I will say it to his face!"

"Patty, Patty, be sensible," Pappa said while he still paced the edge of the light. He began to tap my whip against his leg. "Do you think you can throw away beaux forever?"

"I know I can. We shall grow old together, Pappa. Who else but I can shave your chocolate? Who knows as I do how to keep your accounts?"

Pappa looked at me then, as I knew he would. Despite his irritation he came near to smiling. "You may keep young Mr. Jefferson's accounts! Of what use to me are all my daughters if I cannot buy with you the finest sons?"

"You might buy him with Nancy. Ask him to wait. She is fourteen already. He will not wait long."

"It is not Nancy with whom he plans to attend the theater on next Friday evening."

"No, Pappa!"

"I have given my permission. You will stay the week-end with Peyton Randolph. It has already been arranged."

"Fine, then!" I said in a confusion of emotion. I confess I wanted to see Mr. Jefferson. I liked the thought of a week-end in the Capital, but I felt a powerful unpleasant current of male determination carrying me. I would not allow this pair of gentlemen to conspire together to arrange my life, yet my strength seemed so puny against their own.

"Marry or not as you will," Papa said. "That is something I cannot control. But if you love me enough to obey me you will let him pay his court to you. I leave it to him to do the rest."

"But Jack has ear-fever! He might not be well!"

"That I leave to God," Pappa said, sounding weary. "There is a limit to what I can do."

WILLIAMSBURG OCTOBER 27, 1770

I carried this book to Williamsburg expressly to record the events of last evening, yet nearly I left it within my box for all my great confusion. I had hoped that my evening at the theater would confirm for me my resolve not to wed, but instead it has proven that I have no resolve. I am gone in two directions. I cannot say what I feel, and there is little time, for Mrs. Randolph plans to take me on a round of calls this afternoon.

I arrived in the Capital at mid-day yesterday, tired from the ride but glad of the thought of two days ahead without any work beyond the unaccustomed duty of pleasing myself. Betty was keeping Jack, who is better now, so I had not even motherhood; I was seventeen again and gay with all the old familiar pleasures of girlhood. My mind was lit by the thought that indeed my life has made a circle. If I never marry, I might contrive to be seventeen again for evermore.

Mr. Jefferson had been invited to dinner. All of this had been arranged by Pappa, and the family left us alone in the parlor before the meal was served. A maid sat by the door, mending linens, but other than that we were as much alone as we had been in the parlor at the ball. Pappa must have seen Mr. Jefferson during the week between and said to him something that made him feel clumsy. Perhaps he confided my aversion to marriage or else he avowed that I was eager to wed; either revelation would have undone so sensitive a gentleman. Mr. Jefferson stumbled over his words and his only favored topic was the home he is building on his mountaintop.

"I call it Monticello. The name in Italian means 'Little Mountain.' I have built there just the smallest room, but in the spring I shall begin a house more suitable for a family. I plan to occupy it room by room. I am so impatient to have it done!"

This topic of his home being built was too well-connected to the misunderstanding which hung above our heads like a sword. He had asked my Pappa for permission to address me, and now he believed that with Pappa's consent the decision to marry was all his own. He was trying me as one might try a horse. I could not announce my refusal to marry since he never yet had posed the question, so all I could do was seem balky enough that this was one horse he would not buy. Given the customary reserve of ladies with the gentlemen who most interest them, I ought to have made myself truly unpleasant. But I could not do that to Mr. Jefferson. I sat there beside him in a stupid silence.

I was silent during dinner, too, but this was for another reason. Peyton Randolph is the Speaker of the House of Burgesses, the greatest gentleman in the colony, an eminent cool mind in a great heavy head with a fancy wig and the grandest clothes. That he and Pappa are friends cannot amend the fact that I am in awe of him. I find myself struck dumb in his presence, and he is so polite to all the world that he finds himself unable to suffer a dinner at which I will not speak. Last evening, though, we were spared his round of questions and my own painful answers because he carried on with Mr. Jefferson a most remarkable conversation. I was impressed by this, not only because they were discussing Lord Bolingbroke's understanding of God, a topic far the weightiest that I have heard at table in a while, but because Mr. Jefferson was so much at ease with the ever so eminent Mr. Randolph.

Dear Mr. Jefferson turned to me when ever there was a silence in the ladies' talk and made some remark meant to interest me, some detail of the way he had built his cottage so the kitchen was conveniently under it or some thought that we might make music together if he called again tomorrow afternoon. Sitting as I was at Peyton Randolph's table, I could give him only single-word replies for a fear that I would make some careless comment and shame my Pappa before his worthy friends.

After dinner came a walk in the garden to view the last of the twilight. It was cold enough for a cardinal and muff, yet I suffered the cold so we would not have to face the family in the parlor. Mrs. Randolph had begun to seem as if we were about to be wed, casting sly looks and smiling fondly and making us both feel ill at ease. I believe that each of us chose the garden for worry of the comfort of the other.

Mr. Jefferson talked more freely in the garden. I heard in his voice a rising desperation as he groped for topics to entertain me, speaking of his liking for Campioni and Handel and asking after the books I had read, but I would not respond. This was half on account of my vow not to remarry, and half, I confess, because I found him delightful. I was quite charmed out of words to say. Soon his coach-boy brought up his phaeton to the garden fence which edged the road. I called for Bett to sit at my feet while Jupiter rode along behind; my Bett made a puny chaperone, but for a widow she did well enough. We rode the little way to the theater in more of my awful, stupefied silence.

I liked Mr. Jefferson so well! I liked his lanky loose-limbed height and the way he had curled his hair for me and worn a blue coat with brass buttons and piping. I liked his voice which is mild and mellow and full of a gentle resonance. I felt a sense of repose in his presence combined with an exquisite agitation, a need at once to cling and to flee. I was staggered and confounded. I could not bear the thrill of it when he bent to comment out of the servants' hearing and I caught a scent of green on his breath which came from within him, fine and clean. Oh my foolish heart! Quite against my will it blushed and flirted shamelessly. I do not wonder that he was perplexed; I found myself agitated nearly to tears. This traitorous reaction of my very soul and all my inner organs seemed a kind of compact with my Pappa. Even dear Mr. Jefferson seemed not innocent.

Gentlemen court most sensibly. All their thought is to name of family and size of the lady's fortune. Yet all my care is for his tender eye and the turn of his hand upon the reins and the look of his thigh within his breeches, the set of his ear against his head, each smallest detail of him yet the more perfect. I could not have my peace of gazing at him, yet gazing at him brought me no peace. Even being so near him was an agitation as we rode close together in his phaeton, pushed indeed so close by its narrow seat that I felt the muscle within his arm as he made a signal to his horse. Blessed horse! was my thought. It shared with him a warm and intimate connection.

Still, I said nothing. I hardly saw the play, which was something from New York that involved two ladies doing a great deal of exclaiming first with horror and then with laughter while a gentleman sat and smoked his pipe. Mr. Jefferson seemed not to like it either. Then came the drive home, a drive so brief there was going to be no time to amend the impression I had made. I wanted to amend it! I had not the words. This being so close to him on the seat made me

---

*T*here has been a break of some hours. As I was writing those last words a maid knocked at my door and said that Mr. Jefferson had come to call. Then did my breast flutter! I dared not greet him for fear that if he saw my face he would know what I had written in my journal. I almost asked that he leave a note, but then I went down. Mr. Jefferson did not look well. He stood by the window in the parlor, and his skin seemed stretched on his bones so tight I imagined I could see the shine of them through it. His nose and cheeks bear a faint freckling which I had not noticed before today, but as pale as he was his freckles stood out quite starkly in the window-light. The maid who had summoned me took her place by the door. Mr. Jefferson waited a moment before he said "Please leave us now."

For him to close the doors and make us alone was an event so shocking that I was entranced. I forgot with the sight of him all my resolve to keep myself aloof from him. Now I wanted just the pleasure of his own dear face, this being drawn to him and yet pulling away for alarm at the thrill of his company. I was charmed when he simply looked at me and said, "Mrs. Skelton, I am not good at this."

He meant, I imagine, that he is not bold at courting a lady who wishes to be courted but shows the customary lack of interest. Perhaps it is this which has kept him single, and it is in truth a sorry pity for I vow that his shyness is delightful. I know I am not the first lady to think so. Our problem, however, was greater than this. He was courting a lady who was enchanted by him and yet was unwilling to be courted by him. I had no words to say this, yet I found that his distress touched my heart most grievously.

"It is my fault, Mr. Jefferson. It is not your own."

He had not expected me to say that. I cannot say what he had expected; he had come to me on impulse with all the desperation of his sleepless night. "I thought," he started to say. "Your father led me to believe," he began again.

"It is my fault," I was saying when he commenced this amazing speech.

"Mrs. Skelton, I knew your husband at William and Mary. He made such astonishing claims for his lady that I thought it must be lover's talk. And how your father praises you! He says you are a lady who reads the Classics, who sings and plays like an angel and who is, beyond that, skilled at housewifely duties, sweet and God-fearing and, he insists, even beautiful! A paragon! So I resolved to meet you. Then I met you, mistress, and from that first sight I could not have cared whether you could read or play a note. The pots could fly away for all I cared."

"I saw you with much the same effect."

He startled. "I thought!" he began to say. Then he had not any words to continue.

"Come and sit by me, please." My breast was fluttering so I thought I could not trust my voice, but I felt I must speak clearly now or gather my gown and fly from the room. We sat on chairs by the fireplace. He rubbed at his forehead as if it pained him.

I would have thought these next words impossible to say, but they flew from my mouth. "Mr. Jefferson, sir, I cannot mislead you. I know that it is your hope to marry, but it is my hope never to marry again." Here my face began to heat. I opened my fan. "This will seem to you the most peculiar notion, but I choose to keep my late husband's property under my own and my son's control."

"On the contrary, that seems very sensible."

I looked at him over the edge of my fan for plain amazement. If my own dear Pappa had not understood me, I would have thought no gentleman could. This empathy of his seemed a bond between us stronger than any tie of blood, for I had a thought of a great comfort that he would understand any thing that I might say.

"Indeed, were I in your place I would do the same." His face which had been stark and grave became bright with the pleasure of this new idea. "I am surprised, now you say it, to see how few widows make your choice. I had assumed some difference in female thinking."

However I now say otherwise, as a bride I truly did love my Bathurst. There is a tenderness of talk between wife and husband and a tender sweetness of the marital bed, and it seems to me that my pain of his Lovey but rendered my love for him all the greater. I know indeed how love fills the breast and addles the mind with a thrilling vapor, and there in the sight of my so dear friend I felt again that exultant lifting. But I calmly said, "Does your head pain you?"

"It is a headache coming on. I should be ashamed to admit my flaws, but I am subject to periodical headaches. The strain of last evening may be prompting one. Or it may leave me. Mrs. Skelton, I am so relieved to find myself not altogether repugnant to you."

"Hardly that!" I felt so gay with him that I laughed, and my laughter made him smile. He truly is very like an egg, stiff-shelled but entirely soft inside. With his smile, his shell once again was cracked and I saw the tender man I had glimpsed before.

"Do you keep your emotional journal, Mrs. Skelton? I confess your notion has captivated me to the point where I wake from sleep with the thought in mind."

I could not tell him I had made only three entries and he had been the subject of all of them. I resolved there and then to write a great deal more about very many gentlemen. Or I shall leave off journal-keeping altogether. One further benefit to remaining a widow may be that I shall no longer suffer emotions.

THE FOREST APRIL 17, 1771

I remember to make entry into my journal only when I have something momentous to write. It has lain beneath my bed these six months past with even its location at times forgotten, so when I thought to write in December I disremembered where it was. Then some duty called me, and before I thought of my journal again it was another season. But no matter. As I see I told Mr. Jefferson on the evening we met, there is no point to recording the small events which make each day much like every other. It seems, however, small events become great when they make a pattern in the cloth which is visible only when the bolt is laid.

Mr. Jefferson greatly tries my resolve that I shall remain an unmarried widow. In Mr. Randolph's parlor I was rendered so foolish by the sight of his dear blessed face that when he said, "May I call that we might share our music?" I said not, "I play only very poorly," but I said, "I have some Vivaldi for the fiddle! You will love it, I know!" and other such-like nonsense. I had boldly shared with him my resolve that I would never again be wed, but it seemed he had heard it as a lively notion and not as any genuine wish of a lady. This I thought with a mix of relief and unease. I would not wed, yet I could not support a thought that I might not see him again. He removed to Monticello at the latter part of November last, as I recall, when ended the sitting of the Burgesses. I thought I should not see him until the spring but he was here twice in December, and I found to my delight that his fiddling surpasses even that of Mr. Burwell's William.

Mr. Jefferson keeps a schedule. He likes to rise early and read before breakfast and often-times we would read together, and then after breakfast we would walk or ride on my pair of grays that I raised with Bathurst. Mr. Jefferson has such an energy that he rides at a remarkable rate, so Bett on her mule could not keep with us and we had to pause often and wait for her. He had come from his early groping for topics suitable for a lady's mind to almost forgetting I was a lady at all, so he told me stories from the Burgesses and the foibles of his gentleman friends, strange cases at court, and once a tale of hunting for a rabbit that kept just ahead so he was chasing it for hour after hour and he lost his way until morning. These were strange conversations indeed for a gentleman in the way of courting a lady. So then it was that I came to believe he had well apprehended my wish not to wed. In saying it out I had freed us both from constraints of expectation, for he need not wonder what I might intend and I need not scruple to encourage him. We were in some adventure of a cross-sexual friendship not meant by the parties to lead unto marriage, which whimsy of a thought sat light on my mind as we sang and conversed on our morning rides.

After exercise I must excuse myself to oversee the dinner. Mr. Jefferson would walk about the farm wearing his habitual expression of interest while he gathered ideas for his own plantation. Then often he appeared in the kitchen doorway when the hour was barely after noon and lured me in to begin our music while Betty made the dinner in my stead.

Mr. Jefferson carries a small kit-fiddle, or he plays my Pappa's ancient cello which vexes us for its loosened joining that keeps it forever out of tune. We prefer the cello to the kit, especially if we play the Corelli or other such-like solemn music. But he is reluctant to break our music as the cello drifts ever more out of tune until its sound is a painful trial for the ears. Many times I have lifted my hands and smiled by way of asking him to tune the cello, until one day I found myself out of patience. I said, "Can you not hear it, Mr. Jefferson?" Then I rose and boxed his ear.

He had not been boxed since he was a boy. He gave me one astonished look, and then he laughed. "Point made! You are right!" he could hardly say for his fit of laughter. Now whenever he wants to bring us a moment of merriment he will pluck one splendid sour note and laugh and duck to spare his ear. But we passed many afternoons just playing our instruments and singing, many evenings when little more passed between us than "More softly there" or "Try it this way" or "Let us now begin again," yet the pleasure of being in his company made me gayer than I have ever been.

Our musical afternoons occasioned another moment that I smile in the darkness to record. On one afternoon very near to Christmas we were singing and playing with special merriment when Mr. Dalrymple and Mr. Smithson came to call. I think it likely they had paused overnight to break some longer journey but it was very like them to call together, for reinforcement or for rivalry. So they were given seats in the hall, where Betty asked them to wait until our song was completed. She told me later how they sat there in silence listening to Mr. Jefferson and me together. Then they gave one another a look and a sigh and went back out the door. That was the same afternoon, I believe, when Jack was breeding another ear-fever and Mr. Jefferson swore to him that only music could chase it away. He set my little son on a chair all bundled in his quilt, and he fiddled for him and danced with such hilarity that they were broken up into laughter together and the ear-fever went away that night.

I have found Mr. Jefferson to be the very kindliest gentleman with a child. He is content to play at checks with Jack sitting most ungracefully upon the floor and talking away with him all the while as if they were both little three-year-old gentlemen. Even our servants love Mr. Jefferson, for he is polite when another guest might show a petty temper and upon each departure he tips them well when many guests tip them very little.

Our friendship as it became in December I can compare to nothing other than that moment of courtship intensely sweet when lovers share an intimacy but they have as yet no sense of a future. This suited my heart for I could not bear to accept him or to let him go, and it suited him as well for his shy reserve made him reluctant to press a lady.

But it suited not Betsy. "You toy with him," she said in her so placid voice. "If you will not have him, let him be. He is too good to dandle."

And it suited not Tibby. She is soon to be wed so she cannot fathom my own reluctance. "You plan to live single for your whole life?" she asked me with great consternation. "How will you find security? What fun will you have? For what will you live? Oh, Patty!"

It even suited not Betty, who gave me her thoughts most baldly of words when we were alone. "He will be your friend, mistress, well enough," my Betty said of her own firm voice. "He will sit in your parlor but soon look elsewhere if he comes no closer to your chamber."

I heard her say this with a constriction of my heart like a cold stone turned within my breast. I could not bear it if he courted another. I would die of that intelligence, were it given me, and to see him but gaze warm upon another would carry me directly to a deathly edge. This is not fair to him. I own it. That I can do no other is my only explanation for what my sisters see as his grave ill-use, and if he courts another lady and I die of it then still I shall say that I can do no other. My life would be a most sunny journey if only I lacked my confounding emotions which bid me now run in two directions. And this is but their latest misadventure. I believe I hoped to master my emotions by the device of recording them within my journal, yet my journal only proves to me how abjectly I am become their servant.

We had snows to the west in January. I imagined Mr. Jefferson could not get through them, but still I feared that he might be ill. Then Pappa saw him in Richmond in February and brought me news that relieved me greatly: Mr. Jefferson had kindly asked after me and had asked permission to make me a gift of a German table-top clavichord which will let us make our music together when we sojourn in the Capital. He has ordered it from England, my Pappa assures me, since it is not covered by the ban upon imports. At this news I confess that I danced the jig I had not danced for him at my Pappa's ball.

The spring brought a resumption of Mr. Jefferson's calls, although I no longer call him Mr. Jefferson. I had tried his Christian name in my mind on many a fretful January night and written it on bits of paper like a love-struck girl. Thomas. It seems a strong and wise and dignified name, yet a gentle name. It suits him completely. So when Suck ran into the kitchen late on one afternoon at the start of March and said there was a phaeton on the road and she fancied it was Mr. Jefferson's, I ran out with her to watch it approach as if I were but another servant. I came upon him directly as I left the kitchen-yard, and this so startled me that I said his name. "Thomas!" My greeting so delighted him that he has told me the story ever since; how he had driven all those lonely hours and then been refreshed all in a moment by the vision of an angel calling out his name.

There was no sense in the spring, as there had been in the fall, that ours was a mere cross-sexual friendship without another thought in mind. Thomas had considered it over the winter and decided, I believe, that he needed a wife to make bearable his cottage on the mountaintop and that only I would be that wife. He stepped from his phaeton in such good haste that his Jupiter was hard-put to catch his horse, and he bowed to me smartly and kissed my hand and looked at me most ardently. I was staggered by his new intensity, as if his very humors were speeding their course.

"Are you well, Mr. Jefferson?"

"Not until this moment! You are the first flower of my spring, Mrs. Skelton. I cannot say how I have survived the winter." The like any gentleman might have said, yet the warmth of his voice made me know it true. And he was so fervently tender to me, so full of joy to be again in my presence that I expected his proposal of marriage from that first evening.

I also had considered it over the winter, safe from the sight of his own dear face, and had become ever more distressed and con-founded. My very need for his constant presence made stronger my conviction that we must not wed, for I could not again love a gen-tleman who possessed the power to betray my trust. I fear that dominion of husband over wife which makes each decision of her life his own, so a husband may send a child from its home or lie with a maid or allow or forbid any smallest thing and his wife may only weep. I thought while I was married that my hurt would be less if only I did not love my husband. Now I think that if I marry again it must be to a gentleman so unappealing that betrayal by him will cost me never a sigh.

Yet such thoughts came easily deep in the winter when I only pined for Thomas's company. When I was full in the sight of him all my thought was for keeping his constant complete attention; my resolve was altogether crumbling. I felt panicked by his power over me, and the turmoil of so much love and refusal made me such a greatly perplexing companion that my Thomas was altogether be-wildered. If he had come with thought in mind of proposing our marriage, he retreated to the safety of our former friendship. Oh, joy in this for me! I had a thought that we might carry on in this wise forever. He called near every week-end of the month of March while my sisters and my Betty resumed their entreaties and I only lived daily for the sight of his face. I said to Betsy once that I would marry him gladly if I did not love him half so well.

He arrived for this week-end on Saturday, having broken his journey at Lawton's ferry and lamed his horse in a rut on the road so he could not leave until today. Pappa has had to be away from Sunday, Betsy and Francis and their baby are on a visit to his kin on the Northern Neck, and Tibby is with Bobby Skipwith's family where she prepares for their wedding soon to come. This coincidence of absent family and the need to rest up Thomas's horse left us too much alone these past few days in the pleasure of our private company.

Even the weather conspired against me. The spring is backward this year, and only now it brings us tender weather. We found ourselves on Tuesday morning reading beneath a blossoming apple on the hillock above the mill-wheel pond. I wore a broad-brimmed straw and mitts but with the shade of the tree and the cool spring light I was able to do without my mask. Trussed in stays as I was I could not lie down, but in truth the stays supported me well. I could draw my slippers up under my gown and sit against my stays on that little hill as comfortably as I sit upon any chair.

Thomas was reading Burlamaqui's *Principes du Droit Naturel.* He would pause now and then and read a sentence aloud and translate it, enjoying the words, how the flavor and the meaning of them were altered with the change in language. I read only very little French, but the fact that I have learned French at all gives us yet another mutual pleasure. So we happily read for an hour or more. Then Thomas turned over onto his back, marked his place with a leaf of grass, and laid his book aside. He put his arms behind his head and tipped up his tricorne to shade his eyes.

"Martha? Will you dismiss your maid?"

"Pappa would object to my doing that." My breast began to tremble as it had trembled when he made us alone in Peyton Randolph's parlor. I could only believe he meant to make his proposal, and I felt too intimate with him then to resist as I would have to resist.

"Your Pappa is not here. And I believe that if he knew my purpose he would not object."

I was more than half way through *Tristram Shandy,* which is Thomas's favorite comic novel, a masterpiece of silly wit that had me laughing even as I marveled at the oddities of gentlemanly minds. They seem to attend very much to warring and the condition of their generative members, yet they sorely misapprehend their ladies and this failing of theirs gives them never a care.

"Martha? Please will you dismiss your maid?"

I must assent. For politeness I could do no other. I nodded once, and Thomas stood to his feet and called to Bett, who was picking flowers, and when he had her attention I was bold to say that she must return and assist her mother. Betty's last pale baby is very sickly and she is worn out from constant worry and having to nurse him day and night.

"Thank you." Thomas dropped to the grass, nearer to me than he had been before. He could have put his arm about my shoulders. I imagined he might try to coddle me into accepting his proposal of marriage as he had coddled Mr. Dalrymple into sparing his postilion.

"Martha. Patty." He had never before used my family name; I looked up at the sound of it. He tried to look at me but he could not. He drew up his knees and looked away. "You have asked me not to talk of marriage but I find I can think of little else. Forgive me if I impose on our friendship but I must ask you to consider it now. You know how I love you. When we are apart I think I could not love you more, then I see you again and my former love is as nothing compared to what I feel. It winds me ever tighter, Patty. I fear I am going to burst with it."

He was plucking at the grass between his knees, watching his hand, not looking at me, while I gazed compassionate upon his cheek with a panic half of love and half of a need to flee. He had in a moment blundered and wrecked our precious, tender friendship. I saw that quickly. And I saw as quickly that my sisters and Betty had been right.

He said, "Forgive me if I presume too much. I had come this time with the firm conviction that if you would not have me I would drive away and not see you again. I cannot do that. You are too dear to me. If you will not marry I shall have to be content to be a lovelorn swain forever."

"Oh, Thomas!" I said beyond my will. "If I marry any gentleman it will be you!"

He looked at me with his face gone joyous. "I can address your objection. We can arrange matters so your property remains in your own name."

"That is not my worry any longer." Neither was Jack any longer my worry. I knew that my own dear gentle Thomas would be a most loving step-father for Jack, and nothing like my step-mother was to me. I bit my lip in consternation. I felt on a balance that had tilted to his favor while I struggled to tip it the other way.

"Then may we discuss it? Will you consider it?"

I had only one remaining objection but it loomed for me taller than Thomas's mountain. How could I express it? Somehow I must. I owed him this much explanation. "I do not weather marriage well," was the closest I came to voicing my worry. "Its customs cause me too much pain." This perplexed him. His hand froze on the grass. "I became too fond of my first husband. Yet it seems I am fonder still of you."

A line appeared between Thomas's eyes. The tree had dropped petals on his hat and queue which would have seemed comical at a lesser moment. "Fondness seems desirable in a marriage," he said when I said nothing more.

The thought of my worry as I looked at him made me envision a husband and his wife together. I well could see him lifting a lady's shift and I knew he would do it with the greatest tenderness, voice very soft and hands as soft and full of expression as they are on his fiddle. My cheeks went to flame; I groped in the grass to find my fan for hiding my face. But then my vision changed and I saw my Thomas lifting the bedgown of a giggling servant. The image was as perfectly clear to me as it had become during all the nights I had wept alone in my marriage-bed. "Fondness makes me resentful." I looked away. "Even of so small a thing as a gentleman's maid. Of so little as that. You will think me foolish."

It took him a moment to understand. Then he struggled to his feet, half-clumsy in his agitation. "Do you think I would do that? You worry that I would do such a thing? God forgive us, this is a monstrous system! That lovers must have such a conversation!" But then he found that he could not have it. Instead he said, "I sponsored a bill before the Burgesses to give us the right to free our slaves. Were you aware of that? Martha? I would free them all!"

I looked up at him. I had not known that. I had known from Pappa that as a young lawyer he had tried to argue for a Negro's freedom on the theory the boy had a right to be free, but he had lost that case. Pappa had not held it against him. He had said Mr. Jefferson was very young.

"But we may not free them!" Thomas loomed with his head among the fluttering blossoms. "We are bound, are we not, as fast as they? We may keep them enslaved and care for them or sell them to someone who will mistreat them. Dear God, what a hideous evil! How did we ever come to this?"

I have never seen slavery as a particular evil. The world is full of evils, and all of them seem equally abhorrent to me. I cannot bear to hear the stuck hogs squeal nor see a horse ill-used nor think there could be anywhere an unloved child. The differences in human station seem to me not even the greatest evil. But I want our Negroes fed and warm and not worked beyond what I work myself, and never hurt. The families must be kept together. I cannot bear to see them whipped, although gentlemen whip them readily.

Bathurst sometimes used to decide that a whole gang was slacking and ripe for correction. He would gather them at sunset in a barn and have them flogged ten or fifteen blows which he swore to me did not hurt them at all but only reminded them of their station and who it was they had a duty to please. The first time I was aware of this it came with no warning, but I heard the commotion begin in the barn not far from my open window. When I understood what it was that I was hearing I began to scream even louder than they so Bathurst had to order it stopped for fear I would give myself an apoplexy when I was already well gone with child. He learned to carry on his correction of his slaves beyond my sight and hearing, but he carried it on. My Pappa does it, too, but never at the Forest; I am told that if a home Negro is troublesome he is carried off to a farther plantation, and there he is whipped. I try not to think of it.

But, as I say, I had seen these evils as part of the natural pattern of evils and had not marked them out any more than I would have marked out one particular tree. So for Thomas to be calling for an end to slavery struck me as astonishing revelation.

"What will be the ending?" he was carrying on. "For there will be an ending, Martha. There is nothing in this world more certain than the fact that our slaves will one day be free. But how shall we free them? We cannot live together. One race will always subjugate the other. Yet we cannot send these Virginia-born to an Africa they have never known! And what of the mulattoes? Which race will claim them? What will they all do to us for having so badly treated them? And what will God do? I tremble for us all when I contemplate the fact that God is Just!"

He was frightening me. The ground seemed to tilt, and tears filled my eyes so I could not see.

"Martha? Martha?" He thought me simply too abashed to speak. He sighed. "I see we must have this conversation. With all the whole catalogue of slavery's evils there is this further cruelty."

"Forgive me" was all I could think to say but my throat was so tight the words would not come out.

He said, "I know no other way to say this than to plainly speak it out. I would never take a slave to my bed, Martha, neither married nor single, were she ever so willing. I would never do such a dishonorable thing. If you have learned nothing else of me I am greatly aggrieved that you have not learned that."

I lifted my face and when he saw my tears his agitation left him. *"Chérie."* He took my hands and lifted me to my feet. *"Ne pleure pas. Je t'aime. Je t'aime."* He put his arm around my waist and dried my cheeks with his fingers; he untied my ribbon and lifted my hat and brushed the petals from my cap beneath. I raised my eyes, very full of the thrill of feeling his own dear arm about me. How my poor breast fluttered! He must feel my heart where it beat against him its desperate plea that he understand all my love and fears and not go away from me. Looking so closely into his eyes where we stood upon the hill with our faces near level I seemed of a wonder to see him clearly, open of eye and honest of heart, a gentleman as innocent as a child. He has an uncorrupted spirit as if each day were but his first, yet with it a wisdom as of an ancient who has lived much beyond one single life. This combination of innocence and wisdom seems to me an absolute summation of him. How greatly I love him! I would spend my life as his horse or his slave or the shirt that sheds its fibers against his skin. But I cannot marry him. I cannot do it.

While I stood within his arm thus confounded and stricken, my Thomas softly kissed me. In truth he could have kissed me before that moment, for custom allows lovers to kiss while courting and my sister Tibby has kissed Bobby Skipwith while they boldly sat in Pappa's parlor. But Thomas's shyness or my own reluctance, something had kept him from kissing me, so I was astonished but greatly thrilled when he doffed his hat and kissed me on the hill. Indeed lovers may kiss with propriety, but their kisses are only the touching of lips. Thomas touched my lips. Then, whether the fault was his or mine, we clasped one another in close embrace and kissed as only husband and wife should kiss. My stays were so tight that I could not draw breath but I wanted that kiss to go on forever.

Perhaps it was I who had the greater fault, for when he tried to draw away I clung the more fiercely.

"My dear!" He disengaged himself. I clasped hand to bosom and struggled for breath. "Martha?" he said as if greatly alarmed. The petals were as thick as a cap on his hair. There passed between us a look of such complete understanding that, breathless or not, we began to laugh. "My dear! Will you survive?" We laughed the harder for our breathlessness which made it difficult to laugh at all. I sat. He fell down onto the grass and we laughed for all the pleasure of laughing and for the sweet relief of knowing we need never again have this conversation.

THE FOREST JUNE 19, 1771

I am undone. The early light falls gray on my table, gray on my paper, and gray on the raggedy crooked quill which is gray from his own tiny fingers upon it. Now he lies forever in the ground. I had thought, for a time, I would die of my grief. I never had imagined I would want my journal, yet here I sit, wondering how to begin, knowing only that I must unburden myself so I can be strong when Thomas comes.

He left us on the morning of the ninth of June. Jack was breeding an ear-fever that came on so mild it seemed our greatest worry then was the flood of the Rivanna River which had borne away Thomas's mill at Shadwell and brought such misery in Albemarle that he left us to see what might be done. He would call again on Friday next to be of the party for Tibby's wedding. Now Tibby's wedding is delayed. She knows not when she can bear to marry.

Jack's ear-fever was worse by evening. Even laudanum could not stem his pain, and his ague was such that he shook in my arms and burned so he heated me near to fever. Betty feared to have her babies near him so she sent them to the quarters, and Betsy debated with Francis whether they might take off their son as well. I knew nothing of this. I only rocked and sang while my baby screamed. I offered up my life many times that night if only God would relieve my child. But it was not to be. Dawn found him in a rigid sleep from which he shook now and then with such violence that he near tore himself out of my arms. Pappa rode for the doctor at Charles City Court-House, leaving I believe before one o'clock, but hours passed and they did not return until the sun was up and my darling Jack was in the sleep from which he never awoke. The doctor said it was a malignant brain-fever and there was nothing he could have done but I was long past anyone's reason. I screamed at them both and beat Pappa's breast that they had not come soon enough to save him.

What can I say about that day? Betty washed and dressed him. I could not do that. I wept until there was nothing left in me, no feeling left, not even pain, and then near evening I went to lie beside him where Betty had laid him on my bed. He looked so like his father lying there. I had always pretended he took after me, but there was Bathurst's sleeping face, his own dark hair and long, dark lashes, his nose that was broad from base to tip and his mouth small and pursed with no lip to it. Poor Bathurst had left but this one child. This felt like his second and final death.

And indeed this was very much like his death, the surprise of it cutting through my life so grief was mingled with amazement. He had gone to Philadelphia to be inoculated against the small-pox, leaving toward the end of the summer and going as much for the adventure of it as for the medical benefit. Perhaps he also went to find some peace. Lovey's baby had been born a few weeks before. He took the cure well, I understand, but Philadelphia had the dysentery and he became so ill on the journey home that he was rendered insensible. His servants had not the wit to find a doctor. They tried to hurry him home instead, and he was four days traveling day and night in a bouncing carriage. He arrived at home near moribund. We could not even say good-bye.

So I lay there spent beside my child, looking at their mingled faces and thinking of Bathurst because I could not bear to think of my little Jack. I sold Lovey off after Bathurst's death. A gentleman took her to North Carolina together with her three children, and he promised he would keep them together. That was all I could do for her. But lying in the quiet, drained of tears, I tried to begin to forgive my husband. I saw with a pain of hot tears running freshly again behind my eyes that my forgiveness of his father is the only remaining gift that I can give to my son.

Bathurst's Lovey had been a gift from his brother when Bathurst was fifteen and she was twelve, and Reuben had then immediately died, after which his widow had married my Pappa. So Bathurst had known his Lovey before he ever knew me. He had loved me, I know, but lying there now I admitted that she had been the love of his life as Thomas is becoming the love of mine. Knowing love better, seeing how it is possible to be seized by such a mighty passion that honor and reason are nothing beside it, I understood Bathurst as I never had done. For you, my little son, I shall try to forgive.

Upon the next morning we buried my Jack in the graveyard near the creek where my mother lies. I was comforted to see him laid beside her. I had a vision of handing him into her arms. But then came the pain! I can say very little of all the days that followed because I wandered through them near insensible. I wept, I sanded floors and scrubbed bedsteads, I shouted at Pappa and my poor little Bett, I brewed small-beer and walked by the mill-pond and wailed and punched pillows with my fist. So many babies die. Wise mothers keep them distant until they are at the age of three. Yet my baby was three! He should have been safe! Oh, I know I cannot marry again. I cannot have another child because I am so entirely foolish that when I love it is without a limit. Loving carries such a risk that I cannot bear this pain again. I shall die of it. This I write. Yet now I look at my words and I know that indeed I shall marry again and I shall have other children. Because I am foolish! I shall know no peace until I hold another baby in my arms.

Pappa asked me often if he might send for Thomas but I could not bear to have him come. He is so tender, and he so loved Jack. Seeing him grieving would have taken from me what little sanity I retained. I found comfort in thinking of Thomas in Albemarle, happily going through his days, with Jack still living in his mind and our whole golden future still before us. It is only this morning that I have awakened feeling well enough to have him come. I could comfort him now. And I long for him so! The hole in my life where my little son was compounds the emptiness I always feel when Thomas is away from me. I shall close this now and write a note that I shall send by Ben, who has been once before to Monticello so he knows the way to ride. I shall write on the cover that Thomas must open his note in private. He will want the grace of suffering his first shock alone.

THE FOREST JULY 24, 1771

*T*ibby has become Mrs. Robert Skipwith, which has been ever her dearest wish. She was married on Monday with great merriment, even as we all still grieved for Jack. There is comfort, finally, in the joy of others, and never was there seen so joyous a wedding. Tibby is my prettiest, gayest sister, with such a merriment about the way she walks and easily laughs in company that people are greatly drawn to her. Betsy is as smooth and placid as a pond, and Nancy at near fifteen is still so childish that she keeps a rag-doll upon her bed. But Tibby at seventeen is become a great lady.

For four days we had fifty people, the ladies four to a bed in the house and the gentlemen banished to a barn and three wedding-balls which were different each evening. Once we wore court-dress with great side-hoops and Tibby and Bobby queen and king on a dais and naught for the dancing but minuets. Then we had the next evening an usual ball, the minuets varied with country-dances, and the last evening we who remained dressed as servants and passed our ball sporting at reels and jigs. Even every breakfast was a great occasion of platters of meats and fruits and breads. Tibby managed it all. She would accept no help. Her husband's people already brag of her.

What mattered to me most of Tibby's wedding was four days of Thomas's company. He had come to me on command of my note, but soon he had been bidden on to the Capital where the Burgesses sat in extra session to deal as they could with the great spring flood. We have had less flooding on Kimages Creek, but they have had in the Tidewater and into the Piedmont the greatest flooding ever seen. It seems the very rivers weep for my Jack where he lies small and quiet in the ground.

My Thomas is an inward gentleman. As Pappa seems to hide a smoldering beneath his jocular surface, so Thomas, now that I know him well, seems mild and good-humored upon his face but so dense with emotion just beneath that often I fear he will shame himself by showing his emotions against his will. So it has seemed to some that the loss of our Jack has brought to him only the mildest grief. All his care has been for me, to divert me with such a round of music and paying calls that I had no thought to spare for Jack. Yet I know him too well. I see how he broods in quiet contemplation of Betsy's son, how he pauses with his hand on the back of Jack's high-chair or stares at a peach-pit found in a corner, a remnant of their games of checks. We comfort one another, and on this week-end it has seemed that we are becoming whole.

Perhaps some of this was due to Dabney Carr, the puckish husband of his sister Patsy, who rode up with him to attend the wedding in a great chair borrowed from Landon Carter, a gentleman who is so vastly wealthy that he will not miss one chair more or less. Patsy is near to me in age. My first sight of her was with lappets flying, rushing into the yard at a canter, the horses wide-eyed and Patsy laughing between two rollicking gentlemen who looked at that moment nothing older than the schoolboys they had been together. Dabney is the finest wit, the most voluble of gentlemen. He is a rising lawyer who is, Thomas says, far the greatest orator, greater even than Patrick Henry and bound to enjoy the most brilliant career of their whole circle of friends. Thomas greatly loves him, for Dabney will not let him keep his dignity but he teases him with an innocent wit that puts my Thomas into fits of laughter.

My dear one greatly enjoys a jest which punctures what ever he holds most solemn, as when I boxed his ear while he played at his music or when once I gave him a series of puns on Portia's mercy discourse from *The Merchant of Venice*. This enjoyment of his well suits my bent to see all from an edge of irreverence so I have fancied myself his ideal companion. Yet while I manage one jest and think myself clever, his Dabney is able to orchestrate a very great crescendo of jests, one built most innocent upon another, until Thomas collapses and weeps of his laughter and all who love him must then laugh with him, which makes the party very gay.

This spring I have met very many other of Thomas's gentleman friends. These he has drawn to him all his life for his mildness of manner and his sharpness of wit; while he has not known how to converse with ladies, he shines in the company of gentlemen. And he has held his oldest friends to be ever the dearest, so he still retains like toys on a shelf the love of his playfulest childhood companions.

The foremost of these great childhood friends are Dabney and his opposite, John Page of Rosewell, the mannerly lord of an ancient Seat of a very wealthy family. I encountered Page in May at the Berkeley Plantation, which is so near the Forest that we could attend a ball there and return the same evening. Page, as my Thomas ever calls him, is a pretty gentleman proud of look. His wife is Fanny Burwell, a delicate lady I knew at Pappa's balls when I was first a belle, and I found her still given to telling gossip and talking of the latest London fashions. So Page and Thomas conversed half in Latin and Greek while Fanny and I made show to discuss certain gambling losses and the sizes of hoops while we cast our gentlemen sidelong glances half of pride at their so learned minds and half of irritation.

I expected Dabney to be much like Page, too full of fine portentous thoughts to give much notice to lesser beings. Far from that! He spoke no language but English, and that half the time in shouts or giggles. His Patsy says he is not always this way but Thomas's company seems to affect him, so when they are together her rising lawyer and my lawyer who is also a Burgess are again nothing more than schoolboys slipping frogs into one another's pockets. This interplay Patsy so much enjoys that she very near makes a third of them, for she will suggest to one or the other what he will then say out most heartily. I liked Patsy from our earliest meeting for her face and manner that resemble my dear one and for her mix of irreverent humor with a plain and practical gravity. Unlike near every other lady, she has but little care for fashion. Her cap is a pinny with lappets down such as only an ancient lady might wear, her mitts are black by day, all her costume is wrong, yet all is worn by her so becomingly that she makes it seem the fashion must be wrong and only Patsy Carr must have it right.

It was Dabney's whole purpose for his four-day stay to press me into setting a wedding-date. I believe that I shall marry Thomas, I come to see no other course, but as yet I am unable to say the word so we go at our marriage by narrowing angles. In an excess of very love for him, I have spent my every afternoon this spring embroidering for him a waistcoat and pocket of green silk strewn with singing birds. For his part, he has given thought to how we might make a more perfect music. Attorney General John Randolph has the finest imported violin, and Thomas has entered some transaction with him to ensure that the violin will one day be his own. And now he most resolutely insists that no harpsichord will ever do for me so he has ordered from England the grandest forte-piano. He expects it in country by the fall. Then we shall see. With pocket and waistcoat ready, with forte-piano and violin, with burgessing behind him for another year and dear little Tibby safely wed, we shall see.

Thomas made excuse of the like to Dabney, but that would never do for him. Dabney said the word "marriage" repeatedly and far more often than was necessary, even for a wedding-guest. Then on Tuesday he proposed that we four should take a walk before breakfast. This was greeted as a happy thought, for we were weary of sleeping four to a bed and longed for private company. We set off together, the Carrs walking first, leading us down a path to a wood. We needed shade, for neither lady had a mask. The Carrs were holding hands. Thomas took my hand when we were out of sight of the house. "Masterful!" Dabney said when he saw that we were hand-in-hand. "You will soften her yet! And shall I kiss my wife? Shall we see what might be the outcome of that?"

He drew Patsy to him and kissed her enough that she put hand to hat and scolded him. "Please! My brother will defend my honor!"

"You have no honor. You are my wife." He looked at us, said, "Damn! Nothing yet," and gave his Patsy another kiss.

My Thomas so enjoyed Dabney's teasing that he did a thing that astonished me. He drew me to him with his hand at my waist and kissed me harder than he ever had done.

"Eureka! We have the secret, Pat. Whatever we do they will copy us."

"I think it not!" she said with spirit.

"Look about. Find some grassy spot where we may lie."

"Sir! Remember yourself!"

He laughed. Thomas was laughing, too, and Patsy was enjoying her husband and her brother with a pride of effortless possession. I felt a sudden yearning to marry my Thomas so sharp that it was near to pain.

"Does it not touch you, Tom? The thought of Skipwith alone at last with his little Tibby? And fancy being alone among fifty people lying like cordwood in all the beds and pressing their ears against the walls. I should be afraid one or the other of us would make a sound."

"Dabney!" Patsy said hotly.

"Now look ahead here. A fortuitous fork. You take one branch and we shall take the other." Dabney went as far as this fork in the path before he drew his Patsy again so close that she blushed a little with her arms around him. "I am sure that you will quite understand my wish to spend a little time alone with my wife."

"Be alone if you will," my Thomas said, "but I fear you will find the softness of pine-needles to be greatly overrated."

"We shall not feel the needles. We shall float on the air. And please, Madam Skelton, have a kindly heart. Be very gentle with this man. He is so far gone in love with you that the wrong word said at the wrong moment will make him shrivel with despair. And Tom, you lumbering farmer's son, will you manage to get it right this time? I have taught you all I know and still you are single. I am very near giving up on you."

"I suppose I lack your silver tongue. Perhaps you will be good enough to make my proposal in my stead."

"I doubt that! There are things, my friend, that a man is required to do for himself. And I," he said to Patsy, "intend doing every one of them at the earliest moment."

They went along the path he had chosen. Thomas took my hand and said, "Shall we go farther? Or shall we turn back?"

"Let us walk for a bit." I wanted above all else the pleasure of being alone with him.

We walked a path dappled with spots of light, with the birds still making their morning music and the cleanly sweet of dew-moist pine. I imagined us in the wilderness. It begins not many miles from here and it stretches beyond what the mind can imagine, just forest forever into the west.

"I like them very much," I said. "Your Dabney and your sister Carr. She makes me think of you, the way she is grave on the surface yet she bubbles with merriment underneath."

"I must apologize for Dabney. He is so innocent that sometimes he lacks propriety."

"I am no blushing virgin, Thomas."

"That I would wish most devoutly!"

Before I could reply he drew me into a close embrace. I had a thought for the Carrs but they were far away on private business of their own; Thomas and I were as much alone as if the world ended beyond those trees. My Thomas's face was tight of a tension born of our solitude and Dabney's teasing and his perfect awareness of what his friend and his sister did together in that moment. I had imagined how he might be in the privacy of our marital chamber, but never had I envisioned that look of his face of pure and ardent carnal feeling. It delighted and alarmed me out of mind so I could not speak or draw my breath. He said, *"Je t'aime,"* and a babble of French so rapid I could not follow it, and he kissed me the ardent kiss of a husband who is making purpose with his wife.

Then did I long to be his wife! I felt a perfect yearning to be his wife and lie with him in the morning wood and let there never be an ending. But I could not breathe. Betty so prides herself on lacing me tight that she still refuses to let Bett do it; she comes in at dawn and sets her child on my bed and draws on my laces as if there were a contest to win if she managed to cleave me full in two.

"Wait! Please!" I said.

Thomas left off his kissing with a great reluctance. He traced my cheek and cap with his fingers while I struggled to draw sufficient breath. I struggled as well with propriety. What we meant to do was shameful; were it known, it would ruin all my life. That was the thought of some small, sane part while all my blood and bones and organs louder said that a whole life's shame was worth one moment in these woods.

"Thomas? I must remove my stays."

We shared a look then of complete understanding. The risk was really very small; Dabney and Patsy made our alibi. Indeed, I thought Dabney might have intended to bring about this very event. Thomas reseated his hat and turned away and caught his hands behind his back. He drew a long breath and lifted his head as if he were searching among the trees. His queue moved slowly from left to right. "We would know," he said.

"No other would know!"

"But we would know. There is nothing so private that you are able to hide it from yourself."

"Dabney and Patsy will believe it whether we do or no!"

"What they believe does not matter. I will not let there be any thing dishonorable between us."

It was these words of his that decided me. I had been walking on an edge all spring, wanting Thomas for my husband yet sorely fearing the awful betrayal of innocent trust. I had for long tried to trust my Thomas as Saint Peter trusted in the Lord enough to let him walk upon the water. I had tried, but always had seen the torrent and tumbled into it most miserably. I had tried. But then in that single moment I heard my dear one's honest words and the water firmed to rock beneath my feet. I watched my Thomas square his shoulders. His resolve decided, he was about to turn again.

Softly I said to his own dear back, "Beloved? When shall we plan our wedding?"

THE FOREST SEPTEMBER 6, 1771

*O*h! I am the most dilatory of journal-keepers. I do not deserve the name at all. Perhaps I had thought to lay this book aside, now that my partner in life is decided; there seems to be little to write after marriage beyond how many beeves were killed this day or where I have found a broody hen with her pilfered clutch of eggs. Are married people allowed emotions? Are they not better off without them? This summer was hardly kind to me, for I spent all of August without my dear one. I never even had news of him beyond messages enclosed in letters to Pappa or even to my brother Skip- with that came too seldom to offer me comfort.

He would not write to me. I apprehend his shyness which makes him unable to write private words for fear of a stranger's eyes upon them, yet reluctant to write an impersonal letter to one with whom he feels a complete connection. He is boxed from two directions so he cannot write. This I most perfectly understand. Yet I find an unease that makes me half-believe as I lie in my bed in the quiet night that he keeps himself away and he does not write for some new-found reluctance to marry me. I needs must recall his gaze upon me when ever I move or smile or speak, his attitude one of such complete entertainment that he makes me feel myself the most beloved of women. It is only my memory of his face as it is transformed when he looks at me that sustains my conviction of his certain love when we are long apart.

My Thomas spent his August at his Monticello, where he over-saw his hands as they cleared the forest and built their offices and quarters that we might begin our marriage in a proper home. He has told me so often how rude it is that all I can envision is the wild forest and a dirt-floored cabin with chimney-hole such as only the worst-kept slaves might use. He assures me it is not quite that. He has left me this morning after two days here during which all he ever would talk about was the eager domestic plans he is making, the farm he is building and the details of our house that still exists only within his mind. He sketched it for me as I watched him do it, sitting with his tongue at the corner of his mouth in an attitude of perfect concentration. From his cabin he intends to build a manor-house with an entrance hall of two stories of pillars and ever so many details of moldings. It plain astonished me to see it. And he has designed it all himself.

"I wonder," I said when I held his vision of the perfect manor in my hand. "Would architecture pay us more than lawyering? And would you be at home more often?"

"Less often. I would have to do more than draw them. They would insist I go out and put them up."

"Then let us concentrate upon farming." For this is what I hope will come to pass. With his lands and those that I have from Bathurst we shall have sufficient tobacco-land to earn us quite a respectable income. Lawyering would have him away too much. I digress. What has brought me to grope beneath my bed and return to journal-keeping once again is a tender remark he made this morning as we stood by the step of his phaeton and made our respectable family farewells when all that we wanted to do was cling.

"I am bound for Williamsburg within the month," he said above my head to Pappa. "That is, if I am re-elected." He paused with his hand on the reins and his foot already upon the step while Pappa said that he would be re-elected or Albemarle was a land of fools. "It is not that, so the election is decided," Thomas said with his own soft smile which graces his eyes more than his mouth. "I shall call again, then, at the end of the month. My brother Randolph begins at the College. He has promised that he will transport my books so I may have additional time with you."

Thomas had been with us for but two days, and that after more than a month apart. The prospect of another month to come was almost more than I could bear.

"Sweet Patty." I could see in his face how my distress was paining him. *"Je t'aime,"* he said in front of them all. We turned from the others and he privately said, "Write what you feel in your journal, Patty. We shall read it together when I come again." So now I write. He has spoken of my journal before; he seems to see it as his key to some more perfect emotional union. If he knew how poorly I had written he might not want to marry me at all, for I fear he thinks me a great deal more clever and far more emotional than I am.

I know but one emotion and that is only the purest, the most uncomplicated love, the tenderest worship that ever a woman can feel for the man she so adores. Foolish word! Love is so readily named in reference to every so pallid affection that I have no word to give a sufficient account of all there is to love about this man. All there is to love! He is the most gentle of men, far the most sympathetic and the quickest of wit. Even saying these words seems to make him less when he is all good things in an infinite measure. Further, there is nothing he cannot do! I vow he might have a dozen careers, whether music or architecture or planting or printing or even his infernal lawyering which has him too much away from me. His Jupiter says that he could even make a blacksmith if he were lowly enough in station, and in truth I would rather have him that than have him even the King himself and far away from me.

I have written these words for you, dear Husband. Husband you will be when one day you read them. I cannot share them with you sooner; I only hope I shall find the courage to share them with you on some distant day when we have long been united and we want for only this grace note of additional sharing to make ours the most perfect happiness.

WILLIAMSBURGH, OCT. 23, 1771

My dear Martha

Your father writes that you have refused to answer my letters because I have not written to you alone. I can so clearly see you saying this, with a stamp of your foot and a turn of your head, that I confess I smiled when I read his letter. Then I found my hat and gloves and went out to pay a call on Miss Dickerson, since she is the milliner that you prefer. My sister Nancy prefers Mrs. Pitt so I may go there tomorrow, although spending what I cannot say because I emptied my pocket on Miss Dickerson's counter. I hope you will like what I have bought. Ladies have very decided notions about colour and cut and such details, and I have learned from my sisters that my own taste runs to the plain and decidedly out of fashion. But I have had Miss Dickerson's guidance. She assures me I shall not embarrass my-self.

Dear Martha, I know that what you hope for from me is a love letter. I love you, soon you will be my wife, so a love letter is what you should receive. You are right to object to finding "Remember me to Martha" at the end of the letters I have no need to write to your father beyond my inability to finish the day without the pleasure of watching my hand write your name.

I can speak of my love for you to others. I do that, in fact, to the point of boring them, bringing up your name and our happy prospect in the midst of a discussion of fines or taxation so men look at me as if I have lost my mind. I have lost it, Martha. My mind is yours, my heart and my soul belong to you. But see, I can't even call you "Patty" in this, which is your very own letter. To write a formal love letter would seem foolish now, with all the understanding that is between us, yet to put into words that understanding is beyond my poor ability; my pen is struck as dumb as my throat. Martha, Patty (I have written the name so now per-haps the words will unstick), you are my light and all my happiness. I can't bear the thought of even the small vexa-tion I know you feel at having such an inarticulate lover. Were it possible, I would be with you now to let kisses and caresses and soulful looks say what I seem unable to say or write.

Please write to me, my dearest friend.

Th:Jefferson

WILLIAMSBURG MARCH 26, 1772

I have longed to write of my wedding these three months past. Already I disremember some details. But my journal is stuck behind the loose bricks in the kitchen at Monticello, and it seems it may be some months more before we find ourselves at home again. So I find I must write on letter-paper and then have later to copy it over if ever again I have time enough for the simple pleasures of journal-keeping.

The greatest inconvenience of married life is never having time alone. But Thomas has just now safely left to attend this day's sitting of the Burgesses, so I hope for some hours' solitude unless the gentlemen should again turn saucy and vex the Governor into dissolving them. Such a great sport it is, this matter of Government! We are out at dinner every night, and every night there is another table of gentlemen urging one another into a further riot of pious speech. They talk treason at their private tables. Oh, I share their sentiments in the heat of it, I think it is all very well indeed to cry that we are badly governed and Britain must change or let us be. It touches me not at all as I go about my daily tasks, but when I hear it so bravely spoken out it seems to me very well indeed.

Then we return from George Wythe's home, or Peyton Randolph's home, or the near-by rooms where grave Colonel Washington stays with his delightful lady or where Mr. Henry stays with his lady, who seems to me really a little mad.

Is she mad? Mrs. Henry laughs out oddly or she stares at a wall seeming most alarmed, but she speaks between times so sensibly that her husband seems determined to believe her sane. Other ladies make a sport of her, but this I cannot do. I see a pain in her. I feel certain that her peculiarities are beyond her control. Dear kindly Mrs. Washington shares my view, and I marvel to see how she can converse right through some foolishness of Mrs. Henry's and never move her eyes, never alter her voice.

So we sit for near two hours at table while the gentlemen declaim their complaints against Britain and the ladies discuss what ladies ever discuss, the clumsiness of servants or the dyeing with indigo or the choice of decoctions to cure a child of rashes or a summer-cough. When the last course is cleared the ladies remain since our apartments have no retiring rooms, so we join in the toasts in arrack and wine which the gentlemen give most ardently. They toast the ladies first, then they make a point to piously toast their sovereign King, after which they ever more ardently toast Virginia's noble soil and their own liberty which never can be subject to a Parliament's whim. We return to our rooms past nine o'clock, very weary and warm of all our toasting. As we wash our faces and undress for bed I say to my Thomas, "Are they not talking treason?"

"To speak your own mind can never be treason."

"But if they act on their words? If they try to evict the British Governor?"

This thought charms my husband. "Is that what you imagine? We shall turn little Dunmore out of his Palace and offer up his rooms to let?"

"Do not make sport of me!" I am near to tears. My husband's lack of fear is a failing I had not known of on our wedding-day, and I daresay if only I had known of it I might have chosen to remained unwed. "Take care that you do not lose your head with all this talk of liberty. Truly lose it, Husband! And you have not the right! Your head belongs to me!" He kisses me then and tells me these are worries that never should trouble my mind. I am safe, for he will care for me and our baby that is already with us and will be born, I believe, near the end of the summer. But my worry is not for me. It is for him! I see how the older gentlemen hush when he speaks and I hear from his mouth the most treasonous thoughts in the calmest, most sensible words of all.

My Pappa has told me in high good humor that the Burgesses are on the edge of revolt and the least British wind will topple them. But they had better win! And this he said quite laughingly, which made the horror of it all the worse. If they do not win, he said to me, there will be gibbets in every market-square and gentlemen's heads will be set on pikes at every doorstep in every town. This the British have done in Scotland and Wales. Where ever Englishmen have revolted they have been crushed. But my husband is just twenty-eight! I might see some sense in all of this if we were truly oppressed, but Britain bothers us so very little we forget that it is even there unless we want a bolt of silk or a forte-piano. And what with the bans they keep putting on imports even that reminder of Britain is less; I vow I hardly think of Britain from one year's harvest to the next. Yet for gentlemen, even knowing Britain is there is like an itch they must scratch and scratch until, I fear, they will have drawn their own poor foolish blood.

Why do I write this? I sat down here in a happy frame of mind to write of our wedding and the baby to come. There is no point in fretting. That I imagine the Burgesses are at this moment marching on the Governor's Palace with my own dear husband at the front of them, fighting with words those British guns, that this thought is now stuck fast in my mind is no reason to ruin a beautiful day.

The sun has risen beyond the next-door house so its light falls upon my pane and sill. The outside of the pane is very dusty from all the traffic in the street; I shall have to call for Martin to climb up and wash it before his master returns. We have rented four rooms on the second floor of Mr. Cary's house, and while we have a room for our female servants the boys must sleep in a cellar so damp that I fear continually for their health.

Now the wedding.

We had thought to be married near Christmas Day, but Thomas was so occupied in readying our home that he did not arrive until the end of that week. Then we had to wait for additional friends, he had to post his marriage-bond, so at length we set the wedding to occur upon the first day of this year. My first wedding was a pious rite with only family in attendance, but this one filled Pappa's parlor to bursting with so very many of Thomas's friends that when came time for us to approach Reverend Coutts I swear we could not part the crowd. I wore for my wedding a new-sewn gown in the very latest London fashion, a splendid yellow silk brocade with gold-embroidered stomacher and petticoat and exquisite falls at sleeves and bosom of Honiton lace so near-transparent they seem just gossamer whispers of thought and hardly lace at all. Such a beautiful gown!

The cloth came from the Eppeses at Bermuda Hundred, who were my mother's people. They are a family near as wealthy as the Carters so all my mother's clothing was surpassing fine, and this bolt was so grand that she kept it whole against some great occasion. When she lay near death of the childbed-fever she bade my Pappa promise that her yellow silk would be saved out for her newborn child and made up into its wedding-gown. So he kept it by for me all these years but he disremembered it for my first wedding, so now there it was to be made up fresh by Mrs. Oglethorpe at Charles City Court-House. Her servants are trained at embroidery, so the gold-thread thistles on the stomacher and petticoat are the finest I have ever seen. I would not have my petticoat quilted despite the month, but I wore beneath it a quilted one. I want to have it for every season, when ever there is a grand enough ball. I believe I shall not shame my husband.

Thomas was speechless when he saw my gown. He gazed at me with his face gone rapt, then he gave to me his deepest bow as I gave to him my curtsey. He had powdered and tightly curled his hair, something he seldom troubles to do, and at the sight I laughed for plain enjoyment of my splendid, splendid husband. He had for his bridesman Dabney Carr and I had dearest Betsy, who was far gone with her second child that is due to be born within the month.

He was nervous, my dear husband. His voice shook to say his vows. He said later it was a factor of the crowd, for he cannot speak above a small group but his voice cracks and fails and goes too soft. It was not, he said, any reconsideration of his decision to marry me. And for my own part, every former doubt seemed as foreign as a tale I had only read of some poor lady tricked by her fate into sorry suspicion and disbelieving. Indeed, I trust my dear one the more for my very lack of prior trust. Life teaches many grievous lessons. We must take care not to overlearn them.

We danced and supped in Pappa's ballroom, where Mr. Alberti fiddled so well that Thomas and I joined him for some of the music. Mr. Alberti is a little Italian man with bowed legs and a most ill-fitting wig who has taught music to us both separately. He vows that now he shall teach us together. When the supper was very well along and some of the guests were soon retiring, Thomas took my hand and we left together to climb the ladder to our wedding-garret.

It was upon the week-end before our wedding that Thomas gave some careful thought to the problem Dabney Carr had posed when Tibby was wed. My husband is too private in his person to do what Tibby and Bobby had done, to choose out some one of the chambers and never mind the ears against the walls. So he found that week-end a servants' garret that is never used in winter for the fact it has no fireplace. He carried up a featherbed and all of ten or fifteen blankets, and there it was that we slept together for the first two weeks of our married life. Perhaps it was this that I wanted most to record of our wedding. You will treasure it, Husband, as I shall treasure it, that memory of climbing into our garret and dropping the door and pegging it and being there truly alone together as we had never been alone before.

It was cold! We could not undress, but we had to hurry into the blankets and talk and kiss until we were warmed and able to begin to remove our clothes. Even that went slowly and with much laughter over how very cold it was; and perhaps we also laughed for the shyness of our being of an instant naked together. His skin against mine was near to fire and very welcome in the cold, yet knowing it was his skin made me blush severely. It seemed my head well understood that what we did was no longer shameful, yet my body retained its former opinion.

I complain much of Bathurst, but he was in truth a very ardent husband. Perhaps it was his practice of Lovey that made him so clever at the marital act, for he had very much practice. He kept his own chamber that I might believe him there when he was not with me, but I knew that he ever slept in my bed or in his Lovey's cabin. I wept very much when I was alone, yet when my husband was in my bed I endeavored to put out from my mind this rival of mine who must be no rival.

How different it is with my dear Thomas! For him I have no hidden rival. I have not the need to show to him a desperate and too-ardent love, nor feel the anger that tainted my bed when I slept with a husband who day upon day gave me further reason for despising him. The intimacy of our days together came into our bed even that first night, so Thomas spoke softly to ask me if he might try this or that and we laughed together over his inventions that came to seem ridiculous. We laughed at the sacred act itself, for Thomas said how foolish he felt to be a gentleman refined of manner who yet is prey to all the carnal urges of a stallion rutting in the stable-yard. This drew us to jesting speculation upon more dignified means that Providence might invent for procreation of gentlemen upon their ladies until we had made ourselves sick of laughter, sore of belly and sore of head.

But Thomas was ardent. We could not play for long before the thrill of it was beyond his endurance and he must press on to complete the act. This he said was a factor of his long abstinence. Although he confessed that as a youth he had copied his fellows and consorted with women of a lesser virtue, he had put this practice by forever when he had resolved at one-and-twenty to hold to honor in his private as in his public life. Dear Thomas! I loved him the more for the fact of his confession and for its substance. Very soon this effect was lost, and he comes now calmly to our bed with the ease of a gentleman who never in his life has confronted an empty table. Yet ever I remember my too-eager husband who could have found no better way to prove that I need never fear a rival. At that moment I was opened to him and united with him, my body and soul. I can write no more of this. My cheeks are smarting. But I do believe that if husbands and wives give full attention to their marriage-bed they can put away many greater troubles.

We never slept on that first night. It was so delicious to be alone and talk and kiss and begin again with the moonlight silver through our little window. Soon we were not cold at all, but we complained in the night of being too warm so once near morning he said, "How can you bear it?" and he stood up so his head was to the ridgepole and he was laughing in the frozen air. To see men unclothed is a common thing on every Virginia plantation, where the slave-boys run about in shirts and they have no Christian modesty. Still I was astonished at the sight of my husband shining like an angel in the dark, his hair upon his shoulder and all his body long and vigorous, so beautiful that I gasped at the sight and now nearly weep to think of it.

They shall not have him. That I swear.

The one untoward event of our wedding was the bladder-fever and strangury which came days later and made me crouch for all of a day in misery over a chamber-pot while Thomas read and fretted. I assured him this had happened before. It had come on repeatedly during my marriage and had given me no small amount of pain until Gabbler, an old woman Bathurst had who was fancied a healer among his slaves, persuaded me to drink of copious water when I felt the bladder-fever coming on. All the bleeding and poulticing and puking and purging had only served to make me worse, but Gabbler's copious water and her foul decoctions of onions and tobacco and poplar bark brought a quick and near-miraculous cure. The bladder-fever seems to be connected with recent resumption of the marital act, for it used to strike when Bathurst had but lately returned from some long journey. To our great relief I recovered from the bladder-fever within that day, and the only effect it has had upon me is my husband's daily concern with my water-drinking.

We stayed at the Forest for those two weeks in hopes of better weather, but the winter settled in with yet more snow and ever colder winds. The phaeton needed a switch from shafts to a carriage-pole and whiffletrees so we might put to it my pair of grays that I have down from Bathurst. Then we set out. We stayed each night at some plantation or other along the road. By the time we reached Tuckahoe, three days later, the snow was falling in deadly earnest and the phaeton was near to losing a wheel so we stopped once again and had it mended. For another two days we made but very little progress, driving swathed in blankets while our horses strained to drag us through the knee-deep snow. By the time we reached Blenheim we knew the phaeton would not make it up the mountain-side, so we left it there and borrowed saddles of Colonel Carter's overseer. There was but one side-saddle at Blenheim. The overseer would not see it go, but Thomas persuaded him with talk of our being only lately wed and eager to be at home alone and this the overseer must understand.

We set out at sunset to complete our journey. The storm had abated to the point where we saw a brilliant orange light which I declared to be a fine omen and Thomas declared to mean specifically there would be a very warm fire laid. We yet had eight more miles to travel, and this through snow beyond two feet deep and drifted as high as my horse's breast.

Thomas had long prepared me for the infant rudeness of Monticello. Then he had spent the summer and fall making it what he said was altogether habitable, so it seemed to him by the winter it had become near the manor-house of his dreams. My former low expectations had been elevated through that summer and fall, only to be dashed all in a moment by the sight of the smallest possible cottage, forlorn and dark and cold in the snow. On the upper floor, where we were to live, there was one little room so crammed with books and the marriage-bed he had bought for me and my new forte-piano and even a saddle and muskets and clothes-press and every thing that I could scarce find a floor to walk.

We tied our horses in the kitchen for want of other space. Poor beasts, they had not even water so we brought them buckets of snow to drink. Then we groped our dark way across the kitchen and climbed stairs to our marital home. No servant was about, it being so late they had given up expecting us and had retired to their quarters which Thomas assured me were very near the house. Thomas grew up there on the wilderness edge, and he has told me stories of Indians coming to call like neighbors when he was a boy. The Indians have retreated far to the west, but that was little comfort to me when I found myself in that small brick cabin at the edge of the continental forest. And there was no fire laid.

"It would be unkind of us to wake them," Thomas said. "Let us see what we can do in place of a fire." He began to grope on a gloomy shelf among his piles of books.

"Is this for better or for worse?" I said it half for jest and half for serious. There is romance to the thought of a tiny cabin, but quite another feel to the reality.

Thomas heard my jest and my complaint at once and smiled a smile I could not quite see so my memory supplied the details of it.

This is a play between us that still continues to this day: I have married him for better or for worse, and after the shock of that little cabin which now is the center of all my life we see it is not always possible to tell one easily from the other.

"What a relief! They have not found it." He took from behind his books a half-drunk bottle of Madeira wine.

"It is for better, I see." Despite my dismay I felt a thrill of joy at the sight of my husband so happy to have me at last in his home that he is carving out of the wilderness. No ready-made house would do for him! He must start from nothing and build the very grandest manor in all of Virginia.

"There are other things, dear Husband, we might do for warmth," I said for very love of him.

He turned to me with a sparkling smile, the sparkle of it all I could see in the dark. He said, "You know, I had thought I was weary but that feeling has miraculously ended."

Then I discovered my forte-piano which I had waited for those six months past. I opened the cover and touched a chord of it, feeling clumsy in my gloves. The keys shone a cheerful blue in the gloom, and the sound of it was so deep and strong that it startled me with the power of it.

"Alberti has promised to come and tune it. Do let us first have some Handel, Patty. Are you up to playing now?"

He found a chair and I sat upon it. I chose some passages of Handel which I can play from memory and we have set to poems that I wrote the last summer for his entertainment. He stood behind with his hand on my shoulder and rising to caress my cheek while we drank from the bottle and sang together for the very joy of being at home.

MONTICELLO JULY 17, 1772

I have for so long meant to continue the account I began in Williamsburg that I feel myself the worst journal-keeper. I almost leave off keeping it. Yet how can I let disappear forever these very most glorious days of my life?

I am happy beyond every dream that I have ever had of happiness. It seems we near re-invent the word, for the union we share is so complete we cannot even have our quarrels but soon we are breaking into laughter together. We cannot speak, but the other will say he had been on point of saying the like himself. I find that even traits which were a trial for my Pappa are transformed in my dear husband's presence, so my curiosity becomes a happy gift for conversation and my willfulness is only a play of our minds which brings to us much merriment. Yet I am fearful. I cannot imagine that such perfection will last for long between husband and wife, or if it does last then the death of one partner will wreak a greater havoc upon the other. So I write now for courage in a darker day when we no longer share such a blessed bliss, or for comfort in that darkest day of all when one must carry on without the other.

I must be sly. Thomas has gone off to Charlottesville for what I believe will be all of the morning. I sent Mary to the well for water and Bett to the quarters to inquire of the slaves if any had eggs to sell to me. Their absence let me retrieve my journal from behind its secret kitchen-bricks. Then when they returned I complained of a headache and climbed the stairs to our little home, where now I sit by the open window for a morning of glorious privacy.

They are with me, Betty's older children. After the session of the Burgesses ended in April we spent some weeks at the Forest, where Betsy was in bed of another boy and I was wanted to manage the house. Then when we were readying ourselves to go my Pappa took me aside and said he meant to make me a gift of Betty's Mary and Martin and Bett and Nance and Bob and Jim. This seemed a most stupendous gift: the value of six so excellent slaves would be well beyond a thousand pounds. Thomas and I had been saying that if only they were not Betty's children we would try to buy the two who had been serving us. Now to have the prospect of getting all six!

Yet I could not take away Betty's children. I sought her out and made her walk with me down through the orchard by the mill-race pond, but even when we were alone I knew not how to raise the topic of what her master proposed to do. I was astonished when she raised it herself.

"Has your Pappa talked to you about my children?"

"Yes" was all I was able to say. I have lost a child for whom I shall never cease to grieve, and now I proposed to take six of hers so far she might never see them again.

"Will you take them?"

"I cannot take them from you! How can I do that?"

"But you must take them. I know not what will happen to them unless they go with you."

"Betty?"

"Look at them! They are useless! Misfits! They have only the slender protection of a master who is here so seldom that I fear for them daily, waking and sleeping. I have not the strength to protect them! The light ones, yes, they are young enough still, and I think Mr. Stevens would not dare to harm them for fear of their father. But Mary and Martin go out to work! Their fellows mark them out as different. Indeed, they mark themselves as different, even though they are black Africa itself and hardly even kin to their own brothers. Mistress, I have thought long on this. It was I who begged your Pappa to give them to you."

I had no words. I stopped and looked at her. Dear Betty looks like any slave, and yet she is nothing like a slave; she carries herself not with downcast look but with eyes clear and frank upon us all. Although we are but thirteen years apart, she has been very near a mother to me.

"Why? Why would you give up your own children?"

"Because I know you, mistress. I have watched your husband. It is said that he will not let his slaves be whipped even if it is out of his sight. I do not believe that, but I do believe he loves you enough to give you the power to protect my children."

So now I have with me this remnant of home which is every day such a comfort. Betty keeps Nance to help her care for the three pale babies that remain, but Pappa has sworn to execute deeds that will bring them all to me if he should die. And it is well that I have them. There were no house-servants here beyond an old-woman cook who cannot cook and Jupiter. Our Jupiter is a fine coachman, but Thomas is so fond of him that he has made of him a most inept valet and butler. Poor Jupiter! The like he cannot do, for his hands are designed for outdoor work so he ever spills and rends and breaks and this distresses him most grievously. Our Jupiter has taken up with Pappa's Suck so Suck is living with us, too, although her title remains in Pappa's name.

How can I describe our mountain-top? The cottage is most finely made of brick, and although it is small there is a curious fact that one's mind adjusts to the shape of one's space so now I have forgotten every larger home and I find it is of a perfect size for a husband and wife so dearly in love. It has near below it a row of offices and quarters mixed together, most new-built last summer so only now the wood begins to weather gray. There is, on the very crown of the hill, a most enormous building-site, the great stone cellars ten feet deep and on the northern end of it a great brick room which has just now become my dining-room. That is all there is of our manor to come, but for the moment that is all we need. We have dining with us every night some various number of friends and kin, and while they can generally sleep in Charlottesville or return to their homes at Blenheim or Shadwell or where ever they live, we had no where to feed them. We have used a barn beyond the quarters which is so far from the kitchen that we never enjoyed a warm dish of food. In summer we have set up a table of boards on trestles under the edge of the trees. Now to have a real dining-room!

Thomas's mother and Colonel Carter's family will be of the party to dine tonight. And he has with him on his visit to Char-lottesville Mr. Walker and his great friend Dabney Carr, who pur-poses now to stand for election so they will be Burgesses together. Thomas is so confident of Dabney's prospects. He swears his Dab-ney is an orator with no equal in any of the colonies, even though he is but twenty-eight and unremarkable in his look. "He is a leader, Patty," Thomas says. "I am no leader. It is difficult to lead when your tongue cleaves to your teeth if you open your mouth in public." So we expect a cheerful party for dinner for which we shall be cooking all this day. I also brewed up a cask of my small-beer that Dabney and Patsy have come to love, although my Thomas prefers wine to the beer and he drinks it only to please his wife.

We have the small-beer as part of the opera which has become our summertime entertainment. After the board is cleared we crowd into our chamber where the early evening is bright as day, and there we take parts of *Love in a Village* and sing the whole opera loudly together amid much laughter and copious draughts to keep our throats in tune. Thomas and I both play and sing. Dabney takes the greatest male part and I often take the female lead, for we are said by all to have the finest voices. So we sing for play until candle-time, when comment is made upon the fading light and the ride of an hour or two or three that awaits between our guests and their beds. Then Dabney remarks that any gentleman not rendered demented by his books would suffer his house to be made of wood so it might be most quickly and cheaply built and his friends could have chambers to take their rest. There is teasing and laughter as phaetons and saddled horses are led up to our door, and so we bid good-night to guests who soon will return to repeat the process over.

With all our entertaining, my great need here is for a very seasoned cook, some well-trained and very capable wench who can teach these girls as I cannot teach them. I only ever helped Ondine and Betty, and without them here I know very little. How I long for them! Ondine could, in her prime, make every kind of delicacy, and she has about her an artist's touch so the dishes come to the table so graceful that Pappa is famous among his friends. Betty has learned very much from Ondine, but she was not able to teach her girls. Mary is willful and will not learn any thing above what she wants to learn, and Bett, who is sweet, is a little simple. So I have asked my Thomas for a cook. He does not want to buy one. He seems to have vowed not to buy more slaves, although he will not tell me that; he says only that they will soon be free, in which case he will be out the money, or then if they are not soon free he will be left forever with the care of them, and either way he does not want more slaves.

My child has just given me such a kick! It does not like me sitting still. Often in the night it will kick me awake for very boredom. I have not been entirely well this summer. Once I had the bladder-fever for four days and nights of misery before the water and Gabbler's my husband so urgently held to my lips both day and night did their work and washed it all away. He was alarmed and would have had the doctor come, but I swore to him it was only mild. I am quit of doctors who are ever eager to bleed me out a flood from the foot and give vile draughts to purge choleric humors that cause the sharp waters within the bladder. I have found in their ministrations no comfort at all but only greater pains from all the bleeding and puking. Before Bathurst allowed me to consult his slave-healer, I often had the bladder-fever weeks on end.

But I still submit to doctors for other ills. We consulted a doctor in Williamsburg for a problem that I had forgotten about until the insistence of this child to be born began to make me see it as a living baby. I was not able to nurse my Jack. In the end he was given to a slave to nurse and Bathurst swore she saved his life, but I vow he was the last of my children to be nursed by a woman not his mother. I described my problem to Dr. Carter and he prescribed the breast-pipes, which I use every evening to elongate my nipples. This occasions great hilarity in our chamber.

We laugh now together so constantly that I smiled as I copied over the pages that I had written in Williamsburg. I had forgotten having been so frightened. The gentlemen still talk, of course. Gentlemen ever love to talk; they make of it the greatest sport. I smile to hear them so intent upon gaining their liberty, these gentlemen who are already so free that they live each on his own plantation that is in itself a very city. If we never had any thing from England again, nor even from Richmond or Charlottesville, we could live forever on our mountaintop and make every bit of what we need. Liberty indeed! Our problems with Britain are ending, yet still these gentlemen so love the word that they speak of this ending with some regret. They have narrowed their whole dispute with Britain to just a quibble over tea, upon which alone is a tax still levied so tea alone is what is banned. But Pappa and I have ever drunk chocolate and Thomas is content with water and wine, so the lack of tea is no lack at all and not worth any gentleman's head.

None of this is what I meant to write! I have consumed many pages and most of the morning in preparing to write about our first weeks of marriage when we gaily wintered at my own Elk-island, the plantation I have down from Bathurst. Now I have no time to write about that.

WILLIAMSBURG NOVEMBER 13, 1772

I am so distracted and near to despair that I take up my quill in desperation. I shall have to resort to copying if I mean to have this in my journal, but I have no care at the moment whether I ever see my journal again. I want my baby to live! I cannot lose another child as I lost my little Jack. That last breath taken in my arms and waiting in vain for another one is a feeling I cannot have again. I shall die of it. Yet she sleeps here sweetly, looking for the moment pink and fed although her bones poke her skin like the bones of a bird.

We have named her Martha after my mother and my sister Carr and after me. This was Thomas's wish, and I did not oppose it for thought it might give her additional strength of her union with three who so greatly love her. Now he begins to call her Patsy, but all I can call her is Child of my Soul. All I can do is beg her to live!

It is not for want of nursing that she is so frail. I nurse her constantly, day and night, and were she awake she would be nursing now. Dr. Carter has prescribed some nipple-glasses to further stimulate my milk, but still for all her sucking and all my trying she seems not to get enough milk to grow.

My husband comforts his worry with the mild good humor which is his habitual attitude. He does not suppress his feelings so much as he simply rises in his mind to a plane so high they cannot follow. I admire that in him, that sweet ability to see beyond what ever is his momentary trouble and comfort himself with any diversion. Last week he comforted himself with a mocking-bird that Martin bought for him among my Pappa's slaves. It sings here now in its little cage, as able as my husband is ever able to look right off between the bars and sing and sing for the joy of singing.

MONTICELLO MARCH 2, 1773

*N*ow I have days and weeks for journal-keeping. I may write whole volumes if I like. My Thomas has gone to Williamsburg for an emergency session of the Burgesses and I have been left behind alone. We are separated, something we swore would never happen in our lives, but Patsy must remain with her nursemaid and I find that I must remain with her.

He left me on Sunday. Now it is Tuesday of the first week without him and I know that I shall not survive this hour. Is it possible we are married only one year? I cannot imagine it. All my self has been so sweetly transformed by love of my husband that I cannot remember what I thought or how I lived before our wedding-day. I feel as if my own body has been summoned off to Williamsburg and now I sit, just the soul within, a wraith that is capable only of pain and the purest, the most indescribable longing.

We have been so much together! From our morning reading and walking and riding through our sessions of music after dinner there never was a moment of the day when we were very far apart. He would come to me hourly in the kitchen with handfuls of two kinds of grapes to taste or the antics of some new foal to describe or nothing to say, just the need to see me as I had constant need of him. No other married couple shares so much! I do begin now to see the wisdom of custom that gives to men and women their separate spheres, lest the unity of the marriage-bed make them blend too much together. It were better for me if I did not so much love him. Better for him if he did not love me. Oh, how does he fare alone on the road? I am pained to imagine he grieves for me as I so desperately grieve for him.

His cleverness in finding Patsy a nursemaid must be commended. I swear he could talk the sun out of rising if ever he put his mind to it. I had for long been wanting a cook, to the point where my desire was a play between us. He would complain that some dish did not taste right and why did I refuse to find a cook, or I would tell him in December we would have had fresh peas, which are then entirely out of season, but I had ruined our dish of peas because I am so unable to cook. He rose one morning in January and said that he meant to buy me a cook. I heard this as a jest so I fell into laughter, but soon I found that he was in earnest. He and Jupiter set off that day to an estate-sale to be held at Maiden's Adventure.

When I describe my new cook you will be laughing, too. She is the most enormous wench, half again as wide as she is tall, fatter by far than Peyton Randolph and even too fat for the smokehouse door. But she can cook! She is a well-trained pastry-cook who can put her hand to any thing. She has cooked for Thomas for only a month, but already he pronounces her such a wonder that she knows she will likely not be sold again and that has made her very cheerful.

With Ursula has come an entire family. She had with her on the back of the phaeton a boy of thirteen called Little George and another boy of three or four. And she carried in her arms a newborn child. Then it was that I discovered my husband's trick. "Here is your cook, Patty," he said as he alighted. "She is said to be an excellent cook. She comes well recommended. She is also a very practiced nursemaid."

"I will not have a nursemaid!"

My Patsy had continued sickly, but I had grown so used to it that I no longer greatly feared for her life. My Thomas had seen what I would not see, that our baby was slowly failing, and while he would not buy a slave for a trivial reason he was glad to buy a slave if she might save our child. It took him three patient days to persuade me. I had to make myself used to Ursula and the way she spoke and the way she smelled. To put my baby into the arms of another is a very intimate thing; perhaps it seemed to me too much like putting my husband into another's bed.

It was Ursula herself who carried me the very smallest final step. She is talkative as she shuffles about in the great soft slippers that she swears are the only shoes she ever can wear for all the bunions on her feet.

"You have a kindly husband, mistress," she said to me one afternoon as she managed four pots at once on the fire and I sat at the table and tried to nurse. "He has promised to buy my King George, and that is a very generous thing. We have been together fifteen years and never did we hope we might share a house. Generous! God bless the master!"

"God bless him, indeed." Patsy was not sucking. It seems my nipples are hard to grasp and harder still to draw, so she gives up unless she is very hungry.

"Mistress?"

I looked up at Ursula. Her great round face which is wreathed in folds was soft with the very kindest concern. I confess my heart went out to her for her need to give us back a gift for the gift that my husband was giving to her.

"May I hold her, mistress?"

I handed Patsy up to her very slowly. That seemed the hardest part of the act; once she left my arms I could watch what followed.

"May I try, mistress?"

"You may. Please."

"Poor mite." She tugged at the top of her apron and popped out one enormous breast. "Poor babe. You have no call to do poorly. You are the luckiest blessed babe."

She had the most pendulous great black breast which dwarfed my baby's little head with its wisps of the palest reddish hair. Patsy took the nipple, and she was engulfed in such a splendid flow of milk that she choked and streams ran out of her mouth and tears came unbidden to my eyes. We cried together that day, myself and my dear fat Ursula. The one who has never since cried is Patsy, and now she grows so hugely fat that her father when he kissed her good-bye told her she would have to mind herself or there would be no stays big enough to hold her.

WILLIAMSBURGH   MARCH 12. 1773.

My dear Wife

I have all six of your letters in hand but I could not answer them until today. Even now there is little time, for our friend has today enjoyed the most glorious success of his whole career and his wish this evening is to be in company where he can crow and be properly preened. He deserves the chance to enjoy his triumph, but the Governor will surely dismiss us on Monday and unless you receive at least one letter you will think me the most undutiful husband. Oh my wife! To say I miss you is to say the day is brighter than the night. I feel a constant aching anxiety, a sense of the world tilted on it's edge, and then I realize it is just the lack of my life's whole soul and center. How do you fare without me? Your letters are so stubbornly cheerful, so very exactly the way you would be if you were as miserable as I feel but set on being brave for me. That makes my loneliness so much worse, that double burden of carrying not just my own unhappiness but yours as well. Be comforted, Patty. I am resolved to beat this letter home, and then I intend never to go away again unless you can be with me.

I am sorry, my dear precious wife, that I have not written for these two weeks. I realize with amazement how dilatory I have been, but writing to you would only have reinforced this awful lack of you. Better to do what I have done, and make the round of tables and then come back and read til the candle gutters out. It was only after your letters came that I saw how my silence must look to you. If I could, I would write you fourteen letters and have them already in your hands.

My two weeks have been well taken up with the sort of talk that worries you, so I have had the thought at more than one dinner that I was glad you were not there. To hear just pieces, as you do, is always more worrisome than hearing the whole. The House remains so troubled by the free-handed actions of our British brethren that today we have done what we ought to have done long months ago, or even years ago. Events seem to have their own momentum. They occur, like births, when their time has come. I will not trouble your mind with the details of what preceded Dabney's great success, but I want to tell you enough of it so you can greet him as the hero he is and stir up the spirits of my practical sister to welcome her splendid husband home. (I was going to say, as Penelope welcomed Odysseus, but then that seemed not entirely apt.)

To culminate our two weeks of work we met today in Committee of the Whole, with the issue before us the momentous one of establishing a committee of correspondence which will let us speak with a unified voice both with our sister American colonies and with the British Councillors. It is, as I say, high time this was done. We have talked and talked to no better purpose than the spoiling of too many pleasant dinners. No one beyond ourselves has heard us before, but now we shall be heard. Dabney introduced the resolution, Patty, and he made in support of it such a speech that I found myself wishing I had been opposed so I could let him persuade me. Our motion carried unanimously, even though I know that before he spoke there were some who were still undecided. Randolph and the others were so impressed that they made him a member of the new committee despite his lack of seasoning, so we shall be serving on it together. Despite his late start, I have the pleasure of knowing that our legislative careers will be served out together, whatever they may be.

Jupiter has been standing here for half an hour while I crouched ever lower and wrote ever faster. Forgive my jumbled thoughts, dear Wife, but I am a half-hour late.

There is one more thing I want to say. Please, when you write to me, be discreet. I know it is only your innocence which makes you write so ardently, but I believe I blushed when I read especially your second letter of March the 8th. Remember that others might read your letters. And please, dear Patty, hide this letter too.

I am your doting and most devoted (if tardy) husband,
Th:J.

MONTICELLO MAY 19, 1773

Once again I must sit and write terrible news, if only to calm my quaking heart.

Dabney Carr is dead at twenty-nine. Dead! To be going along so gaily, past and future in an infinite line, and then of a sudden to have no future. I understand it less with Dabney than I did with my poor little Jack; children die. Mothers are commonly told they must give one up for every one they keep. But Dabney! He was so much alive!

He was stricken with the bilious fever while he was down at Shadwell. Our mother is inept at business matters, and Dabney thought he might help us all by getting her straight with her overseer. While he was there he was stricken so greatly sick that Mother sent off for Dr. Gilmer, but nothing that was done was enough to save him. Poor Patsy was still at Spring Forest in Goochland. She has six children! One has only just been born! Yet three days after Dabney's death I continue to see fresh horrors in it that have me weeping as I write these words. How very much better for her if she had never loved him half so well! And how much I wish that I loved less, for just my awareness of Patsy's loss fills me with a terror for the pain I risk. Yet I must not think of that. I must think only of my poor bereft dear sister Carr, and of my dear beloved husband who loved his Dabney so.

And now I look back and find another death I never have written in my journal. Four months gone by, there came a tragic sorrowful letter from my brother Skipwith to say that Tibby has died in childbed. Her new-born child has died as well. I have not seen my sister for near two years, indeed not since the week of her wedding when my Thomas and I walked in the woods in company with our sister and brother Carr and I found on that day sufficient trust to agree at the last that we might be wed. Dear Tibby and Bobby have lived at Prince William, where he manages for his father two great plantations. Tibby little cared to write so I had no letter from her at all for the whole half-year before her death. She is fixed in my mind as safe to the north. I shall need more than a letter to believe her not safe. But Dabney has been so constantly with us, so full of laughter and so much alive! I fear that my husband may not well survive this.

THE FOREST JUNE 7, 1773

$\mathscr{I}$ vow this is the worst year of my life, although I dare not even say that aloud for fear of something worse to come.

Our next calamity after Dabney's loss in this awful, awful spring is the death of my own dear wonderful Pappa. I can hardly bear to write these words, except that I have learned by now that it comforts me to sit and write when ever something happens so terrible that it could not other wise be borne. Thomas has left for Williamsburg to help to settle Pappa's affairs, and his phaeton was only out of sight when I rushed to Pappa's desk for quill and ink.

Pappa!

They say he was taken of an apoplexy and he did not last the morning. Ben rode for Dr. Sequeyra at Charles City Court-House but Pappa had died before they returned. Betty assures me he did not suffer. He was only surprised. He smiled at her and said, "Am I dying?" and then he died.

Betty is the worst of this for me. I want to sit and write about Pappa but my mind keeps turning back to his Betty. He loved her. I know that he loved her and he lived with her very like a husband, and yet now I find that she did not love him.

This morning Betty and I were washing linens for Betsy, who has taken to her bed of her grief. I had seen Pappa not once these six months past and I find there is a comfort in that; as with Tibby, so with my Pappa, I can be here and not much miss him except when I am reminded. But Betsy saw him every day. She is despondent unto despair at his death.

I had remarked in this past week how little Betty had seemed to grieve. I would have expected her to be prostrate with every bit of a widow's grief, yet she went about her quiet business with a pleasant word and even a smile. As I bent for more linens from the tub this morning I said, "You need not pretend strength with me, Betty. Please weep if you like. It would surely help you." I wrung the linens and handed them to Betty, and as she took them I looked at her.

"Poor mistress. How little you understand."

"Please weep. You know I would not mind."

"Do you think I grieve?" she said so hotly that I paused half-bent back into the tub and looked at her in plain amazement. "Mistress, he was your Pappa. To me he was nothing."

"He loved you! He was like a husband to you!" I straightened from the tub so quickly that I cricked my back.

Betty said, "I have a husband! Do you even know that? I have my own husband! When your Pappa cast his eye on me he sent my husband to Guinea Plantation. He came back for me, poor desperate man, and your Pappa sent him away in chains. That was more than ten years past. I am told he is at Guinea Plantation. I am told he has taken another wife, but I will not believe that unless I see it. Do you want to see me grieve? Then say his name. Abraham. Now you see me grieve!"

There rolled down her cheeks two tremendous tears and then a shining flood. I comfort myself to believe that she was weeping for them both, but she remained convinced with a certainty that her heart had room for only one. And I confess to my shame that I knew about Abraham. I remember the commotion, the hunting for him, the naked black man chained in the cart who cried out her name as they hauled him away. I believe I was but thirteen then, but I remember. And I remember that Betty watched that cart from an upper window as it left, her face serene with a perfect blankness I have not forgotten to this day.

"But why?" My voice was the palest whisper. "Betty? Why did you ever stay here? Pappa would not have kept you here against your will."

"You are a mother, and you can ask such a question?" Betty said in her voice of fury, the voice she keeps so carefully hidden I believe she shows it only to me.

"Betty?"

"It was all I could do for my children! Why are you unable to understand? Mary! Martin! My poor black children! When I see them so content with you I know I was right to make my choice." She pinned the flapping linens to the line. "I did what I did for the sake of my children. And I was always fair to your Pappa. But mistress, do not expect me to grieve!"

I bent to my tub. My cheeks flamed hot, although for what reason I cannot say, whether I was shamed to have been so unaware or whether I felt for my poor Pappa some monstrously greater, more piteous shame. He knew her heart. Or he should have known her heart but he did not. I cannot say which is the greater shame.

MONTICELLO SEPTEMBER 9, 1773

I have for long meant to continue my journal but my husband has been so constantly with me there never was time to retrieve it, write, and put it back before I should fear discovery. Now he is gone for these few days to my Pappa's Poplar Forest, and my sister Carr nurses colicky children so we shall not see her here this day. If I do not take this chance to write, I may not for many months have another.

This remains the very worst year of my life, yet even with all our daily pains there come indications of a better year to come. I am with child again. Our baby will be born in the spring. And Patsy thrives! She does so well under Ursula's nursing and Mary's care that I was at the Forest until near August and came home to find her doubled in size. Our Mary has finally found a task that she will trouble herself to do. She plays by the hour with my little Patsy, carrying her on her hip like a servant's child and dandling her to walk in her pudding-cap. Mary has her own child, too, a boy very near to Patsy in age, who rides often-times on her other hip and struggles with my Patsy over every toy until Mary, if she sees me by, will wrest it from her own child and give it to mine. Still, Mary does well. My darling Patsy will not see a year until the end of this month, yet already she walks almost by herself.

It is well my child thrives in the care of others for I have been much occupied. The hands at the Forest are troubled each summer with the intermittent fever, and since Betsy was too distraught to tend them I must remain longer and tend them with Betty. We went from cabin to cabin for week upon week dosing them with the Peruvian Bark, and we were blessed this year that only one was lost and that an old man who was long past work and so crippled with the rheumatism I thought his death must come as a relief to him. Then when at last the fever lessened and Betsy was up again from her bed we came home to find a different pestilence running through our own quarters. Thomas has hired an overseer who was trying to dose the sick himself, but we called in our dear friend Dr. Gilmer and again no one was lost. To our great relief the babes near by the house and my own dear little Patsy were spared, although my sister Carr's youngest have it now from contact with the Shadwell servants. My sister Carr has spent her summer at Shadwell across the Rivanna River, which is so near by to Monticello that the drive can be made in beneath an hour. She seeks there the comfort of her mother's arms.

Patsy's mother, and my husband's, is very tall and mannered like a duchess, although she is so Randolph-dark that in work dress she might be a lighter servant. There is nothing servant-like about her manner; she is stern of eye and vastly proud. I find it difficult to befriend our mother for we are not alike at all: she shows to the world a cool insistence on every detail of propriety which makes me feel as if each thing I do is not entirely right. Thomas swears our mother approves of me, and I find that after near two years I am becoming warm to Mother as I find endearing flaws in the perfection she endeavors so much to keep.

Mother is widowed these fifteen years, yet she remains so inept with money that she lives on an edge of penury. That Thomas must repeatedly rescue her exasperates him, for he believes that she refuses to learn from a wish to keep her older son attending her. Yet I find it all so endearing, her ineptitude and her maternal clinging. I find her reluctant unbending to take some part in our evening operas and her rare, unwilling laughter at the antics of babies at her feet to be so inexpressibly endearing. I see the loneliness she hides out of pride, the sense of superfluity, and I see how now she blossoms with warmth for the chance to comfort her poor widowed daughter come home again with six little children, the youngest a baby newly born.

Thomas and his sister have been much together. They were not especially close before, but they share now such a grievous loss that their greatest comfort is in one another. Dabney had been buried at Shadwell, but once Thomas returned from Goochland with Patsy he had him reinterred in a graveyard he had new-grubbed from the side of our mountain. He and Dabney had played there as children, reading beneath one certain tree, and they had sworn that when one of them ever died the other would see him buried there. So now my husband and his sister go daily to grieve beneath that tree. Of late they return to me more refreshed, and I begin to find in my husband again the cheerfulness and the joy in life I had thought for a time might have died with Dabney.

Thomas distracts himself from his grief with very much attention to his growing fields and his foals new-born and his chariot new-bought which needs now very much cleaning and painting. He traded the chariot from Mr. Meade for his better phaeton and eight pounds to boot, and even in its former unpainted state it greatly improved our journey home. Thomas repairs his older phaeton that he might use it when he travels alone, but never again need I travel with him and find that my scalp beneath my cap and the very most private folds of my skin bear grit worked in from the dust of the road. And Thomas is further distracted by his lawyering, which takes the better part of his every day. Besides his own practice he has Dabney's practice and much now to do for my Pappa.

It seems that Pappa will leave us wealthy. I had thought of myself as an heiress to Bathurst and never considered my Pappa, yet he was a man very rich in lands and surpassingly rich in many slaves. It is yet unclear what I shall have but it seems Poplar Forest will come to me, together with Elk-hill which is near by Elk-island and land on the Fluvanna and on Judith's Creek. I am to be left more than ten thousand acres and something over a hundred slaves. And I know these lands, for I ever reckoned my dear Pappa's plantation accounts; they are, for the most of them, greatly productive. My husband cannot guess how rich he will be. And my sisters will be likewise enriched, for Betsy inherits my Pappa's Forest and Nancy will take the Guinea Plantation. Nancy was married to Henry Skipwith in July. Now her rag doll sits on her marriage-bed.

My Betty is also at the Guinea Plantation, although her title has come to me. I would have brought her here, but I made the mistake of telling my Thomas all her story, and when he heard it he would not think of putting her any where else but at the Guinea Plantation. I would have brought my Betty here, if only to protect her from what must be a grievous pain at Guinea. Her Abraham has taken another wife and had with her at least two children. If it were not for this I could have persuaded my husband to bring them here to us, but Thomas would not have our happiness spoilt by what ever strains may likely develop when Betty attempts to win him back. She wants to be with him, so with him she is, although I miss her dearly here.

I have thought very much upon Betty's choice.

I had not until she told me her story ever placed myself into the mind of a slave, and that I had not done so seems to me now to be very strange and shameful. I had but felt a general pleasure in having been born to my own race and station, while having assumed without further thought that I could have been born no other way. This seems shameful now. I look at servants' faces and imagine myself within each of them, and I find that the thoughts this brings to me are rife with new emotions.

Ursula's King George was bought this summer, his purchase having been delayed by the value placed upon him by his master and by all the events of our terrible spring. He is a most impressive giant, tall and broad and fearsome of face but so quick to learn that he has taken on the general role of a handy-man. He makes repairs and carries things and fills in where ever he is needed, which means that he is much about the house. I see him with Ursula, how they coo and flirt as if they are but newly in love, and I think with amazement how hard it must be to be lovers this way for fifteen years and only now to be living together.

And to make Betty's choice!

I study my dear so precious Patsy who is growing so to favor her Pappa, and I wonder whether I could put him out of my heart if it would give her a better life. Could I do it even for four little Patsys, knowing that if I remained with my husband they could hope for only the hardest service under the cruelest of overseers who bore in his fist the most vicious whip? I could not. I know to my shame that I could not give him up, not even for a hundred helpless children. So I stand in awe of my Betty's choice and I am, if possible, gentler still with these children of hers she has entrusted to me.

My dear dear husband has asked me again when he might read my journal. His loss of Dabney has been his occasion for new examination of his mind: where once he had seen his life unfolding in the close enjoyment of blessed companions, he seems now to come to a comprehension that his life's great companion is himself. I find a new subtle strength beginning which gladdens my heart most joyously, for I had feared with Dabney's death that it might be blow enough to fell him. It has not done that. Indeed I believe that in the end it will better him, but I cannot see what contribution he might ever find in my own poor journal.

My husband believes my journal to be something other than what it is. He thinks to find here pretty verses, a thought upon the shade of a flower's petal or the trill of a bird at day's first light. It would delight us both if it were that. But I seem not to want to write about swans who crook their necks to the shapes of hearts. What I want to write, have the need to write, is some awful unburdening of my mind which will lighten me so I can give to him all the gaiety that he wants from me. He has been pained, I know, by my womanly fears which have made him need to guard his words. Far better that I write upon paper every fear and vexation, every troubling thing, so I can be gay and hear his thoughts as the gentlemen do, most approvingly. For he shares with me now all the masculine thoughts that he ever has shared with his dearest friends. He began with only mutterings, the smoke from his roiling hidden fires, and when he found that I accepted these and even asked him sensible questions he came to speak very much more plainly.

I ask him questions.

"Shall we separate from Britain, then? Is that where all of this will end?"

We are swinging our hoes in the garden plot which we ever enjoy to cultivate beyond where our house rises very slowly, a forest of timbers and a half-wall of brick, the builders intent on their patient work.

He says, "I do not foresee a complete separation. We have the right to govern ourselves and I think we need but claim that right. But we must look beyond our own country, Patty, and toward uniting the continent. They can subdue one colony. They cannot subdue us all."

"But if the King will not give us our right of self-government? What shall we do about it then?"

We are riding the roundabout that encircles our mountain. He is showing me where he means to construct a deer-park like the parks of great English estates.

"Why then, my dear, we may be forced to assert our right more forcefully." Here he remembers my old notion of evicting the Governor from his Palace, and he smiles. "We do nothing wrong. Self-government is the base of English law, and farther back it is the natural law. We claim no more than what we own." He reaches for my hand between us and says, "This has little to do with Britain, Patty. Forget about Britain. Focus upon us."

"But will they not fight us if we do not yield?"

This is my great fear. We have paused in our afternoon of music; I am turned so he cannot see my face.

"I doubt they will fight for us very hard. We shall appeal our cause before the court of nations and when the justice of it is seen by all the British will be forced to yield us up. They are less than we are, Patty," he says with an air of gentle impatience that tells me he has heard my fear. "Britain is to America as a flea is to a dog. It may bite, but it cannot harm us much."

I listen to him most cheerfully as he says these reckless, dangerous things. Then I hurry to our chamber for quill and ink and write down in secret my terrible fears that I dare not keep for journal entry but must burn at once, that very night, when it comes time to poke up our chamber-fire. I could not have him know my heart. He would think me foolish and cowardly, he who is so devoid of fear that he laughs when I hotly insist to him that I will refuse to attend his hanging. Or he would think me Tory, when in truth I am nothing so honorable nor so well considered.

I love. That is all that is true of me. I love my husband and my child and the home we are building and our mite of a babe who is not yet born and the servants who daily toil with us and my sister Carr and her orphaned babies and our mother, so full of stubborn pride, and this, our beautiful, glorious country. Britain touches none of what I love so I think of Britain not at all. It will harm us only if we throw it off, and the weight of it is so little to bear that its throwing-off cannot be worth the cost of any harm to what we love. I try to imagine what a battle might be, how we could run to the forest with all our people and come out again when it is safely won. But I know that my Thomas would never run. He is the county lieutenant of the Albemarle militia; if they march to fight, he will be leading them.

So I write these hard thoughts and the writing frees me to be my husband's true companion. But I realized now as I write these words that my husband must never see my journal.

MONTICELLO APRIL 23, 1774

I came near to burning this over the winter. My fear was not that Thomas would find it, but that Mary or Ursula or some other servant bent upon cleaning the kitchen floor might tug at my two unmortared bricks for curiosity. I had chiseled out those bricks myself and been so proud of my secret work that I had clung to it for far too long. After thought, I have brought my journal up and secreted it deep in my press in the folds of my yellow wedding-gown. This lets me retrieve it quickly and tuck it away again as quickly, and I find that resting my eyes on my press now gives me the greatest comfort. I can better attend to those I love if I keep for myself this vice of recording my thoughts so trivial and, I fear, so treasonous that I dare not whisper them aloud.

I am lately in bed of another girl. We had both so very much wanted a boy! This bringing of boys comes so easily: my sister Carr has three little boys, my sister Eppes has two little boys, and even the servants bear boy after boy. I daily am confronted by Ursula's three. Yet I bear girls! This infant's sex distresses me far more than it seems to distress my husband. Mrs. Sumpter had no sooner dressed the babe and laid it mewing on my arm than Thomas came up at Betty's bidding. He bounded robust up the stairs and called out very merrily, "What a relief to have a girl! Now you will be eager to try again!"

To say such a thing in front of others is an act so greatly unlike my husband that I knew he said it only to comfort and cheer his wife. Yet he smiled to find the babe safely born. He admired its hair of a shade of red as bright as the edge of the setting sun and pronounced it near as beautiful as its mother. "Are you very surprised?" he said to it as it stared with such astonishment that its parents laughed. "Where else had you expected to be born?"

"She had hoped for a house of more than one room. I shall describe for her the manor to come. I expect that she will be willing to wait."

We have named her after our mother, Jane Randolph Jefferson. The idea was my own, which Thomas has plainly said to Mother, with the result that she was less pleased by me than she was dismayed by him. I have said to him that if she could but do it, she would have me out and she would be in my place.

Betty is here to attend me by grace of my sister Skipwith. She brought just her very youngest, Sally, a child born after my Pappa's death, but we think now to send for her other children. Betty has told me little of her life at Guinea, but I know from my sister that Betty's husband has not put away his other wife. They have such fights, all three of them, that my sister prays for me to keep Betty here. I want her here, but I know not how I ever shall raise the matter with her. That she is my property and I have the right to keep her here or bid her go is a thought that will not rest in my mind when I find her face in front of me. We sit and nurse our infants together. Her youngest of my Pappa is the palest of all, so pale you would swear she could not be a slave, and this is a fascination for me.

Just two days gone my husband left me to Burgess at the Capital, and I shame myself to admit that he is very glad to be away. I am at a loss of patience with our slow construction that changes but little from season to season. They fire great mountainous thousands of bricks, they erect a frame that weathers gray, they plod along planks with their hods and barrows, yet still we live in one single room! Jane cries often in the night, and this wakes Patsy, who soon cries too, so we never have a peaceful sleep. My husband would have me give my Ursula all three babies at once to nurse, my two and her own little Archy besides, and indeed he even would gladly have them sleep with her to give us peace. But I have kept my Patsy with me and continued to nurse her myself at night, and I will nurse my Jane. I am their mother.

So our prospect of six weeks or more apart was not a painful rending. He made a jest that in the Capital he might recapture the sleep he has lost, and this I chose to hear not as a jest but I told him that if he stayed a year he might store up sleep for the year to come. I regretted my anger within the hour and wept for it and wrote him a letter. Now I long to see him, but still I believe this time apart is what we need. In truth, our chamber will not hold all four of us.

So Betty and I nurse our babes together. On yesterday morning we were alone, for the girls were weeding in the kitchen-garden and Ursula had taken to her bed. Without Thomas here we have not the continual round of guests near every day, and this has made us glad to cut back our dinners to what we can find to hand.

"Bob has shot a rabbit," Betty said as we sat at the table and nursed our babes. "He wanted the skin. I have told him he might sell you the meat. We might make a stew."

"He will ask too much. That boy! He tried last week to sell me a hen. He asked a whole shilling! I later found he had bought it from Ursula for only half a bit, but he thought if he praised it well enough and perhaps if I were hungry enough he might talk me into paying any thing."

Betty smiled. Her Bob is twelve, and he grows so to favor my Pappa that it pains me to look upon his face. The thought of her Bob and the sight of her Sally and the nervous awareness at the back of my mind that soon we would have to talk about Guinea made me say out a thing I never would have said if I had given it but half a thought.

"Betty? Do you much mind being a slave?"

She gave me the look of astonishment that she so often gives to me when she sees me notice the gulf between us.

"Do you much mind being a lady?"

"Oh! Do I mind?" But before I could answer, my Betty commenced this fervent speech.

"Do I mind that my life is not my own? Do I mind that my children are not my own? That your husband might die, and all in a moment we might find ourselves sold off to the rice-lands, never to see one another again? Would you mind that, mistress?"

"You would never be sold! I would not allow that!"

"But what if you should die? What if you had died of the baby you are suckling now?"

"Oh! But!"

"No, mistress. I find that from day to day my harness does not chafe me much. I have never once been struck. I choose the work that will fill my days. But my mother was whipped near to death, mistress. She was whipped and branded. Did you know that? On the orders of the kindly gentleman who fathered the baby in my arms, my own poor mother was whipped and branded. Think a while on that, then ask me again whether I very much mind being a slave."

"Oh!" I had no words to speak. The color was burning in my cheeks. Betty saw this, and perhaps she repented to give me a shock so near my childbed.

"Be comforted. I long since forgave him. I find I have so much to forgive that I am become very good at it."

"But how could he? Why?"

"She was a runner. Mistress, please. The look of your face is frightening me."

"Would you be free, Betty? If I could manage it?"

She smiled. She has a most handsome face, the features of her two so different parents having blended well into long, dark eyes and a nose somewhere between broad and fine and a mouth I find quite hard to describe, the lower lip most full and soft and the upper firmly chiseled. She said, "Mistress, the day you free me is the day of my birth."

"Then I shall do it," I said to comfort us both. "If there is any way I know that my husband can find that way. Now let us talk of something else. Of Bob's rabbit. Will he sell it to you more cheaply?"

We have not mentioned it again, but the flavor of our conversation lingers between us like a lovers' kiss. My Betty trusts me to do for her what ever I might promise to do, and perhaps that trust will make me bold enough one morning soon to tell her that my sister will not have her return to Guinea.

Oh! And here is another story I very near forgot to tell, yet I must tell it now since it so completely explains my husband. Thomas had long negotiated to buy a tract of near-by lands which he wanted so we might make of Monticello more of a true plantation. All mountain and wooded land that it is, our Seat cannot support itself, so those near-by very fertile lands began to seem to him to be greatly important. He bought the lands. Then came in the fall a Florentine gentleman named Philip Mazzei, a small dark man so mild and cheerful that Thomas was greatly drawn to him. Mr. Mazzei told my husband in gay detail of the vineyards he meant to plant to the west, and when Thomas heard that, nothing else would do but that Mr. Mazzei must plant his vineyards right here. Can you envision it? Soon after this my Thomas executed a document to make an outright gift of his lands so recently and so dearly bought. He gave them away to Mr. Mazzei for the planting of his vineyards, and he believes he has gotten the best of the trade because he has purchased with his lands so voluble a Florentine neighbor!

So that is my husband. All this long spring he has passed in the company of cheerful Italians, improving his fluency in their language, wearing an Italian hacking-coat and pleasing himself to label all his vegetable rows with Italian names. He is much delighted with Mr. Mazzei, although he declares that at last he has met his better when it comes to talking. I am glad of this chance my husband has to think of things other than the British troubles. Mr. Mazzei cares nothing for the politics. A number of times he has been of the party when we have dined with Burgesses, and to watch him participate in their talk when he finds it an utter puzzlement is so delightful that my husband and I must laugh about it afterward.

He came to us one afternoon with a packet of the papers from Williamsburg. It was January or early February, a sunny afternoon so greatly cold that we were sitting by our chamber fire. Thomas was reading aloud from Shakespeare while I embroidered his new waistcoat and rocked with a foot the cradle where our Patsy slept her afternoon nap. Mr. Mazzei came up the stairs, all brisk and ruddy and giving off the very breath of cold. Thomas called down to who ever was below to quick make for Mr. Mazzei a toddy. Then while Mr. Mazzei doffed hat and greatcoat and rubbed his hands at our chamber fire my husband fell to studying the *Virginia Gazette*. I saw at once that the news was troubling.

"Hey! You got a beef you can maybe sell?" Mr. Mazzei said cheerfully. I cannot reproduce his talk, which saddens me, since it is so diverting.

"What are they making of this in the Capital?" my husband asked most anxiously.

"This? This?"

"The troubles in Boston. Indians throwing tea into the harbor."

"Oh! This! This, they say, is a terrible thing. Then, some say, it is not so terrible. It is good enough for that tea, they say!"

"I suppose they are right." My husband stood with his slippered foot high up onto the window-sill and his elbow on his knee and his chin on his hand, looking out the window.

"Of course, I never drink tea myself," Mr. Mazzei explained to me. "Who cares for tea? Hey? You got a beef?"

I said, "I am sure we have a beef to spare, but would you not rather have hog-meat? The killing is a month gone by. We have much to spare. Would you rather have that?"

"Do they expect retaliation?" my husband said with his eyes fixed on the snow outside. The sun made it sparkle so he must squint, but I saw in his face a painful worry.

"No!" I said. "Is there trouble? What has happened?"

"The India Company has sent inexpensive tea to try to force us to pay their tax. Now in Boston, rather than turn it away they have thrown the British tea into the harbor. It is just such an act that the Parliament hopes to provoke from one of the colonies. Now they can carve out the Massachusetts Bay and punish it for destruction of British property. Next they provoke New York. Then South Carolina. By the time they come to punish Virginia we shall be standing all alone."

"All of that for tea?" I could not believe it. All the leaves of tea in the world together are not worth the cost of one single life.

My husband turned and looked at me. His eyes are of an unusual shade, light blue that is heavily flecked with brown, so the angle of the light on them makes them now one color and now the other. His eyes were quite dark as he looked at me. "You have asked, my Patty, how it might happen. This is how it is going to happen. A gang of fools will drink too much and paint their faces and throw tea in the harbor, and now when the British retaliate we must see it as an attack upon us all. We shall find out very soon, I think, just who is with us and who is not." His foot made a weary sound as he drew it down off the window-sill. "But meanwhile let us find for our friend a side of beef."

MONTICELLO MAY 25, 1774

It is ever my thought that when my husband is gone I shall sit by the hour and write in my journal. Yet without him here there is nothing to write! He is gone now the month, and the Burgesses will likely sit for two weeks more.

I do have comforts. I am well supplied with memories, that way he has of folding his arms so it seems a tender hug of himself and his walk that is light upon his heels as if he were reluctant to crush the grass. I have myself, for so much do I feel that I am become a part of my beloved that I nearly can supply what I lack of him from out of my own substance. I know what he would say to any thing, so I sit here now at our chamber table and believe that if

I make a remark I shall hear his answer from his chair behind me. Yet I do miss him! Whether waking or sleeping, I feel at each moment such aching loss. My sister Carr talked often of her loss at a time six months after Dabney's death; she talked not at all of it, then talked much, then never talked of it again. My feeling is very much like hers, a tearing away of roots within, a cleaving of some essential limb. Yet I am not widowed. And because I am not widowed, I bear this pain with a most relentless cheerfulness for fear that if I do not bear it well, some judgment will be rendered to widow me and prove that this little six-week parting was truly a very tiny pain.

Today I miss him the more for a worry that the comfort of his presence would surely allay. I have a pain of my breast so greatly sharp that I cannot bear the press of my stays and I weep for the pain of my infant's suckling. I am truly this morning so greatly pained that I have given my Janey into Ursula's arms, with the thought that I shall only need one day and then I shall be able to nurse her again. My Betty says not. She believes I am breeding a very grave milk-fever, and now I must leave off nursing my child or endanger my life. She has poulticed my breast. I sit here in loosened jumps which smell of molasses and vinegar, and I watch out my window while she and King George attend to what ought to have been my duties.

We have not now an overseer at Monticello so all of that work has come down to me. We should be leaching lye and boiling soap and putting by the herbs and mending, but our house-work has fallen far behind as I go out each morning to see to the hands. There is so much toil! Here we grow mostly the wheat and corn but we try upon some plots to grow tobacco. And we have had extra work this spring because there came a frost in early May that killed all the growing grains and the fruits and withered the leaves from off the trees. I had a letter from my husband by Jupiter telling me at once to re-seed the fields, and this we did, although it meant that we were working with lanterns all that night.

I have found our King George to be a very zealous leader among the hands. When I go to the fields to oversee the work I have begun to carry him along with me. I discovered in him this leadership talent in the panic of re-seeding of the fields when the hands would all have quit at darkness, that being their customary quitting-time. But King George called out, "Do you want to eat? Then seed the fields! The master will never starve! It is we who shall starve!" And other such-like sentiments. He bade them run and get the lanterns and called girls to bake hoe-cakes at the edge of the field, and he worked there with them all that night so the fields were safely sown when came the dawn. I gave him a tip of six bits, which was all of the money I could find in the house.

My husband does not like King George's name. His former master so hated the King that he found much sport in mocking him, yet my Thomas considers the name to be an insult to the slave as much as to the King. Yet King George much admires his own name. Thomas tries to get around that by calling him Great George with a cheerful voice, yet within his family he is King George and my Ursula believes that he always will be.

I so long for my husband! His letters come twice each week by the Post and often another by Mr. Mazzei. I keep his letters on our chamber-table and read them over every night; he writes as he speaks, so I can see his face and I know when he would smile or when his eye would flash. I swear that at times I can smell his skin and feel myself safe within his arms. He never writes of his loneliness. He writes very little of the politics, so most of his letters are just about which vegetables have come to the market now or what we might change in the plans for our house. I write to him the like, how his garden does and what his workmen are about this day. How much of love do we convey with just such homely sharing!

Our construction goes on very slowly. The slaves do not care if a brick is laid and the workmen ask such questions of me that I am in truth unable to answer. I must say, "Leave off that wall until the master returns and concentrate on this other one," or, "Build only the interior of that wall until we have made better bricks for its face." Indeed we are nearly out of bricks. A new brick-maker will be needed this summer, and that means more of the heat and smoke and smell of the infernal firing-kiln. Our middle-building has had its walls half-high for so long that seems its final shape.

We had hoped to have our parlor this year and my husband's library right above. There is a chamber in the attic above our dining-room where Mr. Mazzei lived with his family while his house was built upon his vineyard lands to which he has given the name of Colle. So we had thought to move our chamber to the library and our babes to Mr. Mazzei's old room and live in four rooms. All in one building! My heart does leap to think of it! But the slowness of construction and the need for new bricks will delay our middle-building by another year, so there seems little point in moving our family to live in Mr. Mazzei's old room. We shall keep that room instead for guests, which prospect does greatly delight my husband.

He is little bothered by our straitened living. One thing he will do now in Williamsburg is to place the order for our windows from England and this he sees as a happy event and not, as I see it, as a great frustration, coming as it does beyond two years past the date of our wedding. Would I have married my Thomas if I had known that we would live forever in a single room? This I ask myself, and then I smile. How ever I am griped by these daily trials, I cannot but know I would have married him and lived my whole life in an open field. But I think it imprudent to tell him that.

MONTICELLO JULY 27, 1774

*T*he crime of treason against the British Crown is punished by not one death, but three. When rebels are convicted of treason they are taken to some public place and there they are hanged up by the neck. Hanging, however, is too clean a death, so after they have suffered it but before they are rendered insensible they are cut down. Then they are disemboweled, and to make this second death complete their entrails are burned before their eyes. Once they are thus irrevocably gutted, their bodies are cut into four large pieces and then, what must be a relief to them, they are at last beheaded.

It was these heads on pikes that my Pappa foresaw when he laughingly told me what the Burgesses risked. He described for me their whole punishment, and I wondered at the time why he did, if he thought to impress me with their bravery or if he meant to make of me an ardent rebel since failure is so unthinkable. I know not his motive, but I know his result. My Pappa's words have troubled my sleep near every night for the past three years, and it is only now that I am able even to watch my hand form the words. I write them to put them out of my mind. I can no longer bear to touch my husband's belly and be aware of the bowels within nor see his loved face for a slice of a moment without his body under it. For I fear that it may come to rebellion. I truly can find no other course. Lord Dunmore has again dissolved the Burgesses, but rather than submit to his will they will meet next week in rebellious assembly. My Pappa would laugh to see me now! I must push past my fears and learn my husband's bravery or I shall be unworthy to be his wife.

The Boston Tea-Party has brought with it the chain of troubles that my husband feared. I could not have imagined it would touch us here! But the British have prohibited trade with Boston, and thus blockaded, the Massachusetts Bay has begged for support from her American sisters. Our Burgesses discussed these events while they were sitting in Assembly, and they determined then upon my husband's suggestion to make of June the First a day of fasting and prayer in support of our Boston brethren. Lord Dunmore dissolved them in a fury so home they came ahead of time, and we had for ourselves on Saturday last our own Albemarle day of fasting and prayer. Then did I feel rebellion on the air! We went down to St. Anne's all together with very many of our neighbors and friends, forming up a parade of chairs and mule-drawn wagons. We brought very many of our servants, which made for them a holiday, but for me it was no holiday. I had come fresh from reading my husband's reasoned summary of our case against Britain. I knew for the first time on that morning that we risk a rebellion and a war.

As is usual, the ladies curtsied their greetings and then went in to take their seats while the gentlemen talked in a group together until the final moment. Whether it was from a shame that I had ever harbored cowardly thoughts, I found a need to remain with my husband. I stood with my hand upon his arm and listened to the gentlemen's talk and made myself nod when ever they nodded and say an agreement when rebellion was proposed. My husband understood that I was under the spell of his document, but the other gentlemen gave me looks as if I had returned to a dining-room after all the ladies had withdrawn. They had repeatedly to curb their cursing, which was a painful trial for them that my husband and I made sport of when we talked about it afterward.

We were meant to pray for deliverance from the grievous risk of a civil war. We did pray, but our Saturday service was less for praying than it was for anger. Reverend Clay called gentlemen up to speak, my husband the first and meant to speak the longest. Then it was that I conceived a pride for which I shall have to account to my Maker, for Thomas spoke so wonderfully! I had come from reading his condemnation of Britain which was meant for the eyes of learned men, and there he stood, saying much the same things in words that any child could understand.

"It is we who own our government! Our government does not own us!"

"We need obey no law we had no part in making!"

"If we do not give our support to Boston, we shall have no support when Britain turns on us!"

"For ourselves we fought, for ourselves we conquered, for ourselves we have a right to hold!"

And many such-like sentiments. He stood very straight beside the podium with his hand at ease on the edge of it and his eyes soft and calm upon us all. While others cheered, I could not suppress a smile so great I had to open my fan for fear that my pride might shame us both. I was so proud!

The common men seethe with a worry this summer that they will be conscripted to fight the British. This fear my husband tried to allay. He stood before them as their county lieutenant and told them in words most firm and kind that there will likely not be a war, but if there is a war it will be over quickly and on their part most gloriously won. For this there were cheers from those standing at the rear and out in the sun beneath the open windows. I found that even his voice was stronger than I had feared that it might be, although indeed it does not carry. It has too much of the sweet softness which makes it so full and rich on the ear. Still, he sounded so fine!

Yet it seems such talk comes easily to families gathered at their church on a sunny morning in July, with the crops in the ground and the rivers high. Bring on the British! I felt no fear then. It was only that evening, when my husband and I had long and repeatedly savored our day, that I began to feel my old panic at the desperate risk to my husband's life. I had to take up his document by candle-light and read it again while he copied it over, and truth to say, while it confirms our rebellion it also brings me comfort. I know at least that our cause is just, what ever now might be its end. I swear we are so little troubled that I am astonished to learn of the grievous pains being suffered at the northern towns. British troops have been quartered on the people. They march in Boston and New York. They even have fired upon the people, and they daily pillage and humiliate and commit the most unspeakable acts. I swear, I had heard only pieces of this and had thought it all so far from me that it seemed but sport for gentlemen. What care I for Government? Only give me a peace that I might live my life! But I may no longer hold these thoughts. I must read my husband's document until its perfect sentiments are part of my very soul and will.

Yesterday, and it was no surprise, my husband and Mr. Walker were chosen out to attend the Convention of Deputies which will meet at Williamsburg on Monday next. They were the Burgesses from Albemarle before the Governor dissolved their Assembly, so now they must attend this bastard convention which meets in defiance of British law. Their wives were not consulted in this; we must bear our worry how ever we might. The Deputies meet to set Virginia's course in response to the Boston troubles and to choose out some few delegates for the Congress of the Colonies. This Congress was proposed in June by my husband's Committee of Correspondence. Delegates from all of the colonies will convene in Philadelphia in the fall.

How this delights my husband! He was so greatly excited when he set off this morning for Williamsburg that he must himself see to his driving-horses and to the saddle-horses for Jupiter and Martin that he insisted must be matched, all bays, to make a better presentation. He paid a great attention to his clothes, to see that we packed his newest shirts which have not an excess of the lace that he comes now to see as perhaps too British. He wanted more of his white silk stockings. He wears cotton only on the road. And had we packed his new waistcoat, the one that bears but a tracery of vines? Had we packed his gilt buckles? I never have seen him so concerned about his clothes!

There was a gaiety to our preparations which came from his eagerness to be gone. Patsy laughed and clapped in Mary's arms. Janey is subject to Jack's ear-fevers and she has been breeding one this day, yet she smiled when her father bent to kiss her cheek. I could not smile. When came the moment for him to take the reins, he kissed me and I clung to him as if this might be our final parting.

"Patty? Patty? The servants!" he said. "I shall be away for ten days at the most!"

He knew it was not just these ten days, but the journey to Philadelphia that I feared. They will surely make him a delegate to the Congress of the Colonies, and the thought of such a dangerous and long separation brings tears to my eyes now as I write. Yet I was brave this morning. I left off my clinging with a better will than I would have thought I possessed and said, "Get it settled with the British, Husband. You have a better use for your time than this."

He smiled to see me so bravely saucy. "I shall tell them unless they yield to us they will have my lady to consider!"

So we smiled together and he was gone. I watched him down the road until the top of Jupiter's hat was lost among the trees. I am able to bear these ten days apart. And with God's grace, I shall also bear what ever more is yet to come.

MONTICELLO OCTOBER 11, 1774

*N*ow do I take a risk! I have longed for my journal these two months past, but my husband has been so constantly with me that I dared not risk retrieving it. Now Thomas has only just gone out to walk our lands with Mr. Cox, who was my Pappa's steward. It appears that Mr. Cox will oversee our plantations that we have from my Pappa at Elk-hill and Cranks, although he and Thomas yet disagree upon what his fee for this will be. And he continues to balk at my husband's insistence that he must not resort to the whip.

"But they are used to the whip! They will not work!"

"If a man is determined not to work no amount of whipping will change his mind. Here we give them Saturdays off if sufficient work is done in the week. Or we kill a beef. You will be astonished to see how cheerfully men will work when they see for themselves some reward in it. Truly, if a man has a rebellious mind to whip him will only make the problem worse."

So my husband says most patiently, and in truth the servants at Monticello are as cheerful as any I have seen. Negroes sing so mournfully that the sound of their singing is near to weeping, yet here the sound from the fields and quarters is lively and very near to gay. Our children here do not just run, but they scamper and laugh like any children. My husband at length resolved that he must prove his point to Mr. Cox by walking with him through our fields and quarters. As they left I hurried to retrieve my journal. With a bit of luck they may be gone the morning.

Where shall I begin? My husband never arrived at Williamsburg for the sitting of the Deputies. He was stricken on the road so greatly sick that Martin was required to take the reins, and they brought him home huddled and miserable with such a violent dysentery that he had to be carried from his phaeton and then he was in bed for nearly a week. To see a second husband carried home was in truth a very shock for me. We had Dr. Gilmer, but no other hands were fit to care for him but my own. He has a strength in him which shook off the illness with gratifying rapidity, so within three days it was just my pleading that kept him from bounding up from his bed and trying again for Williamsburg.

We had sent off his document by Jupiter. I swore to him that its presence there was better even than his own, for the Deputies would consider his words with all the respect due final words, since such they must think that his writing might be. This did not appease him, but still he yielded when he saw that I was near to tears. He understood that Bathurst's death had given me a fear beyond the ordinary.

So I sat beside my husband and read to him. Within a day or two he was so very restless that nothing I read would engage his mind, so then I thought to teach him how to use a needle. This diverted him until he saw how slowly a flower is built up stitch-by-stitch.

"I shall be the morning at this one blossom!"

"Not at all. Not much beyond half an hour."

"How can you bear it? Does your mind not wander?"

"Indeed it does. I sing or converse while I work. I find it most enjoyable."

But he had not the patience. It seemed to him too much effort spent for too little reward. He is possessed of such a restless mind that he has not the patience to use his hands; whether designing our manor or laying gardens or smithing a lock or any thing, he envisions the work quite thoroughly and he loves the very thought of it. So he begins. But then his hands are too slow to complete what ever his mind has begun before his mind runs far ahead and he must hurry after it. In truth, his mind is his master and it drives him hard.

So I tried every topic to interest him that had not to do with the British Crown nor the Convention of Deputies at Williamsburg nor the Continental Congress for the fall. He worried that he might not be chosen to go, and indeed my husband was not chosen. This was likely due to the single fact that they thought he must be too ill to go, but still he finds it a trial and a humiliation to be dealing with his overseers while others contend with his Government. I tried every topic, but it was only by accident that I hit upon one that seized his mind. And then we opened such a painful boil that I was sorry for having raised it at all.

One early morning Betty came up to take off our babies for Ursula to nurse. Patsy at two is nearly weaned, but often in the morning she pleads for Ursula so we allow her still that single nursing with her sister at the other breast. We do it in part for our Ursula's sake, for her own little Archy has died in July so she finds in nursing our children together a very great comfort. It was so very early when Betty came that the light was soft and lacking in color, yet if he had been in proper health my husband would have been about his day. As it was, he woke to Janey's cry and he watched as Betty took them away. I knew this, for I was watching him. He turned and saw that I was awake. As is his habit, he drew me to him and kissed me for good-morning upon my nose and cheek and where ever else he was able to reach.

I said, "You are feeling better this morning."

"There are just twenty small, angry people with pitchforks running inside my belly. That is an improvement over one hundred. A very great improvement."

I returned his smile. I greet the morning with reluctance while my husband greets it with a very great glee, so we make an effort to meet at the middle.

"Betty seems quite happy here. Does she no longer wish to return to Guinea?"

"We have never talked of Guinea. She expects that I shall free her soon."

My husband stiffened in all his limbs. "Have you promised that you will free her?"

I saw at once that he was going to be reluctant to free my slaves. Knowing this brought me near to panic. "Of course I have promised! Why should she not be free? You have said that you would free them all!"

"Oh, Patty. You should not have promised before you had first discussed it with me."

"They are mine! They come from my Pappa! You have said you would let me control my own property!"

"All right." He sat further up against his pillows. "Let us suppose that you have my permission. How then will you go about freeing your slaves?"

"You will show me the way! If you are so very clever, sir, then show me the proper way to free my slaves!"

"There is no way."

"Of course there is a way!" I sat up straight on the bed and paid no mind to the morning's chill. I would not continue to lie beside a gentlemen who refused to free my slaves.

"The only way to free a slave is to transport him beyond Virginia. If he remains in Virginia, any one who pleases may take him up and enslave him again."

"Very well! We shall transport them beyond Virginia!"

"Them? Betty and how many of her children?"

"All of them!"

"All ten of them? Even the babies who are your father's children?"

"Of course! All of them!"

"Hush, Patty. Be calm. They are working below. You must not let them hear you."

"I cannot bear to hold them against their will! I must free them!" I was near to crying. Indeed, I was crying but I refused to cry so my tears but stung and blinded me.

"Patty, listen to me. She cannot support them. And even if we sent her money in what ever far place she was able to find, she could hope for only a Negro's life. You have been to the towns. You have seen how they live. Your Betty would have a worse life as a free Negro than she ever could have living here with us."

"But she should have that choice!"

"Should Patsy have the choice of whether or not she wanders near the stairs?"

"It is not the same thing! You vowed that if you ever had the right you would free your slaves. What happened to your vow, sir? Have you grown more cruel as you have also grown older?"

He folded his arms in a hug of himself and looked away from me. "I meant to free my slaves once I had that right. I thought to hire them back for something over what they cost me to keep, and we would all be happier. I believed I would do that. I do not believe it any longer."

"Why?" I felt very near to panic.

"I wanted it for myself even more than for them. My conscience plagued me. I would ease my conscience. So you could ease your conscience now by packing Betty up and sending her away, and she would wave most joyously as her wagon passed beyond your sight. You could hold that image forever after and feel yourself the most generous mistress, when in truth your salving of your conscience benefits not even Betty. It accomplishes nothing!"

I stared at my husband. He had grown so fervent that truly I feared for his fragile health. "The problem is not just with us, Patty. The problem is with slavery. The whole system! To properly undo it now we would have to turn time back a hundred years, and failing that the best we can do is to find a solution which cuts the knot and does not only untie one string of it. We cannot abandon our slaves to suffer. We cannot walk away and think ourselves pure because we had no part in creating slavery, for slavery exists and we hold these slaves. We have no honorable exit."

"But I want to free my slaves!"

"And so do I want to free them. The very moment I can manage a world in which I believe they can make their way I shall free them. At once! But until that day comes I know they are better off here with me. I find that bitter, but my conscience must live with it. And so must yours. I will not free your slaves."

I groped within my mind most desperately to find the error of his reasoning, yet the more I groped the more I saw that his position was as just as was my own. I shrank from further thinking then, for I saw beyond our little dispute a whole vast weedy field of worries stretching yet farther than my mind could reach. I saw with a feeling like my stomach shrinking upon a morsel it was bent to reject that there might never be a solution. We might suffer with slavery for evermore.

"But will you ever free them?" I said in a voice so meek it was surprising to us both. My husband turned his eyes unto me.

"I will free all the slaves. And more than that, I will find a way for them to live with dignity. I swear that every day of my life. I cannot yet say how I shall do it, but I will free them if I ever can."

This conversation with my husband left me with the taste of ashes in my mouth. There were ashes dry behind my eyes and in my belly such a knot of pain that I feared I was breeding my husband's sickness. I wish I had never given thought to slavery! When I saw it as a natural fact I could please myself by being kind to my own and never give a thought to any others. That my Pappa was an importer of slaves even seemed to me for all of my life to be nothing worse than the fact that he was also a lawyer.

Now is my peace torn apart! I look freshly at the gangs of slaves all bent and toiling in the fields, at the corpses on the gibbets on market-days, at all the silent faces. That I cannot imagine how we would live if we had not these hands attending us only makes my misery all the greater. My husband sees how I suffer under the burden of my new awareness. This is a pain he has borne for so long that he has made some peace with it so he offers me consolation in our usual manner, with sly and gentle humor.

"Take heart, my Patty," he says to me. "You might try praying St. Augustine's prayer: 'Lord, make me good, only not quite yet.' "

Or, "Be glad that we need not free our horses. Imagine how we would strain to pull our own wagons!"

Or, "You might learn to draw your own stays, Patty. That would be a wonderful kindness to Bett."

He says this as we struggle to draw the stays which are the latest London fashion, so high in the front and coming down so low that I must walk with only little steps and I find it a trial to sit at all. They are, in truth, more modest since they do not expose the top of the bosom, but to wear them I must modify my gowns. I swear I am near giving up on fashion.

MONTICELLO MARCH 22, 1775

I have passed this morning in the gay amusing reading of passages from my journal. How discouraging it seems! Who is this lady who frets so much over every thing? I resolve now to write of these past five months just as they were lived, in perfect bliss.

I continue to rejoice in my husband's fortuitous illness which kept him from the Williamsburg Convention and then from the Philadelphia Continental Congress. Indeed he was there in greater part, for friends of his printed his document in a pamphlet which I rejoice to see does not bear his name at any place. His "Summary View of the Rights of British America" was read among the delegates. They thought it too radical on the whole, but we are told it led many lively discussions in the ordinaries near by the Carpenters' Hall. This, I comfort my husband, was even better than his having been there in very flesh, since he is only one gentleman and he is ever uneasy to speak in company. For his part, he reads his pamphlet again and frets that the editing is not right, the words may not be perfectly chosen, and had he but known it was going to be printed he might have written it differently. So the Congress had its pamphlet, but I had the best of it. I had my husband!

We passed the fall season here at our Seat while he settled up our business affairs. What with Pappa's added plantations, we have four overseers now and many hired or indentured workmen and so exceedingly many slaves that my husband wrote down every one of their names and still we believe we have not counted all. He numbered 187. This seems a very grievous number for people so determined as we are determined to free them at the earliest date.

Much work has been done upon our construction, which lifts my heart to see the site. We had the hire of Mr. Pond last summer to fire some further many thousands of bricks, and by this spring the walls are past the second story on our middle-building. The foundations are laid for our chamber-wing. I truly do begin to see the shape of our house! We had given thought this summer past to completing our chamber-wing before the winter, but we shall need more bricks of a new-hired maker. Indeed, I have for so long lived with my family all together in one room that I tell my husband gaily I prefer it so, for if we had a chamber and a parlor together we might too seldom see one another.

So our middle-building takes its shape, although as yet it has no windows. The Continental Congress has so admired our Virginia Association's bans upon imports that it has imposed them continent-wide, which means that we must surrender our windows as the ship that carries them nears our shore. So our workmen have set about constructing windows from glass made in the colony and near-green wood cut upon our mountain. Truly American our windows will be, however warped might be their frames and waved with lines might be their glass. The separatist sentiment within the towns has lately become so very strong that every smallest thing is styled "Liberty this" or "Patriot's that." So I tell my husband we shall have "Liberty windows," and I make my eyes cross to prove to him that how ever fine might be their politics we truly shall not see out of them. He laughs at this. He swears that if the Burgesses had anyone of my irreverence they should long since have come to fighting.

How ever much work was done on our house we could not be

in it before the winter, so in December we removed to my Pappa's
Elk-hill plantation on the James which is very near by my own Elk-
island. Elk-hill has an old brick house which leaks cold air at every
seam, but this was a winter so very mild that we needed only fires
to keep us cheerful. We had come and going the winter long some
many various friends and kin who stayed within our vacant rooms
and helped, as we said, to warm our house. Our mother came with
her Randolph and Nancy, and my sister Skipwith came with her
Henry, and my sister Eppes with her two little boys, and John Page
and other of Thomas's friends and my own dear friends and some
Burgesses.

As a belle I had my three good friends. We disported at the
balls together and we sewed together the forenoons long and rode
out for pleasure in the afternoons, so it seemed that we nearly lived
as a group and moved together from house to house. Now my
husband so completes my life and his friends are so constant in
their attendance that I little feel the loss of my friends, who live for
the most part far away. It is just when I greet some one of them
that I feel brief bereft that our lives must be separate. So there
came in this winter my friend Penny Morris who is very lately widowed, and she so grieves for her husband that I have a thought she
might go the way of my sister Carr. My sister Carr will not remarry
for none can take her Dabney's place, and in this I greatly encourage her. Penny has but one breast. And while our babes played
at our feet she told me what had befallen her breast in a voice most
alarmingly calm and mild.

She had a cancer. This her physician said must be removed or
it would claim her life. They did not name for her the day, but only
they arrived of a quiet unexpected morning and sent all her family
to a near-by farm. The doctor brought his four strong men who
held her still upon her kitchen table. They gave her to chew upon a
wooden spoon, and the doctor required that she nod her head before he would begin to cut. This she would not do, but she conjured in her mind the faces of her helpless children and her head
moved, she said, quite beyond her will. The doctor took most of the
breast at once and the blood was so great that they covered her face
that it would not find her eyes. From beneath the cloth she meant
not to scream but her pain was beyond endurance, and for this the
doctor later reproved her that he finds it hard to cut if his victim
screams.

"But that was not the worst," my Penny said. She has little

changed from our girlhood days, so she yet has her still and tranquil face and she seldom smiles, but she wears her look as if she
keeps some merry secret. "He must have every bit of the breast,
right to the very bone beneath. For half an hour he paused and
scraped, then paused and scraped and paused again. I could not
plead that I would rather die, for he had tied that infernal bit to my
head."

"Would he give you no laudanum? Not even rum?"

"No laudanum. He once took the breast of a lady who had so
much laudanum that she died while he cut, and this was for him
such a grievous shock that he would not risk it more. I later tried
laudanum for the after-pain but very little did it do. This is not a
mild pain. It goes to the bone."

"And not rum?"

"Never rum. He disapproves to see a lady drink."

"Indeed. And you were careful not to offend him."

At this my dear Penny gave me her smile which is lovelier still
for its rarity. She said, "Were I ever to do it again I would drink me
down a gallon."

So I had my dear Penny, but ever our guests were for the most
part my Thomas's friends, his school companions and his fellow
lawyers and very many Burgesses. The foremost Burgesses who
sojourned with us were Benjamin Harrison and Richard Henry Lee,
who had been to the Congress in the fall so they brought Philadelphia to our table. Oh, to have the wit to describe these gentlemen!
Mr. Harrison is greatly fat, fatter indeed than Peyton Randolph.
His face is greatly round and red and he needs much attendance
from his servant who goes with him even to the privies. Yet Mr.
Harrison has a clever wit, a great good cheer that lights a room, so I
find much pleasure in his company. Beside him Colonel Lee is
greatly tall, so thin you would swear he had not all his bones and so
fiery of look you would think he must hold a flame within. His face
seems all part of one great beak, and it bears that same distracted
look of very much going on inside that I see so often on my husband's face.

Thomas much attended to Colonel Lee. This gentleman
speaks like an orator if he has an audience of only one, in a deep
round voice most firm and strong as gentlemen ever love to speak.
"We must watch New York! She is a Tory sewer if ever I should use
the word. And South Carolina is plain complacent. She will fall
away at the earliest strife. Then there is New England! Never you

saw such a collection of independent minds. They are hot for liberty, that is sure, but each gives the word a different meaning. I vow they would rebel for the pleasure of it and that, my dear Jefferson, is the seat of the problem." And many such-like things he said while my husband gazed upon his face with a yearning that made me grieve to see it. He would have been there, my dear one, in the place of his pamphlet.

With so many people here in the winter we held three very impromptu balls that were all the gayer for their utter lack of planning. Beside the splendid balls of the Forest, which often gathered a hundred guests, these parties of twenty were little more than dinners with a bit of dancing to finish the evening. I played while they danced a harpsichord so ancient it cannot keep in tune, and my Thomas fiddled by my side as we watched our dancers in gay assembly. The hour was so early that children danced. Little Jacky Eppes gravely danced with my Patsy, the neither of them yet three years old and my sister Betsy leading them through a most peculiar minuet that had us laughing for the love of it, yet unable to laugh since the children were so intent upon their dignity.

Yet even with so many people near we were very often alone together. My husband continues to keep his schedule, although he prefers now to work in the mornings and exercise in the afternoons when he claims that his mind is of a lesser strength. How fiercely it drives him! He feeds it the forenoon long and often for much of the afternoon lest he suffer a growing restlessness as if his hungry mind were showing teeth. Our guests assume he must work at the law but he has not been a lawyer for beyond a year since our farms and plantations can well support us.

Still, he works. My Thomas travels with crates of books which he lays out open upon the floor and he joyously moves among these books on the trail of some most earnest issue. It might be a question of architecture or a play of Euripides raised at table, or he reads upon natural religion or the role of a government or cartography; what ever thought has alarmed his mind he must harry and pursue it to its end. He commonplaces as he goes, or often-times he writes a letter. He groans and sighs and laughs aloud with the flow of his internal conversation. He tells me words, although I never seek to grasp from him any whole idea for fear of being seized as he is seized. So all through our merry winter together I made his excuses to our guests that he might have his mornings to give to his work. I saw to our children and directed our servants that everyone might be warmed and fed. But I spent very much of my time in the mornings sitting to read near by his side or writing letters to sisters or friends or settling plantation accounts or mending. We passed whole mornings as close companions with very little said, yet our current of tranquil communion together made us even breathe in harmony.

In the afternoons we walked or rode with any of our guests who would take the air, our horses so very fresh with the cold that we had on some occasions much jumping and kicking. Once I rode a filly but newly saddled and sworn to be gentle by Ambrose, the horseler. She was a very pretty filly, a bright red-chestnut well marked with white, but she truly would have nothing do but she must be in the next county at the earliest moment. My Thomas saw that she was too fresh for a lady. He said we must pause and exchange our saddles, but I ride more than passing well so I assured him I was not overmounted. In truth, I rather enjoyed her capers. So we rode on. We were a party of six but I was the only lady, and since in the party were Colonel Lee and Mr. Walker, lively indeed was the gentlemen's talk. We had taken a foot-path along the James which is our favorite riding-path for its views of the river and its frequent fields which make an invitation for galloping. I wore a cardinal and a handkerchief to mask me from the sun and wind, and soon there was enough of wind that my red cloak flapped and my white mask flapped and my filly grew more alarmed by the moment.

"We must change horses!" my husband said.

"I am fine. She shall not succeed in gaining her liberty from me." This I said, then at once regretted it for the fact that we were not alone and Colonel Lee, with his pious air, could never find the fun in it. My husband loves my sauciness, which he swears he needs to keep his mind in balance, but some other gentlemen find it shocking. For this, my husband allowed me to ride yet farther on ahead of the rest. He and Colonel Lee were deep in talk upon varieties of peaches, for Colonel Lee's Chantilly is a great plantation famous for its splendid trees.

I proposed a trot. This was assented to, and merrily we trotted on while the sun played upon us through the trees. There was no snow and the ground was soft but only crisped at the top by cold, which curious footing I could feel. My filly, so very fresh as she was, chose to find this form of surface alarming. She became so very quick and gay that I knew that indeed I was overmounted. I tried to slow her pace, but my greatest pull was without the very least effect. Then ahead I saw the start of another field.

"Thomas!" I only had time to say when my filly began her galloping. The next county beckoned! I tried to circle her, but she was unaware of her reins and my very presence was alarming to her, with the flapping of cloak and gown and mask. She had been saddle-trained by the horseler and never yet ridden by a lady.

A side-saddle is a secure enough perch if the horse is not eager to be rid of its rider, but my filly jumped and turned as she ran. I grasped the pommels between my knees and clung with all fingers to the mane while I waited for Thomas to catch my horse. My Thomas is the finest horseman in Albemarle, and I knew that even as I bravely clung he was whipping his own horse after me. Yet I could not wait. Near across the field my filly either jumped or slipped and I was flung from her back with a violence that made me insensible for a time. I know not for how long. It seemed at once that I looked up into my husband's face, yet his frantic fear made me well aware that I must have been asleep for some little time.

"Patty!" He held me in his arms and he was rocking me, which I could not tell him compounded the awful pain of my head. The other gentlemen stood above so I could not let him shame himself. Since he made so much of my accident I ought to have managed to die in his arms, but I could not do that. Instead I thought to startle him into sense at once.

"I am Lysistrata," I said with what faint voice I was able to muster. "Keep thee from my bed. I shall prevent a war." It was a feeble jest but all I could manage. He knew that I never would do the like. Yet did I have my Betty's strength, I fain would organize all the ladies and we would erect our barricades so wars would be ended for evermore.

Oh! I had meant to write of my Betty and now the morning is nearly gone.

My Ursula could not remove to Edge-hill so we carried my Betty in her place to nurse my Janey and to manage our kitchen. This went on fine into January when Thomas and I thought to visit Guinea, which now my brother Skipwith has most grandly styled his Hors du Monde. So Thomas and I went in January to visit our sister at Hors du Monde, and we carried only our personal servants to spare our children the strain of the journey. My Betty discovered while we were gone that Hors du Monde is actually Guinea. Upon our return we found her enraged, yet as is her habit she hid her rage beneath an iron tranquility. Seeing her anger, I thought it best that I not be alone with her. This resolve I was able to keep until the second morning of our return, when we had a breakfast so inedible that we wondered what she might have put into it. My husband sadly set down his fork and said, "Perhaps you should speak with Betty."

I went out to the kitchen through a pelting rain which was a near duplicate to my mood. I knew my Betty. I knew precisely what our conversation would be. There were others in the kitchen, and this for a moment seemed to me a kind of reprieve, but a look at Betty's face made me well aware that she would speak her mind if others heard or no.

"Please leave us," I said to the other servants.

Betty would not wait until we heard the door close before she said, "I will be free now, mistress."

"It is not yet the time."

"I will be free! Do you care so little for me that you will go to Guinea without telling me so? I have cared for you and cared for your children and still you think so little of me?"

"I thought it best not to tell you."

"I think it best that I be free!"

"It is not the time. What will your freedom bring to you now? A life in the street? No clothes? No food? The freedom to watch all your children starve?"

"I will be free!"

"Think, Betty. Think beyond the word. There is not a better life for any Negro in America than to be a servant of your own good master. It is not right!" I said louder as she began to shout. "But it is true nonetheless!"

"I will be free! No! I am already free!"

She tore from her waist her apron-strings and tidied her cap and handkerchief while she said in a voice most clipped and calm, "I shall go to Monticello for my other children. Then I shall return to Guinea. I am free at this moment. I have the right to go to Guinea and live with my own husband."

"But his wife is in bed of another child!"

This she was unwilling to hear. "I have been patient. I have remained while you recovered from your birthing. I have been fair to you. Now it is my time," and other such-like things she said. She was far beyond any reason. She would not listen even to my husband, who talked with her for nearly an hour and came from the parlor shaking his head.

"She is free," he said with a look at me which was oddly both amused and pained. "I could beat her to death and that would make no difference to her. So she is free."

That decided, Betty set out to make her escape from us. She fomented her small rebellion among other slaves who were her friends and resolved to make their escape with her. This they all three said to my husband at Betty's instigation, and he patiently told the law to them, how he could not legally set them free and he thought them better off owned by us and he knew of no place upon this continent where a Negro might live without fear of enslavement. But they would be free!

I was sorely afraid for my four dear servants and for the three babies they meant to carry, yet all I could do was to give them money. My husband found for each something more than a shilling. Then he also found that he could not let them run away from us on their own for a worry that harm might come to them or they might be stolen upon the road. He had a thought to visit our Seat and see that it weathered the winter well, so in the end it was their own dear master who drove the wagon in which they made their escape.

My Thomas was gone for more than a week, and when he returned he would not tell me whether my Betty had traveled to Guinea. His face bore the look of entertainment that I so often see upon it when he has discovered something new, some facet of the world that he had never guessed, but he would not say a word about Betty. He only said once that it seemed to him that escaping now and then might be a very good thing.

So I thought very much upon my Betty in the weeks that remained before we all went home. We went home some ahead of time because the nursemaid Betty had found for my Janey was a callous wench who made us long for our own dear servants. Yet while we remained, I thought much of Betty and of all these servants under us who bear the choice of being bondsmen for life or of living in a welter of misery. If they had that choice! We cannot give it them, for like children offered poisoned sweets they might choose their misery over their bondage. This very word, liberty, is so much with us that it cannot but affect our servants, and I grieve for that. I wish above all that we might find a way to give them what they so desire.

We had thought to remain at Elk-hill until after the sitting of the Delegates, but this we could not wait to do so home we have come at the middle of March. Now am I amazed! My husband had hired in January a likely carpenter named Joseph Neilson, and he was here upon the day when Thomas drove his escapees to Monticello. My Thomas swears that Neilson looked at Betty and she at him and there was from that moment never a thought of escaping any farther. Joe Neilson and my Betty have taken up so well that I blush to see their affection, and Thomas has been forced to remind Neilson of how they must be when there are ladies present.

But my Betty is happy. It seems she is so very strong in her mind that she could not leave off her Abraham unless it were by her own will. All must be by her will. Had we commanded her to share her bed with our carpenter she would have demanded to die instead, but now all of it is by her own will, her being at Monticello, her loving Joe Neilson. So she is content. When she saw me alight from my chariot she ran to me and greeted me as if there had never been strife between us.

So we are at home. I look out to our garden-space where servants are breaking the clods and sowing, with the earth the rich shade of that chestnut filly and the sun shining full upon their backs. And the smells! There is no where on earth that smells as Monticello does in spring, with the sour earth and the sweet new greening and the breeze so high and distant that it carries every essence from far away. All we lack is my husband. He is gone to Richmond for a week-long session of the Delegates, who meet to discuss the first Congress past and give charge to the second Congress soon to come. They meet in Richmond for its central location and its distance from the eye of Governor Dunmore, who would not approve their defiance of Britain and might disapprove it with the guns of his guard. I can say this gaily. Having heard of the very great troubles of the northern colonies, I have come to believe that our Governor is in truth afraid to challenge us. He is not my worry any longer, and the lifting of my fears thrills my heart most gaily. Now I await just my husband's return, and then shall truly begin my spring!

THE FOREST JUNE 12, 1775

*V*ery grievous woes have befallen us. I know not even how to begin yet it comforts me to write, so write I shall, although in after life I shall skip these pages for the very pain of reading them.

My husband is sent to Philadelphia.

I had thought the Congress was a danger past, but our Delegates when they sat in March have named my Thomas as an alternate Congressional Delegate to Peyton Randolph. Mr. Randolph is the Speaker of the House of Burgesses and the Burgesses were called to sit in May, so home came the dear accursed Mr. Randolph and off went my Thomas in his stead. I have sent a second husband to Philadelphia! He went from Williamsburg on yesterday for a journey that will take him beyond a week, and every passing minute, every word that I write continues to carry him farther from me. This should be woe enough. Yet there is more.

Our troubles began at the end of April, when truly it seemed that Governor Dunmore lost what ever fragment of his mind remained. His British Marines under cover of night came from a schooner in the James and stole gunpowder from the magazine which was kept there against any untoward event, a rising of slaves or an armed invasion, and not as any threat to him. Yet he stole it, and only promised to pay when pressed by a most indignant crowd and the threat of militias being raised to a number of ten thousand men. Now it is said that he fortifies his Palace and even that he spirits his family away. This astonishes me. Who would ever molest them?

So we were already much exercised when came very terrible news from Boston. They have had a battle at Lexington. The story comes in contradicting parts, but it seems there was an invasion of the British into their peaceable country-side to fire upon the planters and pillage and murder and burn farmsteads along the road. Then gathered militias from towns around and fired upon the Regulars, and killed very many. They say some hundreds. Oh, our militias had trained before, but now in good earnest do they train!

Only yesterday there came past our door a company of long-rifles from beyond the Blue Ridge and headed down for Williamsburg with the thought of marching to the defense of Boston. This one of them explained to me as I ran out and walked beside his horse. How fierce they smelled! Blood and skins and sweat! There may have been twenty of their company, all dressed in skins and stern of look and bearing at ease across their saddles their rifles longer than I am tall. The servants came running from field and kitchen and stood transfixed along the road, while only I had the bravery or the folly to try to converse with them.

Are we at war? Is this a war? When does it begin?

Thomas would not leave us at Monticello while he traveled so very far away. He was greatly alarmed at the Lexington news and the news of Dunmore's gunpowder theft, and he worried the more from all that he had seen and heard in the Capital. He wanted us safely down in the Tidewater, near by the Capital and the raised militia, what ever now might come to us in the months when he will be away. So we were at our Seat for a bare six weeks while we saw to the planting and set forth the tasks, and then at mid-May we came down to the Forest. Here we remain until my dear one returns.

Yet it carries with it a great excitement, this exercising unto a war. My sister Eppes and her Charles-City friends have organized their Ladies' Association for making replacements for every item that they can no longer buy from England. They drink teas of herbs and buy wool in the dirt which they help their servants to spin and weave, and they gather to sit and stitch and knit, they gather for dyeings and quiltings and spinnings. Never have I seen ladies so aroused! There is one among them who has ten servants and knits the stockings for all ten of them, and another who will wear just homespun garments even to her cap and shift.

This, I understand, we are all to do. There is a banning of every use of goods from England. Yet I cannot carry it to this end; it seems to me ridiculous. I have had nothing new these three years past beyond one pair of stays. My last new gown was my wedding-gown, and I turn and re-make and style again my mother's press of ancient gowns. My caps are no longer very white and I have many stockings and many shifts which seem to be made of darnings and mendings, yet still at the parts that might see light they are the fine clothing of a well-born lady. My Betsy's friend in her homespuns looks like a small-planter's wife from out of the woods. Does she not shame her husband? Does she not shame herself when she is forced to scratch where she is most chafed?

Here there is little for me to do beyond these exercised meetings of ladies who mean to fight the British with their needles. I work with my hands when they are not about, but often when they meet I find a willfulness that will make me stop working to play with my babes or walk to take my air.

Patsy grows quite big. She will soon be three, and she takes so closely after her father that she very nearly wears his face and she speaks in whole long sentences. All of this, and she is not yet three! Other ladies leave their children wild until they are even six or eight, but my Patsy wears her stays and her neat white dress and she spends her days close by to me. She loves to help with the care of her sister, who is growing now quite big as well. I rejoice to find my Janey safe past her first year and already sturdy upon her feet. So we walk out as ladies, all three of us, slowed to the pace of our youngest member, masking our faces and wearing our mitts and pausing to study each tiniest flower and every smallest wonder of beetle on a leaf or precious humming-bird. How much joy they bring me! How greatly I love them!

Janey, I fancy, takes after my mother, wearing as she does her very red curls and her fragile look of lady-like leisure. She has suffered much with ear-fevers and other complaints, but now in the summer she grows much stronger. She has had nothing trouble her these two months past.

So I have my children and my sister Eppes, but already I grievously miss my dear husband. I hoped until yesterday to have a reprieve, some word sent that he would not go at all, but late on yesterday came back Jupiter, riding dejected on a spavined horse. Thomas means to hire a postilion so he directed Jupiter to come back and protect me here, and this the poor boy seeks to do to the point where I must insist that he give me distance. He and my Thomas grew up together so now his love and loyalty are complete.

PHILADELPHIA   JUNE 26. 1775.

My beloved Wife

I have written to our brother Eppes a letter which you might want to read if you suffer any curiosity about political events. I believe you will ask our brother to throw his political letter into the fire, and since I hope for this one a better fate I shall write in it only of my love for you. Oh my dearest

Patty! If I had known what lonely miseries I would suffer, I would have carried you with me at any cost. Few delegates have their ladies here but there are some you might improve since they seem just pallid copies of their husbands. What a humorless lot! I smile to think of what tumults you would bring to their midst, making them challenge their complacent assumptions and all of you coming off better for it.

You would not, however, care for Philadelphia, which is busier and dirtier than Williamsburgh. Ladies wear clogs here even in summer for all the filth that lies in the street and the smell of the place is hard to describe, richly strong but not altogether unpleasant. After less than a week I have come to enjoy the convenience of book-sellers and abundant markets so much that I almost begrudge the hours I must spend in tedious assembly. I can't say what I expected to find at the Congress but I know I never expected this. We had arguments aplenty in the Burgesses, but there they were on principles which all could apprehend and agree were important and we only differed in our points of view. Here, however, are sixty men who are leaders in their colonies, and each is so bent upon his own prestige and defending the honor of his own country that principles and even the future of all must bow before every imagined slight. Such posturing! Such talking on hour after hour in the heat while the flies buzz and the fans wave and the gentlemen doze in their dreary seats! The only thing they have managed to do in the six weeks they have been sitting here is to name our great friend Washington as Generalissimo of all the troops in North America. Here is a single spark of wisdom.

You know the Colonel, how he bears himself modestly but he knows very well his place and rank. It seems he would not politick, but he wore from the first his militia uniform saved from the French and Indian Wars as a reminder, if any needed reminding, that he is the best soldier in America. His nomination came from John Adams of Massachusetts rather than from our own countrymen. In fact, I am embarrassed to say that Pendleton and some others saw a need to oppose it. Yet wisdom prevailed, and barely in time, for there has been further strife in Boston at a place called Charlestown which I shall not describe for fear you will toss my letter down in despair. (Be comforted, Patty. We shall show our strength and this will be over very soon.)

Washington set off from here on Friday last in a show of military pomp which I enjoyed all the more for having my own insignificant part in it. He had an escort of mounted and uniformed militia and many other officers besides, and then on horseback or in carriages the Massachusetts delegates and many from Virginia and other colonies, all of us cheering as lustily as the townsfolk cheered to see us pass. What a display we made! I am a county lieutenant, Patty, but having seen genuine officers now I think I shall not have the face any longer to train my own militia.

My greatest satisfaction in my first week here has been in meeting the Massachusetts delegation and finding them to be all that I had expected them to be, and more. The Adams cousins lead the lot and I find them so hot for their liberty, so fearless and clever in defending it, that I am confirmed in my belief that a union of the colonies is near at hand. I must keep my eyes fixed on this goal and try to manage a greater patience with all the wavering delegates who still believe we might return to Britain. That we cannot do. Our fate is sealed now in blood. The sooner we can agree on that, the sooner and the brighter will begin our future.

Now my candle burns low and my hand wavers. I truly must soon take to my bed. My dear precious Wife! I find in writing to you the greatest comfort, as if in imagining your eyes on this I can feel myself almost in your dear arms. I need you with me so very badly that my mind has begun to supply your remarks: I will be listening to some wrong-headed delegate, barely able to contain myself, when my small Patty-voice will say something witty which calms and delights me back into patience. I do adore you my precious Wife. Believe that you are the very soul and the center of all the aspirations of your doting Husband,

Th:J.

THE FOREST JUNE 27, 1775

If this is my emotional journal, then must it truly suffer my emotions. Am I a Tory? Are my sympathies improper with my own dear husband off to the Congress? Oh! I am so very angry that I must write this now to calm myself.

We have had for these two weeks past the company of our sister and brother Skipwith, dear Nancy and Henry, come in haste to comfort their poor lonely sister Jefferson. I had written to Nancy in misery when my Thomas was but two days gone, and rather than write she has come herself. Nancy is grown to nineteen years, her rag dolls and childishness far behind, and through exchange of letters we have become better friends than we ever could have been as children when our every attempt at friendship was foxed by the eight-year difference in our age. Now we feel no difference. With her company and Betsy's I am almost a carefree girl again; we laugh together in such high foolishness that truly our children believe us mad. Nancy's views of the politics are near my own, which is to say that she has no views. She nods and smiles to what ever is said and then she speaks on to other things. Betsy, however, as mild as she is, has become an ardent Patriot; what ever she says has a fire to it and she has begun most firm and quiet to wear her homespun wools and linens. Her fellow-Patriots meet here often to sew and knit with righteousness, and their visits have become a painful trial because of their so righteous anger.

Such suffering this blossoming war has brought! We have had not a shot fired in all of Virginia, we expect an almost immediate ending, yet every where is pitted friend against friend on this matter of the politics. Some of our very dearest companions have failed to pass their political test. They are forced to band together in fear, and many contemplate removing to England which is indeed a foreign country since all have lived here for generations past. How can I not grieve for the Tories' pain? And some of them are not even Tories. Dear Attorney General Randolph, well-loved brother to Peyton Randolph and as good a gentleman as ever breathed, is rumored to be settling his affairs and planning to remove to England for no other reason than that he cannot agree with those who call for separation. He has sent me a note to let me know that Thomas may have the violin he has coveted now these five years past so the instrument may be spared a damp sea-journey. My husband will be glad to have the violin, but he will grieve to have it at such a cost.

Yet the ladies of my sister's Association are able to see only Tory or Patriot. When first they met me I was seen to be a lady of perfect politics for my husband's attendance at the Congress and for his well-known very ardent voice. Their belief that I must be right-minded lingered, indeed, for several weeks, until they were sewing in the parlor this morning and Nancy and I went past their door in our usual fit of high good humor. "For shame!" one lady was brave to say. "Your husband fights for your liberty and you will do nothing? You only laugh?"

"If my husband fights for any thing it is for my right to laugh," I said before I saw Betsy's face gone pallid for my shameful anger. At once rose in me the indignant thought that I did no more than to defend myself, but I knew that mine was the greater fault. I am her sister and I live beneath her roof. I should have curtsied and said my regret and hurried on away. "Forgive me, madam," I made myself to say, and I dropped for my accuser my deepest curtsey.

"She is not well," my Betsy said. "She has a fever of the kidneys." This is not true, for I have no more than a tenderness at the small of my back that aches a bit from the press of my stays. I feel but very mildly unwell, yet Betsy has told all of this to her doctor and now he wishes to bleed me for a fever of the kidneys.

"Were my husband at the Congress I would do my part," my Betsy's friend said to another friend, who then bent deeper to her sewing.

I had a stern look at my accuser. She wore a homespun gown, yet her cap was imported and her stocking was of silk. I would not join them in judging people's minds by the clothing they wore upon their bodies, but if I did so judge her she would rank at a place between my Betsy and myself.

"Forgive me, madam." Then sprung to my mind her name. And with it came the memory that she was a feather-merchant's lady who might indeed not be well enough born to comport herself properly in company. "Mrs. Curtis," I said the more gently for this suspicion I had that she might be coarse-mannered, "I just prefer to take no part in any political meeting. But I sew in my chamber. I do assure you of that."

"Think, Mrs. Jefferson! Think how you might inspire us with the words of your noble husband!" This came from Mrs. Pratt, who knits her servants' stockings.

"I am not my husband. I cannot speak for him."

"But you have news of the Congress? You might share that," said Mrs. Lee of the homespun cap and shift.

"The delegates are sworn to secrecy. I know no more of the Congress than what you know. Indeed, I know less, for I do not read the papers."

"You do not read them!" said Mrs. Curtis. Yet she seemed less incensed, having garnered the favor of my attention. Seven faces turned their light unto me with a rapture that put me back a step against Nancy. I saw that they but hungered for what ever little glory I might reflect.

"Make a speech," Nancy said so only I could hear her. "Stand for election. Now is your moment."

"I am proud of my husband," I said out firmly. "His politics are indeed my own. But if he were a Tory I would be no less proud and his politics would be no less my own."

Here Betsy blanched further. Ladies drew in breath. Nancy, behind me, said, "No, Patty!" but I felt myself seething with thoughts so urgent that I could not pause to consider them. "How is this my rebellion? How will it alter my life if I am governed by Whig or Tory? To my husband it matters, so from my soul I pray for his quick and certain success. But I feel myself foolish to sit and sew while he places at risk his very life. Still, I sew. Yet I would to God that Britain had governed us very well so there had never been need for a rebellion and my husband would now be safe with me!"

"Tory!" said Mrs. Curtis. "You hide behind your husband!"

"She is unwell. She is unwell," my Betsy said in her gentle voice meant to soothe and comfort. Yet while she said it, I had a look from her eye that showed she quite agreed with Mrs. Curtis.

"Do we not copy our husbands' politics? Would we not all be Tory if our husbands were Tory?" I said from my rising desperation as I saw that none of my words had touched them. She who will not perfectly hate her neighbor of imperfect politics is imperfect herself, and worthy of hatred. This I saw, and only this, for Nancy took my hand to draw me away.

So am I Tory? Should my husband put me by, as was said in the room after I had gone? I do love my country. Were she invaded, I would defend her at the risk of my life. Yet my country as yet is not invaded and what is asked instead is my husband's life. I try so to cultivate the mind of a Patriot where always has been the mind of a lady who loves only peace and harmony. I nurture in myself a political fire that goes out again and again of its own, for never can I find enough fuel to feed it. I cannot hate the British. I can see too well why they are indignant at our rebellion. Far less, then, can I hate the Tories, who two years gone were our dearest friends, and least of all can I welcome a war which might cost us everything we love while it promises nothing more than a change of government. If these are Tory sentiments, then I am a Tory. May God have mercy on my soul.

My Betsy has kindly forgiven me the tumult I brought to her Association. She only asks that I absent myself when ladies meet within her parlor, and she pleads with me most earnestly to offer myself up to be bled. Dear Nancy professes to agree with my view, yet I fear that she does not apprehend it. She agrees so the politics will not come between us. I love her for that. Yet I feel so alone.

PHILADELPHIA   JULY 4. 1775.

My precious Wife

I have in hand yours of the 27th. Each time I read it I suffer an increase of an anger so foreign to me that I am at a loss to know what to do with it. You are no Tory, Patty. If you would please me you will not change even the smallest detail of your delightful mind which I treasure above all things in this world. I am impatient with men who let their tempers rise too easily for trivial reasons, yet here I sit in a perfect rage. Were your friends all gentlemen I would soon be dueling and that would be an end of it.

Dear Patty, my Wife, my soul and treasure, believe that there can be no forbidden thought. If liberty means anything it means freedom of the mind, and if your friends can't see this they are not patriots no matter how earnestly they may knit. I decry this labeling of people's minds. I am impatient now for separation, yet I wish that we might move so slowly that even the most reluctant of rebels would have time enough to find our point of view. There are few real enemies among us, Patty. There are only fearful people, scrupulous people, people whose business might be hurt by separation and people with friends and family in England. They might be won, if we but had the time. And they are, as you can see (and I love you the more for seeing it) all good people.

Ladies should not concern themselves with politics. Their constitutions are too delicate, their minds on too elevated a plane, and when they parrot their husbands without understanding they bring no honour upon themselves. But you, Patty, do me the immeasurable honour of cultivating your own pure thoughts while you still support me in mine. I would have you no different by a single inch. Just the thought that you might change yourself to suit the narrow dictates of someone else's conscience has me fully as outraged as I would be if someone had presumed to rearrange my face to make it more acceptable to him. Your mind is exquisite, tender and sensitive, sharp and wry and unlike any other. Please keep it for me as gently as you keep our children. Feed it and protect it from harm, for I can't bear the thought of returning and finding you changed in a single detail.

Nor can I bear the thought that you might be ill. Why did you never tell me you had pains in your back? To read that you have been pained for weeks but you never said a word to spare me worry only makes me worry more. What else have you kept from me? I find faint comfort in your assurance that your back-pain has now blessedly lessened, but I do support your determination to deny your sister's doctor a blood-letting. This bleeding of the sick in my experience does as much harm as it does good, and it seems too often to be prescribed when the doctor has nothing else to offer. Drink water, Patty, as diligently as if your husband held it to your lips, and drink a dose of Gabbler's for good measure if you can find the ingredients. You will be fine, I know, for I cannot bear to have you other wise.

My trials are trivial beside your own but you will smile if I mention that again I find myself a pace or two ahead of the rest. As happened when I entered the Burgesses I was asked when I arrived here to draft a document, and again as happened in the Burgesses it appears that my draft is unacceptable. They have argued in committee for more than a week over my Declaration on the Necessity of Taking Up Arms, and now Mr. Dickinson of Pennsylvania has drafted a Declaration of his own. His draft is not very different from mine except that it holds out to Parliament a last small hope of reconciliation. This seems to better suit Congress's mood, although you well know that it little suits mine.

Sweet Patty, my beloved Wife, I can't bear this separation. Your absence is a constant painful distraction made worse by my awareness of the miles between us. Were you ill, were you dying, I would never know. I sit here not knowing what your health might be, and if I let myself really dwell on that I come to an edge of insanity. My country has the right to ask many things of me but truly it may not ask this, that I chop off the finer part of myself and yearn for it with every breath I take. Dear Patty, I know your aversion to travel but if you suffer at my absence as I suffer at yours I hope you will be willing to join me in the fall. It is rumored that we shall adjourn within the fortnight and reconvene in September. Will you return with me then? Your Betty and the others can care for the children very well, and we shall not be away from them long. If you are here no one will question your politics and I shall always know the state of your health. The journey is not rigorous. Our chariot will make it easily, or we might rent a carriage or even buy one if good enough can be found. It is not right that husband and wife should be apart.

Adieu, mon coeur. Toujours je t'embrasse.

Th:J

THE FOREST SEPTEMBER 30, 1775

I am too ill to write. That I put quill to paper shows forth my sorry need for a comfort which never will be my own again until I see in heaven my poor dead children. Yet to write for comfort is become my habit. So I write.

My husband came to us at our Seat at about the end of August. We had passed through Richmond on our journey home and I had thought to see him at the Assembly there, but in Richmond I found a willfulness that would not let me see him once and let him go. I bade my Jupiter drive on past the very building where the Assembly was meeting while my heart tripped fast and I hugged my children close. It was a willfulness, or a new shy fear that my husband, not seen these three months gone, was become too grand and distant a man to suffer any interruption from me.

So home I drove to await his arrival where he would well expect me to be. My Suck came running with the first alarm, and we ran out to see his phaeton approach in a ray of yellow light through clouds which had hung about us for nearly a week. I swear the light even moved with him. When I reached the phaeton it was full upon us, and he leaped down heedless of his horses and took me into glorious embrace all careless of the servants and what they saw. How we kissed all over one another's faces! How we laughed and stumbled breathless together and spoke silly words and whirled and whirled in a giddy sweet embrace of bliss! Patsy ran to greet him, saying her "Pappa!" Behind her came my dear, dear Janey riding safe in Mary's arms, with her face which nearly was my mother's face tipped like a flower into the light and squinting and smiling and clapping her hands, each smallest detail of her yet the more precious. Thomas took them into his arms at once, and while Janey seemed not to know him well, Patsy kissed his cheek most cheerfully.

My Thomas had attended but the end of the Assembly when he passed through Richmond on his journey home, but that had been enough to let them select him out once again to return to the Congress. This was a tragedy so much expected that he did no more than to remark upon it as we started up together toward our house. He said, "Will you come?"

I said, "Yes." I had not known my answer, but in that moment I could do no other. Foolish word! It was a challenge to evil Fate, which then intervened quite heartily.

We had finished our simple dinner of corn-porridge and bacon and a kept-for-a-day squash-pudding. Yet my husband must eat, so my Ursula made for him a salad of greens and a quick-bread beside and a stew of peaches she had made on a thought that he must soon return. This he ate in our chamber while the children begged for morsels they did not crave to eat but only wished the pleasure of taking from his fingers. Then we played with our babies. My heart shrinks with pain at the memory of Janey upon her feet in her white dress stitched by my own hand, the lace cut from one of my mother's gowns, so caught up with laughter at her father's antics as he played the horse that Patsy might ride but he must rear up to have her off. They played at a foolish fox-and-geese until they near upset the table and then he set about to teach them checks, the which I could not sit to watch for the awful pain of my memory and now cannot think of lest I weep.

He thought the children must be taken off that we have our peace after his long journey. My Ursula's cabin is too rude a place for babies ever so gently bred, but Betty's family lives in a fine stone cottage where there are babes like of age and a swept board floor. We made a play of packing up their toys that they might find it an adventure and not an exile. This they did, the both of them eager to go and laughing aloud their infant pleasure, although my poor Janey did reach for me when she found that my Betty was to take her away. I write this, and I weep. These are tears on the page that I shall weep again to see in after-life.

Yet I did not know what was to come. I sought just the comfort of my husband's arms, never mindful of the risk of bladder-fever but glad of his eagerness like unto the night when we first came together. And as on that night we did hardly sleep, but we talked between times and over again we came together of a comfort and a pleasure the greater for our long practice. Could I have the gift of extending one moment of my life for evermore, I would choose that blessed night in our chamber and my own dear husband's tender voice and his skin against mine and the shock of my delight at being of a sudden within his arms after all our long separation.

My strangury began on the following afternoon of a pain most violent. It came on not slowly, but with a sharp awareness which bade me at once drink of copious water and bade my Thomas send slaves out running to search for the makings of Gabbler's potion. I was on that evening greatly ill of a fever more severe than any I have known, yet I would not have a doctor. I but drank and drank and had it all back up again, at which I drank yet more. I would not let my body have its will, for it ever seeks its foolish immediate comfort.

I felt improved enough by the following evening that we said the potion must have its effect. We blessed my dear Gabbler, who is many years dead, and we began to find a humor in my long crouch-ing on the birthing-stool that my Betty had found at the quarters to set above my chamber-pot. At candle-time my husband assisted me to stand. He found a fresh shift and helped me onto the bed and washed my face and hands most tenderly. He talked of all the gunpowder we might have made had we but saved my water, surely powder enough to supply the deficit of all of General Washington's army.

"We have not seen the children all this day," I said while he yet washed my face.

"They are happy, Patty, never fear. They spent this whole day with Betty's children playing along the Mulberry Row in such a state of uncleanliness and disrepair that it was very well indeed you did not see them."

"Oh, Thomas!" We both most firmly believed they must begin their lives as ladies, yet we knew how they yearned to play in the dirt as the servants' children love to play. We smiled for the thought that their wish was fulfilled despite all our anxious care of them. "We must kiss them good-night," I said, but when my husband protested I did not press him. I felt an urge for my chamber-pot and a chill of the fever again rising, and I knew that indeed I was less well than I had thought for a moment that I might be. So we did not summon them. Here is a pain that I shall feel for as long as I have life.

It was early on the following morning when Betty came running up our stairs with a banging that sat us straight upright. "Is Jane here?"

"No."

Then down she went.

My Thomas was off the bed and into his breeches before we heard the door close below. He ran down after her, tucking his shirt, while once again I found my chamber-pot. I had slept so little that Betty's words had no effect upon my mind. There was a haze of illness between myself and the world as real to me as the morning light. Soon thereafter came up my Bett, sent by my husband to be my nurse.

"What has happened, Bett? Where is Janey?"

"She wander, mistress. Me think she find the corn-crib."

Bett is not clever. My Betty finds in this an exasperation, but I find in it a kind of grace. There blossomed in my mind a vision of my child sleeping like an angel upon the corn, since I did not know that the cobs may shift and the slaves find such a danger in the crib for children that they bar it stoutly and forbid them away.

So I was comforted in my deluded vision and clouded in a tranquil haze of illness. My mind could encompass only drinking and drinking and crouching above my chamber-pot. It was near the hottest part of the day when came back my husband, still half-dressed and his face unshaven and his hair loose and wild upon his shoulder. "Leave us," he said to Bett, and he lifted me from my pot and set me sitting upon the bed. Then it was that I saw his own stark face. My haze of illness was dispersed at once, and I knew before he spoke what he must say.

"Oh, Patty, I would die myself a thousand times before I brought you such news as this. I cannot bear to hurt you."

He was near to weeping, yet there rose in me an altogether unexpected rage. "Tell me!"

"Janey wandered in the night. She shared a pallet with Nance so far from the door that none could dream she would ever reach it, yet when they woke this morning she was gone."

"How did she die? Tell me!"

"She fell into the well. Some of the palisades had rotted away. We have just this minute found her."

"Murderer!" I shamed myself by saying. "If we had our house she would be alive!"

Yet saying that word, "alive," made me know that she was otherwise. I fell into such a fit of weeping that my husband drew me close against his breast. To what I know must be his own vast shame he also began to weep with me, my cries very ardent and his near silent and muffled altogether by my hair.

There passed three weeks of which I have not the heart to write. They laid my Janey where Dabney lies while I had not the strength to follow her coffin, and I gave myself up to my illness grateful to suffer such trivial bodily pains. Having buried my Jack, I knew very well the horror of a mother's grief, so I welcomed my fevers and the pains of my back and the grievous pains on my chamber-pot. Dear Thomas patiently tended me and bore my intermittent weepings and angers with a gentleness that shames me now as I remember it. From whence came my anger I know not, for even in my deepest rage I did not truly blame him. My Janey's death was a tragedy as random as the fall of a leaf in a gust of wind. This I know. But in my dementia of pain her death made a focus for ancient hurts so shameful that I could not entertain them while I was yet sane.

I told him that she would be living still if he had but managed to build us a house. This cut deep, I know, for his frequent distractions and constant small changes to the design have made of our construction an endless trial. I told him with fury that he did not grieve, for he had been away from her for much of her life. I told him, and this is my greatest shame, that if he loved me he would remain with me. I felt so impatient of our separations and knowing that I could not travel so far for the risk of bladder-fever and for the grievous risk of leaving our remaining child. "Have you not done enough? Can you not see a duty greater than the duty you owe to your country?"

This I said, and he had no answer for it. His day for returning to the Congress came and went without a sign of his wish to be gone, but he only tended me the more gently for my very anger. Yet as my illness lessened I recovered my mind, and with it a growing bitter shame. "I am sorry," I said to him a hundred times as he combed my hair or fed me a broth. "I did not mean it. You are so good. Please forgive me, dear Husband. I did not mean it."

Ever his answer was, "Hush. I love you. I understand. Now drink this down." Yet I felt grow dense between us an estrangement like a wall of glass at my sorry treatment of him. There came to me knowledge of a certainty that I had broken the perfect friendship between us. This pained me so greatly that there came an evening when I could no longer bear the sight of his face. From my ever bitter misery and shame I said to him, "Thomas, you must return to the Congress. I am well enough now. You must be gone."

At this he stood from the bed where he had been sitting to talk of the tobacco-cutting which goes on apace at our Poplar Forest, from whence we had that day had a slave come riding to beg of us our surplus hands. "I cannot go until you are well," he said in a voice so thin it seemed not his own.

"I am well enough now. You must be gone."

"Oh, Patty." He walked into the light of the table-candle, then out of it into the light of the fire. "I have no wish for the journey. I cannot bear the thought of my yearning for you which will be the greater since I shall daily fear a return of your sickness. But my dear, we must give what our country demands. I have no choice but to go. The Assembly has vested in me a trust which I cannot put aside for personal comfort. How can I fail my country and live with myself? How could it ever but harm our marriage?"

And other such like-things he said while I said each time he paused for breath, "You must go. I do quite understand." He protested the more for my very willingness to have him gone out of my sight.

In the end he went. I lived for two days more so shamed that I could not look at his face, yet I hoped that just my willingness to send him would heal every rift there had come between us. That it could not do. My final desperate act on the evening before he went away was to place my hand upon his thigh in our old plain signal.

"No, Patty. You will have back your illness."

This thought of his alarmed me. Did he mean that we might never again be as husband and wife? Would he then take a maid? "I will not have it back! It happens but once after any separation!"

Still, he would not yield. So I did to him things that I knew would overcome his will, and he suffered them longer than I thought he could. He made no effort to defend himself. His pain at our rift was as great as my own and he would not risk a wider one, yet I was willing to put between us a very canyon if only he would lie with me. Still, it made no difference. I found in our union no comfort, no hope of our former friendship. I saw him off on the following morning with a renewed bladder-fever already beginning but refusing to admit the least sign of it until he was gone beyond my sight.

I have written this over two days of time. I am too ill to write any more. My grief which his presence so blessedly lessened is upon me with a force so great that if it were not for care of my remaining child I would now most joyously follow my Janey. I feel myself some reluctant Medea, murdering her baby against her will to take a revenge that she does not seek upon a husband she truly and deeply loves. Yet I see how unworthy I am to be this perfect gentleman's wife. I share not his politics, and I have not the goodness to offer him up with a generous heart. Best if he find some Philadelphia belle to do for him what my body is too weak to do and what my mind is unwilling to do, to be in all things his compliant wife.

PHILADELPHIA   SEPT. 30. 1775.

My very dear Wife

I am with you in all but flesh and my very flesh aches with the lack of you, I am sore of my head and sore of my belly and miserable to my very bones. I can't bear the thought of your least distress so my memory of your grieving face is a constant torment whether waking or sleeping, an agonizing reproof to me. I feel myself not in any way worthy beside the gentle strength of my own good lady who can yield up her husband with a generous heart at the moment of her own greatest need. Oh my dear, please forgive me for leaving you as I know I never shall forgive myself, and know that if I had the choice again I could not drive away from you.

After such a lonely remorseful journey, I arrived here this morning and went to the State House for an afternoon of arguments over the appalling possibility that Pennsylvania and Connecticut might soon be at war over their boundary along the Susquehanna River. Our own boundary with Pennsylvania must also be settled or we risk a similar sisterly conflict at a most inconvenient moment. These disputes between provinces have some delegates fearing that the northern colonies might seek to impose their will upon their southern sisters. I doubt that, for the army at Boston was raised from the whole continent, but late at night it gives me one more worry for a head more rational by light of day. Oh my dear, I am weary and must take to my bed but I can't sleep well without a kiss from you to dispel every trouble from my mind.

Dearest Patty, we are parted for less than a week and already I am pushing the minutes past until the blessed minute when I shall see you again. There is no bright colour, no exquisite note except in your presence. My former hope that you would be with me now makes desolate my lonely room and the silence which does not contain your voice. I can't bear the thought of more months apart. I only comfort myself that I can hurry an ending to what must be temporary confusion and strife and bring closer the day when I shall retire to the tranquil pleasures of our fire-side. My ardour for that day makes me more impatient with the tedious progress of a Congress which debates for long and laborious hours on details which little bear upon the matter at hand. I had forgotten, my Patty, the tone of this place, but after one afternoon I now remember too well.

My dear, you can't hate these separations more than I completely hate them. I see ambitious men all around me, eager men like John Hancock of Boston whose hunger for acclaim is a marvelous force. I feel no similar ambition. I feel instead an aversion to public life, to the self-aggrandizement and the lost hours and the conflicts which some inexplicably relish. My every humour inclines me toward domestic harmony and the peaceful life on our mountain-top where our fiercest conflict is with the weather and the most revolutionary event which occurs is the turning of summer into fall. Please write to me quickly, my darling Wife. The gravest worry in my night-time head crammed full of worries is that you might have suffered a return of your troubles. Please write to me unsparingly, for I would rather know the truth than to be left in doubt.

I wish you had carried Betty to the Forest so you might have her care and comfort there, for I have developed the peculiar conviction that if you were ill she could make you well by the simple device of demanding your health. I hope that you will not for long allow our terrible accident to come between you, for Betty is the last one on this earth who would have wished any harm upon our child.

Her Bob does very well with me, although he shares his master's loneliness. I had thought to make him just a postilion, but he is so very quick to learn that he serves me now as messenger and body-servant. He carries himself well in company, although his colour has occasioned comment since few have ever seen a slave so pale. This they are free to say in front of him, which the poor boy protests with a childish anger that I must severely reprimand. I am ever aware of who his father was, for I see in this boy the same good humour covering a most choleric temper. It distresses me more than I can tell you that I must curb his impulse to defend his honour and teach him instead that he has no honour. My comfort lies in the knowledge that within our family he may develop a dignity which would otherwise be denied him, yet the boy is so charming that my awareness of his slavery cannot but trouble me.

The condition of the freed men here is no better than what it is in Williamsburgh, and worse, for there are fewer slaves so they lack a ready connection to the white community. We truly must end this evil, Patty, and cut the knot for all of them, slave and free. I come to believe that their only salvation may lie in their removal to a country of their own where they need not fear any future enslavement nor contend with a stronger white society which will only ever despise them. Such a separate country would end this mixing which creates poor bastards like our Bob who will never be accepted by any race. There is ample room in the interior of the continent for us to establish such a country under our united protection until it is able to stand of it's own. I am thinking as I write, yet the notion appeals to me. We truly can't continue as we are.

Now I must take to my bed. Having written to you, I feel a little measure of the perfect peace which being in your arms would bring me. Oh my dearest Patty, you know how I love you, how miserable I am when we are apart, how much every happiness of my life has come to depend on your certain love. Our hearts are so conjoined that you know all of mine and I fancy I know all of yours, and nothing is more important to me than our sublime communion. I love you my dear precious Wife. Please write to me quickly and relieve my anxiety about your health. Know that at every moment you fill the thoughts of your devoted husband

Th:J

PHILADELPHIA   NOVEMBER 7, 1775

My dear Wife

I have written to you on every Tuesday here but one, and each time I took my pen in hand it was with the thought that the next day's Post would certainly bring me news of you so I really ought to delay my letter. Yet I am here now five weeks, Patty, and I have not had in all that time one scrip of a pen from your dear hand nor any news from our brother Eppes. For too long I have comforted myself with the thought that the post-rider must have been unhorsed or taken by Indians or smitten by a damsel or run off to the Regulars or any thing. The suspense under which I live is too terrible to be endured, as I can only conclude that we must have suffered some misfortune so great that no one has yet had the heart to bring it to my attention. What has happened, Patty? What ever it might be, I would a thousand times rather know it! You would have written to me if it were in your power so I can only conclude that you are very ill, but then why has our brother Eppes not written? Pray ask him to write and tell me every thing, sparing me not the worst detail, that I may end this uncertainty.

My anxiety for you is made still worse by the intelligence which continues to reach us concerning the actions of our late Governor. I think it important that you understand that we are now most certainly at war, my Patty, for our enemy is sending a force to subdue us. It is thought on advice of secret dispatches taken when a few of their ships were boarded that they mean to split us in two at New York and harry us severely from the north and west. On Ld. Dunmore's entreaties they also mean to mount an invasion into our own country, and this I tell you only because I know you will hear of it any way and I want you to know the truth of it. There is now under sail on it's way from Britain a fleet of frigates and smaller vessels, and with these Ld. Dunmore means to sail up our rivers and lay waste the river-side plantations. We have urged the Virginia committee of safety to move at once to fortify the rivers and to do what it can to subdue Ld. D. at his base at Norfolk. It appears that some of the townsfolk there are giving him assistance, which news, if true, will make his defeat more difficult. You must be careful, Patty. That the Forest is upriver from Williamsburgh does give me a measure of comfort, but I urge you in the strongest terms not to venture onto the James and to keep yourselves out of Williamsburgh, for if they gain the river they will make for the Capital.

My dear, are you refusing to write in a fit of temper? That I would certainly rather believe, but I can't believe it for I know that you would not so spurn my heartfelt letters which must be thick on your table now, each one more contrite than the one before it. If you are still angry, my precious Wife, then write to me that you are angry, write even that you refuse to see me, but write that you are alive and healthy. There may be ten letters in tomorrow's Post. If I can convince myself that the post-rider has at last rescued himself and damsel from a wild bear's den and is even now galloping for Philadelphia I may be able to sleep this night. I love you, my dear one. Care for yourself as the center of all my happiness, and know that you are the greatest treasure of your devoted husband

Th:J

MONTICELLO DECEMBER 14, 1775

We have been at the killing all this day. When I thought to record in my farm-book the numbers killed then I thought as well of my forsaken journal, but for the afternoon long I could not entertain the thought that I might open this book. Then eventually my fear of my previous entry began to make essential my reading of it, so here I sit at my chamber-table writing by the light of a stub of candle and by the greater light of a cheerful fire which Patsy makes play is her kitchen-fire. She sets upon the hearth her little pots which were made for her by Barnaby, and she swings them on a crane he smithed for her yet ever closer to the flames so I must repeatedly intervene. She knows the risk of skirt-fires, for my Ursula suffered one some months gone by and it was only the blessing of a water-bucket set by chance for the washing of greens that saved her from a most appalling fate. Yet children are heedless. My little Janey had no thought in mind for her mother's pain when she set off through Betty's cabin door and sought the adventure of the well.

It is only in reading my entry written when I was in my deepest grief that I see how far I have traveled in three months' time. For long I had numberless causes for weeping, so I could not hug my Patsy without craving her sister and I could not set eyes upon my Betty's Sally. It was partly for this that Betty remained here when I returned to the Forest, and partly for her guilt which made a strangeness between us despite my resolve that I must not blame her. She could not offer me comfort for all of her anger against herself, and this I know made her angrier still. I could not comfort her, for my every attempt brought forth from her a torrent of bitter words. "It should have been my child," once she said. Or, "Leave off! How can you forgive me when I cannot forgive myself?" So in the end I left her. I had not the strength to contend with her grief beside my own.

How I have made myself whole now I cannot say, but I recall the moment when it began. From my bed at the Forest I had a view of the orchard, where one bright morning I saw the boys out gathering the cider-apples. Then in a flood came back to me my memory of the day when I met my Thomas; he had come to our ball on a random whim and very nearly not come. I came near to not meeting him. So I wondered at my fate, which seems to be random yet it operates with a great precision. That I am born to my station, that I have my dear husband, and even that I have my grievous trials seemed to me of a sudden to be not random. I knew it of a certainty that let me not even name the agent, whether God or Fate, whatever it might be seemed less important than my realization that it could not be random. All makes up my life, the evil with the good, and I must take the one to be given the other. Mine was the choice to face calamities and swallow them down like a black potion and not, as I had feared, to be consumed by them. One must eat the other, and I chose in that moment that I would eat my pain so it would not eat me.

I can say it less well than I would like, for in truth it was a feeling near to joy when I saw that the choice was indeed my own. There was a power to that feeling which delights me still when ever the thought of it returns to me.

I had much time so to think at the Forest, for I was greatly ill of a kidney-fever. It was slow to yield, although I was twice bled and I left off stays and lay upon my bed with a poultice of my back for week upon week. Then as it lessened I found beneath the fevers a cause for illness which brings me joy, for it seems that I am with child again. My baby will be born at the end of June. I yet am not altogether well, but the coming of this baby so lifts my heart that all of the events of my life are brighter as if of a sudden the sun were up so the night-time shadows are dispersed.

Even I am reconciled with my Betty, for I come from the Forest to find her also with child so again we shall sit and nurse our babes. Betty finds in our shared condition a bond which improves a healing time had well begun. What remains of her anger at herself only softens the anger she had built against me, for if I have taken her children's freedom then she has taken my child's whole life.

There may be in this a balance of pain that lets us resume the genuine friendship there long was between us when I was a child and I knew not the difference in our stations. I had endeavored to keep her friendship, but ever I knew that my Betty was my slave and I could bid her give me friendship as I bade her complete any other task. While another slave might have found no shame in such a kind attention from her mistress, for my dear proud Betty just my own awareness that she was of a lesser station had been enough to build her wall of anger. She had granted me her friendship as she had granted my Pappa her comfort in his bed, but she had borne for neither of us any genuine love. Now I see that love cannot cross the bar that the weak erect against the strong. But my own dear husband has shown me in truth that all are equal before the Lord and our greater rank but gives to us a greater duty. Of a sudden I see my Betty as my equal, fully equal as it were beneath clothes and skin, and she for her part is so startled by her mistress's forgiveness of the loss of my Jane that she is tender to me as she has not been tender since she gave me love and comfort when a child. So we begin a new friendship. I cannot name it, but I find in it a very great joy.

My Betty brings now her eleventh child and none has yet died, which is a passing wonder. She is able to tell her infant's sex by the quality of her sickness, and she assures me now that we both carry boys, which intelligence I scarcely can dare to believe.

I am come from the Forest at the start of December despite the insistence of my sister and brother that I am not altogether well and I must not live alone upon my mountain. I assured them that Joe Neilson and others are here, but this caused them all the more alarm for it is not proper for a lady to live alone among her slaves and workmen. Yet I must return. December is the killing-month, and I had a further worry as well for seeing that all was in order for winter and tending to my Ursula's lying-in.

It also seemed to me that Monticello must be safer than the Forest, for the war is well begun at Norfolk. There Lord Dunmore's Regulars face from their ships our militiamen and harry the inhabitants of the town. While each side waits for reinforcements, he for his fleet and we for artillery, they fight little battles to try their strength. These battles have seemed so alarming by the time some word of them would come to the Forest that I began to fear to look out a window and see red coats upon the road. Then my dear husband wrote again to say that we must keep most strictly from Williamsburg, and I needed no further prompting than that to pack up my child and find our way back to home.

Lord Dunmore has given a proclamation for the emancipation of our slaves, which chills us all with the fear of a rising. My brother Eppes is a most stern master. I did not feel safe among his servants, who have good reason to rise against him, but here among our own I am safe enough without the protection of gentlemen. Still, my sister complains that my husband will not be pleased to hear of our return. He has but lately been told of my sickness, for I could not write for beyond a month and then when I wrote I made it seem only mild but he took it for a grievous risk to my life. I have had four letters so strident with worry that I have written to make a sport of him that he might be startled into sense at once. The Congress has granted itself a free use of the Post, so I told him that now I may afford to write since he left me without so much as a farthing.

I am glad of my husband's worry, although to be glad of it seems quite shameful. My reading again of my September entry recalls to me the awful loss I imagined of not just my Janey but my Thomas as well. All love was gone, for I did not merit love. Yet my own dear husband patiently loved me even from his distance of hundreds of miles until my certain knowledge of his love made me feel again that I might be worthy. I tell myself that I must not depend upon my husband's love to feel my own value, for if I lost him I would lose myself. Yet so it is. I ever have defined myself by the love of my Pappa or sisters or husband; true it seems that I do not exist except by reflection of the love of others.

Although I have one strength found just today. The memory of it confounds me still. Today we killed eight hogs and two beeves that we might supply the workmen, a thing which I have not since a child been ever able to hear or see. As they drove up the beasts to the killing-frame set below the end of our Mulberry Row, I was seized by my old childish panic and I ran for the safety of my house. Yet there as I sat I came to worry that the boys would kill with more than necessary pain. This fear became more of an agony than my fear of the sight and sound of dying, so I upped and ran from out of my house and down again among the shops and quarters.

They were on the point of beginning the killing. Four boys had a hog by a chain on its leg that they might drag it to the killing-frame, and it squealed of its pain where the chain tore flesh. This I said that they must stop at once, but I bade them lead and coax the beast with a hand of corn. They must hang it by its leg to bleed it out, and this I then was forced to direct for my command had made me their overseer and they would no longer work on their own. So I superintended the applying of the chain and then the hoisting into the air, and I bade my Great George stick it deep and cut it deep across its throat that it might more quickly meet its end.

All of this, and I but a pace away, and the great hog squealing with its final breath, and I only eager to hear it go silent and know that it would never suffer more. A part of me seemed to stand far back with wringing hands in a great amazement, for who was this lady? She dared to touch it! She directed the catching of its blood! I found to my surprise that what I had most greatly feared had been my own anxiety to hear the squeal, yet I could stiffen myself to listen to it and only care that since the hog must die it but do it with the least of pain. Now we plan a great killing at the end of the month of a herd driven up from Bedford, and I thrill myself to say that I shall superintend every step of that killing from start to end.

My Ursula is in bed of another boy, which lifts her heart after the loss of her Archy and lifts my heart to see it. "I shall have milk for you, mistress!" she said out gaily when the babe had only just left her body and before she even knew its sex. So she will have milk. And I have a thought that I may give her my next child to nurse from its birth, for its health is more precious than my wish to nurse it. This I write, and I am surprised to find so little pain in the writing of it. If I can learn to swallow my grief for my Janey so in the end it will not swallow me, then I can swallow as well many lesser pains.

MONTICELLO MARCH 31, 1776

I am so weak abed that to write this I must sit against my pillows with my ink-pot stood upon a book and my journal wedged between breast and thighs. This seems odd indeed, but I can scrawl quite smart if I have a care not to upset the ink-pot. I must write. I have longed these many weeks to write, even shaping words together within my mind as event closed fast upon event. Now at last I may write, for my husband is bidden to attend to a great calamity which I shall save to mention last of all lest the pain of it overshadow my other trials that have begged for a voice these many weeks past. I know not even where to begin, whether the ravages of my country or the ravages of my body must seem the more important to me. Although I write for myself, I have a thought of other eyes upon my journal. I must not seem self-occupied while my dear country fights for her very life.

Britain now occupies Virginia soil. That Virginia is indeed British herself and has been so for near two hundred years is a wonder to me now, when Britain is our enemy with her teeth locked into our bone and flesh. Lord Dunmore has lately occupied Norfolk and much of unfortunate Princess Anne, where he sails the Chesapeake as a very pirate and burns and lays waste the undefended plantations. He burned Norfolk town to ashes on New Year's Day, which news struck a spike into my soul. Its people had succored and provisioned him. If he dealt so with them, what may he do to us?

New rumors come to us every day. We hear that Dunmore retreats or that he waits for reinforcements, that Tories are commanding North Carolina, that Charles Town will be taken by the British or indeed that it is already lost. Canada is lost although my husband will not admit that it is lost, but General Arnold was repulsed at Quebec so Montreal cannot be held. Without Canada we may not hold New York, so then the continent is split in two. Can we hold New England? Shall we crumble and die as Britain subdues us one by one?

Britain is so strong that our fiercest blow is the brush of a feather against her teeth. She makes a sport now of gentlemen who pull all together to tweak her whisker, but once she is aroused she will crush us as a cat kills a bird she is weary of baiting. Yet we are British ourselves! That we must of a moment call Britain our enemy seems like some grievous bodily sickness, as if Britain were a poison of Virginia's blood that has come to its head in the ashes of Norfolk. Anciently I felt an agitation at the thought that we might provoke a war, yet my fears then seem but childish now. Then I was safe. I knew not what a war might be, although I did imagine it a fearsome battle that we must run together and swiftly flee. Now I know war to be a dread in the belly that never leaves me, whether waking or sleeping. It is a grievous loss of internal peace; to lose peace external would be easier to bear. Even having a battle so it might be over would be a lesser pain against this dreadful waiting.

My Betty sits by my window now in the white light of a cloud-covered day and knits so fast that her needles blur and their clicks are one continuous sound beneath the distant song of servants hard about their planting. I had thought to dismiss my Betty so I might find my journal, but then with a sigh I directed her to retrieve it from the folds of my wedding-gown. I can find no better expression of the understanding there has come between us than to say that she retrieved it without a question and to add that I felt no need to warn her that it must forever remain a secret.

My husband returned to me at the turn of the year. The Congress had resolved to sit through the winter, the which he found that he could not do for worry of my health and for dread of Lord Dunmore and what more he might destroy in Virginia. So I have my dear husband, but since his return he does seem near a stranger to me. His mind which once was all my own is full of the worries of Quebec and the desertions of soldiers from out of New York and the getting of powder and the printing of money and the disputations unto a war between Pennsylvania and Connecticut over the Wyoming Valley. His mind is now become continent-wide while mine remains tight within my own Virginia. There is a strangeness between us like a difference of language. We cannot converse, for he speaks to one subject while I answer him upon another. I have found the space between us to be so grievous that I complained of it one morning a month gone by while he held a draught of Gabbler's against my lips. "You are returned to me a stranger, Husband. I know not what to say to you."

I had said it mildly, but he stood from the bed in a very great agitation. His features were sharp, as if his skin were gone tight. "It is you, Patty. It is not me. There is a softness gone out of you. I know not how to name it."

"Indeed there is," I said with a heat that surprised me to realize my own anger. "I have buried two children, and now a third. I live here alone with my slaves and workmen. I kill my own hogs. I do not wonder that I am become less soft for you."

He turned. I had a thought of sparring and drawing blood with one perfect thrust of my knife. "You might visit your sister Eppes," he said. "You need not remain here."

"Whether I am there or here if I am not with you there will come an ever greater strangeness between us. How much were we together last year, Husband? Was it three months? Was it four? And how long will you remain with me now before your body returns to where your heart remains?"

"My heart is with you." He stood with his arms hugged about himself and his eyes fixed upon the window-sill. "I shall hate to go. I have no wish to leave Monticello ever again in my life. But our union of the colonies has become so tender and the dangers press from every direction so the absence of even one of us now might settle events against our success. This summer will determine the course of our lives and our children's lives. I am needed there, Patty."

"You are needed here more."

He gave me a look of strained amusement, as if he meant to make an awkward jest. "When ever I return I bring you pain. It might be well if I did not come home at all."

Upon my husband's return we had most gaily come together as a husband and wife. We felt only joy in our bed that night; we had spoken too little to find our separation. While I suffered some remnant of a kidney-fever, on that night I truly did feel myself well. But my bladder-fever began days later and brought with it such violent fevers as never I have known in all my life, so my mind wandered far and I lost all sense. What I recall of it is my husband's voice as it came through a roaring of my ears and the candle-glow of a night most bitter when my body shed my son before his time. I never saw him. He never lived enough to cry. Betty says he was the size of a gentleman's thumb but she swears to me that he was a male, which news seems the end of a curse of bearing girls forever. It seems odd to say it, but knowing he was male is a joy that nearly smothers the pain of his loss. I shall bear other children. I have a hope now that I shall give to my husband the son he desires.

Yet the loss of our fetus compounds the unresolved pains and angers of our Janey's death and deepens our grievous chasm of strangeness between a husband who thinks to his continent and a wife whose mind is fixed upon her hill. There was much that we must say but no words to say it. When he said he thought it better that he not come home I chose to hear his words not as a jest, but they drew forth from my deepest heart my very greatest fear of all.

"You have a mistress. Do not deny it! Tell me this: is she black or is she white?"

His look of amazement said with certainty what his every protestation might only suggest. Indeed, he did not wait to protest but he ran to the bed of a single bound and burrowed into it beneath the blanket all heedless of waistcoat and shoes and breeches. He kissed my belly and breast through my shift and emerged from the bedclothes near by my face to kiss my cheeks and lips most ardently. "Oh, Patty, do not dream of it! Do not imagine it!"

The strength of his emotion startled me, so my breath trembled tight within my throat. I apprehended his fear that my very suspicion might sever the tender connection between us. My voice shook. "Then stay with me, Thomas, please. I cannot but think of it when you are so long away."

"I will not leave you ill. I promise you that."

So he said, and my heart opened like a flower. I felt a sweet return of all our understanding. He still moves about me half a stranger with his mind fixed upon the continent's cares, but beneath the difference he is himself and I know he is not lost to me. To hold him here when he is wanted elsewhere seems to me half a dishonesty, but he has given to his country now the better part of these eight years gone. He has done his share. There are others whose wives do not need or love them half so well.

So I am weak abed, but I am not so weak as my dear dear husband believes me to be. When the slave came this morning to summon him to Shadwell I begged him to wait while I was dressed, but he could not wait and he told me sternly that I am not well enough to leave my bed. Our mother has been stricken greatly sick of a very grievous apoplexy. There came another slave an hour after my husband rode in haste to be at her side, and this second servant announced to me what my husband would never want me to hear but from his own lips, most tenderly. Our mother has died. While Thomas worried for me, Fate has taken from him someone else altogether.

To know that she has died is a very hard thing. I have tried to please her, and while I lie now and listen for my husband's boot on the stair I must admit that our mother too did try to cultivate a love for me. But she felt most keenly every loss, and the loss of her children most of all, so she held my sister Carr close by to her and she held close her Nancy who still is not wed, and she held close her Randolph despite his wish that he must live away from her. Dear Randolph is a boy of twenty years, most playful and simple of his mind, whose greatest pleasure is to fiddle in the quarters and dance with the Negroes half the night. He lasted for only months at the College, since he has not the taste for words and books. Now he soon should come to a man's estate, but his mother insisted that he was not fit so he must remain longer to live with her that she keep him cared for very well. She tried in like manner to hold my husband with every pretense of needing his attention, so I was but a rival for the love of her son. She never could have felt a great love for me.

I know not what to say nor how to comfort him now, for he suffers so greatly with his grief. He craves his Dabney to this day, with the sudden death near three years gone. His mother's clinging made him put her away more than might have been common for a loving son, and the guilt of this will compound his suffering to know that she is lost to him.

THE FOREST MAY 14, 1776

I sit again beneath the very tree and upon the very mill-pond hill where first my dear husband proposed our marriage. This is even a day very like that day although the trees have shed their petals, but the touch of the breeze and the whisper of the brook make me so greatly wish for my dear one's presence. Beneath another tree near down the slope our Patsy sits with my Betty's Sally to learn from Nance the slaves' ancient art of plaiting their wound-grass baskets. Sally is so pale a child that her mother masks and mitts her as if she were white, and there they sit, the slave but two and the mistress a lady nearly four, they both so intent upon Nance's fingers that Sally topples herself now as I write.

My Patsy has chosen Sally out to be her close companion. She so greatly misses my poor dead Janey, and this is Janey's nurse-mate and near the same size, so Patsy coddles and admonishes her as once she so ardently mothered my Janey. Nance cares for them both, which relieves my Betty to give full attention to her new-born son. Betty has given to him the name of John. My heart yet thrills as I write these words.

We had Granny Smothers for her lying-in. I would not trust my Betty's life to any but far the most practiced granny, and this good woman had lately attended at the childbed of my dear friend Maggy Lee. Granny tended Betty while I washed the babe drawn fresh from the body of its mother, and I marveled as I washed at the size of the child and the way it had grown within a woman's body and passed through a tunnel surpassing small. It seems indeed hard that the man creates the child but the woman must grow it to such a size.

"It is near as light as Sally," I said to my Betty as I put it safely into her arms. It was yet fierce with its infant rage that it was born into the world at all, so it waved its arms out of its bundling and wept a fury. Betty lifted her head where she lay against her pillows that she might have a good frank look at the child. Then she lay back again of her weariness and gazed up warm into my face.

"He is John, mistress. I shall call his name John." John! For John was my Pappa's name, and in using it she gives to him her love and forgiveness. John might be also my little Jack so she does what she can to give me back my son. That she names her child John is a gift of love to the mistress who has found not a way to free her, and I understood at once all the love and the gift. I did not, however, speak it out. Had I done, my Betty would have said the like of "Well, but I cannot name him Joseph."

She is in a very rage at Joe Neilson. I doubt not that they may resolve this yet, but they have not spoken kindly for some few weeks and my Betty came with me here to the Forest with her babe not even two weeks old.

I find a fascination in thinking upon the love they have borne for one another, for I come to apprehend that what people love is the image that we hold of our beloved. That they fell into love at a single glance is not now hard for me to believe, for Neilson saw in Betty a pretty wench he could woo and bed without regret while Betty saw a man with a white man's power who had as well some qualities of the other race in that he worked with his hands and he bore himself mildly. Each saw a perfection in the look of the other. Yet each saw blindly! Betty is in truth the very obverse of any meek slave wench, while Neilson is but a common man who bears nevertheless much arrogance. Each is near the opposite of what was sought. How soon they each saw this I cannot say, but it seems the very disappointment of it was a challenge to them each to remake the other. They persisted the fiercer in their love of the image and punished the reality wherever it differed so all their year together has been fighting and wooing. To have them now apart seems a great relief.

So I think, and I savor the thought of it to have puzzled out an element of human nature. I ponder now whether there might be some relation to the love that I bear for my husband, whether he or I might be blinded too and struggling in our blindness to remake the other. I think it not. We never quarrel as others quarrel. I read through my prior entry before beginning this and I see there what my mind had forgotten, that once in his distress he did say out that I am become less soft to him. He thinks me softer, indeed, than I know that I am, greatly sweeter and gentler of my temper, but these are genuine qualities that are born in me out of my very great love for him. When I am in his dear presence, I am that better lady he perceives me to be.

And I do see him truly. While he has made a study of every science in all the world, my own dear Thomas has been my whole study. I have watched him of my love and of my anxious awareness that upon him rests my entire happiness. Indeed, I know him so very well that I know what he will do before he knows it himself, so this time I knew that for all my jesting that he never leaves me money of my own he would make a show of giving me a great sum of money. And this he did. Upon his departure-day, he took from his pocket-book two five-pound notes and he laid them careless upon the table and said, "Here, Patty. Now you have your postage if you wish to write a letter to your sister."

My husband is gone to Philadelphia. In the end I could not hold him here, but I kept my dear one for all of the spring by the luck of a great periodical headache that seized him after his mother's death and clamped him into misery for day upon day. He rose well enough upon each morning, but the headache would grow so he must take to his bed and then it would not leave him until after darkness. I feel a shame to say that often I thought that headache a gift and not a curse, for it persisted unto weeks until I came to believe that I might keep him there in my arms forever. We laughed together in the darkness and we softly talked in his pain of the day and while it sounds hard, I know, just his need of me came to seem to me a kind of gift.

I am blessedly recovered to much of my health. It seemed we restored our health together, so even when at last he was well enough to contemplate his return to the Congress we came to-gether as a husband and wife and I suffered not thereafter a return of my sickness. I find now a very most curious thing, that cooling foods will improve my health. Ever the doctors when I had my fevers would bid me eat of naught but animal-foods, and this I have endeavored to do although my Thomas little cares for meats. Then when we were ill he swore the meats were the cause so he set us upon a plan of cooling foods with no sweetmeats and no bite of a sausage, no eggs nor milk nor any warming foods, which diet would greatly dismay any doctor. Yet it restored us both, this diet of greens. It made me feel well as I have not felt well in so many years that the feeling was lost, so even though I have my kidney-pains and now and again another fever I do feel myself again very well. I am not with child, the revelation of which is a great disappointment to me, but I shall bear again and yet again. My mind is the master of my body.

PHILADELPHIA   JUNE. 11. 1776.

My dear Wife

I think of you at every moment. The health you were regaining on the day I left has continued in my mind in two directions, so I am half the time annoyed at my own reluctance to inflict upon you the risk of the journey and half the time frantic to imagine you so sick again as you were in the winter. Do write to me very often, Patty. You can't imagine the delight with which I see your dear handwriting on the page and know that at least at that recent moment you were safe and well.

I have lately taken new lodgings with Mr. Graaf at Seventh and High Streets in a hope that here at the edge of the city I shall find a breath of a breeze, but it's so hot that the breeze is the breath of a furnace and no help to me at all. And we shall be sitting here at least the summer. I write those words with a misery which only you, my precious Wife, will understand. I worry at every moment about your health, but the most terrible thing about our separation is the lack of your ear and the terrible lack of our sublime communion. I never knew loneliness until our marriage, but now I shall never again know peace unless you are beside me.

We have had at last a resolution moved for declaring our independence from Great Britain, and I am glad to tell you that it came from our own countrymen. On Friday last R. H. Lee moved on instruction from the Virga. Convention that we not only declare our independence from Britain but that we move with speed to confederate and to form our foreign alliances for trade so Britain will not do by starving us what she cannot do by force of arms. I have had a letter from Page in which he sensibly suggests that we shall win this war in the bellies of the people, for if they suffer want then soon enough they will abandon their leaders and make their peace. (I write this, then I recall my reader and nearly move to cross it out. But never fear, Patty.)

We met on Saturday last and again on Monday in committee of the whole, where it was seen after long and phrensied debate that South Carolina and the middle colonies are not yet ripe to leave the parent stem. That found, a vote on Lee's resolution was deferred until the first day of July. I doubt not that the people of Maryland and Penna. are farther along than are their leaders, but still I am frustrated to see us kept from advancement by our fainter members. Until we separate from Britain we can't form a confederation and we can't treat with all the foreign countries which worry over losing their own colonies so they must have a cloak of legality. With a war long in progress to the north and also now begun in the south, a simple declaration of the fact that we are not connected to our enemy seems to me a very mild step.

We shall fill this month of ripening with committee work on the elements of Lee's resolution, viz. the drafting of a declaration of our independence and the forming of a plan for our confederation and the drafting of terms thought proper for our foreign alliances. I am appointed to the first committee together with J. Adams and Doctr. Franklin and two other members whose names you will not recognize.

Dear Wife, I can't tell you how eager I am to be gone from this place. The other committee members are amply competent to draft whatever document is wanted here, while I fear that without my presence at home Virga. will not take the chance of this moment to establish a government worthy of her. Independence is nearly decided upon and the document just a formality, while decisions being made in Williamsburg now will decide our fate down to the tenth generation. Were I there, I would also be with you and know that you are safe and well. Your health is a constant worry to me, but I worry less for your safety now because intelligence which we have lately received suggests Ld. D.

may be preparing to sail. He has abandoned Norfolk for Gwynn's island in the Chesapeake, and deserters report he has the small pox aboard and he cannot long endure. But he may have some mischief to deal us yet, so I had rather have you under our brother's protection than at home where you must rely on servants.

Oh my dear Wife, I so desperately wish that I could be at home with you. To be sitting here in exile while the Virginia Convention drafts a constitution and forms our government is as hard a thing as my country has ever demanded that I do. Forming our government is indeed the whole point of the exercise, for if a bad government is decided upon we might as well have kept our former bad government and spared ourselves the expense of the conflict. I had hoped to be recalled and one or two left to represent our interests before the Congress, but despite my petition that is unlikely. Here I am, and here I shall remain.

I write to you as I speak to you, without any guard of common sense. I see I have written pages of what I can only call a whine of frustration, and now I am comforted much as I would be comforted if I had spoken with you. I ought not post this letter for fear that someone will read it and think me cowardly, but I lack the energy in this heat to write you over a better one. I shall seal it well and hope for privacy. (If any stranger has read thus far: For shame!)

My very dear wife, I pray that you are well as I never have prayed for any thing. Kiss Patsy for me. Is she learning her letters? Tell her I shall expect to find her able to recognize the alphabet. Oh my wife, you are my very soul and the center of all my happiness. Be assured that at every moment you fill the thoughts of your devoted husband,

Th:J.

PHILADELPHIA   JUNE 25, 1776

My dear Wife

It is so late that I am uncertain whether my candle or my mind will be first extinguished, but your letter has lain here for four days now and it weighs so heavily on my spirits that I can't face another attempt at sleep until it is well answered. Your joy in the thought that we may now end slavery and your innocent belief in our certain success only pain me the more, because I share your hopes but I can't share your certainty. There is a distance, Patty, between our assertion that the slave trade is an evil inflicted on us by Great Britain and our decision finally to end that evil. All I can do in drafting this declaration of our independence is to avoid giving comfort to those who would keep slavery and to lay a ground upon which we can end it. This is a justification I give myself for remaining here when I am eager to be gone, that in drafting this document I may capture a consensus which every man of honour and good will can share and lay a ground of our common understanding upon which a good government can be built. Had any other sought to draft this document, he would have claimed our ancient right to life, liberty and property without a thought, but I know too well what comfort that single word "property" would give to the holders of slaves. I have rather affirmed that all are created equal and claimed for all our right to pursue our happiness, that none may seek to call another man his property and look for comfort here.

Oh my dear Wife, nothing would delight me more than to assure you their freedom is near at hand. For us to declare our right to liberty while we hold a subject people in thrall is almost to render absurd our claim. But we must do what is possible, Patty, and leave for later what will be possible later. If we move more than a pace or two ahead of the rest we shall lose them altogether.

From your sweet sheltered place it seems a simple thing and accomplished by a single stroke of the pen. But it is not simple, and if simply done it may prove a worse injustice than slavery itself. I have talked out of doors with some few members, not arguing my position but sounding their own, and done this the more since your letter came so I might know what to write to you. I have been dismayed by the little concern that most members give to slavery, seeing it not as a cancer of our liberty but only as some unfortunate fact with which we shall have to contend and again as we labour to frame our confederation. There is little wish to end it, but there is instead an irritation that it exists at all and a hope, I judge, that if it is ignored it may yet heal itself all on it's own. The truth is that we are embarked on a course which is fraught with risk and it's outcome not certain. Once we have freed ourselves, we shall gain the power and develop the will to free these others.

I worry further, Patty, that the freeing of slaves will create a permanent class of Negroes who live in misery and want and without a hope of improving their station. Truly, freeing the slaves is but half the task, less than half the task, and the easier half. I come to believe that an end to slavery must be most diligently planned, that the result might be dignity and a chance at happiness for these our servants who have suffered so much. Do let us not talk of freeing them now, but let us rather give thought to how we might perfectly free them once our war is won.

Dear Patty, I am so weary that my pen is shaking in my hand. I must tell you that the committee all together has approved my draft of our Declaration and has made to it so very few changes that it will go to the Congress almost all my own. There is in this a feeling of triumph for me, that I have at last drafted a document not so far beyond the sense of the body that it must be put into milder form. But now it must face the whole Congress assembled. I doubt not it may weather some battles there. Adieu, mon coeur.

Th:J.

THE FOREST JUNE 26, 1776

*N*ow must my journal comfort me. I have seen this day a horror far the greatest I have ever known and I doubt not the sight of it will never leave me.

Dear Betty this morning came to the parlor where I sat with Patsy and Sally in the breeze from a window to teach them a lesson of the needle-work, for Patsy how the needle must be held and for Sally the names of the bright yarn-colors. To this gay morning scene my Betty came in an ardent fury.

"You must come with me, mistress. Here is Nance for the children." I saw her agitation and rose at once, but when I knew that she meant to go outside I started up the stairs for my hat and mitts. She said, "Leave your hat! Your face may brave the sun this once!"

So I went out the door of my Pappa's house to squint my eyes tight in a blinding sun. I was so sun-stricken that Betty took my hand and she hurried so we were nearly running. I could not guess what great calamity might provoke from her such an agitation. She drew me past the gardens to the woods behind and into the quarters and down to a shed, where she put away a blanket from over a door and led me into a gloomy space. It smelled of sour earth and of dusty chickens roosting and clucking in the heat. With the blanket away there was light to see, and my eyes made a sense of the shapes and shadows until I saw at once a sight that made me clap hands to mouth that I might not scream. Upon a pallet lay a very young girl. She was curled like a child with her hands beneath her cheek and her feet, light below, were nested together with the heel of one clasped in the toes of the other. This curious detail I fixed upon that I not look again at her poor frail body so bloodied and beaten that her human eyes were surely the greatest horror of all.

"Look at her!" my Betty said.

"What? Why?"

"Look, mistress. I want you to look very well that you will never in your life forget this sight."

"Who did this?"

Betty drew me out and let the blanket fall. I resisted, for we should have bathed the child and comforted her as best we could. The hands were then all in the fields so there was no one near to tend this girl.

"You must buy her, mistress," Betty said beneath her voice for fear that the child in the shed might hear.

"What happened to her? You must say at least that!"

Betty gave me her look that made me know that again she was weighing how much of the truth her fragile mistress could safely bear.

"Tell me! I command it!"

She took my hand and led me away from the shed. I resisted, for I was pulled to remain by those eyes that I felt still upon my back.

"Do you recall her? Dinah? Lame Mary's child?"

I did recall Dinah as a little girl who had made of every task a childhood-play, so she danced fetching water or she talked to vegetables and tucked them like babes into her gathering-basket. I had found an affection to see her play when slave children ever so seldom played, for I did not then know that their lack of play was any but a natural thing.

"She grew up too pretty, mistress. The overseer took her when she was but thirteen."

"Poor child" was on my lips but I did not say it.

"He liked her so well that he tried to buy her. Your sister's husband would not sell. Then later they quarreled, whether for that refusal or for some other disagreement I cannot say, but Mr. Stevens came near to quitting his post. They made a peace, but then your sister's husband must prove that he is the master here. He took that girl to his bed but once. Now Mr. Stevens has nearly killed her."

There were in this speech so many horrors that as they burst in my head one after another I came near to losing all my sense. Betty put me down on a bench while I tried to keep the harsh light of the sun and the glare of so many so terrible horrors from taking away my mind altogether. So many horrors! And not the least pain for me is the fact that they are married, the man and the gentleman. Their wives must mean as little as does the slave or they could not so readily betray their trust.

This bedding of slaves is a recent thing, for it hardly occurred in my mother's generation. Indeed, that I have my Betty at all is due to its very novelty. When Betty's father knew he had begotten a child he begged my Pappa to sell him the girl, but that my dear Pappa never would do for a mixed-race child was such an odd thing that he wanted to see what she might become. There on that bench I first understood that my Pappa had carried the experiment on by what he had begotten of his own body.

"You must buy her, mistress. They will kill her between them."

"But I cannot!"

Here is another great horror, that my husband might ever know aught of this. He is so tender that the sight of that child would have put him into a painful frenzy. And he greatly cares for his brother Eppes. He very truly must never know.

"If you might save the girl but you do not, then her blood will be upon your hands."

This my Betty said as if through her teeth, most low and terrible upon the ear. With her words I found a frantic sense which made me stand at once. "We must tend her first."

"I shall see to her. Go and buy her, mistress."

So she said, and all heedless of the sun I set my feet upon the path. I made to run, but my stays took all my breath and the sun took my vision so I scarce could see. All my thought was for where I might find my brother without the awareness of my sister; he often works the mornings in his chamber, and Betsy likely would be at the kitchen. My thought of Betsy made me hurry a route through the high grass around the blind side of the kitchen, so I gained the house by way of the front and tarried within the door that I might find my breath. My eyes blurred of spots in the welcome dark. I held to the banister to keep my feet.

My brother Eppes was indeed in his chamber, the which I could see from the top of the stairs. He is a large man, not so tall as my husband but large of his bone and now running to flesh, and his hair is as curled as my mother's hair so his queue is a tube against his back. At the sight of that queue against his yellow waistcoat my mind seemed at once to resume its thoughts as a head comes through water and gasps for its air. I had not wondered what I might say to Francis, but in that moment I had all my words. He surely would be glad to be rid of the wench and he long has coddled me for love of my husband. I need but make my request of him and he would most gladly make me a gift.

"Francis?"

He turned with a start.

"May we speak?" I must not enter his chamber, yet I could not speak from beyond the door for fear of what the servants might hear. We must not be private, yet we must be private. I turned my body that I not see his bed, and all of a sudden recklessness I stepped within and closed the door.

Francis stood from his chair so rapidly that he had it over with a crash. He looked at me alarmed. "What is wrong? Is it your husband? You have had a letter?"

"No. Forgive me. I only must ask if I might buy a slave of you. Lame Mary's Dinah? I had liked her when a child, and now I have just seen her again. I know not what her value might be." So I said in words grown soft unto silence, for when I said out the name of the slave my Francis gave me a look of horror. His complexion grew a mottled red, and he turned and walked as if he needs must walk but I would not allow him to leave his corner.

Then did I feel such a shame as I have never felt in all my life. What did I do? Where was my mind? That I accosted my brother alone in his chamber and chastened and alarmed him of his sin was far the most shameful thing that I have ever done in my life. I thought to run, but that I could not do for fear it would alarm him further. I but caught my fan where it hung from my wrist and fluttered it to hide the red of my face. The snap of my fan in the morning quiet struck Francis as if it were a physical blow so he winced of it, the sight of which wince inflamed my shame the more.

"What is her value?" This my sister's husband said as if he spoke unto the wall. With his words came crowding into my mind thoughts separate, and yet coming all at once.

Francis is the son of my mother's eldest brother. He brought much property into his marriage and he could have lived well upon his own, but so much did he admire my dear Pappa that he occupies now my Pappa's Seat and he seeks to take there my Pappa's place. But he has not any of what Pappa had, not the wit nor the strength nor the ease of power, so he looks, now that I see him closely, like a boy caught wearing the clothes of a gentleman. And there he paced as my Pappa had paced by the bed where my own dear mother had slept, by the bed where now he slept with my sister in all her innocence and trust.

"Her value may be less. She has been injured." This I said from out of an anger which I must not feel and must not say. The saying of it shamed me all the more, for I saw by his blush and by his blink that he well understood that she had been injured. He had been there agitated at his work, for he could not send his wife to tend her. Indeed, the very fact of her injury was likely to make all known to his wife and cause him much inconvenient strife, for all that he had only been correcting his overseer. And the overseer, too, had won a point which my brother must think out a way to counter, for a slave was damaged and a threat was made that Mr. Stevens might inform my sister. My brother saw that his bedding of the slave had been foolish but he knew not a way to regain his feet.

"I would buy her, Francis," I said out softly from a newfound compassion for my brother's worry. "I have ten pounds of my husband." This I said from my own new worry, for I had not a tenth of the wench's value. I could not beg the money of Thomas, for he would see my agitation and soon know all. Yet the very mention of my dear pure husband was a further blow upon Francis's shoulder so he threw back his head of the pain of it. "The Continental bills are affecting the money. It may be that she is worth less in good Virginia currency with so much Continental money about."

"Yes. True."

"I want her for Poplar Forest. I never would have her at Monti-cello. My husband has ordered me to buy no more slaves. I must ask you ever to keep my secret."

"Of course. That I will."

"And my sister, Francis. I must beg you never to tell my sister."

He looked at me fully for the first time and a breath of air went out of him. I gazed up calmly from behind my fan and tried to say with clear look of my eyes what never my lips must ever speak. "How does your kidney-fever, Patty?" Francis said while I looked at him.

"It does well enough. I thank you, sir."

PHILADELPHIA   JULY. 4. 1776.

My dear Wife

I have by the same post and folded one within the other a cheerful and healthy letter from you and one from our brother informing me that you are gravely ill. I am lately come from the Congress and I must go out far into the night to compare the text of our Declaration of Independence as it is converted into print, but I can't go until I have first written to demand that you reveal to me the state of your health. Are you ill? Pray tell me, Patty, that I shall not labour under this uncertainty. I cling to the cheerful tone of your letter, while the tone of his makes me almost frantic.

These have been four exhausting days but the matter at last is decided, dear Wife. The Congress have voted on the second instant to declare our independence from Great Britain and voted today to accept the form of my Declaration of Independence. We have signed the written copy which I submitted with the changes noted in marginal form, but we shall need copies printed for dispatch to the colonies and that will be my task for this night to come. When they have already made so many changes I can't risk some inadvertent change which may do still greater damage.

Only you my Patty will understand the misery with which I have sat these two days and heard my work debated line by line and altered severely. J. Adams tried to cheer me with every change and I told myself it was all for the good of my country and the fact that such careful attention was given would make it a document to forge our union. But

Patty, I had worked so hard to make my document a perfect expression of our common sentiment, and their changes seem to me arbitrary and in some cases frankly damaging. And they have cut altogether what J. Adams refers to as my philippic against the slave trade. We claim our own liberty while refusing even to allude to the fact that here in our midst are men who have been denied their rights by act of the very same oppressor. I have written this out of my own frustration and I realize now how much it will pain you. Be comforted, Patty. The freeing of our slaves is not the work of a single day, but it must be accomplished by uplifting the masters to a greater state of enlightenment. They can't live for long in their own freedom before they come to see the slavery of others as a shame and a horror.

There is much other news but no time to write it. Our affairs in Canada go still retrograde, with half our army there down with the small pox and pressed severely by Genl. Burgoyne. New York suffers treasonous betrayals by officers which I may not discuss, and she is soon under attack by Genl. Howe who has arrived at the Hook and has landed some horse on the Jersey shore. It is thought by all that the next three months are the only ones in which our trial can be severe, so we work now to send what support we can and to rally the spirits of the people. Do you Patty show a cheerful spirit and let all know that the war goes well and will likely soon be over.

Despite my request that I be excused, I have lately received word that I am elected again to the Congress. I wrote at once to Pendleton to request that another serve in my place. Now I hope to leave within the month, or whenever our plan for a confederation is set, and to be with you my Wife very early in August or even some days sooner. I had formed this plan before receiving the latest favour of our brother Eppes, but now with his news my resolve is decided and I shall depart on the earliest date. You must write to me the moment you receive this letter and assure me of your perfect health or my own will be destroyed by my terrible worry. Oh my dear, you can't imagine the yearning I feel at this moment to be in your arms.

Th:J.

PHILADELPHIA   JULY 23, 1776.

My dear Patty

I have had no letter from you for a fortnight past. Why the devil don't you write? Our brother Eppes writes that you are gravely ill and then you write that you are not ill and then he writes that indeed you are ill and then no letter at all. If you were an enemy bent on torture I would own that you had found the perfect method and now I must do what ever you require that you end this awful suspense.

Dear Patty, I must believe you are well or I shall lose my mind. I had rather have you refusing to write in a fit of feminine temper, and as odd as it seems I am comforted by the memory of your refusal to write before we were wed. Perhaps my letters have been lost in the Post or I have said in one something that angered you. If I have done, my sweet darling Wife, I regret it from the depth of my soul and I beg that you forgive me for a clumsy husband who still has not the wit to write to you the tender letters which you deserve. I know no other way to say this Patty than to tell you that you are every breath I take and every beautiful thing I see. Truly I can't live at all but in the light of your perfect love.

Perhaps you are angry that I keep myself away even while knowing you may be ill, but I must stay here until I am relieved and I have begged for relief these two months past so I know not what more I can do. It has been decided that our Declaration of Independence must be inscribed upon parchment as it was altered and then signed again and the first one destroyed. As I wrote it, I ought to remain to sign it. But I do now promise you dearest Patty that I will leave this place on the 11th day of next month, barring only a delay in the signing. I will come home even if I am not relieved, for truly your need of me is the greater.

I have written to our brother some news of the war, which goes well to the southward but ill to the northward. Our situation in Canada goes still ill, although we do not quite despair. That Charles Towne has repulsed it's attackers and Ld. D. has quit his attacks on Virga. is a comfort for those of us who live to the south, but it frees our enemy to concentrate it's pressures northward. A fleet is now under sail for New York and likely to arrive within the month.

General Washington has but 15,000. active men at New York, and despite the imminent threat of attack the recruitment for his army goes on slowly. Men who would fight on their own farms find a harder task in defending their country and a still harder task in defending a country which is not precisely their own. When Virga. and Penna. have lately been at skirmishing along their western border, it requires an effort of mind for their inhabitants to believe that their interests are now in perfect alignment. Yet this they must believe, and soon, or the Genl. will be fighting almost on his own. A flying camp of militias is forming in the Jerseys which we hope now may destroy Genl. Howe's force before Admiral Lord Howe's fleet arrives. (These men are brothers, Patty, the General and the Admiral. Never was there thrown a more infernal litter.)

Now it comes to seem that events of this fall will decide our fate. I doubt not it will go well for us, but meanwhile we shall need all our courage. That I can't bear to think of you distressed or at any risk at all for your safety is but another reason I must go home when I need no further reason. Oh my dear Wife, write. Be angry if you must, be sad or lonely or even ill, but write to me that I may survive these few more weeks. Know that everything I do is for you and all that I wish for in this life is the true and perfect communion with you which is my entire happiness.

I can't bear this, Patty. Please please write.

Th:J.

MONTICELLO SEPTEMBER 13, 1776

*T*hat I needs must seek a time to open my journal when my husband is out upon his business is a joy to me now, when for so long I might have written the day long but I would not. I had no great sorrow for which to crave from writing an active comfort, yet I suffered a daily misery of loneliness which the writing of it could but increase. Now gladly I write! My husband is returned from the

Congress but four days past, and the joy of his return is such a violent delight that unless I write I may die of it. He has gone off to Charlottesville to contract with a layer of brick that we might close our rooms, so for just this moment I am alone. Now very joyously do I write!

Our work goes on. I have a hope that we shall be in our house before the Second Coming of Christ, when, I suppose, we shall have no more need of it. The bricks for the middle-building are near about laid and those for the chamber-wing are well begun. A year gone by, my Thomas has bought the indenture of Billy Rice from Philadelphia to cut the stone columns that my so dear husband yearns to see standing before his house. These the man labors to cut very well, although in making the first he got the wrong dimension so now all the front must be re-cast to fit this column's symmetry.

My Patsy at four may not share our chamber when her father and I are together within it, so before his return I have sent her to live in Mr. Mazzei's old room above our dining-room. She cried out of loneliness her first night there so I must be summoned to comfort her, but now she finds a pride that she is the first of the family to live in our manor-house. And it is well that I thought to send her away, for we had upon the night when my husband returned such a quarrel as never we have had before and devoutly I wish that we shall not have again. I had not thought to write of it, but now I see that this is the cause which drives me to my journal. I must cleanse my mind of it. My journal must bear the pain of it how ever it may.

I shall pass over the joy of my husband's arrival, the which occurred along about candle-time. We had Patsy up again to kiss her Pappa, and we had together a supper of greens and peas and a corn-porridge which we playfully mixed like swill all together upon our plates. He had come home in a terror over my health, so the while that we ate he looked at me with a smile on his face and a gaze of wonder to find me altogether well. Our brother Eppes had written to him that I was gravely ill, for our brother wished that Thomas might soon return and my face might be removed as a reproof to him. I had written to my husband that I was not ill, but then indeed I had fallen ill and remained so for the great part of July. The lack of my letters unto weeks had made him believe our brother Eppes, so the sight of me smiling and laughing was to him as if he had been given back my life.

He had for me very many gifts. It seemed every time he had a worry for me he must comfort himself with his pocket-book, so he had gloves and shoes and crooked combs and yards of linen and of sea-green lustring, laces and cap-wire and pins and buckles and butter-prints and soaps and every thing. We were at opening boxes for near an hour, and at each new gift I must kiss him again until the thrill of it threatened to arouse his passions so he stood from the bed where we sat with gifts in piles by the wavering candle-light. "We must discuss this, Patty. I had thought to wait, but I see that clearly it cannot wait."

"This looks more blue than green," I said of the lustring whose bolt-end I held to see by the candle. "You say it is green? Oh, I cannot wait to see it by the light of day!"

"Patty, listen to me. Ever since last winter when you were so ill I have tried to avoid a decision that I know I must make or I shall endanger your life. Now my worry while I thought you were ill again has firmed my resolve to do what is right. Patty? My dear, look at me."

I looked up at him with his back to the fire, so I saw him in shadow but he saw me well. His arms were folded tight and his chin very high. He said, "I have decided that we must have no more children."

This announcement was so far outside my expectation that at first I misapprehended it. I thought he must disapprove of Patsy. I said, "She very well learns her letters!" But then as I made this foolish protestation I came to understand my husband's decision. I said, "No!" and stood. "You shall not put me away! I know I mean more to you than that!"

"I do not intend to discuss this, Patty. I have thought it through. I will do what is right."

That he stood in the gloom seeming near a stranger and I could not even see his face gave a greater force to his plain cold words. What I best recall is the scents of that moment which made more dreadful its reality, the dear familiar scents of our so tiny room of smoke and books and ancient cooking and the scent of Philadelphia still about my Thomas so he smelled of sharp scents and nothing familiar.

"I do beg you, sir, to reconsider. I truly am well. You need have no fear." This I said, but then I needs must recall that indeed I had been ill in July. I had felt so well that I had begun to eat of meats and sweetmeats, so I had suffered a recurrence of a kidney-fever and a very violent strangury which kept me to my chamber for much of that month. Yet in risk of the loss of my husband's love I must recall that illness as nothing at all. Indeed, it was nothing. I fought the memory, that he not see its guilt upon my face.

"I will not risk it, Patty. I love you too well to see you die."

"I shall not die!" I said to the dark stranger who narrow stood with his arms tight folded.

"Your health is too precious," he said with patience. "We need not have more children. We have Patsy. We have our sister Carr's children. Truly there are many children about."

This he said, but all my thought was for his need to escape when he felt the yearning of a husband for his wife. He would quit my bed. My only thought was that he had resolved to quit my bed. I said, "Shall I leave here this very night? Shall I live now with Patsy? Or must I go farther?"

"You shall live where you are. Do not play upon me. Do not attempt to change my mind."

This he said, for I was saying on, "Will you divorce me to marry another? Or will you be content to take a maid? And may I ever see you? For I do still love you, for all that you do not love me." Here tears began so fiercely that I could not control them. Gasps rent my body most painfully. I held fast to the post of the bed while I strove to control my furious weeping.

"Stop it!" he shouted with surprising anger; the shock of it put me out of my weeping. "I will not change my mind! That I will not do!"

My Bathurst ever had shouted at me when he was most grievously in the wrong, so I knew male shouting to be a weakness and not a strength. That my dear husband shouted while he spoke so cruelly gave to me a peculiar comfort, for it showed that his position might not be firm. My gasps still tore me with violent hiccoughs, but since he had ordered me not to weep, then I would not weep. I looked at him through streaming tears.

"Oh, Patty," he said with such pain that my eyes grow moist again as I write. "You know how I love you."

That he spoke thus to my inmost self was greatly worse than his former shouting. I felt it as a cut from a weapon most cleverly used where I had no defense. I said, "We cannot live but as husband and wife."

"That is not true! Do you believe that I have no control at all?"

"Come and kiss me as you ought and say again that we can live together as a brother and sister."

He waited but a moment before he strode across the boards and put his arms around me. I trembled of weeping as he tenderly kissed and then kissed the more quite beyond his will until I heard his change of breathing which said he still did most completely desire his wife. "This you see," I said against his coat when he ended the kiss that he not do more.

"We have no choice," he said against my cap. "Oh, Patty, I cannot live without you! That I cannot! I very truly cannot!" Yet even as his mind made these protestations, his body was sensible of our long separation. It clung to me so well that truly it seemed he lacked the power to pull it away. He said while he clung, "I would not take a mistress. I swear it, Patty. Nor even a maid." Yet while he so spake, his body louder said that he could not well live celibate.

"Indeed you would take a maid," I said, and I looked up fully into his face. We were turned so I could see it by the fire-light, and only the close full look of his face was a thrill of my heart which I feel again as I recall that moment. Then I first understood that he would do for me even what he believed most wrong, that he loved me more than even he loved his honor as a gentleman. I said, "We must come together as a husband and wife. And I promise that I shall not be ill. I have drunk Gabbler's daily for a fortnight past that we might come together upon this night, and so we shall come together. I do promise you that."

So I said boldly to my husband's dear face while my eyes yet blurred and gasps of hiccoughs seized me again beyond my will. While he gazed at me, I removed his coat and began upon the buttons of his waistcoat. I saw in his face all his tender concern intermixed with his natural sanguine humor; so much as he may imagine me at risk, he cannot believe it in his heart. He fears for me, and yet he does not fear. I apprehended this most clearly. I need only be to him again as I had ever been to him, and his terrors born of our months apart would dissipate as mists are put away by the sun.

"You are a most impertinent lady," he said as if he said to me words of love. "I know not what to do with you." I had his waistcoat off and began upon his breeches, the which he first once tried to defend, but then he sighed and put one shoe off against the other. "I had meant to say that if you love me you must not attempt to change my decision. I had wondered what rules we might best make upon length and degree of embrace or kissing. I really had given this much thought, Patty, which you cast aside as if it were nothing." So he said. Then very soon thereafter he had not a mind to speak at all. I had afterward a strangury so mild that it was cured by Gabbler's and yet more water, and we speak not together of that night for my defiance of him was very shameful.

What greatly alarms me of that night is his first resolve which he almost kept, for we cannot live but as a husband and wife. To end our marital comfort now would end our close communion of our minds, and to live together separate would be greatly worse than if we were parted for evermore. And he would take a maid. However much he now says not, he is a man and he would take a maid.

So I put that aside with a great relief. I ought now to mention the politics, for I have a thought that in after-life I shall want to know my own thoughts upon these changes of our government. Very much has transpired in these three months past. Patrick Henry is elected the Governor of Virginia, although he lies so ill of bilious fever that my husband's friend Page must serve in his room. Our Page is the President of the Governor's Council and second now in the colony, the which so greatly delights my Thomas, for all that my dear one now has become nothing more than a Delegate. He had his fine moment of service in drafting a Declaration of our Independence and in shaping with the Congress our confederacy so the colonies might act with a unified mind. He is glad now of his Declaration, for all that the Congress have made to it changes which still severely vex him. The fact of our independence pleases him greatly, and he speaks with a lightness of that moment to say that in truth it was a plague of flies which tipped the balance for our liberty.

There was near by the room where the Members debated the Declaration of their Independence a livery-stable with its attendant filth, and heat enough that they must open all windows. This produced in the room a swarm of flies which attacked the gentlemen's legs through silk stockings, so they lashed their legs with their handkerchiefs but they could not keep the flies away. My Thomas jests that it was this vexation as much as any aspiration to liberty which made them at length put discussion by and affix their names that they might escape.

Yet he jests not upon our constitution, which troubles his mind most grievously. When my Thomas knew that the Virginia Convention would write our constitution in the spring, he drafted and sent his own constitution that his voice indeed be heard. But Mr. Mason's constitution prevailed over his, and this is a tragedy for us all, for Mr. Mason gives us nothing more than what we long had of the royal will. My Thomas would have ended the importation of slaves! He would have given us freedom of our religion! He would have let female descendants inherit in equal status as if they were males, the which so very greatly delights me. He ever does have a care for his wife. And his constitution benefits the common men, for he grants to them each his fifty acres that he might keep his family and have his suffrage and live with a hope to better himself. That these good provisions are lost to us because the Convention heeded not my husband's constitution is a tragedy that briefly troubled him until he recovered his usual humor. Now he swears that when the Assembly convenes he shall effect these same results by changing the law. He sits the morning long and reads his politics and very intently drafts his bills that when the Assembly sits in the month to come he will make a perfect use of it.

So this will be our life, and I rejoice. We never shall ever live apart again. The war continues in colonies north, but the British have been repulsed from Charles Town and Lord Dunmore is gone away to New York so it seems the British have yielded the south with scarce a fight at all. There is very great fighting at New York, the places lately unknown to us but now upon near every lip, their islands of Long and Manhattan and their towns of Brooklyn and Jamaica and Harlem. The British fleet there is in the hundreds of vessels and the army in the tens of thousands of men, and more arrive daily, the which cannot but trouble us even so far away. Indeed, they may well take New York. They may take New

WILLIAMSBURG DECEMBER 3, 1776

I see the break of my final sentence and the blot of ink where I closed the book quick and recall what gave me such a start. My husband surprised me at my journal. I so was enjoying the play of my words that I did not hear him enter below, and his head cleared the floor and I looked up alarmed and slammed the volume shut.

"What do you do, Patty?"

The look of guilt I wore must make him believe me a criminal. "I do nothing." I made haste to push the book aside but he came and retrieved it from beneath my mending.

"Do you still keep your journal?" This he said with amazement. He held the spine cradled in his hand and turned a page to see what it was.

"Please give it me, Thomas. Please do not read it."

"Why may I not read it?"

"Because it is my own."

At this he looked most closely at me as if he looked down the length of his nose. "Do you keep a secret from me, Patty?"

"I do not. I only wish to have one thing that is all my own."

He looked down then at the open book as if he read a sentence of it while I felt I must writhe to see his eyes upon it. I saw in his face how alarmed he was with a very great curiosity to see the thoughts within a lady's mind, and that his own lady. He would have read the book and not so much as moved to sit upon a chair. "Please, Thomas."

At that he looked at me. His hand that cradled it closed shut my journal with a great reluctance. "I keep no secret from you, Patty. All that I have written is yours to see." This he said, for I ever read his commonplace books and his draughts of his letters and all that he writes. I might suggest a change to make a better sense, and this he greets most cheerfully.

"I have not written it fit for any eye but my own. Please, if you love me, do not read it."

"Why should you fear my eyes? What have you written?"

I stood to my feet for what ever small advantage that might give me. He still was taller by a foot. I said, "You are a gentleman. To you belongs all the world. I only ask that you let me have this small book for myself."

"But I allow you to read what I write."

"That is not the same thing!" I saw in a panic that he would press me and press me until I yielded. "Can you not see, Husband, that our lives must be different? You are a gentleman! You own every power! But I must live beneath every gentleman and curb my every unseemly thought, so I must have a place where I can speak out freely. You must not see that speech. Oh, Thomas, do not risk a change in your opinion of me."

I saw that my words but enlivened his interest and gladly he would have spoken further, but the look of my face did give him pause. "Nothing you have written could alter my opinion of you," he said in a voice which held a weak conviction.

I curtseyed gravely with head fully bowed. "Dear Husband, I do now beg your leave to keep a private journal."

"Of course you may keep a journal! You do not need my leave!"

"If you read that book now, then I may not keep it."

He saw the sense of this. I lifted my eyes. After pause, he handed me back my journal. "May I ever read it?"

"Some day you may. I do believe that some day you may."

So I said. Now I have a gladness to know that I may leave my journal any where, for since he has vowed that he shall not read it I know that verily he will not read it if it lies on the table under his hand for beyond a hundred years. Now that he is over the shock of it, I believe he finds a pride in knowing that I keep a journal so full of spirit that I dare not let him read it. He has jested of it when we were private, but gently so I might hear his pride.

This is a lovely day, for all that it is cold enough that I must wear gloves within doors. I sit at the window in an upper chamber of this fine brick house of Mr. Wythe's and look out upon the Palace Green where now our Virginia militia trains. I hear their commands right through the glass and see their bold stern faces, and I wonder how much of this is ardent feeling and how much indeed is a show they make to encourage their fellows and themselves. Williamsburg has a hospital where they care for soldiers stricken in the war, and these walk about to take their air with bandages on their arms and heads as a warning to the fresh militiamen who soon must go out and take their place.

Oh, the war to the north goes very ill. Our good brave General Washington has not been able to hold New York, and the tales now told by our returning soldiers are such that I must weep for him. I cannot think of him as a fighting General, but I see him still as but a gracious gentleman. When first I joined my husband's circle it was Colonel Washington and his lady who befriended me. He is a gentleman as tall as my husband and possessed of a very great dignity, so he gives an odd impression that the force within him is greater still than what is seen. When he is in a room, he is the center of it. All within it must defer to him. Yet upon my arrival at my earliest dinner when I was but a bride, this gentleman and his patient lady sat with me and talked most tenderly to tell me how greatly fine was my husband and how I was far the loveliest lady and I need not be shy, for the gentlemen all were eager to pay to me their attention. With the great Colonel Washington by my side I was the center of that dinner and the next, until soon I was at ease and very well launched and I no longer needed his encouragement.

I cannot forget his kindness to me. What ever he may do for all of his country says to me less of his character than does his soft voice and his so rare smile to put a frightened lady at her ease. Yet now he flees with his beaten army from Long Island and Manhattan and all of New York, the colony indeed so filthy with Tories that they danced in the streets to welcome the British. They did not deserve the service of so greatly noble a gentleman who fought for their freedom when they would not claim it. Indeed, they nearly sold him out to the British. He scarce escaped the colony with his life. Oh, his poor poor lady! What must be her thoughts as she reads her papers day upon day? Now the dear gallant General Washington flies with his army down the Jerseys while General Howe and his army come near to overtaking them at every river-ford. The war comes so near to Philadelphia that the Congress may be forced to leave the city, and only the thought that my own dear husband was in that city scarce three months past puts a terror into me. I did not then have any thought of his grievous risk.

Yet I must not fear. I look upon my husband who never has entertained a fearful thought, and I see how he greets each new calamity with a thought for how it might yet be countered or even how it might bring a greater advantage. So long as I remain close by to my husband, indeed I can feel no fear at all. There is less of fear too in the very air, where once fear thickened as a noisome vapor that ofttimes would catch within the throat how ever we might strive to make ourselves brave. But there is less alarm now among the common people since they no longer fear a prompt invasion, and with the worst of the Tories gone from our midst there is a peace made among those who remain as of people conjoined in a common effort. No longer must we dress for our politics. I have had made this year three beautiful gowns and much of personal silks and linens, and only the comfort of dressing well does make me believe that we have won our peace.

So I work to cultivate a courage that I might serve my country if ever it should need me. There is a story current of a Quaker lady ardent for her liberty who greeted General Howe and his fellows as they harried the Patriot army in flight. This lady so charmed the enemy officers and graciously plied them with food and drink that they rested in her home for beyond two hours until our army had made its escape. How the thought of this thrills me! One lady was given the grace alone to save her country. That I fain would do if the chance of it came, but I cannot do it weak with fear. Verily fear is a useless emotion, for it renders helpless its fearful victim and thereby makes likely the very calamity which courage might with luck prevent. So I shall be brave. What ever now may come, I shall be a lady worthy of my fearless husband.

We move today to rooms at Pinckney's, for Mr. Wythe has returned from the Congress and he needs his house. I worked with my husband and servants below to pack up the last of our household goods, but I am three months into a pregnancy and breeding another kidney-fever. My husband liked not the look of my face so he ordered me above that I might rest.

"Very well," I said to him. "I shall find my journal and write what I think of gentlemen who order about their ladies."

"That you surely will do," he said with a smile as if my journal were a bond between us. I shall write and write for all of my life and then in the end he will know all.

My Thomas is ever so happy here. He has found at last his calling, for the joy that he finds in making the laws is beyond any joy I have seen in him. Yet the Congress refuses to yield him up. They shamefully prey upon his guilts, for they nearly have forced him to travel to France and once again leave all that he loves.

This calamity fell on the eighth of October when we had but arrived in Williamsburg. A messenger Express came from the Congress to pound upon our door while we sat to our boxes, and he stepped within as if he conquered the house with his voice and mudded boots and his dust of the road. He bore a letter from the President of the Congress most cleverly and devilishly written to command that my husband sail for France if ever he loves his countrymen. My husband was made a Commissioner with Dr. Franklin at the Court of France. He must leave at once. There could be no denial.

Here was a terrible conversation ever to pass between a husband and wife. My Thomas dismissed the man to Southall's while he handed me the letter that I might read it, so when he turned from the door I but looked at him. I had not any words to speak. "They make it difficult," he said as if greatly weary. "Winning France to our side will give us the war. And if she sides with Britain, then the war is lost and there is no where on earth that we may live."

I found voice to say, "Will you go then, Thomas?"

"How can I go?" But here he must turn and pace from hall into parlor and back again, from hall into dining-room to hall to stair while his jaw moved as if he chewed his thoughts. "I cannot leave you. I know the hell I suffered when we were just six days apart, so how can I put us months apart? And we are at war! How can I leave you, Patty?"

"Would you have me go?" This I said with my throat gone dry for the thought that if he bade me then indeed I must go. This must be all his own decision or else he only will ever despise me.

"You are not well enough to travel," he said. Yet he looked at me as if he saw me freshly, to see if indeed I might stand the voyage.

"It must be all your decision, Husband. If you go and leave me I will not complain, and if you bid me go with you then I will go."

This was a speech unlike his wife. While I bend to his will when I must bend, I retain still such a willfulness that he swears that even my yielding to him is my cleverest tool to make him yield to me. Yet these words were no such artifice, and this he saw at once. He stood with his hand upon the newel while his body lost a stiffening, as if he had steeled it for a battle with his wife that now would never be. He straightened then and stepped to the parlor. His face was gone bright, as if his mind rose above this great new worry of his posting to France so his only thought was to his papers whose unpacking we dared not entrust to servants.

Thus we lived together for near three days while the messenger waited at his ordinary and Thomas and I spoke of all the world, but we never mentioned the name of France. I sought to read in his face what his thoughts might be, but I saw there just a firming of resolve and I never could guess in which direction. I only was comforted that he did say once that Dr. Franklin is a gentleman of surpassing wisdom and able ever to present our case without a help from him.

Thomas rose on the third day very cheerful. He jested of the cold which kept me abed until our Bob had poked up our chamber-fire, and he jested of my casting about with Bett to wonder which gown I had a mood to wear. He said that he had but three pairs of breeches and only one clean so he thought to wear that. While he sat to wash his feet as he does on every morning of his life he said, "There is a letter on the table, Patty. You might read it over to approve its style."

Then I found on the table the letter he had written by the candle while I slept. He declined most respectfully his posting to France in a belief that another could better serve, and because a circumstance peculiar to his family would let him neither leave us nor carry us with him. I read to those words. Then I splashed the basin over in my haste to be held in his arms at once for my very great joy to know that truly never again must he leave my side. His love for me is greater than his love for his country. Naught can she ever do to trouble me more.

I so rejoice in my defeat of my rival that I can share my husband with a careless ease, as if I were the mistress and she but the wife so he pays her his attention for decency's sake. Still she tugs at his coat, his poor sorry country, and she begs that he give her a little time for he is at the head of the Assembly now and one of the leaders of the colony. He has already this session done very much to disestablish the Church of Virginia and to pass to common men the western lands that other wise would go but to the gentry. So he gives to his country what attention she begs while his heart and his love belong to me, and I pity what for long seemed my greatest rival. She does seem in truth to be a female spurned.

My Thomas makes haste to ensure that the gentry will claim very little of the western lands. He says that he mistrusts the gentry despite their zeal to win their freedom, for gentlemen cling to what is their own and they seek not the broader common good. If we would keep our freedom and build our own country it will be with every man's heart to the contest, and all of our precious western lands must be given to the people who most need them. This he says. It needs a stretch of my mind to think of our gentlemen as aught but worthy, for these who risk the most have been at the front in the fight to win our liberty. Were it not for my husband and his fellows we would live for ever beneath the Parliament's boot, so it seems very hard that their reward must be a lesser right while the common men gain a greater. This I think. Yet the common men share the fight so perhaps they have earned each his fifty acres, and there is land enough upon the continent so each may have his own small kingdom. My husband has a very great wisdom which lets him see to each action's distant result and to the result beyond that, and yet farther still so it seems that he nearly sees the farthest future. If he says that each man must have his fifty acres or our venture is spoilt before it is begun, then I know it to be true.

Perhaps then we also might free our slaves and give to them

each his fifty acres. Here is a thought! Can they truly live without our guidance? Perhaps if we can but educate them they may live well enough all on their own. Oh we would still need them, but we might have their hire and each might return to his lands at night, or they might live here and keep a farther land so they have a where to go. How this would delight them! I see my dear Ursula and her Great George with all of his dignity, and to say to them that they have their freedom and a fifty acres to call their own would be such a joy that I foolishly smile alone in my chamber to think of it. And my Betty! I would not have her go, but if she stayed only of her love for me I would know that truly I have that love and she does not only coddle her mistress.

I cannot see as my husband sees, to each action's third or its tenth result, so I cannot think beyond their joy and mine in the moment of their freedom. We must talk more of an end to slavery when our greater war is nearly won. While my mind cannot untie the knot, my dear husband's mind will surely untie it.

MONTICELLO JANUARY 13, 1777

*O*h, my poor New York! We hear now such tales as should cause the very stones to weep of all that has been suffered within New York by those who struggle for their liberty. I had thought the whole New York must be only Tories and glad of the arrival of the British. Their members at Congress even near disapproved my husband's Declaration of their Independence, so cool and craven must they be. I had thought them unworthy of our General's aid and the blood of our so precious men. Yet I am wrong! Many soldiers leave the army now where it winters in the Jerseys, for our gentlemen in the Congress swore the war could not last beyond six months' time so they made the terms of most but six months long and these return now to defend their Virginia. Yet such tales they tell! I cannot bear to write them as plain as they are said in town, and this even in the presence of ladies.

New York is lost to us. Our States had only been styled United when the British cleaved them full in two. This my husband insists is not a fatal loss, for New England can well defend itself, yet still we are cut off by land and Britain rules the sea. The Canada indeed is nearly lost, and the British press down upon the Hudson River and so harry and excite the Indian tribes that they war now upon us from the west. We have had much trouble of the Cherokees within our farthest western counties, yet far enough away that I heed my Thomas when he insists they must not trouble my sleep.

Yet how greatly grievous is the pain of New York! There was upon Long Island and onto Manhattan much looting and burning and the taking of women, and some of these were ladies gently bred who could not flee with sufficient haste. Many such ladies were raped by the soldiers so some must die and others go mad, and this against every dictate of honor and the duty of the strong to protect the fair. Are their officers not gentlemen? I cannot imagine the fear of those ladies at their so cruel fate, and the shame of it that their honor is lost and with it must be lost their husbands' love. Yet even more fearsome than the evil British are the terrible Hessian jaegers, who will not take a prisoner but they kill them cruelly or they beat them most unmercifully. They make a vicious sport of some they take and cut away a poor wretch's generative parts and leave him to live as no man would live. Can these Hessians be men? I see them in my mind as furred and fanged; I cannot think them human.

It seems that if the winter had not come our army would have ended at our very door. They nobly fought, but they were over-numbered unto triple or more of well-supplied troops and they had not even boots nor powder nor blanket for cover in the cruel snow. We are appointed now to gather up every blanket we can spare for dispatch to these troops, that they survive the winter and with them survives our liberty. Greatly pitiful are tales of the rags with which boys and aged men must wrap their feet, and the blood of their sores runs upon the snow and still they march and fight. How fierce is the human need for freedom! How great the shame of the British tyrant, with so much blood upon his head!

Yet after so many so terrible tales we have lately had a word of such high hope that our only doubt is from its perfection. My Thomas seeks a confirmation of it when he meets with his fellows in Fredericksburg to make there together their new committee for the reformation of Virginia's laws. It is told that our dear brave General Washington left his winter camp on Christmas Day and crossed the Delaware River and took back Trenton and captured nearly a thousand Hessians. And that not enough, but word has late come that he has seized back Princeton in the Jerseys and he carries on farther with his so few troops that he might re-take New York. And this in full winter! The tales are told that he rides before his men into the British guns so his army prevails by his will alone. This I can believe from what I know of him.

Verily I had not wished for this war. Long would I have lived beneath a great oppression that we not risk a harm to all we love. Yet now that it is entered, I find a fire of a very surprising Patriot feeling, so I swear I could never live with the British and I must have my liberty what ever its cost. Only the thought of our so dear General riding before his soldiers into the battle thrills me beyond my fear for him and far beyond any weak fear for myself. I fain would see a battle, to see what it is and whether it is as I have thought of it.

I said this to my husband as we packed his box that he might make his journey to Fredericksburg. He is gone now on yesterday for it may be a week, and this journey very greatly delights him for he meets with four gentlemen of the Assembly that they might re-write Virginia's code of laws.

Here at last is his calling. Indeed we have found it. My husband loves best not his lawyering nor his legislative work nor the act of governance, but what he greatly loves above all other duties is the new-creation of a government. I jest with him that if there were but the need he might peddle his governments upon the road and live in perfect happiness. This he cannot do for there is not the need, but he packed his box for Fredericksburg with all the delight of a youth setting out upon his whole life's journey.

"Have you ever seen a battle?" I said to him as I better folded up his shirts while my husband made choice between two of his waistcoats. I knew his answer, but I felt a great interest which forced from me the question.

"I pray never to see one." Then he looked at me and saw my lively interest, and I saw that he perfectly shared that interest what ever he might pray. He said, "You are a most confounding lady! I thought you were terrified of the war."

"That I am. I only wonder what a battle might be if we were ever to see it. Would there be naught to see but smoke and flash? And naught to hear but firing? I have watched them train and I have heard such stories. You cannot be surprised that I wish to know more of what a battle might be."

"Oh, Patty." Here he set down his waistcoats and he came to

hold me warm in his arms. "All the war talk is taking your inno-cence. Were it in my power I would completely protect you." This he said most nobly, but I had a thought that I do not wish to be completely protected. If these are human facts, the war and the fighting, then I fain would have a sight of them. "Never think of the fighting," my husband said, and he kissed my face to comfort me. "Think in its stead of the life we shall have very soon when we have won our peace. I shall order the floor-boards on my return so we shall very soon be in our house. And you carry another baby. Think instead about that, for you never will be happy my dear if you think too much about the war."

MONTICELLO JUNE 15, 1777

*T*oday I have buried another child. I have no heart to write; I sit to write as if it were the bitterest medicine. That I knew from his birth he was meant to die and that when it came his end was God's own blessing cannot ease my pain that he is gone from my sight and his poor small body is gone from my arms. Yet writing is my comfort, so I write here now while my husband reads behind me in his chair that he might comfort me if again my sorrow should rise beyond what I can bear. I know not what comfort I may find in writing. I am beyond comfort. I am near beyond pain. The story is very simply told: I have brought another son before his time. Yet there is in those words no comfort at all so I must write on yet more.

We thought at each moment of my pregnancy that I might be very greatly ill, but indeed I was well as ever I am until the six-teenth day of May. Often I seemed to breed a kidney-fever but it ever was so very mild, and the child did quicken most ardently and all did seem to be very well. My husband was so anxious after my health that he bade Dr. Gilmer attend to me upon every sneeze and every hiccough. But I kept most perfectly to breads and vegetables and often I drank of Gabbler's tonic, so I had not even any bladder-fever. My husband must attend the Assembly in May and we thought it better that I not risk the chariot upon the rutted roads, but I waved him out of sight so gaily.

I write this as if I write out a lesson. The effort it takes me to dip and write makes my hand seem to weigh beyond a thousand pounds.

What came upon me at the middle of May was a very grievous fever. It began as if I but took a chill from having slept imprudently with windows open, but it grew most greatly worse. Betty nursed me together with Nanny Brewer, the wife of Mr. Brewer who makes for us bricks, but the Brewers only came here late in April so I did not feel at ease with this woman who speaks out coarsely, and she is not clean. I wanted my Betty or one of my sisters or I wanted my dear husband, and when I said his name from a fevered sleep my Betty sent Jupiter to summon him. So my Thomas came. I heard his familiar voice from wherever I was, neither awake nor sleeping but wandering within my mind that was become a track-less waste of fever. Sounds were louder there although I did not hear them, but his step on the stair and his voice I heard. "Patty? Patty?" His hand was cold. His voice was near to panic. "Bring Dr. Gilmer! Never mind the hour!"

This I heard him say, and the words remained most firm and strong within my head to repeat and repeat and over again. I assembled a strength to say very softly, "Dear Husband? What is the hour?"

"It is ten in the morning," Thomas said. I saw that indeed it was become day. I did not know until he later explained it that he had summoned the doctor at two in the morning, and Dr. Gilmer had then both come and gone while my husband's words rang inside my head.

The time was intermittently lost to me, but it seemed that three days more must pass and then my body must give up its effort to carry my child. I was recovering my health so I knew that my body's decision was only greatly foolish, for I had the strength to carry it on. In this Dr. Gilmer disagreed with me. He told my Thomas that the child might survive but if I carried it further I might not, and this was all that my husband need hear for him to plead and then command and then plead again that I give up resisting the pains of my labor and allow my body to deliver the child.

It was clear when he was born that he could not survive. He was scarcely bigger than my husband's hand and his cry was only the mew of a bird. Yet moment by moment he lived on, he lived to be washed, he lived to be dressed, and he would not suck but with a tube into his mouth he could be fed milk and he could swallow.

Indeed he lived for beyond a fortnight, and never I put him out of my arms for a thought that while he was in my arms he would be safe and he could not die. Foolish thought, for my poor little Jack could die while he lay within his mother's arms, and he a great child twenty times the size of the mite I held both day and night.

His name was Sweet. I only ever called him Sweet, for had he lived we would have named him Thomas but that name must wait for our certain worry that he would not survive. Yet he might have survived. He died of a fever that came upon him late on Friday last, and it took him off on Saturday evening while I still held him fast within my arms.

My Thomas has only just said to me now that I have written here for more than an hour. He would see what I have written if I offered it, but he has too great a respect for me to make a request when my refusal of it would be shameful between a wife and her husband. Oh, dear man. I thought on my wedding-day that I did very greatly love my Thomas, but such mild feelings of a widowed lady were as nothing to the love that I bear for him now. Never was there born among all of mankind so good a man as my dear husband. He deserves a living son, and he shall have a son. That I vow to my Jack and Janey and Sweet and to the mite who was born but the size of a thumb. So many so very dear dead children. I have a thought that if my earthly family may be small, I shall live in a very crowd in heaven.

MONTICELLO SEPTEMBER 1, 1777

*M*y poor forsaken journal has lain forgotten upon the table these three months past. It has lacked even the dignity of a hiding-place but has reposed forlorn beneath a pile of books which we have little used, so they bear a dust blown in through the window from our Mulberry Row.

I find a shame to write of my happy summer when I read of the loss of my little son. Yet I have had with me the summer long the presence of my so very dear husband, and never can I ever be sorry for long when he is by my side. We have had such carrying-forward this summer, such coming and going of friends and kin, such fine delightful entertainments what with picking-parties for every manner of berries and fish-feasts along the Rivanna River and dinners and operas and every thing. We had even two very careless balls upon the under-floors of our new-made parlor, with all the doors open and the dress so careless that ladies wore the gowns they had worn by day and gentlemen danced in their shirts and waistcoats. These balls were the merrier for their careless ease and we said that indeed they were more American, for now that we are severed from England's rule and we seek full rights for every man we must live more like the common people with whom we make our common cause.

And upon this night I first understand the meaning of this commonality. We have had today for our dinner-guests six officers and soldiers of the Continental Army who encountered my Thomas in Charlottesville, and nothing would do but he must house and feed them. I told him when we retired to our chamber that I would sit and write awhile, but now he is abed and he begs for me to extinguish the candle. Yet I write on. I have heard this day such a very remarkable conversation that I fear may be lost unless I write it down.

It being Monday and our week-end guests having only left us early this morning, we had not thought of a proper dinner but we had planned a cooling salad of fruits and greens. My Thomas went to Charlottesville upon some business of the militia, and he came to us near dinner-time with six most dusty and rowdy men whom I took to be further British deserters he had hired on a whim to help complete our house.

That they were not. He gave me to know upon introduction by the kitchen-door that these were soldiers late of the Continental Army and bent upon a re-enlistment, and not only soldiers, but one was a major and another a lieutenant. I made my curtsey to the officers, assuming they must be gentlemen, for all that they were coarsely dressed and they wore rough trousers like common men. But they made me only clumsy bows, and one seized my hand in both of his and kissed it. The other but shook my hand and said not, "I am charmed to make your acquaintance, madam," or suchlike formal pleasantry, but, "A lovely mountain you have, Mrs. Jefferson! Fancy living here above the clouds!"

This hand-shaking is a custom of the common people which gains some currency among the gentry, for all that it seems more warm than bowing although it does show less respect. But never is a lady's hand shaken. I was quite alarmed out of words to say. This my Thomas saw, but he could do naught but lead our boisterous guests away and leave me with my Betty and Suck to make hurried dishes for a better dinner.

That the meal must be delayed from four until six mattered less with the days still summer-long. So we ordered killed a goose and this we filled with forcemeat. We cut a cold ham and made a hurried stew of the venison remaining from our week-end dinners. These meats with potted fish and pickles and salads and stewed fruits and a cornbread bought from Mary must do for our dinner for the Continental soldiers who go now to fight for our country's life.

We had the windows open in our dining-room and a cooling breeze of the late afternoon. The soldiers took their ease along our dining-table which was spread with cotton new-woven this summer of red and white and green intermixed, which the slaves find very cheerful. Every proper cloth had been used on the week-end, so this our cotton must be brought from the weave-room and cut in a hurry from the bolt. We grow cotton here these two summers past and spin and weave it here ourselves, and we find that we can clothe many of our servants. This economy does greatly please my dear husband.

Such talk we had at table! This I meant to write, yet the coming to it has consumed much ink.

Three of the soldiers had been with General Washington at Long Island and the fighting upon the Manhattan, and very nearly they turned the war to hear their own account of it. Each shot very many of the enemy and killed some others with knife or hand as effortlessly as they would wring a bird's neck. And this they said, even though all knew those battles to have been very great defeats. "We gave them a fine account of the Rebels! We taught them how to fear a good Yankee!" they said while their forks ever flew to their faces leant out to inches above their plates.

My Thomas was eager to hear what details they might give us of those famous battles, and eager the more, for he knew that I sat very anxious to know what a battle might be. I would have spoken had they been gentlemen, but I knew not how to converse with soldiers. Then while I yet labored to compose a question suitable for talk between lady and soldier, the one I thought the youngest said out words far the most appalling that I have heard. "There were days we had naught to eat but mussels pried from rocks in the bay," he said. "I did not mind that, for a mussel resembles that part most delectable of a woman's person."

I looked up alarmed. I did apprehend what it was he thought a mussel to be, for I have thought the like myself but never imagined that any would dare to speak it out. I could not look at Thomas down the length of the table. Any thing he did would be very shameful, for he could neither reprimand a guest who had so nobly fought in the war nor suffer so grave an insult to the honor of his blushing lady.

"Pray forgive me," Thomas said very mildly. "We have a custom at Monticello that we never speak of mussels at the table."

At this the shamed soldier was poked with elbow by his fellow who sat upon his left, and they gave one another looks abashed and they dared a look at me. They had indeed forgotten that I was there and had thought themselves at ease among rough men, and seeing that made me only wish that I could be as if unseen. If that were a sample of plain male talk, I was curious indeed to hear the rest.

They spoke on chastened of gentle things until once again I was forgotten. They ate great mountainous plate after plate of every dish so hurriedly made and pronounced all very grand and delicious, and they said that never was there spread a table like the table of a Virginia gentleman. I watched them as they ate, for they charmed me with their loud gay voices and their so rough manners. They were indeed so very young and the youngest were boys still in their teens, their cheeks sun-reddened and their eyes very bright with a warm and lusty humor. I found them most appealing, for they had an innocence as of colts grown wild at their summer pasture, and they fought for my country. I would have loved them for that if they had come to me filthy in skins and rags.

The men talked but little of the course of the war, which seems to me not a course at all for little happens for good or ill and it may go on for ever. Yet now we have a development, and none need wonder why they re-enlist for General Howe's fleet has been sighted off the Virginia Capes but a fortnight past. My husband insists that we are safe since the British cannot pierce the Tidewater swamps, but Williamsburg and my dear dear Forest are too close in their way. "They make for Philadelphia by the Chesapeake," the young lieutenant said to us. "Washington waits there the summer long. I doubt not that we shall see a battle now."

My Betty and her sweet willful Mary were clearing the cloth that we might have our wine. I saw the soldiers' faces as they looked at my Betty and at her pretty young blacker daughter, and I knew that they saw but female bodies who lacked the protection of husband or honor. There swelled in me a most unseemly rage.

"What think you, sir? Do women have souls?" This said the lieutenant to my dear dear husband. It seemed that I was forgotten again, but this is a topic I have heard at table with even the most genteel companions. Ever some playful gentleman will make an artless sport of the ladies by asking whether any believe they have souls. But I was at that moment not disposed to find any humor in the question. Nor was I of a temper for the subtle doubt which rises when ever I hear the question, for if my body must be less than the male's then may I be in other ways deficient. I have friends among ladies who say right out that they are glad they do not have souls, so when they die they will close their eyes and that will be an end to it.

"I am certain they do, sir," Thomas said in his gentle voice meant for me alone. "If heaven lacks females it cannot be heaven, so certain I am that they must have souls."

"Well, at least those do not have souls," a soldier said with careless nod at my Betty's back. Then could I have struck him! I hoped my dear Betty had no awareness of what he said, but I saw in her face when she turned again that very well she knew. And I saw further with a terrible shame that she found it entirely unsurprising for common men from out of the woods to believe her not a human creature.

"I fear you are mistaken," my Thomas said. "All people have souls, and those of lesser station may well have the greatest souls of all."

I looked to Betty, but my husband's concern was for Martin, who waited with his tray of wine. Martin is a full-grown man of twenty with far the noblest face and bearing, and he bears a disdain for common men as if he were the greatest gentleman. He bears also much of his mother's temper and in his youth he does not perfectly mind it.

"Do you then, sir, think them equal to the white?" asked out that youngest heedless soldier. Close behind him stood my stiff proud Martin. I looked at Martin sharply to give him warning.

"Indeed I do," my Thomas said in a voice that let me know how shamed he felt to be having this conversation before our servants. Here three of the soldiers fell to heated discussion, one supporting my husband and the others denying, and while they were distracted Thomas took Martin's wine and bade him with gentle voice to leave us. I touched Betty's hand where she held a dish and bade her with eyes to follow her son, and Mary hurried after them. Very glad they were not to wait on us while we must defend their humanity. Bereft of his Martin, Thomas poured the wine and passed the glasses hand to hand.

The major was the only older man. He bore a rough unshaven look, and he sat as if he were not used to a chair nor even to a fork or table. His beard-ends were gray upon his cheeks and they glistened in the sun where it hung so low that its light came nearly across the room. He seemed with it all a more sensitive man, and he seemed alone to apprehend that his fellows had discomforted us. "Pray forgive these fools," he said to Thomas. "They cannot afford a slave themselves. Yes, beyond your two," he said to a soldier who was bent upon protesting his words. "It is but an envy of their betters. You would have done well to have fed us from a trough set out beneath the trees."

This speech charmed my husband. He would have spoken most cool and polite while we drank our wine, but hearing such an ingenuous speech made him look at the major tenderly. "All men are created equal beings," he said to this man, although he addressed them all. "If you do not think yourself less than I am, then you need not think yourself greater than they are."

"A pretty speech, sir," that owner said of but two slaves. "I cannot imagine you believe them your equal in courage and wit and integrity. In ability, sir? You cannot think it, no matter how nobly you speak it out."

At this my Thomas set down his glass while I watched him down the length of the table. What he said for answer I was eager to hear. I had not much considered this question, but I see it had made a constant worry lying close beneath my thoughts. I had not dared to think of it. If the Negroes are not competent, well it may be that they cannot be free.

"No," said my Thomas as if the effort of saying the word itself made him weary. "I would devoutly that they were my equal in every manner of ability, but I cannot deny what I plainly see. They may not be in all ways my equal. But that matters not!" This he said so firmly that some sat straighter on their chairs. "They come from

their Creator my perfect equal and they have their rights that are
equal to mine. If I have a finer wit, that is a blessing to me but it
carries with it a greater burden. Nothing about it can give me a
right of any description greater than their own."

"How then do you justify owning them?" said that owner of
slaves, half-belligerent.

"I do not justify it. I awaken each morning and find myself
again today an owner of slaves, and since that institution wants a
remedy I must keep my slaves with me until it is found." Having
said this and thus unburdened himself of what I know is a shame to
him, my Thomas seemed near jovial. He poured the wine and held
back the dregs with all of Martin's care. There was upon the
beaufet a second decanter, and this he stood pertly and stepped to
retrieve. I thought that his waiting upon the soldiers was an effort
whose symmetry greatly pleased him. "A toast, sirs," he said as he
returned to his place and stood in the light with his glass upraised.
"I give you these United States of America, where every man is of
right and ought to be free."

Even the owner of slaves must drink this toast. My Thomas
drank it deep. Then the colonel gave the lady Mrs. Jefferson, which
toast should of right have been the first one given, and others gave
General Washington and the army they rejoin and the death of
tyrants and then one even gave the Continental money, that it not
depreciate to the point where a dollar's bill is worth less than its ink
and paper.

At this they all laughed of the wine and the sunlight and their
bellies contented with so much food. While they yet laughed,
Nance came to the door with Patsy and Sally hand by hand as she
is wont to do of an early evening when Patsy and Sally are soon
retiring. Sally at nearly four sleeps in Patsy's room, for my Betty is
occupied by little John and her infant Lucy lately born. Sally shares
the pallets with Nance and Thenia and Critta. They have a very
crowd in Patsy's room.

The children came to kiss me good-night, their sweet breath
warm upon each cheek and their lips like the brush of a wild bird's
wings so delicate and precious. Then, "Pappa!" said my dear little
Patsy who no longer is so little at all, for she is turned five years and
tall for her age. They hurried to him the length of the table and
Thomas drew them gaily up onto his knees. The little slave Sally is
so sweet and charming that he drew her up beside his own and they

both most sweetly hugged and kissed him. "Good-night, Pappa!" said they both together. Betty's Sally has for long called my Thomas Pappa to copy my Patsy in all that she does, but she is old enough to learn her place and this I daily mean to teach her. Yet Sally is such a charming child that when ever I am bent upon her correction I think she might have one more day in which she need not call her friend her mistress.

"Good-night, little cherub-faces," Thomas said. "And these men are soldiers who fight for your freedom. You must bid them good-night as well."

So the children slid from my husband's lap and curtseyed as well as I have taught them to curtsey, low and gracefully with heads fully bent. I saw them and thought with a queasy shame that I must correct Sally this very day for she thinks herself a lady.

My Thomas watched the children turn for the door and upon his face was a look most lively. He bade our Sally return to him. "Go along, Patsy, and she will follow. She will be up directly."

Sally is a bold sweet child well aware that adults are charmed by her. To be thus called back while Patsy must go seemed to her a very victory, so she went to my husband with a fond shy smile and climbed up confident onto his lap.

"This little girl is a slave," said Thomas slowly and most thoughtfully. I saw that he meant to give a lesson, but he knew not what that lesson would be so he thought it through as he yet spoke. "You cannot see to the freeing of slaves because you cannot see beyond their shade of skin, but here is a skin you recognize. And yet she is a slave."

These words of my husband's meant nothing to Sally for the plain word "slave" meant nothing to her. She smiled the more for my husband's attention and for her new awareness that she has a status that Patsy does not share. Yet as I looked at them, I saw to my horror that every soldier there must assume that Sally is my husband's child begotten upon his maid. "She is the child of my own Pappa's maid!" I said before ever I could stop myself. This seemed as I said it but a confirmation that likely she must be my Thomas's child, and I blushed as never I have blushed before. I seized up my fan most desperately.

"I have inherited her," Thomas said. "She is not my child. But that is not the point I make. When you look at this child you must believe that she has a perfect right to be free, and so must her darker brothers and sisters who are of her own family. God and blood make no distinction, and so we must not. Never has there been on this earth a greater evil than slavery."

"You cannot free them," the lieutenant said.

"Indeed we can. We yet lack the will, but soon it must arise from our present struggle. Free men must recoil from slavery, sirs; the darkness cannot survive in the light. Yet we must free them wisely, that we end the evil and not create a permanent under-class to bring to us I cannot say what pain. We must raise and educate this generation of the age this little child is now and free them as they come to manhood and give to them each his land and his mule that they might better themselves and live truly free and not like the freedmen in the cities." His dear face shone as he said these words with more than the light of the sun upon it as he said out plainly his great solution to the worry which so much troubles me. Above the child's head, his eyes came to mine. I smiled too widely and bit my lip.

None of the soldiers spoke for that moment. They likely were more transfixed by this interplay between husband and wife than they were by my husband's plan for freeing the slaves. Then the owner of slaves said low and softly, "You cannot mean it, sir. No one would live with Negroes free upon the near-by farm."

"Then may we free them farther away," my Thomas said very cheerfully. "They might be given a state of their own, and if indeed they can govern themselves and better themselves and quite confound you, then, sir, you might be glad if one of them might be your neighbor." This brought a murmur from some of the soldiers which Thomas spoke above as if he heard it not. "I think it better that we live apart while we and they adjust to their freedom. Slavery brutalizes the master as it does the slave. Neither will ever be at ease with the other. I know not whether the white and the black can ever live together at all, but if we can it will only be after we have taught the Negro to govern himself. After all that we have taken from him, it is only just that we should give him that."

"Govern himself!" said the holder of slaves. "He has not the wit to even feed himself!"

"I think you wrong, sir, but that we cannot know while he yet lives here in servitude. We must free our slaves, and at the earliest date. Yet freeing them is not enough. To abandon our slaves to freedom now is an act as despicable as slavery itself, for the sorry state of the Negro freedmen must not be extended to the whole class of slaves. These freedmen have no human dignity and never any hope to better themselves so they must hate us and we despise them. We cannot live for long so unequal. A war of extermination between the races must be our only bitter end."

He looked alertly from face to face as if he judged how well he had persuaded them. I thought them not persuaded, but him I thought well satisfied that he had planted seeds which might bear later fruit. He said, "That we shall free them is a certainty, so we must begin now to plan for their freedom. There is land enough beyond the Mississippi for them to have each his fifty acres. And if we are apart, there need be no mixing. We need not create others like this child, who every time she confronts the glass must see there the face of her oppressor."

Sally bore my husband's speech passing well, the adult words in his so dear voice all seeming in some wise a tribute to her. Yet as he came to the end of it his voice became dense with a perfect fire, and she heard his last words with a new-found doubt which I saw at once upon her face.

"Come, child," I said, and rose from my chair. "It will be soon your bed-time." I could no more bear that doubt on her face than I could have borne it on the face of my own. I lifted her from my husband's lap and held her close as I made for the door, that she know that what ever be her legal status she is a pretty child and she is loved.

My Thomas stirs now from deep in his sleep. The quill makes a low and patient scratch which seems indeed to comfort him, but it stops and starts as I dip for ink or choose a new quill with a better point. It has become now very late, but I am not tired. I shall write on.

The state of my health is quite confounding. Again I am altogether well. I was so ill unto death in May that it cost us the life of our little Sweet, yet once I was delivered my health improved while I kept most strictly to my proper diet and drank of my Gabbler's and copious water. This I did along into July to prepare for a resumption of our marital comfort, for certain I was that my so dear husband again had resolved that it must end. He had resolved. Yet he would not say it out for fear of the tears and the pleas of his wife, so he was to me most cool and tender and he kissed me well but not with any passion and as I recovered he contrived each evening to set himself a task which put him late to bed. I knew this. I knew so exactly how the thoughts were arranged within his mind. So I went to bed obediently and contrived a false sleep that he might soon come to bed himself, and for weeks while I recovered I let him believe that his wife would not oppose him and he would prevail.

I no longer very greatly fear that my husband might take a mistress, for he loves both his wife and his honor together and the love of one alone would keep him pure. My greater fear now is of a greater loss, the loss of our communion of our minds, for if our bodies be separate and uneasy together then soon must our minds be like the same. Yet I could not but lay my hand on his thigh and hope that he would yield. He had yielded to my pleas that single time for their unexpected strength had disarmed his mind, yet now he expected my arguments and he had his answers for a perfect armor, so pleading alone would never let me prevail.

Very many evenings came and went while I could not find my proper courage, but upon one evening in full July I found of a sudden recklessness that the night had arrived and I would be my husband's true wife if I should perish for it. I was willful and would not take to my bed until the sun was set and the stars were out, and then I moved restless and I would not sleep, so my Thomas worked late by candle-light. I had thought he would have to be very weary, yet then I began to have a worry that his weariness might instead work against me. Ever I would have but this one chance.

At length my Thomas blew out his candle and found his night-shirt and his cap and fumbled out of clothing in the dark and weary came to bed. He must be well asleep, so I waited longer while my eyes moved restless by the moon's full light to search out the features of our so loved chamber which soon no longer will be our home. Our middle-building is roofed and windowed and in it are many of Thomas's books, although the floor is not laid and we think now that we may not be in our chamber until the spring. With that day soon to come, we find a new reluctance to leave what has been our only marital home. We neither say this, and yet I know that we both feel alike the same foolish reluctance.

Thomas slept. I waited until his breathing was slow and deep from the depth of him, and then I crept with a quiet stealth to hover like an angel near above. I cannot now say what I did to him for modesty and memory alike forbid, and I had not known but only had guessed that his body could be severed from his mind. It seemed quite scientifical. I had a thought that my experiment would interest him if ever we could talk of it, although that seemed unlikely.

I had a hope that he would awaken near the end of the act and be relieved to find our decision made so we might go on as before. But he might awaken early and fly from me, or then he might not awaken at all and I become pregnant and he be unpersuaded that he and not a stranger was the infant's father. Beset by these doubts and yet defying them, I laid back the blanket from his so dear body and by subtle touching with hands and lips I claimed its most fervent complete attention. His mind slept on, or it nearly slept so he flung his head and mumbled words and his hands made ineffectual motion. I had meant to bestride him. This I nearly did, but as I loomed above him he came awake and he caught my arms and flung and pinned me to the bed. "What do you do? What?" he said in a rage half of fear and half of indignation, yet there his body lay close above mine most firmly intent upon its own purpose. It was a near thing, but his mind cleared of sleep in time to gain dominion of his body. He fell back away from me as if in despair.

"Please, Thomas." I was near to tears. I did not know what he might now do.

"Must I sleep elsewhere? Is that what you wish?" he said from his ardent wounded pain.

"I wish to be your wife."

"You are my wife! But we cannot risk it! That we cannot!"

"Then I am not your wife. It is I who must go. I shall leave you in the morning."

My words or my tone affected him, and he turned his head upon the pillow. I felt his gaze but I dared not meet it for fear that my sorry lack of tears might mean to him a lack of love. His look commanded that I turn, but I would not turn. Then gently he spoke. "You do not understand how completely I love you. My dear, I would live a thousand years celibate rather than bring to you the slightest danger, and still you must attempt such a sorry trick."

"If you live celibate you shall live without me."

"I will not live without you!" His voice held a stridence not heard by day, so I had a thought that the procreative need in truth is a very great male weakness. My need to prevail was confirmed yet more.

"If you give not to me your masculine attention I ever shall believe that you give it elsewhere. You are a man, and the quarters hold women. Ever when you travel to the towns there are women. You could live your life celibate for a thousand years and for those thousand years I would think you not celibate so you might as well have your mistress, Thomas. I shall believe it whether you do or no."

Here my eyes made tears enough that I could turn. I turned, and a tear fell onto the pillow. His face became soft, as indeed it must do for sympathy of his wounded wife. Only my look made him need at last to move upon the mattress and have me into his arms. "Oh, Patty. You cannot carry a child. You must not risk it ever again."

"Indeed I can!" I said with heat. "My fever was not a kidney-fever but just some random illness, and had it not struck we would have our son beside us now! I swear that I will give you a son. Oh Thomas, even if I die for it then I die very glad that you have a son and that is my right, that I die for a cause which I think is worthy of my life."

"Patty, Patty," he said for my terrible agitation.

"I mean what I say," I said against his breast. "If you will not have me I shall go, for I cannot live with you and be not your wife."

"But I can live celibate. I doubted it, too, but we have lived this way for two months now and it has a charm, Patty. We may indeed be better companions for it."

This he said, but while his mind yet reasoned I captured the attention of his body as ever a wife can do for her husband and she knows how to do it very well. He choked on his words. He said, "The Devil take you for an obstinate creature!" But as he spoke his mind gladly joined his body; his words were sweet words of a perfect love. "Only not the act," he said from out of the last small resistance his mind yet made. "We may do all else, only not the act." So we avoided the act. Indeed, we never missed it.

Now my husband awakens from his sleep and he says, "Patty, come to bed! The sound of your pen is making me dream that I am chained to a desk and I must write forever. Now come you to bed!" And so I must. Never would I defy my dear husband.

WILLIAMSBURG NOVEMBER 7, 1777

*M*y very dear Sister

Your letter traveled first to Monticello, and then it followed us to Williamsburg when Jupiter brought to us a wagon of chickens, for you cannot imagine what they cost us here. I am much delighted to have your letter for I think of you so often, and I share your hope that we soon may meet despite the distance and the war.

It is likely now that we shall prevail, for as you must be well aware we have had a great victory at Saratoga in the eastern New York and the capture alive of their General Burgoyne and his troops of near five thousand men. I write these words more gaily than I have ever written any thing, for we have lived two weeks with this intelligence and we scarcely dared believe it for its very perfection. We had suffered the season long with our great defeats at Brandywine and German Town, and then suffered more from the terrible news that General Howe has taken Philadelphia and the Tories shamefully dance in the streets. To hear the intelligence we daily hear I have feared that we must lose our war, for if a war depends upon battles won then ours must soon be lost. But my dear wise husband is ever so hopeful and never cast down by any defeat, and now Saratoga has made him so cheerful that I fear he might dance in the street himself. There is a new joy in the Capital, too, as if our victory is nearly won, for people are weary of this war and eager that they soon find their peace.

Now see. I had thought to write a letter to my sister Nancy, for I have from her a most painful letter that her Henry has gone off soldiering and left her miserably quite alone. But she will find no comfort in news of the war so my letter to her is safely spoilt. I must begin again a nonpolitical letter. Perhaps I shall save this for my journal, since there I have one certain friend who receives what I write without a judgment so I can tell her any thing. I shall tell her yet more. I cannot imagine what cheering thing I may write to Nancy.

We sojourn in Williamsburg now for the Session, and here we remain until the turn of the year. We have pleasant rooms on Francis Street so we are off the dust of Duke of Gloucester Street and nearly into the country side. Indeed, here we have our five bright rooms and a quarters for our servants and a stable for our horses, every thing such a comfort that we rent by the year, so when we come for the Assembly we shall have a home. I come to believe my Thomas will be a Member of the Assembly all the rest of his life, which suits me well if they can cut the time to the six weeks it was before the war. Six weeks in the city in spring and fall and with it a gay round of dinners and balls makes of politics but a gay diversion and little inconvenience.

My Patsy sits beside me with her book. I must and again interrupt myself to say a word that she cannot read, and soon she will stand in her great impatience and say that we must take our air. She is lonely here without her Sally, and lonelier still for the lack of Sally is by her own command.

I would have had my Betty with me here but she spares her infant the strain of the journey, and Bett too has lately borne an infant son so she has remained behind as well. Yet I have with me Mary for my cook and Nance and Thenia for my maids, and we have with us Bob and Jim and Martin. We have very many of Betty's children, and although they are young they make a fine attendance. Fain would I have brought our Sally, too, but Patsy said to me one day that she thought it best that we not bring her Sally. "She is a slave, Mamma," Patsy said. "I must not have her for my friend."

"What? Who told you this?"

That she would not say. But of late I puzzle out that it was likely Nance who turned her mind, for Nance is resentful of her so pale sister who earns much attention from her betters. Nance demands now that Sally call us master and mistress and not address my husband as her Pappa, the which brings to him a mild relief for he knew not any better than I when the moment should be when she must learn her place.

Yet I grieve for my Patsy, for she bears her father's shyness without his friendship talent. I seek now some lady with a like-aged girl of Patsy's proper station. And I hope that when she again sees her Sally she might fall into their former friendship, for I wish for them both the same tender understanding that their so different mothers have for so long shared. We have quarreled indeed, and the space between us has seemed at times a very canyon, yet in this whole world there are but two people who know and love me to my soul and these are my husband and my Betty.

Oh, my Betty! She is far the most astonishing creature. I swear to her that her infant Lucy is a fine revenge upon poor Joe Neilson, but she says that it may be a fine revenge upon all of mankind without discrimination.

The father of Lucy is a bold young hand far younger than Martin, scarcely older than Bob, far the handsomest slave that I have ever seen, for he bears himself quite tall and erect with a fine and noble presence. This is a commonplace of Monticello slaves, that they carry a certain dignity, and this our young Charley is so greatly handsome with the bold strong look of a fine young creature as if he had been bred like a horse for his beauty, and that for many generations past. When I arrived as a new-wed bride he was but a skinny strapling child, and when I looked again he was at sixteen years and nearly as tall as my husband.

Betty saw him when I did, in the heat of the summer when she still so bitterly fought with Joe Neilson. Charley came to the kitchen with Ursula's eggs, for she makes a great commerce in selling to us. Indeed so many of our slaves sell us chickens and aught that they grow within their gardens that they soon possess all of our ready money and my husband must borrow it back again.

So Betty took Ursula's eggs from Charley with a full bold look into his face. "Who are you, boy? You cannot be Charley! Little Charley?" So she made a sport of him.

"Yes, mistress," he said with a dignity which made me believe that I must protect him. I hesitated for a fear of her temper, and then as I watched I found a tension between them far more complex than the words they said.

"Do you not know how to address your betters? You must bow!"

He bowed, but not like a gentleman with pointed toe and sweep of his hand. He bent but little from the waist, and his gaze was full upon her own. "You must curtsey, mistress."

"You dare speak to me so! Where are your manners, boy? I should take a switch to you!"

"That you may not do."

"I may if I will! You are but a hand! I may deal with you how ever I like!"

I thought he surely must look to me for he knew that I would not let her beat him. Yet he looked but at her. "That I am but a hand I cannot change. Nor may you, mistress, change what you are."

I thought this a most intelligent speech from a boy so young and so over-mastered, but it drove my Betty to a perfect fury. "Speak up for yourself! Are you not a man? Demand of them a trade! Demand freedom, you bastard, if you are a man!"

Then I must intervene, for I could not have her sow an insurrection among our slaves. "Charley, leave us now. You have other work." I very nearly pushed him out the door, for her eyes and his were so locked together that neither paid to me any least attention. "You must not suggest that he demand his freedom," I said to my Betty once he was gone.

"He is fine," she said while she took up her work but she gave another glance at the door. "Did you know our little Charley would grow to be that? Good Lord in heaven! Charley?"

I thought no more of it, but scarce a week later we heard a commotion upon Mulberry Row while we made ourselves ready for our bed. We seldom have fighting, for Great George forbids it and that far better than any white overseer. He out-ranks every slave but Betty's family, so when for more minutes the shouts continued we knew they must be among the Hemingses or among the white workmen who like their rum.

Betty was standing at her cottage door berating poor Joe Neilson. We could not see her, but close by our window we heard her very well. And I seemed to know before I heard what she said that Joe had come hopeful to her cottage door and found her there perhaps in her bed with our surprising Charley. We caught few of her words in the summer night, for there were other sounds and the wind blew against her. But she did say, "He is worth ten of you!" and "I purge myself of all white men!" and things far more alarming.

"Is it Betty? Is she mad?"

"She has taken up with Charley. Do you recollect our little Charley?"

"Oh, give us peace!" my Thomas said and he closed the window.

For some weeks thereafter my Betty could not forbear from tormenting poor Joe Neilson. Charley was so love-struck by her attention that he followed her where ever she went, and she for her part claimed his work for the garden that she might have his constant presence. My Betty is some past forty now for I am lately turned twenty-nine, and that she threw him over for a young slave-boy was for Neilson such an indignity that he never has recovered to this day. He keeps himself apart, poor sorry man, and he drinks such a quantity of rum that my Thomas must reprimand him for it.

My Betty yet carried on with her Charley when we left for Williamsburg in that fall. This tormented her sons, and especially Martin, who keeps himself well aloof from the hands for he swears that they are stupid and they are not clean. Her older daughters envied her and her younger daughters tittered, and through it all my Betty passed serene. She would have her Charley, and they were her children so they must bear her whims how ever they might. We came from Williamsburg into December and found that Betty had left off with Charley and she lived quite alone with her youngest babes. "I am quit of men," she said to me although I did not ask a question. "If you show them a kindness they resolve to possess you. Ever they are naught but pomp and show. Mistress, if I may find one advantage of my condition over your own it is that I need not suffer a man. So I shall make the most of it."

MONTICELLO FEBRUARY 1, 1778

*I*s there a God? Here is a question so vexing it were better indeed not to ask it at all, for it cannot be proven of a certainty and to posit an answer in the negative must make of life but a monstrous terror and of death a black horror of an ultimate ending. Yet never to ask it is to carry through life as heedless as a beef within its stall, for without a subtle doubt there can never be either virtue or joy in any devout belief.

I have lived my life always greatly glad that I am born a lady, so I need not think upon troubling things but I may leave their contemplation to gentlemen. When ever smallest doubt arose that we might be praying unto empty air I could look at so many so solemn male faces and know that if they prayed then must God exist. Yet as I grow older I come to fear less, and I see now with an eye made clear that gentlemen do not always think with perfection. Only look upon the present war, or look indeed upon any war and see the bitter fruit of errant minds made bitterer still by their arrogance which lets them not admit of any mistake. Indeed, gentlemen err. No longer can I trust in their wisdom from my soul, which doubt most greatly troubles me.

Our dear Reverend Clay has within the past year altered our St. Anne's to Calvinistical Reformed, so we worship now in a manner far plainer which my dear husband likes very well. I like it not, and I find that my aversion to it comes from this most singular doubt, that if men might choose to so alter their worship then might they but invent the Deity worshiped and alter Him as well to suit their changed taste. I find this possibility greatly distressing. We are late come from Williamsburg so this is our first Sunday within our own parish, and the altered worship from Bruton Parish has caused me such alarmed agitation that my husband has reminded me of my journal and begged that I write my worries here.

My dear one has not a doubt of God, for he long since has reasoned the matter through and he finds the Creator just a certain necessity evident to him in the fact of Creation. He likes well the teachings of Jesus Christ and he models his life by their perfect light, and with this his certain awareness of God and this his Christian doctrine he finds a most tranquil religious contentment. He cannot fathom my agitation. Indeed, he enjoys the profusion of sects which follows his late change in the law, for Virginia no longer supports Episcopalian clergy nor makes of other preaching a very crime. Now all may preach who would like to preach and each looks for payment to his own parishioners, as if religion were but another good to be bought in a shop of one's own choosing. My Thomas so loves the profusion of sects that he gives to all that beg of him, and this with a delight that he thus contributes to the freeing of every human mind.

"All minds are different," he says when I make sport of him that he gives his alms even to support a Popish priest. "Each must approach his Creator in the way that his mind and his conscience make plain to him. If some cannot find God but through a Pope, I am glad they find a way to God at all."

"But what does God want? How can the versions of God be as different as if men had conjured Him within their minds?"

"Read your Gospels, Patty. There is the plainest view of God that ever you will find. If He has a preference, that must be His preference."

"Then must we all worship Him as He prefers!"

My husband is impatient with all my insistence, for he finds a pleasure in so many sects and the proof they bring to him that every mind must indeed be as different as every face. He likes even the religions of the Indian and the Jew, who have not a thought for Jesus Christ. But I cannot share my husband's contentment. God, if He truly be a God, must prefer one particular mode of worship, and any lack of care makes a great suspicion that He may not even exist at all.

I think much of late upon my dear Pappa. He was for all his life a professed Christian, but he held a fond humorous view of religion as if mankind were but a sport of God to alleviate His eternal boredom. He liked to read religious books to find the humor in them, and of these far his favorite was St. Augustine's *Confessions* wherein he found the spectacle of a man impaled by God as a fly is stuck upon a pin. He would read it and smile and laugh aloud as the saint made his ineffectual struggles, and this so greatly alarmed and appalled me that never I have read it to this day. Yet I have my Pappa's book. I took it from his chamber when I entered it very soon after his death, and I keep it here with my store of books upon female sciences and my myths and my *Iliad* and *Odyssey* translations and all my such books that my husband likes not so I keep them separate from his own.

Oh, my dear dear journal. But the writing of my doubts has comforted me of the worst of them, so I still must fear the lack of a God but I find in that possibility less distress. My husband does most completely believe and his mind is of the greatest honesty, so only my knowledge of his certain belief nearly tips the balance within my own.

Now the war carries on like an endless sickness. I cannot recall the way we lived before, but I think of our life before the war when we had not a shortage and never a fear as some lost Eden. So careless we were! I told myself I even wearied of balls. I would not stew a peach that bore a single bruise, and I spent I cannot say how many hours at the matching of gown to petticoat. Now we jig in the parlor and call it a ball and we stew up any peach that is not full black, and my hours must be spent at the reckoning of money that loses its value by day upon day and the feeding and clothing of these my slaves that they not be made to suffer. Now I have a great care to take naught as my own, but every least thing seems the greatest gift.

The armies rest now in their winter camps, the enemy in comfort at Philadelphia and our poor poor remnant of a Continental Army at Forge Valley in the Pennsylvania. There the soldiers suffer yet more than they have suffered even in the winter past, and all the food and blankets we can send to them may not be enough to preserve their lives. It is said that dear brave Mrs. Washington joins them at their winter camp, which intelligence, if true, shows a very great courage for they daily risk attack by the fiendish British.

These British have most cruelly dealt with Patriots who remained in the Pennsylvania. Tales now current I shall not record for I cannot bear to preserve them, but if half of what is said is true of the British and their terrible Hessian servants then heaven preserve us if ever we are so bereft of luck as to suffer them here. And they yet use the Indians! This must be far the greatest of their so heinous crimes, that they stir up the savages and send them down to murder the helpless planter families who brave the western wilderness and live too scattered for effective defense. My husband and the Governor and his Council have become so alarmed by this border raiding that they have commissioned Colonel George Rogers Clark to try to subdue the Illinois country.

Here is a very devious trick. They dare not say a public word for fear of alerting the enemy, so my own dear husband and the Governor's Council alone know the extent of all they plan. It is said that Colonel Clark will take his militias west to protect the Kentucky, but far beyond that he intends to venture north and west to the Illinois to clear away out of our whole north west both enemy and hostile savage alike and preserve to us nearly all of the continent clear to the distant Ohio River. He may take Detroit, which fort has become a center of the terrible British evil. There greatly monstrous General Hamilton buys from the savages bloody scalps which were cut from the heads of women and children dreadfully murdered in their beds. Oh may brave Colonel Clark succeed! I cannot sleep for thought of the mothers huddled in terror in their beds and kissing the dear small heads of their children while savages chop away the door.

Colonel Clark I must describe, although words written out cannot convey his bright alarming presence. He is a man still in his infant twenties and possessed of the same great energy which made my husband so charming to me when he was like of age. He moves with agitation and readily laughs as if his laughter were smoke from some fire of joy which he banks, but it burns in spite of himself. He is manifestly appealing and manifestly wearying. I jest with my Thomas that he is a man very like a human nutmeg, for a little of him well flavors the evening but too much of him is far too much.

Yet my Thomas cannot have enough of him for evening after evening. Colonel Clark is come from Albemarle and he is a great reader and his hair is red, but these similarities cannot but hint of the friendship which rapidly grows between them. Colonel Clark must dine with us every evening while we were in the Capital, and this was well enough when there were other guests but time unto time there were no other guests and Colonel Clark alone came to dine with us until it seemed I nearly had a second husband. We dined, and when was removed the cloth they talked long together over wine. "Might you reach Detroit?" my Thomas said, so I heard him as I played my music. "Think you it really is possible? Oh, devoutly would I join with you!"

When first I heard him say the like I found it most alarming, but certainly as I knew my husband I knew that he never would be a soldier. It was the thought of the wild country that he loved, the seeing what never has yet been seen. So they talked together unto candle-ends while I played to calm their minds my ancient spinet which still I prefer to my forte-piano, although I would never tell my husband so. My spinet has a delicate sound so you hear not the instrument shouting forth but you hear instead the music.

"We must have it all!" my Thomas said when after long delay we might take to our chamber. The spice of Colonel Clark so clung to his mind that I nearly smelled nutmeg in the room. "We cannot let the Spanish or the British have it. We must claim the continent to the farthest coast. We must have Canada! We must take the Floridas! Once we fix our borders it will be too late!"

So he talked on even while abed, well fired by his vision of our confederacy full-grown until it is a continent wide. Yet to conquer so much against the might of Spain, which holds the Louisiana and holds the Floridas and even holds fast to the farthest coast is beyond what can be done, when Spain is France's ally and we beg most earnestly for help from France. Without France we might not win our war, but we might be worn down until the British prevail of our very weariness. I must find a way to calm my husband's mind that he might relax to sleep. I said, "But we scarcely can hold a confederacy of our thirteen so small colonies. Think you, Thomas, of the manifold troubles of holding a country many times this size."

"It must be done! Why can you not see it, Patty? Here we cling to the continent's edge. We cannot suffer foreign powers to hold the land to our rear and flanks, for then we never shall be safe. We shall fight this war for evermore."

He says this with a perfect eagerness for his vision of the continent all united, while I sink alarmed beneath my blanket until it is fast above my head. I have fixed all my hopes upon the war's rapid ending, and now he says that there may be no ending. Yet we must have an ending, and that very soon, for I am become with child again.

This intelligence I yet keep from my husband for fear of his great distress for me. He thinks he has found the most perfect solution, that when we come together as a husband and wife we avoid the act which might create our child, or if we wish the act that we have a care to end it before any certain emission. In this I perfectly yield to him, for when he is intent upon the act I am often-times able to distract him enough that the act is complete and the dear small homunculus well sent upon its internal journey. But a month or two, and I am with child. I have not the heart to tell him so.

And since he must not know, I must guard my health that it not betray my secret. I have bought in Williamsburg some Jesuit's bark which is a sovereign cure for the intermittent fever, for since my fevers come intermittently it may be that the bark with my draught of Gabbler's may keep me very well. I have lost my old fear of a rival mistress in my certain awareness of Thomas's love, but as I lose my old fear I find beneath it an ever fiercer craving to bear him a son. Oh my Thomas, if I may but give you a son to carry your name on after you then aught may befall me as it may. I ask no more of my life than that.

MONTICELLO JUNE 19, 1778

*B*ut a few weeks more and I shall bring another living child. My Betty will not assure me that it is a male but I feel very certain that it is a male, and if it is not then it is a girl and strong indeed from the feel of it. I must keep my mind most perfectly calm, that God may deem me worthy of a living child. I grieve to my soul for my so dear children who are gone forever from out of my arms, yet I must not grieve. Grief pollutes the blood and weakens every bodily humor, and it may be that my very grief has cost me the lives of my little sons. So I will not grieve. I but offer up my four dead children torn from my arms, that God may have a pity for me now and grant to me a living son.

I had further sworn away kidney-fevers, my mind the master of my body, but all such resolutions could only delay these pains of my back which put me fast abed. My fevers are mild, and my strangury has come but twice only very mild, yet my husband is frantic for my health. He swears that his resolve is decided and never we shall ever risk another child, and I oppose him not, for if I carry a male I may well make my peace with his wish. If I carry not a male, I shall better turn his mind if I have a care not to harden it now. So I lie obedient upon my bed on a day so hot that my only cover is two lengths of our homespun cotton sewn by my Bett to cover my legs. My child makes a perfect slanted table if I have a care not to take so much ink that it runs upon the page. If I survive my lying-in, yet I may not survive my husband's anxious frenzy of a love for me.

Thomas took willingly my every excuse very near until we left for the Assembly in April, that I had random fevers, that I but gained of weight, that ladies often grow broader of waist as they near the age of thirty. I wore my stays tight to keep the child within and let him not see my body clear, but his hands gave him awareness that his eyes were denied. Soon before we left he insisted to me that I must certainly be with child, and that I could not well deny. My confession so alarmed him that he nearly kept himself from attending the Assembly session, which he must not do, for the law requires that the Members attend upon pain of arrest.

"I cannot leave you now! And we cannot take the risk that the journey might deliver your child! Why did you not tell me? How could you imagine that I would never know?"

"But I am well, Thomas. I truly am well. We might make the journey slowly."

In the end we went as ever we travel, with Patsy and Suck and Bett in my chariot and Jupiter driving and Jim riding postilion and Thomas in his phaeton and Martin and Bob riding one before and one behind. We went along slowly at always a walk that Jim might find the best track of the road, and we paused at the Forest for near to a week that I might recover from a bladder-fever. We did again the like upon our return, the horses at a walk, the stay with Betsy. Indeed, I survived the journey well. But my kidneys came to pain me on the homeward leg and there came soon after a more violent fever, so now here I lie upon a kidney-poultice and here says my Thomas I shall remain.

It was well that I was with him in Williamsburg. His fellows have used him very ill. They put him up for Speaker of the House, and this when he was reluctant and shy but he would have been the Speaker for his country's good and he would have been the finest ever seen. They put him up, and then they chose the vile Mr. Harrison in his room, and that by a rout of double his votes so he must be shamed indeed. Why do they so little apprehend a man so completely and so perfectly good? A few shamed him very greatly more by saying he must accept the people's will and he must put a gay face upon his loss and take it like a gentleman.

That he is. But he is ever so gentle a man, and his work for his country is a burden to him, yet he gives to it all of his blood and his bone for it merits nothing less. To be thus rejected when he likes not to serve but he stays in the service for his country's good is a rejection of his very inmost self, that he has given all he can and been judged not worthy. Oh greatly do I wish he would cast it aside and not serve his country ever more, for he has done his share and far more than his share. If his country cannot give him its gratitude then that should be only his country's loss.

I had no words to give him when he came at dinner-time of a bright spring day and said that Mr. Harrison had been chosen. I could not show him my anger and shame; I could not shout that all the Members are fools; no emotion of mine was of the least value and naught could I say to comfort him.

He said, "It may be for the best. None should serve in a government post beyond a few years' time, for the power of it is very corrupting. If I were made the Speaker of the House I might very well be corrupted, too."

"That you never would do!" died within my throat. At last I said, "It is a blessing, Thomas. You love the creation of a government but the running of it would only bore you."

Yet still I can see his very great hurt that he has been judged and deemed not worthy. His rejection for the Speaker has made him now but turn to his law-making all the more that he might the more perfectly serve his country. This rises in me a most unseemly anger. He is ever so faithful and good to his country, while she is so faithless and cruel to him.

He labors ardently the summer long to write a statute of the criminal laws. He works in his library in our middle-building, where now are removed his shelves of books so we must spend every day apart. I had thought we would remove as some grand event, but in truth our removal into our house has carried on for the past six years. We shall have our own chamber before the winter. What should have been the first has become the last.

My Thomas sits with me in the afternoons and reads of his Bracton and makes his notes, or he tries against my mind some thought of his of how might be punished a crime of assault or stealing or some such other crime which is far beyond any thought of mine. "What think you of adultery, Patty? Does that not seem but a private vice?"

"I think if you punish every man for adultery you soon will have naught but women left."

He burns with a very zealous fire for his revision of the criminal laws, to make all consistent and more humane and to lessen the sanguinary punishments. He has written a statute for religious freedom and further many statutes for freeing the lands and establishing schools and every thing, and now he plans for the freeing of slaves and he thinks and writes on the politics as if all must be perfected this day and naught may be left beyond Saturday week. "This is the certain moment," he says when I complain of his work at the height of the summer. "While we have our common enemy we must form our government and free our slaves, for when the war is over every man will return to only his own private cares. This is the moment! We must cut every chain, for any that stay will remain with us long. We have but one moment to set all to right. I cannot waste this summer."

My Thomas begins now to free our slaves. If naught ever comes of the war but this, then the blood and the pain of it are very well spent. He has set the steps unto an abolition very firm and clear within his mind, and the first must be an end to the trade which brings new victims every year. He has worked for beyond a year gone by to end this importation of Negro slaves by the drafting of a bill and the patient talk with Assembly delegates out of doors where persuasions can be made and never is any one forced to the hardening of his mind. Many come to see the sense of it. My Thomas now does truly believe that soon we shall see an end to the trade. And I have embarked upon the second step, which is the education of the youngest slaves, although I am found to be so inept at it that never should I ever have tried at all.

When came we from Williamsburg in the winter I thought to make a school for Patsy and add to it slave children like of age that they might be taught to read. Happy thought! It came to me all in a moment. I shall teach my slaves to read! My Thomas was pleased by my sudden notion, and more pleased the more he thought of it. He is troubled by a worry that their minds might be in subtle ways deficient, and this what he calls my experiment might put his worries to their rest.

Yet it came to be a difficult thing, for I must have students for my school and when I set out to gather my students their mothers were afraid to yield them up. Try to fathom the mind of a mother who looks with terror when you say that you would take her child the morning long and teach it how to read. They could not refuse me any thing, but I could not bear their fearful looks that I might take their children and return them changed or return them not at all. "Yes, mistress. Thank you, mistress," they said to me while they held their babies desperate close. After I had made one turn of the quarters upon a Saturday afternoon and seen the word pass ahead of me so mothers pulled their children from the street, I came away chastened and went in the evening and brought with me Betty and her little Sally. Here was a slave-mother very eager to send her child to school.

Well, she was almost eager. Betty cannot read, but I know full well she has the wit to read. She has wit enough to look at my gift and see the risks within it. "You must not begin what you cannot finish," she said to me as we walked to the quarters. "For your sake and theirs, you must not awaken what might be better left to sleep."

Here was a strange speech from my Betty. I would have thought her my ardent advocate that I teach and free them every one, so to hear her say that their minds should sleep was a shock which gave me a great amazement. Has she changed her wish for freedom? Oh, what can be the thoughts within my Betty's mind? But I could not make inquiry into her thoughts for a fear she would answer me very well and with fierce proud look she would say out things which would show me to be a fool that I had never seen them. I have learned not ever to question my Betty, and we never speak now of slavery. But only the fear that she might turn upon me and say out things which would show me the fool made me say, "But indeed we shall free them, Betty! We do intend to free the children!"

"Do not promise them freedom. Promise only that further skills will make them better slaves. Tell the mothers their very cleverest children will learn trades or maybe earn a house-servant's place. Do not promise freedom. They never will believe you if you promise them that."

The sight of Betty's Sally was no comfort to them, for her face and straight hair and Patsy's outgrown dress made her look to them to be nearly white. But my Betty they all love and respect, and her patient talk did persuade four mothers to venture for their children an education. With Betty's Sally and Peter, four and seven, and with Mary's Danny who is nearly six I had seven slaves to join with my Patsy and sit in their circle at my kitchen chair and learn there how to read. Thus we carried on for a week before my Patsy must be banished from the circle. She begins to read words passing well while the slaves just begin to learn their letters, and this great difference must shame the slaves and make my Patsy proud. To prove to the slaves that they are stupid is to settle my experiment before it is tried, so although I had begun my school for Patsy I soon must banish her to my chamber to sit and read while Nance must sew and fetch me up when Patsy has a need of me.

Once Patsy was gone, my dear little students began very tenderly to take their lesson as if I had commanded that they learn so learning had become their grievous work. Each looked to the others, yet none would make bold to correct the mistake of another child so all agreed upon an alphabet which was said out different every time. One there was, Hanah, a child of eight, who always said it perfectly, yet she never would correct another child and all of my urging but frightened her. "I will give you a book, Hanah," once I said, "if you will correct our Danny's mistakes. I will give you this book of poetry."

I showed her the book which fell beneath my hand and said the last word once I saw what it was, an *Othello,* far the least suitable book which ever can be thought of for a child. But Hanah hungered for the book and she made bold twice to correct our Danny, and this was so greatly painful for her that although Mary's son still said it wrong I gave her the book and greatly praised her. But never on another morning no matter what inducement I offered her could I make our Hanah say aught again to correct the mistake of another child.

I also taught them numbers, and this went better for some had learned numbers in the quarters. But numbers beyond twenty and the adding of them brought again that agreement with each child's error, so the sums were different every time and they could not learn at all.

We carried on in this wise for two months' time, until our journey to Williamsburg intervened. By my very great effort and holding my tears I made most to learn the alphabet. Most learned numbers to fifty, and some learned more. Yet while I taught them I also taught my Patsy, and the slaves were so much slower to learn that their dullness was alarming to me. What ever could I tell my Thomas? I dared not say to him any thing beyond, "They learn very well, dear Husband. You surely will be greatly surprised." If ever my Thomas believes them stupid he may lose his faith that they can be free. Foolish lady! Such a fool I was to try to teach them any thing. I am a sorry teacher. Now my clumsy failure might tip the balance against their freedom. How much I repent! I am spared now by my illness and my lying-in, but my husband expects that in the fall I shall return to my teaching of the slaves and give to him a group he can show as proof that they are able to be free.

MONTICELLO JULY 17, 1778

*W*hy may a person not decline to be a part of history? Mankind is so given to committing follies with his history that it seems but just that there should be a way that we might plain decline it. "No, thank you, sir," we might but say, and the triumphs and the pains would carry on without us. I would not even wish to know. I have no ambition but to live my life.

So the people of the Wyoming Valley would gladly have opted to live their lives. Yet they had not the choice; all the whole great valley have been murdered in the greatest agony of pain. We hear the stories yet worse each day, and even in my bed I am forced to hear, for ever when servants go down to the town they bring back tales ever yet more dreadful. These they are in such a panic to tell that their stories float in with every breeze. The Wyoming Valley is greatly disputed by Connecticut and Pennsylvania, which states have sent many innocent planters to claim its land for either side. Thus they have lived in great contention for a matter so small as the bound of a state, and then in a moment came down Tories and Indians to murder those innocent planter families. They have burned them alive so they might dance by the light. They have chased them unclad through beds of coals and roasted the children upon their spits or cut them to pieces while they yet lived and those who loved them must hear their cries.

There are told so many such desperate tales that I have no heart to write them all. Two families lived close the one to another but far from any pretense of a town, and these were taken to an Indian camp and the women and girls even down to infants were raped by the Tories before their men. At length these greatly dishonored females were shut up in an Indian hut and the Indians made sport the whole night through at the torture unto death of all the men. Every male to an infant of not yet two was murdered in the greatest agony, and their poor bereft wives and daughters and mothers must lie through the night and hear their cries. But one survived. One woman escaped to tell this tale, and she left at the camp her two young daughters for a fear that no one would learn the fate of her family and the treachery of the fiendish Tories. But consider that. She must abandon her children lest their torture and death go unavenged. I can write no more. It seems that I can better bear the murder of very many than I can support the thought of that desperate mother as she gave to her children their last farewell.

MONTICELLO SEPTEMBER 4, 1778

*M*y child is a girl. I have taken a month to write those words, and there in the writing is so much pain that I must write on yet more. She is a very pretty child, as pretty indeed as was my little

Janey. I rock her cradle with my foot while I sit to write within our chamber, and there she so sweetly mews and smiles and yawns and makes her ineffectual fists, quite unaware that she is a girl. I have not the heart to tell her so. We have named her Mary for Thomas's sister Bolling and for a fancy we have of the name and because it sounds well with Martha's name, to make of them a pair of Biblical sisters.

We have removed to our chamber. Oh, blessed house! We have slept here but these three nights past, for it was only then that Thomas pronounced me well enough to remove across the lawn and up the steps and fast into bed. Even now he would like it not to know that I am sitting out of bed, but he sees to his crops. Great rains in the summer and now the predations of the Hessian fly have ravaged the grain as it stands in the fields so we might not have a crop at all. I like well our house. It is very plain for we have not yet the Palladian orders nor paint and plaster every where, and the windows are unpainted and the stairs so rough that they catch at my gown when I ascend. But here I sit in a great plain room with the windows open so blows through a breeze that brings up the scent of the wood and the plaster as sweet as if the house were newly born. My Thomas likes very well our house, for his library is but a door away. I may sleep, and he be able to work and hear any sound that I might make.

I lately have been most grievous sick. I still am not yet perfectly well. It came on me a fortnight before we thought was the time I might deliver my child, and so greatly fevered did I become that the child was delivered before its time. I fought my pains for fear of the memory of my Sweet who was born too small to live, but my Mary came big as a full-term child and she cried out strong and hearty. While Granny Gaines drew her from my body and Betty and Bett supported me, I could see very well by the light of the candle that she was born a girl.

"A girl!" I said from out of my pain, not knowing even that I made the cry, but my so dear husband waited below and the tone of my voice panicked him. He came up the stairs while they yet cut the cord and Betty made haste to clean the babe, which was far the strangest thing I have ever seen. Never may a husband see a baby's birth.

"It is all right, Patty!" He sat on the bed and leant to have me safe in his arms, all sweating as I was and still in labor for the after-birth had not yet come.

"A girl, Thomas."

"It matters not. Oh my dear, it matters not at all and you must never have another child!"

The pain came fierce to rid the after-birth. Many ladies cannot bear this childbirth pain, so when the birth of the baby has nearly come they are stood and bled out from the arm until they faint away. They come to their senses blessed slow to find themselves delivered, and this by some is thought a wondrous thing. I cannot think it so. If this is pain, it is my very own pain and it is my own dear blessed child and I will see it born if any see it born. Yet I would not have my husband know my pain, so while he was below us in the kitchen I had held my cries the whole night through when ever pain must come. It was then beyond midnight and very black and I was weary unto sleep, but one thing more I was bound to do and I could not have him see it.

"You must go, Thomas. This is not fit." Then came a spasm to cut my words and throw my head on the pillow.

"Patty!" my Thomas said frantically. Perhaps he thought I was meant to die.

"Come out of here for the love of God!" said my fearless Betty to her master. She took him by his shoulders and drew him up, very slim and small beside the height of him, but her hands on his shoulders were very firm. She coddled him as ever she had coddled my Pappa. "I shall make you a toddy. Come down the stairs. Would you not like a toddy to help you sleep? She is fine, I do assure you. Right down the stairs, master. There you go. Would you not like some honey and toast?" She later said she made him a toddy and toast and she sat with him while he ate his food, then she brought a pallet for the kitchen floor and laid him there to sleep.

I thought my husband's visit but a small event, a dream-product of so long a night, but the fright of his seeing me in helpless pain has firmed his very most certain resolve. He will have no more children. I beg that he wait and we not discuss it until I am entirely well, but he refuses to wait for a fear that I might find a way to put aside his decision. "We will not have more children, Patty! We will not discuss it ever again! I had rather have my wife than a hundred sons! Come to sense now! We shall leave it off!"

So I may not speak. I must look to my health and make myself again perfectly well so when the night comes to conceive our son my husband will be glad of it.

My so dear husband still must labor to write his laws this

summer long. We have had few guests for the state of my health, but Betsy and Nancy were here in June, and the Bollings, and the Carters came up from Blenheim, and the Mazzeis and such-like friends and kin came and went enough for a happy commerce so we thought ourselves not bereft of friends. I could not bear to wear my stays for the heat of the season and my growing child and for the frequent pains of my back which the wearing of stays could but increase. My dear dead mother had an ancient bedgown not of cotton but fashioned of the finest silk, and jumps of black velvet and a fair loose gown of dark green satin trimmed in lace. These she ever wore when she neared her confinement, yet I in my pride long forebore to wear them. Then the summer past I cast pride to the wind and I wore her silk bedgown the summer long, and thus attired in the greatest comfort I shared pleasant dinners with our so few guests, who swore me so becomingly arrayed that bedgowns will surely be the newest fashion.

Indeed, for all that he is glad of guests my husband liked the lack of them, for he labored at the laws and when he tired of that he could labor at our gardens and at our house and play at his scientifical pursuits which are for him the greatest sport. We had in June an eclipse of the sun which thrilled him for the chance to measure it, for all that it was clouded over and his watch not answerable to the task. He measures the air-temperature twice each day, once upon rising and once before dinner, and he daily makes notes of rains and winds and aught that we might see of weather.

Now he plans in good earnest for our splendid Seat with its gardens and orchards and lawns to come and a deer-park he buys now fawns to fill. He has been so much away and our house has been so long abuilding that to have it up and the gardens to lay and all the refinements now to provide is a thrill as if it has become his toy and he is a child for evermore. He even thinks to make an orchestra. Here must I laugh! We have very many workmen about so he thinks now to bring from Italy where music is the country's whole life's blood some workmen who play at clarinets and bassoons and such-like instruments. Oh, my husband! Thus does he rise in his mind so his cares can never trouble him. No event so trivial as a civil war can cast him down for long.

For we still are at war. I do believe that we shall be at this war for evermore. The British army has left Philadelphia, which gay intelligence gladdens our hearts, but they have fought but little this summer long beyond a battle at Monmouth in the Jerseys. Our Captain Paul Jones raids the English shore, which exploits do greatly astonish us, and Colonel Clark enters the far north west and meets there some success. But it matters so little! All events that seem hopeful ever turn again to have no effect. The armies but move of a grim broad dance and capture one city and leave another, and naught has been changed for good or ill but still more blood is spilt. My husband has made a calculation that from Lexington and Bunker's Hill until Saratoga the enemy has lost ten thousand prisoners and nine thousand killed and eleven wounded, full thirty thousand casualties of this war which he thinks they certainly cannot sustain so soon they must retreat. I cannot share his belief. The British expect to win, and if they suffer losses they will fight the more. Indeed, to see all that they have suffered only makes me more fearful of how they will treat us if in the end despite all our struggles they should yet prevail.

The French have signed treaties in the spring which briefly made us think our war was won, for we had prayed for treaties these two years past until it seemed just the signing of those treaties would surely be enough to win our peace. That it has not done. We wait for word that Britain has entered a war with France, but it does not come and we conceive a fear that Germany and Prussia might enter a war and thus divert France from her attentions to us if she sides with one of them. Oh, the fortunes of nations make my head to ache. I cannot think of them. The greatest effect of our French alliance is their sending of merchantmen to trade for tobacco, and the price of tobacco does come to rise but every other price has risen yet higher so we must be poorer than we ever have been.

A chicken has come to cost a whole shilling! Once our Bob tried to sell for a shilling a chicken he had bought for half a bit, and the very great humor of such a price I had made a jest against him. Now I jest no more, but the jest has turned and gone in his direction. When he comes in the morning to build our fire, if he finds himself in a merry mood he will say the like of, "Will you have your boots, master? And would mistress like a chicken?"

So my husband laughs and even I laugh and Bob but wears a sly droll face which makes us laugh the more.

MONTICELLO NOVEMBER 28, 1778

*M*y husband is arrested for his nonattendance. Two trusty servants of the Sergeant-at-Arms have arrived this day at our own house-door and given his note which demands that my husband attend the Assembly as his prisoner.

"I shall go," said my dear so blessed Thomas. "Of course I shall go. I shall be right along," he said while he held me in his arms, for I stared and wept to see them appear there bent upon taking my husband away. "It is all right. It is all right," he said to me patiently. "Patty? Be assured they will do me no harm."

This I knew upon some surface level, but deep and much stronger was my desperate fear. I have held for every day of my marriage a terror that my husband will be arrested and tried most cruelly and drawn and quartered, for all that he fights for our liberty. I have seen his head upon a pike on many a desperately worried night, and there was that pike before me now.

"Will you be so kind as to give me a moment to comfort my wife? I shall send my boy to pack my box. I shall be with you directly."

The pair of servants stepped down the gallery to where our Caesar held their horses. Behind them, Betty closed the door to shut them fast away.

"Why does he do this? What have you done?"

My Thomas bade me sit on a parlor chair and he sat down there beside me. "Dear Patty, please listen. You must stop weeping. Please listen to me." Then he called to my Betty as she passed our chairs that she must send her Jim out to harness his horses and send her Bob to pack his box.

"Will he put you in a prison? May I not go with you? Oh, Thomas! What ever will become of us now?" So I said on foolishly while he held my hands and wiped my face of tears. His gaze upon me was so warm and kind that a surge of my love made me weep yet more.

"The Assembly has been sitting for these six weeks. You know

Mr. Eppes has warned me, Patty, and I wrote to promise I would certainly attend before the end of this month. He has done me the favor of waiting until now and he only holds me to my promise."

"But he will arrest you!"

"Just until I have paid my fine. Please, my dear. I cannot bear your tears." He smiled at me most tenderly. Just the memory of his so gentle smile clamps my throat tight in a painful spasm.

"Leave off with your country! She uses you ill!"

"But a little while longer and I shall leave off. Please, my dear. They must have a quorum of members or they cannot conduct their business. Will you smile? Come and smile. If they meant me harm I would be out the door and carry you away. You know that, Patty. Will you smile for me, please? I cannot keep the memory of such a face!"

He held my eyes until I nearly smiled. To prevent it I must look fast away. "Virginia uses you very ill, Thomas. She does not deserve you. In truth she does not."

"It is my fault," he said with a sigh as he stood and lifted me to my feet. He must change his clothes, for he wore leathern breeches and an old shirt and waistcoat meant for work, and he wore with them old stained cotton stockings which no one beyond the family must see.

"I wanted to work on the criminal laws, and here I have my books. But I meant to attend before mid-November. I certainly should have been away before now." So he said while we went out the parlor door. There is beneath our chamber a drawing-room which Thomas had meant to be our chamber, but my sickness and his need for his library have kept us to sleep in the attic-room. So it is that we must climb the stairs, although Thomas had sworn when we left our cabin that never would he ever climb stairs again to sleep within his bed.

I would not let Bob dress my husband, but that I must do to his small-clothes and shoes and I washed him myself, from his head to his feet, although he said it made him feel like a witless child. He bore my ministrations with a patient grace, well knowing that in dressing him I comforted myself. I was not prepared to see him go, for there could be no thought of my going with him. My Mary, who gains the name of Polly, is nursed by three women in their turn. Betty and Ursula are at the end of their nursing and my own milk is meager as ever it is, but with the three she has enough.

"Must you shave me, too? Might Bob do at least that?"

"I shall shave you." This I did then try to do with a towel to protect his shirt and stock, but his fear and my determination soon had us breaking into fits of laughter.

"Leave the nose!" he said. "Take the chin! Leave the nose! I can live without a chin!"

By the time he was dressed we were nearly merry, and merry all the more to hide the dread that we must endure so many weeks apart. He will not return until the Assembly rises, and this not until the end of December. But all such terrors we must put away as he stepped out onto the portico between the pillars cut by Billy Rice. Then Jim brought up his phaeton. There was to that moment a fine appearance, the gentleman tall between the pillars and the two servants standing by their horses. I stepped to the servants and politely said, "I thank you very much indeed that you do my husband such an honor." This I said by way of encouraging them to treat my husband very well and by way of shaming them for stealing away such a good and noble gentleman. My Thomas stayed for me, since I was not well. They should be much ashamed.

Ashamed they may be, but now I must suffer emotions even more wretched than shame. I sit to watch the sun set beyond Mont Alto and I see the pink light upon the page and think how only the evening gone by we walked together in our garden where we found the season so blessedly mild that lettuce yet grew in a sheltered spot and we wished we had sown some latter peas so we might have peas at table now. Such gentle talk between a husband and wife we so take for granted that we remark it not, but oh, I would give many years of my life if I could have that conversation with him now!

He must leave the politics. This is no way that we can live our lives. Word has come that in the month gone by the Assembly have enacted his law to ban the importation of Negro slaves, so Virginia has become the first state upon earth to ban the importation of slaves. From here he might work to free them further. He need not remain in the Assembly. I shall swear it is corrupting him. I know not what ever I shall say, but he is not meant for the Government. He does say himself that the finest of minds must be spared for scientifical study, for wrong it would be if a Newton were wasted upon the mere creation of laws. But he is greater than a Newton! He has no peer! Who would care to know the height of a mountain? Yet he has bought a theodolite in the summer past for the making of his geographical measures, and he sights from the roof to know the size of the mountains and nearly to measure the size of the sky. Oh, he is not meant for the Government. That he wastes his mind on its Government is far his greatest sacrifice for his country.

MONTICELLO JANUARY 22, 1779

*T*oday have I seen a thing quite amazing. An enemy army is within Virginia! We have built a Barracks upon a hill at Ivy Creek near Charlottesville, and there we have installed near four thousand soldiers who were taken with Burgoyne at Saratoga. Only knowing they would be coming here has made me distressed this winter long, to have an enemy here in our country and we not able to defend ourselves. "But can you not refuse them?" I said to my Thomas ever and again upon many a night. "If the Colonel refuses them from Albemarle, they cannot be forced upon us here."

But my Thomas was delighted to have them here. This I could most plainly see. He said it is little enough to do when the Continent asks this service of us, and they are harmless withal for they have not weapons and they wait for hope that they will be exchanged and even despite our loss of the harvest we can feed them and they are not a burden. So he said on and on with an eagerness that made me know he is delighted to have them. He seeks the acquaintance of his enemies with a joy that he will know their minds and know what stamp of men they are. He made many visits to their camp to help them be settled and more content and to make the acquaintance of officers. Some of these officers he likes so well that he calls upon them now to remove to Colle when Mr. Mazzei goes to Italy, and that very likely in the spring.

My husband often begged that I go with him to make the acquaintance of enemy soldiers that I might give up my fear of them. "They will not harm you, Patty! What do you think, that I would carry you if there were any risk?" So he said and again and over again, but no such honorable plea could move me. Thus it was that at length he gave me a reason that he knew would win my heart. "There are women and children there and some are not recovered from their march. They have marched seven hundred miles from Boston, and that in deepest winter. We might carry to them some blankets and meat, and I know it would cheer them to see a lady." So I must go. Indeed, the more I thought of the children the more I must pack up yet more gifts, lengths of cotton and wool and a loaf of sugar although sugar has become so very dear.

Scarce was I prepared for the enemy camp. I had a thought of soldiers in lined-by tents with their coats very red and their muskets by, all well under guard and sharp to salute and all in finest fettle. What I found instead was a hill churned with mud and clustered with the very meanest huts, the men thick about all dirty in rags which once might have been for them uniforms but now the red was turned nigh to brown and the blue was turned to gray. It was thus that the British could be told from the Hessian, for indeed very many of the soldiers were Hessians. As I rode by the fence in my cleanly chaise I saw a woman contending with the top of a tree, she struggling in her skirts beneath all the branches while three dirty men in their blue made gray were hauling with ropes upon the trunk. I looked about for Thomas that he might command that the woman be relieved, but he had ridden far ahead to direct our Jupiter in driving our wagon-load of gifts.

This gathering of gifts is a common thing we have carried on now these three years past. We have a barn near the end of the quarters which holds out gifts meant for the army. These our friends carry when they visit us or they send by a cart with a trusty slave, and with what we can gather from out of our own we often can send a wagon down with provisions for the army. But all such gifts are for the Continental Army. They are not for the enemy. When I knew that my Thomas meant to divert to the Barracks some of our so precious gifts I said, "But they cannot have the army's gifts! Not the army's gifts! That you must not do!"

He said patiently, "We have blankets now that we could not move north before the spring, and here we have people who need those blankets. A soldier without his musket is just a man and not an enemy any longer."

This I resisted until the moment when I saw that woman standing in the mud contending so stubbornly with a tree. I saw children stand and gaze at my chariot, brown with the mud but for their eyes, and cold, I was certain, for they had not gloves and only rags upon their feet. So wretched did I feel that I would have denied them any smallest comfort!

If there were in that camp four thousand of men, there may

have been the like of women and children. These my husband tells me have suffered greatly, since the British would allow but few on the ration no matter what the reality. So all these enemy women and children must forage for food along the road, yet the British ever punished any soul caught stealing and they whipped poor mothers whose only crime was their need to feed their children. I swear, I have thought that war is evil but never have I known it could be so evil.

My Thomas and I had an escort to us of our good Virginia militiamen, and but for them we would have been smothered by the eager women who pressed us close. Their men were ashamed to beg of us, but the women were not ashamed if it were for a husband or a child they begged. I heard but pieces of what they said, that one must get to England for a dying sister or another had a babe bereft of milk. So piteous they were, and yet each seemed to be a woman who had followed her husband to war and then had been captured and made to walk, and still she must every day tend her children and mend and wash and find a pot of food. That they had suffered and brought their families through it made a dignity to shine upon every face, as if they had stared down the Devil himself and naught could ever alarm them now. While my husband directed two militiamen to write down every woman's request, I gazed long upon them. I could not hate them, for women are never the enemy. Indeed, I am sure they are not glad that they have invaded our country, but they only loyally follow their men. There can be for them naught but pride in that.

I did not want to keep myself from my Polly, who now may be breeding an accursed ear-fever. She is a babe most wondrous cheerful so she laughs at every smallest thing and she seldom weeps, but if ever she weeps but to make a face at her will begin her laughter. Yet that infant whine and that rub of an ear are symptoms I have come to know well, and she showed them this morning as we readied to go. I would have stayed, but I had made a vow to my husband so I gave her into my Betty's arms. Now she sleeps here quiet in her rocking-cradle and her ears for the moment are at peace, but still I worry that she might begin this curse that tormented my Jack and my Janey.

For worry of my Polly I could not do what Thomas meant for me to do and spend some hours with the Barracks women to comfort them and learn their needs. I know him so well! He has brought me at last to cultivate an ardent Patriot feeling, but now of late he is much distressed that I come to hate the British. There within the Barracks he meant to temper my mind with a tender sympathy, but this my one sight of the woman in the mud would most completely serve to do.

"Come and see how they live, Patty. Look in one house. May we enter here? Will you show us your house?"

A woman thin and plain of face inclined her head and put aside the filthy scrap which served her for a door. She lived in a hovel eight feet wide, and that she said with five other people, with a table cut of half a log and ends of logs cut to make out chairs and naught for the smoke but a hole in the roof. By the side of such misery our slaves live well, for all have tables and wooden floors and many now even have glass for their windows and they have for their fires full wattle chimneys. If ever we kept them as these are kept I could not live for the shame of it. "Would you like more dishes?" I said out of my nervous awareness that I must say something. "Do you live here with your family?"

"No, madam. My man die at Saratoga. My girls die in Boston and on the road. Now I and my son live with four good men who share their food. I wash and cook. We make it an even bargain."

I could not bear to look at her face, so dreadful was her tale and so calm the voice in which she came to tell it. Yet what touched me most of her poor Barracks hovel was my tender awareness that it was clean. The woman had swept her earthen floor and her blankets were folded and her pot scrubbed with sand and her one platter clean upon the table. Brave woman! Even in so desperate a place she still would create her family home.

I would not see further beyond that hovel, for their misery was very painful. As we left it I said, "I shall enlist the ladies of Charlottesville. I shall term it a matter of Patriot pride that we care for our prisoners very well and the ladies all will be eager to help. You need not worry more." So I said to my husband while I made for my chariot. I felt very anxious to be away. "Leave the harnesses on!" I called to my Jupiter, who then as I spoke was beginning with Bob to hook away the traces from the whiffletrees. The horses stood to their ankles in mud and the suck of it was alarming to them. "They have rested enough," I said to Bob. "They will be very glad to be quit of this place. We shall go on slowly. Will you come with me, Thomas?"

My husband well knew that my alarm of that place was fully as great as my need for my Polly. Yet one more thing he meant me to see, for he yearned to perfect my compassion for them that I never would hate our enemy more. "I must visit the wounded. Do come with me, Patty. In but another moment we shall take our leave."

So I gathered my cardinal with a patient sigh and turned to where my husband made gesture of his hand at a hut some larger than the others. We walked with care from height to height to overstep the ruts where black water stood so a freeze might have been a surprising blessing. My Thomas had warned me to wear an old gown and clogs upon shoes which were already stained, but the filth was as if it hung in the air and it clung to every surface. The smell was of rot and of standing water and many such-like putrid scents. I would have masked my face with my handkerchief, but I could not bear to shame those people whose living together had produced this air and they must breathe it in if they would or no.

What my so dear husband meant me to learn by the sight of the wounded enemy I cannot say, because he would not wish to create in me a violent pacifism. He loves not the war, but to his perfect mind there are causes which merit the going to war, yet for me that one sight of those wounded men has made of me a pacifist for evermore. Oh, the stench of that place! The groans and faint ravings like no human sound in a foul near-darkness of stagnant air. There was no window, and the only light came in chinks where board could not meet board. It was this blessed darkness that let me enter before I could see what lay within, and there beneath me and thick about me were bodies on pallets upon the floor.

Before this day I have seen wounded soldiers. They walk about in Williamsburg to take their air, so to see there a man with a sullied bandage has become an event of no great remark. But any wounded enemy able to walk would never have suffered so vile a stable, so those upon the floor were so greatly maimed that they were not able to move at all. Any battlefield wound to head or torso is very likely to be fatal, but those to arm or leg might be survived if the wounded limb is cut away. This I now well understand, for the sight of that place so greatly dismayed me that my dear dear husband must enter my chariot and comfort me for the long ride home. He explained their amazing lack of limbs, and some were missing two and one man even three, by saying this cutting of the wounded parts was but a better effort to save their lives. It was not, as I had feared, some infernal torture inflicted upon them by our own.

Oh, the pain of that place! As I came to see clearer the floor first seemed to undulate, and there beneath me was that piece of a man with both legs gone from above the knee and one arm at the elbow, and his one good arm he raised into the air. Very nearly I screamed, but as the sound rose within me I saw his face and I could not so dishonor him. It was but a mild and usual face of a large pale man not twenty-one, and he looked up at us as calm and mild as if he believed himself nothing remarkable. My husband took his hand and spoke to him. For all my horror I heard not his words, but only I heard the soft sound of his voice so dear and so familiar to me. He very briefly spoke to some few others and took what hands they offered him, but he did this always with an eye upon me and he saw near at once that I must have air.

My dear husband sits there now to work at peace within his library, and I write in our chamber by my single candle so as not to disturb his solitude. He comes now and again to lay his hand at my cheek and ask if I am comforted of my journal, for he feels a guilt that he has misjudged my mind and thought it capable of bearing such horrors. I assure him that I am well recovered and I have a greater strength than what he sees. I fain will wait until he finishes working and go with him together to our bed. Now, as upon no other night, I need the sweet comfort of his arms.

MONTICELLO FEBRUARY 3, 1779

*G*reatly I fear that our cause may be lost, but I never can tell my husband so. What ever can I write to comfort myself? Where will be our certain haven now?

The British army have captured Savannah and marched across Georgia west from the sea and taken Augusta the capital, and all these defeats in one month's time so our best defense is only grass. We could not stand against them. We had within Georgia our Continental Army of the Southern Department which lately had suffered a great defeat of its expedition into the Floridas. It was routed from the Floridas, so they say, for it joined together soldiers from both Carolinas who despise and greatly disdain one another so they cannot make an army.

Oh, the pain of the poor sorry people of Georgia! The British have run through the streets of Savannah and bayoneted the women and children. They burn every town and every farm from poorest planter to great plantation so the people must flee with their beds on wagons, and this in darkest winter. There are stories terrible of roads so full of people fleeing the monstrous British that the ground cannot be seen for mile upon mile and those taken ill must die where they fall for their families cannot help them. It was told of New York and Pennsylvania that Tories came to welcome the British, but there in Georgia many whole towns of people have taken the oath for the British King. And still of these towns, some are pillaged and burned.

We had come in Virginia to think of the war as very nearly won. Even I had believed this of my soul, how ever I still might fret and fear, that the war would gutter out to the north and soon our peace would come. Now every one feels a great alarm in Charlottesville and towns around, a bright alarmed feeling of a new-found fear which peculiarly is like to a giddy joy.

"Might they come this far?"

"There are two states between!"

"If they conquer Virginia the war will be lost. All the Continent surely must come to our aid."

"But they might not help us! We might be alone! So Georgia thought, and now she is lost!"

The like is now upon every lip. That is, it is now upon every lip but those of my dear husband. His sanguine humor will admit of no fear but he says, "Oh Patty, they cannot prevail and you must not let them trouble your mind. We shall drive to the south and have back Georgia. Only look at your face. My dear, will you smile?"

So smile I must, and I cannot tell him how greatly I now begin to fear. My Pappa foresaw it. He was born in Britain and knew her power as a boy, and ever he said we were fools to rebel because Britain has not the heart nor the sense to ever yield at all. She will hang by her teeth if we fight her hard, but her teeth are in our throat and she will win. Ever as I think of my Pappa I hate so many of the things he said, but much as I hate those many things I know that my Pappa was ever so wise and always for the most part he was right.

Yet he would have been wrong about my dear small Hanah. She would so greatly astonish him. Now here is a better story to tell, for if aught can comfort me of my fear it must be this great most singular hope that indeed the Negroes are not stupid. Certain it is that they can be free.

I never have resumed my teaching of slaves. My husband asked me late in the fall if I felt well enough to begin it again, and since I could not have him think me ill I made for him feeble explanation. I told him that I but kept our Polly from exposure to the slaves' disease, but this was transparent for they had no disease so from this he knew that I wished not to teach them. I comforted myself to tell us both that soon again I would begin my school, but well I knew that I never would try. I could not take the risk that I might again fail and doom the race to slavery for evermore.

Then one morning some beyond a week gone by, my Betty and I were planning a dinner and I thought to describe my visit to the Barracks and say how much better we house our slaves. This mild observation did not much please her. "We had rather have hovels and with them our freedom," she said to me indignantly. "Chains with beds and glass windows are chains nonetheless. And what has become of your wish to teach us?" Her words alarmed me, for naught could I say. She would see the lie in any least excuse. "Have you then given up on teaching the children? Can it be that your wish to free us all was just some foolish lady's whim?"

"That it was not! How can you speak so, Betty? Certainly you know me better than that!"

"Then what is it, mistress? Sally yet asks me. When will you again find the time to teach her?"

"It is not over Sally." I must give her the truth, for truth she was strong enough to hear. I put my hand upon hers where it lay on the table and looked most earnestly into her eyes and said, "I am a sorry teacher. I fear that some may not have the wit to learn, but if any have the wit to learn I am not a teacher worthy of them."

I had buried my doubt of their strength of mind within my greater doubts of myself, but that central doubt was what she heard. "You fear we cannot learn! Can you be such a fool? Oh mistress, you do so greatly try me!"

So she said while she stood up from the bench and went most furiously out the door. I looked up shamed at Suck and Mary who stirred the pots upon the fire, but they turned their backs as if they had not heard for they would not risk this clash of giants. My Betty is ever so gentle with me but she shows me at times near a mother's vexation, as if she expects so much of me that my failures must be to her a grievous pain. Now that I am a mother, too, I apprehend this confounding of a mother's hopes, and when I see in my Betty these her angers I am warmed to my soul to see her love.

I had thought she but removed herself to avoid unseemly words between a slave and her mistress. She startled me when half an hour gone by she appeared again at the kitchen door. "Now, mistress," she said with a smug excitement as if she had found out a honey-tree, "sit you down and listen. Just sit you down. We shall see who has the wit to learn."

I sat on my chair with my eyes upon her so I did not at first see my little Hanah. She hung back beyond my Betty's skirts so Betty must tug her by the arm, and when I saw her face I saw her near to tears. "Oh, Hanah, what ever can be the matter?" I looked alarmed from face to face. "Betty, stop at once! You frighten the child!"

This I said, for my Betty had forced our Hanah to sit down hard on the table-bench. "Say it! Say it!" Betty said. She leant down close to Hanah's ear. "You must say it now. So help me, girl, I shall take a switch to you!"

At this the tears broke and rolled dark streaks upon the poor child's dusty face. Her hands clung together for a desperate comfort. Her shoes began a frantic desperate dance, for they could not reach the floor. "Act One. Scene One," she began so softly that above the sound of kettles she could scarce be heard. "Venice. A Street. Enter Roderigo and Iago. Rod. Tush! Never tell me; I take it much unkindly that thou, Iago, who hast had my purse as if the strings were thine shouldst know of this." And on she went. I did not at first make out very many of the words she said, but then with a chill that pricked my back I clearly heard some words of the play. The child was saying out the whole *Othello*.

"Dear God in heaven."

"There. Enough," my Betty said. "She reads by night and recites by day. Some there are who think her mad and themselves very clever to have saved their own children. There, Hanah. There is your penny now. You did it very well."

We said nothing more once the child was gone, for indeed there was nothing more to say. I lived for days with the glow of knowing that indeed my slaves are able to learn, but when I thought again of beginning my school I seemed still to feel my old reluctance. It was not until just three days past that came to me why I yet felt reluctant. Indeed my Hanah learned, but I did not teach her; perhaps they can learn but they cannot be taught.

This was, I believe, upon Friday last, for that was the day my husband trained his militia so he was gone to Charlotteville the morning long and near it was until dinner-time. My husband is not a battle-officer as once and for long I so greatly feared, but he is the executive of the Albemarle militia who bears the title of their Colonel and often-times he presides at their training. So Thomas was not at home when came my thought like a revelation that well enough they might learn to read but still it seemed they could not be taught. I could not ask the question of my Betty for fear she would make me appear the fool. Soon she must lose patience altogether and the love between us must be spoilt.

Yet I knew none other whom I could ask. We have for our overseer Johnny Brock, who is but our latest of this dreary breed. They are all of them bullies and natural tyrants, and when Thomas endeavors to reform their minds they up and quit or they plain defy him or else they turn to dreary drink. This Johnny Brock does none of these, but he is so shiftless that he lies late abed and he ventures to the fields only now and again. He likes to turn his hand to the carpenter's trade, which Betty's former Joe is pleased to teach him. So we pay an overseer to be a half-hand carpenter. This we find our Negroes like so well that my Thomas says now we might give a thought to leaving off an overseer altogether.

We have little need for an overseer because our dear Great George daily rouses the slaves and carries them out and directs their work. We style him our foreman, but well in truth he comes to act as our overseer, and this he does the better for he works with the slaves and he works the hardest and the best of all. So at length, when I could think of no one else and my need to ask my question near burst in my mind, I left my Mary and Ursula and Suck where they began to make the dinner. I went and bade my Bett call up our horses that we might ride out and take our air.

The hands were clearing a stand of wood far down the hill where it comes more level. Tobacco is an exhausting crop which sours any field within a few years' time so planters must ever be clearing new fields and leaving the old to grow up weeds. When after long riding we found the work by following its singing and chopping sounds, I bade my Bett summon Great George to me. It was not fit that I should search for him through a dark wood full of slaves at work.

That was a very pretty day near to the end of January, with the sun very bright and a cooling breath of new-turned earth and fresh-cut wood. I found a pleasure in the clean pure air which had stripped away every breath of green and left just the scent of the wild raw earth which smelled near as if a deep enough breath would discover the very scent of life. With my stays so tight I could not smell it, but I found a certain comfort in that. Ever I find comfort in my thought that but for my female disabilities I might conquer or discover any thing.

When came my Great George from out of the wood I knew not what to say to him. He is greatly large and greatly black, and his features are enormous upon his face with his nose greatly wide and his mouth as thick and enormous as a hole above his chin. Looking thus down at his ugly good face, I knew not what to say to him.

"Have you need of me, mistress? Is something amiss?"

"No. Nothing." I dismounted from off my horse, and this he could not help me do for it was not fit that he should touch me. "I would talk with you, George. I must ask you a question. Bett, take these horses over by that tree." So she did. He watched to see that she stayed within sight, then warm and polite he returned to me. I knew not what to say, but sure I was that he expected that I would speak, so naught could I do but to speak out plain while rose a blush that I could not hide for I did not have my fan. "George, do you know our little Hanah? Cate's child Hanah?"

"That I do, mistress."

"She can read, George. Did you know she can read? But I did not teach her. I could not teach her, for when I tried to teach the slaves how to read the whole lot of them refused to learn. Think you they can learn but I cannot teach? Or how is it that Hanah learns to read? Oh, devoutly do I wish to understand their minds!"

Great George looked down at me very calmly. His head went to tilt as if he all but said what Betty would have said out plain, that I am a greatly foolish lady and nothing there is that I will understand. This he would not say for his great politeness, but I blushed yet further for the look of his face. "They can learn," was all he said. "If they see a sense to learning, I dare say they can learn very well."

"Then how can I teach them? I must not promise that they will be free this very day, but George, consider their freedom now. They never can be free if they will not learn!"

I had said too much, for never should I have talked to Great George of that forbidden freedom. I saw that he was alarmed of the word, as if I had said it to test his mind and now he must renounce the very thought of freedom or surely he would suffer his master's wrath. Our Great George once had a very hard master. His back bears the scars of terrible beatings. He keeps his back covered in the hottest summer but through his sweated shirt can be seen the scars, and as I thought of them I felt the keenest shame. Then a change came mild upon his face. "You taught them wrong, mistress." So he said. "You ordered them to denounce their fellows. Never a slave will ever do that."

"But I would not have punished them for their mistakes!"

"How could they know that, mistress? For all they knew you would sell any child who differed from the others. To learn is as dangerous as not to learn. It is better that we all be just alike."

"No!" The plain sense of this roiled my mind.

"Yes. It was said in the quarters then that those who learned to read would be sold away. What good is reading here? Only give them a reason. Give them a reason, and never demand that they shame another slave before your face."

"Oh, George." My breath came so sharp that the press of my stays must make me gasp. I looked to find a stump and sat upon it. "I am foolish!" I said. "Oh, my poor poor Hanah. Does she now fear that she will be sold away?"

"You think us stupid, do you not?" my Great George said. "You are too good to hope that we are stupid as all the white masters so devoutly hope, but you think it. Mistress, we are not stupid. A stupid man cannot survive as a slave."

I looked up the great distance to his face, dazed by the blow of the sun on my head. My hood and my mask had slipped away and I had not the sense to put them back.

"Hanah will not fear, mistress. I shall explain that you never meant to do her harm."

"Harm? But I meant to help her!"

I saw that George had said his piece and he meant to say no more, but when he heard my well-meant but so foolish words he lifted his head in a reckless shrug. "Would you truly understand the mind of a slave? The cleverest slave is the one most stupid. The quickest slave is the one most slow. If a slave can convince you he cannot work or his leg is lame or he has taken ill, then he has won, has he not? Only look upon a slave and see a perfect idiot, and the man you look upon is surpassing wise. The stupid ones you can work to death, mistress. The cleverest ones work the least of all."

I looked up at my George right into the sun, dazzled by his vision of a life inverted so good is bad and dark is light and the right must plain be wrong.

"Some slaves like not to work for me since I am smarter than the white and me they cannot fool. But your husband has the sense to reward his slaves, and those who work the best get the best reward. He is kind to us, mistress, but a slave is a slave. To fool the master still is the greatest good."

I saw that as he spoke he began to repent, for he gave away secrets to an enemy and he did not know but I might have a way to use it all against him. Thus it was that he spoke to praise himself, who other wise never would brag at all. But still he was uneasy so he said to me last, "I have too big a mouth and too much escapes it."

"No, you must not say that!" I touched his hand, but from this he recoiled as if I had struck him. "I am sorry, George. Please. I would not betray you."

"Well, so now you have your answer, mistress. You may not wish it, but still you have it."

"Thank you."

"Now I shall return to the work. Not a tree will have been cut while I am gone."

He turned and walked back into the woods, this man who was born within Africa and stolen from it while yet a boy and now by the vagaries of what ever fate his life is linked with mine. I knew even then that what he had said was more than he ever will say again, and indeed he never shows by word or look that he even recalls this conversation. Yet the more I consider it, ever the more it does so greatly astonish me.

I have been so foolish! I have thought us alike but for our skins and but for our minds, although now I believe that the Negro's mind is fully the equal of my own. Yet I see that we are different, the which my Betty ever has patiently tried to teach me. Different we are, and as different as if that very earth of Africa had been removed to dwell within our quarters. They are to me so greatly familiar, and yet what I see is not true at all for they live within a different earth! Only think of the questions. When ever I recall my Great George standing in the wood, his so wise answers inspire in me questions which I can scarce articulate. And of these, far the most alarming is this: why ever do the Negroes submit? If they are fully wise and strong, how is it that they consent to be slaves?

The Indians will not be slaves. A century gone that experiment was tried, but the Indians plain refused to be slaves and they fought and died within their chains and never any would submit. My Thomas greatly admires the wild Indians how ever grievously they try us now, and he says that certainly they have their minds and spirits equal to our own. And his proof is this, that they will not be slaves.

It near seems to me as if the very fact that a man is willing to be enslaved will decide his fate for slavery. Only those can be free who insist with their lives that they must be free.

MONTICELLO MAY 2, 1779

*W*e depart for Williamsburg on Tuesday next and we shall not return before the end of June. Since I intend not to carry my journal with us I have a thought that I must catch it up, for much there is to say of these past few months which other wise I shall not recall. I do love my journal, but I love not its burden. Years past, it seemed that I had my right whether I would write again or no, but now that my journal carries eight of my years it demands that I must keep it for evermore. Yet there are now scarce fifty pages remaining. I know not wherein I shall write after that.

My husband has seldom left my side, for I have again been greatly ill. Yet it was not my kidneys, but a fever of my lungs which I suffered for beyond a week gone by until I was cupped by a Hessian surgeon. Now my husband has gone this day to attend to the needs of the Hessians at Colle, for he thinks me well enough to be left alone if I have my Betty by. So I write.

We traveled for the month of February and carried with us many of our so dear servants, for I must have my Betty to nurse my Polly and I must have my Bett and my Mary to cook and they each brought their infants and we brought Betty's boys so we carried altogether beyond a dozen servants with the women and the children in a covered cart where they sang, which made the journey very gay.

We went first to Elk-hill upon the James, for Cox leaves off as our overseer there and we have hired Billy Chisholm in his room. My Thomas was eager to see Mr. Chisholm and counsel and instruct him very well that he not abuse our people. We spent two nights at the Elk-hill house, and there the roof well comes to leak. If they do not soon repair the roof the whole of the house will rot away.

To travel in winter is preferred, for in spring we have the mud and in summer heat and in fall we have either the mud or the heat and often a plague of biting flies. But we have had this winter a plague of mud which dragged upon and greatly wearied the horses, so we moved on slowly and we stopped at every plantation-house along the way. From Elk-hill we went to Hors du Monde to visit our so dear sister Skipwith, but we could not tarry. My Thomas must keep an engagement he had made in Williamsburg to meet with his great friend Mr. Wythe and discuss their revisions of the laws. We were in Williamsburg for more than a week, crowded into rooms with the patient Wythes, and they had there no quarters for our servants so we must find their lodging where ever we may.

In Williamsburg we found that the war alarm had greatly enchanted all the people. They live nigh unto the mouth of the James so any sight of any sail at all must thrill and alarm them over again until it is seen that the ship is a merchantman bent upon doing no one harm. The British still hold the state of Georgia and none can guess where they will next appear, but certain it is that to win this war they must take the Capital of the greatest state. So Williamsburg finds itself the seat of all hopes. At this it is altogether transported, and such an excitement pervades the city that to breathe the very air must make one weary.

But there was in this atmosphere of war alarm one tender touch of our life gone by. Late in February there was given at the Raleigh a ball for the sake of the General's birthday. Such a joyous ball! I would have worn my yellow gown and been far the grandest lady there, but sadly it remains fast packed away. I know not when ever I shall wear it again. I had nothing splendid, but I wore the best gown which I had carried against some elegant dinner, my gown of the blue-green silken lustring that my husband bought while he was at the Congress. Mrs. Wythe had a petticoat and stomacher that could be pinned to fit me passing well, and these were of a white brocade with flowers nicely wrought in thread of gold. But to dine and curtsey and dance and laugh and never talk of war the evening long was an event so joyous that I shall live for long on that one sweet ball.

When at last we were quit of Williamsburg we journeyed to the Forest, there to see my Betsy's baby girl who is well nigh unto Polly in age although she is not nearly so pretty and cheerful. My so dear sister now has four sweet children, her Richy and her Jack and her two little girls, and she lives indeed a blessed life for never one has died.

Her very dear Francis is made still uneasy by my purchase of his slave-girl three years gone, and this, although I have told my Thomas not a word of what transpired that day. Indeed, my Thomas has no awareness that he is the owner of one more slave who lives now at our Poplar Forest and I hear that she does very well. But Francis cannot forget his own shame. Thus he believes that neither can I forget, although in truth I never think of it until his unease calls it back into mind. My Francis suffers me when Thomas is not about, and I think him not uneasy with Thomas alone, but when we are together he blushes and sweats as if we three share a compact to hide from one another his grievous shame.

We stayed for but two nights at the Forest before we went on to Spring Forest in Goochland to see our sister Carr. I do most greatly admire my dear sister, for she lives a sole widow and she tends her six children. Ever she still is so greatly cheerful, with her costumes not matched and her sly droll wit and her sense like my husband's that all will be well and naught can ever be improved by fretting. But she suffers some want on account of the money. She has sold some lands and been cheated thereby, and I like not to know her private affairs but my Thomas does suffer some alarm of her. Now he wonders whether it might not be meet if she sold all her remaining lands and removed to Monticello.

"Oh, Tom, you talk nonsense!" dear Patsy says, and she gestures at her roving laughing children. "Do you want these wild demons living with you? Only think of Patty! She could not bear these boys."

My sister Carr has three pretty girls, her Jane and her twins who are near about ten. But beneath these are the three little boys at nine and eight and six, and they are for a truth the wildest children that they grow up there without a father. Her Peter is a charming rogue and Sam is like the same; her Dabney who was born at his father's death is the only one who puts me in mind of him. In truth, it would be hard to have her boys.

We returned from Goochland well into March to find the vegetation far advanced, for the month of February was exceedingly warm as if it were the month of May. In the previous year my husband has planted very many fruits and flowering trees, and to find these in bloom to greet us here made our coming to home completely joyous. Alas, our joy must be short-lived, for within the week the weather set in cold and killed all the fruits which had blossomed forward before it set in mild again. Our spring has continued in this wise, alternating warm with cold, so the gardens have suffered and the trees have been blasted that chanced to be budding in tender leaf when ever cold would come. It puts me in mind of that ancient year when came that very great frost in May so Great George and I must re-seed the fields.

Now comes to me a use for my journal, for I read back and see that was in 1774. I have paused yet further and read yet more of that ancient time but five years gone, and it seems to me as quaint and dear as very ancient history. Mr. Mazzei had newly come and his Colle was abuilding. Our house was abuilding, and its slow pace of work distressed me when truly it never mattered. So much that seemed important really mattered so little! We felt our so indignant emotions which trembled for liberty in every breast, yet then in that year we could have turned from the war. That was the final year when naught had been broken and well we could have kept our tie with Britain, for in the next year came Lexington and I see no where to stop from that day to this. Should we have stopped? And would we have stopped, had we known that our way led to endless war?

I do believe the common people would have stopped if they had known what was to come. Not my so dear husband nor any of his friends, but the common people who suffer now had never envisioned so severe a war. Now their minds are hardened, but then, at the first, they would very gladly have turned away. But should it have been stopped? Then I would have said yes. Had ever I envisioned but the smallest of the distresses to which I am accustomed now, I would have flown from the war as from a pestilence. How greatly adaptable is the human mind! Now I will not yield if I die for it, and it seems indeed that the fear of a pain is greater even than the pain itself. I cannot yet say if we should have stopped it. Surely if it costs my husband's life then naught could be worth so great a cost, but absent that we may come to say that glad we are that we have had this war. If we can end it now. The longer it goes, the greater must be its final prize.

So now we have had our peculiar spring in which we must plant and plant again, and this has created a further hardship for the prisoners living at the Barracks. When came we from our winter journey my husband resumed his frequent visits, and once I went with him upon his insistence that I clear my mind of my painful vision of mud and lost limbs on their winter hill. In truth they get on better now, and the Barracks begins to be a good-sized town well enclosed within stakes and guarded, yes, but tidy with its houses and neat fenced gardens where now they contrive to grow their food. With trenching and privies all the mud is gone. Indeed they become quite settled there. Then late in March there came to us word that the Governor and Council meant to move them again. They had but arrived there three months past, and that after walking seven hundred miles, and they had worked and struggled for a proper home and spent for seed and planted it, and no sooner had they become well settled than they must be taken up and moved again.

This intelligence sent my gentle husband into a frenzy of an anxious rage. He must sit and write for an afternoon and then for nearly a night gone through to compose his plea to Governor Henry that they might be left in peace. He bade me read his letter while first he wrote it and when I took to bed and then again in the morning.

We must not move them, sir! my husband wrote. They are perfectly placed for health and defense. We yet have sufficient food to feed them. And to move them now would fix upon this nation a character of whim and caprice and cruelty. We cannot move them! So he wrote on and on, with argument after argument. I think it was a letter of seven pages when he copied off his final draft. I pity Mr. Henry his receipt of it, for he cannot stand against such a mind. My husband cannot bear to see anyone wronged, not even if it is his own enemy wronged. Mr. Henry leaves off as Governor in May and none yet knows who will replace him, but I doubt not that my husband can persuade the next Governor. Our prisoners are blessed to have such a friend.

For we have made among them very many friends, a merry social circle. General Phillips and his family reside at Blenheim and General Riedesel has many Hessians at Colle, so we dine with our enemies several times in each week and we share with them dancing and cross-country riding and music and such fine entertainments.

The British are a vexing uneasy lot and not so charming as the Germans. General Phillips ever must have the lead, the which brought a greatly perplexing round of invitations snubbed until we understood that he must say who will dine and when. He is the ranking Englishman. He feels himself to be far above the German general and a whole world above any provincial gentleman known to have the character of a rebel. Thus it was that when came my husband's birthday near about the time when arrived at Colle General Riedesel and his lady and children, I could not arrange a birthday dinner.

I sent upon Saturday to Blenheim and Colle my notes of invitation for a dinner on Tuesday. My note to Colle went unanswered, but then from Blenheim came upon that Sunday next a most formal note which declined for them both. Yet by the same servant came an invitation for a dinner to be given on Thursday and word that the guests would include the Riedesels with particular mention of their daughters. While the servant yet waited I wrote to accept, and I wrote by separate cover an invitation for the General and lady to attend upon Wednesday. I had a thought that a dinner one day past his birthday would yet please my husband very well. But then on Monday came the General's refusal, with excuse that upon that Wednesday next he would dine with the Riedesels at Colle.

So my Thomas had not his birthday dinner. We had in its room two days past the date a dinner at Blenheim for beyond thirty people at which my so dear blessed husband was the only civilian gentleman. But imagine the scene! The British wore their red coats with white breeches and ruffles, all very clean, and proud as if the sight of their detested coats must not inspire the most complete revulsion. The Germans were in blue and yellow and white which made them look enough like Continentals for their appearance to be more pleasing to us. They seemed altogether younger and kinder. I told myself these were the hated Hessians, but I could not imagine such gay young gentlemen committing the acts that are reported of the Hessians of rapine and rape and mutilation. But to hear their sweet words made greatly charming by their clumsy German voices has made me altogether resolve to doubt every future report of this war.

The British ladies were ancient friends who little wished to add to their number. They wore the fashions now current in England, and with but a glance I could certainly see that while once we dressed in London fashion now Virginia is become sadly out of date. They wore the most elaborate feathered hats and gowns puffed up in polonaise style, and they carried not fans. In their opposition, I wore my finest cap and fan and a small-hooped gown of flowered chintz. I had thought myself a most fashionable creature, until with one look at the rest of the party I found myself as dowdy as my sister Carr.

General Phillips was a very congenial host once he felt respected of his rank. As he bowed to me he said, "My dear Mrs. Jefferson, I had heard that you are a beautiful lady but no account of you has done you justice." This charmed me, so then his large pale face and his hair as powdered and curled as a lady's became handsome enough that I could overlook the hue of his infernal coat. But it charmed not the several British ladies. She who flouts fashion cannot be a beauty, and well I was revealed as a provincial hag.

Those cool proud looks of the British ladies upon my sorry dress and figure must throw me for companion to General Riedesel's lady. German she is, but she speaks a fair English and she has a ready wit to mock the British, having lived in England for almost a year. She found their cities sewers and their food but a pap and their wits so phlegmatic that they called her Red Hazel, and they thought if she was foreign she must be French for their minds could not encompass any other country. Fritschen was my friend for a fortnight, until in one moment was ended our friendship. My husband assigns it to me. I retort that he may fight this war in his way, and I for my own part shall fight it in mine.

Baroness Riedesel is a large fat lady who sings and touches the keys very well. She has three delightful daughters of the ages of seven and five and three, and with Patsy now six these three little girls are a bounty of charming gentle friends. While they speak little English, they speak it enough for checks and cribbage and cards and quoits. So we brought our daughters to the entertainments, and while the gentlemen smoked and played at cards and my Thomas played chess and he played at his fiddle with charming delightful young Baron de Geismar, my Fritschen and I would sit and converse and watch our children at their play.

My dear husband greatly does come to love the Baron and

certain other Hessian officers. He speaks not the German, but with French and Italian and English they get on very well. And their pride is not engaged. While the British must ever be handled with the greatest tenderness, the Hessians make play as if their sojourn here were meant entirely for their pleasure. Even this is true of Baron de Geismar. His father is so ill in Germany that Thomas must write to beg of the Congress that he be exchanged for his father's sake, yet still the Baron can laugh and fiddle. Ever he enjoys to tweak the British.

The drinking of healths is a peculiar problem when those who dine are enemies. Beyond the ladies, each of whom is fervently drunk, and such good wishes as pleasant weather, there is naught that can be drunk that will not give offense to some or other members of the party. "I give you generals!" said Baron de Geismar once, with grand gesture at the two there present. "I give you peace aplenty!" "I give you God's heaven!" "I give you good Virginia hosts!" These were well enough, but after some dinners he went on to giving the death of tyrants. "Why you not drink that?" he said most offended when the British set their glasses down. "You king is a tyrant? Oh, heaven deny! I never say so, Georgy!" He drank his wine glass to its dregs. One by two, even the British did the same.

This subtle sport that was made of the British by some of the Hessian officers did not set well with that Hessian lady who ever herself likes to mock the British.

"He have no respect!" she said of Baron de Geismar when once we sat in the hall at Blenheim and watched our daughters at their play. We heard from behind us in the dining-room the last of the toasts being merrily drunk, and one was to the health of British mothers that their sons be soon at home again. Then Baron de Geismar added the hope that the mothers should not whip their sons too severely for what they have done to so fair a land. At this there was a round of uneasy male laughter.

When Baroness Riedesel complained of him, I felt that I must defend the Baron so I said, "He speaks the certain truth that they are the invaders here." Then I said, "England is as a flea to a dog. We do no more than to scratch it away."

"England is great!" said the Baroness. She sat to her height, most greatly fat and her face most round and proud. We had gaily come to using our Fritschen and Patty, for we said we must be friends as our children are friends, but now she said, "Mrs. Jefferson, do not forget that yours is a very backward land."

"That it is not!"

"That it is. The people have no civility. They spit tobacco upon the street. You yourself are a lady, but I have seen America and I say for the most it is a backward land."

"That it is not!" I said in a perfect rage. And this I said, even though I suspected that verily she might be right.

"Even you are backward, for you have slaves. You have slaves, Mrs. Jefferson! Consider that!"

The Baroness has three maids and a man who in dress and in manner resemble our slaves. She has told me they beg to be dismissed from her service and returned to the comfort of their own land, but she will not allow it. So are they not slaves? I said, "You have your slaves as well!"

My retort was too close to an uncomfortable truth. She stood up indignantly onto her feet and said, "They are not slaves! They are free! They are free!"

Then it was that I should have made my curtsey. We both were guests at Blenheim, true, but she was the guest from beyond Virginia so mine was the offense that I quarreled with her. Yet I would not yield. Although my face went to flame and I trembled with shame upon my chair, I said, "If my slave wished to go back to Africa, gladly would I send her with my own money. And soon we shall free them! I promise you that! Europe will ever have its lowest classes, but once our slaves are free we shall all be equal!"

Our shouts had brought the gentlemen running, and Thomas the first for my shouts were the loudest. They drew us apart, each husband alarmed and very solicitous of his wife. I know not what the Baroness said, but I told my husband through bitter tears that Fritschen was an evil abuser of slaves and I never wished to see her more.

In this I nearly had my wish, for soon thereafter I took to my bed with a great lung-fever. Dr. Gilmer was gone off to Williamsburg so General Riedesel sent his own doctor. Thomas would not have me bled, but the dear Lieutenant has dry-cupped me twice and this did slow improve me.

Lieutenant Hayer is a small frail man with a great addiction to horseflesh. I have seen this before, that the smallest of men are often times entranced by the greatest of horses, and the Lieutenant has bought a great seventeen-hand gelding upon which he perches like an overmatched boy. My Thomas has a homebred colt first used upon mares in the previous spring, and his foals are now born so surpassingly fine that the Lieutenant goes the county round to buy a mare good enough to put to our stallion. Dear Thomas has promised him a free cover if ever he can find the mare to suit him.

Caractacus approaches seventeen hands, and at four years he is a colt still growing. Upon each forenoon, once he has seen me, the Lieutenant goes eagerly to visit the colt, and then he returns very full of the robust pleasure of an excellent horse to touch my cheeks and temples and suggest to my Betty some addition or other to the fever-tonic she gives to me by draughts and not by patient spoonfuls. Never will my Betty do any thing patient.

One day I heard him saying to my Betty that General Riedesel builds a house for his wife and all it will lack is a forte-piano. "She have one at Wolfenbüttel. She play it so fair! A pity she cannot have one here."

I alarmed them by speaking, for they thought me asleep. I said, "She might have my forte-piano."

"Oh no, madam!" said the good Lieutenant Hayer. He feared that his words had bade me offer it and I did it only to be polite.

"I insist. She must have it. Please see to it, Betty."

That a woman inert should develop a will caused a rush of activity all around me. Thomas came to talk with me warm and kind, and my Betty talked and the Lieutenant talked, and all the while I lay on my bed and said that she must have my forte-piano.

Ever my husband makes impulsive gifts, as when he gave away the lands for Colle, and he knew that I must have become contrite of the rift I had put between myself and Fritschen. So he yielded to my wish with a sadness to remember our whole life together with my forte-piano, and yet with above it a greater pride that I am so generous with my enemy. I could not bear the sight of his sadness, but I was thrilled to my soul to feel his pride. Perhaps I may yet become as good as my husband.

MONTICELLO AUGUST 12, 1779

I have so very much to tell that I have put off my writing the summer long, for when I sat to write I must write for hours and I did not have the time. I know not even where to begin, with the invasion of my country or the invasion of my life. Yet my life now seems the greater loss.

My husband is the Governor of Virginia.

Mr. Henry could not serve beyond three years' time so we knew another Governor must be chosen, and I think indeed it was his very awareness that he would be put up for the Governorship which made my husband bid us stay at the Forest. That, and because he did not wish to risk our safety in the Capital. The British have lately been plundering the South Carolina coastal rice-lands, laying waste the plantations and carrying off slaves with a promise that they shall have their freedom. Then, it is said, they transport the slaves and sell them again in the British Indies. Such evil! If they will leave them be, our slaves will certainly soon be free!

Then came the British early in May to carry on a vicious attack upon Portsmouth. We had but lately arrived at the Forest, and we heard naught but the most terrifying rumors until my dear husband visited us there to try to make me cheerful. "They only try us, Patty. They do no more. The Capital is certainly very safe."

He said this, when in a week of fighting they had burned the most of Virginia's fleet and burned the town of Suffolk and sent their raiders far into the upper Chesapeake Bay. Still I hear stories these three months gone of the murders of innocent women and children. But then I only knew there was fighting at Portsmouth, and that just a day from Williamsburg. "You cannot go back!" I foolishly said. "Leave off with the Assembly until they move the Capital!"

For this they have lately resolved to do. They make plans to move the Capital to Richmond town at the falls of the James, but the move will not be made until the spring. And my husband now presents his greatest laws upon which he has labored these two years past, his criminal reforms and his bills for the granting of universal education and religious freedom. Even as I begged him to stay with me, I knew he would not leave the Assembly now.

But what I did not know until weeks gone by was that the delegates were split upon the Governorship. They had put forth as candidates my own dear husband and his ancient friend John Page of Rosewell, and had I known this I would have made myself most frantic for worry of the end of it. My Thomas is too tender to lose an election. I could not beg him to refuse the post for a fear he would despise my interference, but I knew that while he would be glad to be elected he little likes the running of a government. And he fears the great loss of his time and his freedom and the pains of holding power at so desperate a time. Oh, he had little wish for the Governorship, but once he was up for it he must win.

Yet how could he prevail against such an opponent? Page is become a hero now for his work on the Council and the Committee of Safety, and he governed Virginia very well indeed when Mr. Henry was grievous sick. I would not have imagined that even my husband could prevail against a gentleman so greatly loved. John Page is as proud as ever he was. He and my husband often disagree, for Page is an earnest aristocrat while my husband insists we must be ruled by the best men out of every class. Yet they remain good friends. To live for weeks with knowing that Thomas must lose the election or he would lose his dear friend would have made me certainly very ill.

I have not the heart to say more than that there were cast two rounds of ballots and out of the second was my husband elected. Page strives to continue their friendship, the which does greatly relieve my dear husband, but Page is so saddened that I think him likely soon to leave the public service. In this I so greatly envy his wife. Since Thomas was elected on the first day of June and until we came to our Seat at the end of July, I saw so little of my own dear husband that I might as well have been a widowed lady.

To return to the environs of Williamsburg and the panic of constant war alarms was odd indeed after spending our spring in happy company with enemy friends. I worried for the Barracks-women and for our Hessian friends at Colle, but Jupiter came past us now and again to carry messages to my husband and ever when he came he stopped at the Forest to bring me word of how our people fared so I rested content that our friends did well.

At the Forest my companions were my so dear Betsy and her ancient circle of Patriot friends, now agitated further by the burning of Suffolk. They met in her parlor two mornings each week and she twice as often went to theirs, and the stockings they knitted and the shirts they sewed were enough to suit a whole battalion. With my husband up for the Governorship I became the center of their circle, courted and all my imperfections forgotten and rapture attending my every word. Their attentions made me feel greatly foolish. Beyond that first week I gave excuse that I must remain at home to tend my Polly, so the only meetings I still must grace were those held twice weekly in Betsy's parlor. Thus I had many mornings alone, and it was at last upon one of these that I dared to speak frankly with my brother Eppes.

I could no longer abide the knowledge that Francis, who ever was my certain friend, has been estranged from me these three years past. Close to him as I must be at the Forest this estrangement became a grievous pain, but still I never would have spoken to him had we not been together in the garden.

It was a May morning with a pearl-gray sky of the sort which little threatens rain. Ladies love such mornings, for even though we still must wear our hat and mitts we often may do without a mask if we walk abroad in the early morning. The dew was yet thick upon the grass when I carried our babies with their garden blanket and set them to play by a rough-wrought bench which is close behind the kitchen. There I sat me down and took up my book, for I have resolved for the sake of my soul to read St. Augustine's *Confessions*. But this I cannot bear to do for love and fear of my dear Pappa. I have carried his book the summer long and refused to replace it with another, yet ever when I sit and open the book my mind runs on to other things. So I found a need to sing for my babies a foolish round of "Ducks in the May." My Polly creeps along very well so often I must keep her on the blanket, but Betsy's Patty is two months younger so all she can do is to sit and look. She thrusts every object into her mouth and wails when my Polly will snatch it away.

The morning and the babies and the Forest garden soon put me in mind of my poor dead Janey. Well it would be if a living child could take away the grief for a child now lost, but in truth it only increases my grief to see in my Polly some remnant of Janey and know again freshly that my so dear baby is dead forever beneath the ground. To put away my grief, I looked off at the garden which spreads for beyond two acres in size as far as the trees that shield the quarters. Women and children were here and there bent to weed among the vegetables, and closest to me was a dark slim child whose quick and cheerful way of moving put me in mind of Lame Mary's Dinah, who talked to the vegetables as if they were babies and tucked them into her carrying-basket.

No sooner did I have that thought of Dinah than Francis came from around the kitchen. He stood with his back to me and looked at the garden to judge, I imagine, if his slaves worked well and what might now be ripe. He wore still his gown, as he often does until past the time for breakfast, and with my Betsy gone the morning long he might wear his gown until the afternoon. "Francis?" He startled at the sound of my voice. He turned and saw our babes on the blanket, and he gave a sigh as if he put away a fear that I had tracked him there. "Good morning," I said. "It is a lovely morning."

It was not a lovely morning to him, for he would have preferred the sunlight. I saw his confusion and briefly thought that I might explain why I fear the sun, but any explanation that I might give would need more and ever more explanations until I could give him some central awareness of all that makes up the mind of a lady. This it was his own wife's duty to teach him. Instead I said without prior thought, "Francis, may we again be friends?"

"Indeed we are friends! Why would we not be friends?"

"I promise you I never have told my husband. Truly from my heart I never have blamed you."

He was not prepared for such plain talk, and for my own part neither was I. I opened my fan with a gentle motion. I did not wish to alarm him further.

"I should thank you," he said. He did not seem grateful.

"The fault is not with you, dear brother. The fault is with slavery itself. Once we end slavery we shall all be free, and we, I dare say, no less than they."

I saw him as confounded by this speech as he had been by my preference for a cloudy morning. Confounded, and growing hostile to think that once again I was bent to make him appear a fool unto himself.

"You are a good man," I said quickly. "Never would you harm another person, but this vile owning of human beings must put you at odds with your better nature."

"Patty," he said with a rising voice, as if he meant to make a telling point. He broke it off. He said, "I love and respect your husband better than any other man, but he and I do not always agree. I do not intend to free my slaves. They are stupid. They need us as much as we need them."

"But that is not true!" I said to him, delighted that he would talk so plain. He spoke as if I were a man, and I felt then such a rush of fondness as if he had given me the greatest gift. My only thought was that in return I must give him the gift of my awareness. "I have a little girl who has taught herself to memorize the whole *Othello*. Even Patsy cannot do that. They seem stupid, Francis, for this brings to them the best advantage, but when they are free you will see them wise."

Francis said, "A good choice," at the name of the play but he little liked the rest of my speech. When I ended it he plainly said, "I have boys who forget how to use a hoe so we teach them over every morning. Girls who cannot spin or weave. Only look at their faces, for the love of God! They are such abject idiots!"

My mouth was open to give him what I knew was my certain perfect answer, but then I fast must close it again. If to make my brother believe them stupid was the only certain defense of his slaves, then I could not strip it away from them when I had as yet nothing else to give them. "All right. Let us frankly assume that the blacks have lesser minds than the whites. Still, they are our perfect equal in every right before the Lord, so to hold them in bondage is a terrible sin against their natures and our own."

"They are too stupid to be free! You may have your pretty lady's thoughts but we must contend with them every day!"

I liked not that swipe at my lady's thoughts. Polly was pounding Patty's head with a stick, the which was cushioned by Patty's hat, but the babe was beginning to seem alarmed so fast I seized the stick away.

"If they have lesser minds than the whites that but gives us a greater duty to teach them. Never can any difference of mind give us any pretense of an advantage over them. They are completely equal with us, Francis. Every man of every rank must now be equal or we fight this war for nothing more than the right to drink inexpensive tea."

I saw when again I looked at him that he was charmed beneath his irritation. His face wore a look as of a man who first sees a monkey on a chain, and he sees with a mix of delight and unease that it wears a shape very like his own.

"Your husband discusses these things with you? He listens when you give your opinions?"

"Yes he does. Only think of the future, Francis, for we cannot go on as we are. If we begin our confederacy and give not rights to every person in it, then all the rights we have so painfully gained will one by one be stripped away. We have only as many rights as the least among us."

"But what of women? Will you lead a revolt of women?"

With this he cleverly meant to trick me, for if I said that women must also be equal he would say that society must soon be destroyed. I would not enter his clever trap. I said, "Of course not. I am quite content to rely upon my husband."

"Does he then agree with all you say? Would he truly go so far as to free the slaves?"

"Has he not said so to you?"

"He never said it so plain. Your husband is aware of his listener. He goes a bit beyond me, but then when he sees that I am not with him he goes no farther."

"Well then, he truly does believe that we must free them every one. He hopes to free them while the war continues, for we might not again find so perfect a moment."

I saw alarm in Francis's face as I bent again to Patty, who was weeping for Polly's tugs of her hat which put it down to cover her eye. I lifted Patty to dandle her and straighten her hat that she might see. As I did so I said, "The end of the importation of slaves is but his first step in a careful process. Now we must raise the next generation and teach and train it to be free, and we must give to the blacks a country of their own where they might make their way. Or they might remain here. Indeed some would remain, but most would be very glad to leave us."

"That is all your husband's notion?" my Francis said. He sounded dubious. When I nodded, Francis said, "He will never persuade the Assembly to set free the slaves. Never! He dare not even try!"

"Indeed he will try. Oh, Francis, we need but do what ever we can do, for mankind improves with each generation. Any thing we cannot finish now will be done for certain by this child's children."

At that we both must look at his babe who bore his face and bore my name. Francis is a gentleman of wavering humors most easily and unpredictably bored, and he little cares to consider his daughters when all of his investment is in his sons. I saw his soured look of impending boredom. I said from my rising desperation, "Can you not see it, Francis? We went so terribly wrong a hundred years gone by, but yet we can right it! Still we have time! And my husband can do it if any one can."

"White and black cannot live together." His boredom so possessed him that idly he bent to pull one weed.

"But we live together now! Oh, Francis, if you love and respect them from your heart you never see their color. I look at my maid a hundred times, and then with surprise I will notice her shade. It is but a trait, Francis! It is no more than that!" This I said, although I cannot know that it is really just a trait. I only know that we cannot think it more and gladly live together.

Little Patty reached to touch the weed, but Francis heedlessly tossed it away. He said, "Your own husband must command you. This is no affair of mine, but I think it better for his sake that you not speak out so plain. He is a man of position and honor. He likely will be the next Governor. You will do him great and foolish harm if you make the world imagine he harbors such thoughts, and that will be all the more shameful, Patty, if the thoughts you express are yours alone."

My cheeks came to sting quite sharp at this, but Francis abruptly turned away. "Thank you," he said as off he went.

This time I thought that unwilling he meant it, as if his heart spoke what his mind withheld. And he treats me gently now, my Francis. This speaking frankly together was an intimate act between a lady and her sister's husband, and the knowledge that once we spoke so plain remains like a remnant of a last embrace. He builds now his own Seat in Chesterfield which he comes to style Eppington, after his name. It may be that once he is free of my Pappa he may be more willing to free these others.

So we departed the Forest late in July and made what seemed a sorry journey to prepare Monticello for our absence which likely will extend for these three years to come.

Oh, our dear dear Seat! We are here so happy and every small detail of our lives is so perfect. I sit to write upon a day very hot, but the windows are open and the breeze is fair and it brings to me shifting scents and sounds, crushed grass or a horse or dinner cooking, a brief bit of chopping over distant laughter. Beyond the lawn a gang has worked the morning long to enlarge the carriage turn-around and they have graced us with the most glorious singing, rising and falling in melodious parts as if their voices make an orchestra. This delightful habit the Negroes have of singing as they pursue their work has so infected my dear dear husband that ever when he walks or rides he sings a minuet or a country-reel. My first sure sign of his return is that first most joyous sound of his voice.

Here close beside me Polly sleeps. She has grown too big to sleep in her cradle, but she craves it when she suffers ear-fevers. I would need my Bett to rock the cradle since to rock a child so large would make it hard to write, but I have here a gentle Hessian lady, Margareta, the wife of an officer. While she rocks the cradle with her foot she makes for me a bobbin-lace. I had hired her for a way to give her money while she yet keeps her pride, but the lace on her spool is so very fine that I mean to use it to edge a cap.

I am abashed to declare that I miss my Fritschen, for all that we so often fought. It seemed that my very great pride in my country must make her ever disparage it, and the more she disparaged the more I defended. At some moments this was a cheerful play; at others it drove us to angry tears. Yet she was glad to have my forte-piano although her husband for honor must insist to pay, and we are friends enough that letters pass between us tender of affection and respect. They have journeyed to the Springs for the General's health, from whence they hope to go on to New York that they might be exchanged. General Riedesel was sun-struck in the spring so severely that it almost claimed his life, and likely it is that a man so ill will pose no further danger.

They carried with them many Germans, yet still we have many Germans here. From my husband's library comes German speech most low and intent as of men at work. Margareta's husband is deep in study with Thomas's good friend Mr. Unger. My husband is gone for the forenoon long to see to the fields with Mr. Garth, but he will not deny them the use of his books. Indeed, his books are in such full use that he talks now of needing a cabinet, some small room where he might read and work safe beyond the reach of friends and servants. That he will not have for these three years to come. He will never have any moment of peace, and reading and writing for his own pleasure will be his dearest memory.

I struggle now to compose myself to become a proper Governor's lady. Quite against my will and indeed to my shame, the thought has come to charm me. The Governor's lady leads Virginia society, the which Mrs. Henry never could have done, but she died soon before her husband's election and he married Dotty Dandridge in her room. Dotty is cousin to General Washington's lady and gracious in her very most gentle way, but she has seemed not aware of her leadership duty to set for Virginia its social pace. She has seemed even frightened of the Governor's role, as if she must for peace of mind believe her husband still a private gentleman. Very well I understand why Mrs. Henry disliked her husband's service, for being the wife of the Governor makes me far too intimate with news of this war which changes not at all from month unto year and it may go on for ever. We have frequent Expresses from Williamsburg, and at first I delighted to hear the state's secrets. Now I ever flee when the rider comes.

Each bit of glad intelligence brings in its trail an even greater pain. Colonel Clark has captured the Hair-Buyer Governor Hamilton at the fort of Vincennes, and my husband has brought him out of the woods and clapped him into the deepest jail. This was just. Only think of the women and children murdered that this fiend might buy their scalps! But the British General Phillips and even General Washington have begged of my husband his clemency, and now we have heard that the whole British nation are enraged that Virginia serves an officer so. This means that to all my previous worries must now be added the further worry of what the British might do to my husband in further retaliation for Governor Hamilton if ever he should fall into their hands.

Yet there is no real news. We have little battles to no account always very far away, and all now believe that the British have no intention of ever invading far. They need not invade. They yet hold New York and blockade the shore to the farthest south, and they need do no more for our spirits to fade and our money to depreciate until for very weariness we shall grant them a sovereignty as the price of our peace. We may yield to them now or ten years from now. To them it matters little. It is said that they offer us terms in secret which the foolish Congress fails to heed, and this word is coupled with a certain belief that if they invade again it will be to the south. Their invasion of the Georgia succeeded too well. They will make a replication.

So all the sorry news in my husband's dispatches and every sorry word to be heard in the towns is some variation of these fears. My husband alone is ever cheerful. For him the check-mate is only ours, that they wish to invade but they cannot, and the depreciation of money and the trials and the fears are but a swift prelude to a British yielding. "We have fought them to a standstill, Patty! The greatest army on the earth, and we have them boxed!"

"Indeed. And if we box them well enough, soon a chicken will cost at least five pounds."

Yet I think of a way to help my husband. My thought is ever clearer. The British are at war with our very minds, that if they cause us to despair we shall have to yield, and it is little wonder we are near to despair when our life has become so devoid of grace. The Capital is miserable for its lack of balls and the severing of its delightful past with naught but war alarms to take its place. My Thomas is the first American Governor with a lady who is fit to bring him glory. I vow that he shall be remembered in history for shaping a grand new society, that he expanded the gentry to include all the people and his lady gave far the most splendid balls.

To this end my Bett has removed from my press my dear so ancient wedding-gown, gay worn but once when in perfect fashion but now become entirely out of date. Mr. Miike, a clever Hessian tailor, works with me to update my gown, and Margareta promises to sell me a hat which she says will suit it very well. She has dressed my hair in London fashion to teach my Bett the use of drop-curls and forms. I shall strive to be the finest Governor's lady. I believe I shall not shame my husband.

WILLIAMSBURG DECEMBER 8, 1779

*W*hen stepped we into the Governor's Palace and looked around at the gloom of the place, at the sabers tarnished upon the walls and the paneling stained where a roof had leaked, my husband stood dispirited. "I had planned to say we have evicted Lord Dunmore and after all you are proven right, but one good look and smell of this place makes me think he went quite willingly."

"At least now we know why he burned our Norfolk. He was all out of temper that we housed him here."

If I had not so gaily anticipated the Palace I would not have been in such despair, but I had dreamed of a great society and I could not base it here. Yet when we toured the Palace, we found that the ballroom and the supper-room at the back off the gardens were in better repair than the other rooms. They needed only paint to make them gay. My husband must attend to his own duties, and I for my part must attend to mine. We came to the Capital late in September, and it took me only a fortnight of work to make so very many arrangements that my head yet spins to think of them.

The quarters at the Palace are so poor that I would not have them for my servants. They have not even wooden floors and the windows are only square-cut holes; how people can call themselves believing Christians and force their slaves to live so poor is a matter quite beyond me. Those servants needed in constant attendance I put into rooms upon the third floor, and the rest I quartered at the Assembly House which is very near by the College. We brought very many of our servants with us, all the Hemingses and beyond them Great George and Ursula and our Jupiter and Suck. We have for our service beyond twenty Negroes, and this above the groundsmen and carpenters and all such like that we must hire.

We would have left Great George and Ursula, for neither travels very well, but our prospect of living years away bade my Thomas make Garth his overseer. Tom Garth is a mild and kindly man, but he bears a resentment for our dear Great George and the easy charge he has of the hands that they work for him so very well. My Thomas and I considered this and we thought it best that George come away, for if he were left there might be strife and we not able to protect our servant.

With my people placed, I must set to work to create a proper household. I have hired Jamey Wray and his crowd of servants to effect the minimal sufficient repairs and make them to last until the spring, when we shall be away. We thought to have Martin run our accounts, but he is well occupied in running the house and with all the shortages caused by the war this purchasing of goods requires a free man's powers. After putting out my need abroad I have hired young Alex Wiley, who is said to be a most zealous man and possessed of a very great honesty. I like him, for he will deal with me and he never demands to consult my husband.

Thus we carried on for beyond two months. We had in that time many pleasant dinners of Delegates and members of my husband's Council, upon which serves our friend John Page and also serves the young Mr. Madison. This latter dear man I have little known, but rapidly we become warm friends for his droll wit and his fragile look and his manners all are most endearing. For all of his life he has been most sickly, for which he yet remains unwed since he wishes not to leave a widow and orphans at his certain early death. He reveres my husband as no other man, and they talk warm together far into the night, their minds leaping each beyond the other so they speak often-times in a short-hand of words so their words need not delay them. Mr. Madison's Seat, which he styles Montpelier, is in Orange County near by to our own, so I rest content we may prolong our friendship when the troubles of this war are done.

Then we might see him wed. I fear that Mr. Madison is less unwell than he believes himself to be, and his lack of a wife is the root of his ills. If he were wed, his wife would do what it is not meet for any other lady to do, just coax and coddle and make light of his pains and turn his mind to other things. Ever I marvel at the ease with which a wife can come to control her husband, each man requiring his different controls and all improved by the fortunate fact that there is one person in this world who knows them very well.

Thus do I know my own husband. Soon I understood that it was not for the repairs that he delayed our ball, but he kept the work ever going on so we never would have a ball at all. I said this to him a fortnight past. "But we need not paint the parlor, Thomas. The guests will be at the back of the house. I fear these delays are but a ploy and you never will give a ball at all. Only think! If we live with no hope and no pleasure, the war is over and the British have won!"

"But of course we shall give a splendid ball. Let us only paint the parlor, Patty. That and the stairs. And we must oil the hall. Would you have it be less than what it was when the British Governors gave their balls?"

It was just on last evening that I lost my patience. We had for our dinner Mr. Harrison and other leaders of the Assembly, and while I little heard their talk I learned in conversation with their ladies that the Assembly means to rise before Christmas. We have our ball now or have it not at all.

When at length we retired to our chamber, I found myself in a shameful rage. I was angry less for my husband's refusal than for his great dishonesty, that he kept me believing like a credulous child and then he would say upon Christmas Eve that the Assembly surprised him by its early rising. I deserved a better regard than that. Although I hid it well, Thomas saw my rage. Even though it gained to eleven o'clock and both of us were weary, he came to me where I washed my face and laid his hand upon my shoulder. This is ever his signal to me, as my hand on his thigh is my signal to him.

We have learned very well to have our comforts with never a risk that we begin a child. So many inventions we have made to create a pleasure between husband and wife that the joy of it is beyond describing. I would have said I cared no more for the pro-creative act when we did so many more pleasurable things, but then of an instant all was changed. I saw in his denial of my ball and in his denial of my son one singular betrayal of his wife.

I turned beneath his hand. I saw him by the candle so my face must be shadowed, which privacy further emboldened me. "I think it not, sir!" I said and slipped away and went to find my sleeping-cap. "I am weary of seeing my children die on the sheet. I never intend to do it more."

"Patty? What ever possesses you now?"

"No important thing. My stays were tight. I have some touch of a female complaint. Good-night, sir."

Never I show to my husband aught but the sweetest and kindest temper. Never have I thought I might speak that way. For his part, Thomas was quite amazed. "Patty?" He sat down on the bed behind me and put his hand upon my shoulder. I could not bear his familiar touch which spoke as gently as any word. The shame of my petty defiance of him combined with the misery of so much loss, and my tears came quite beyond my will. I choked the sobs away that he not feel them. "Please tell me what is wrong. I will mend it, Patty. Any thing at all. My dear? Will you listen?"

"Treat me like an adult!" I turned to him hot. My tears so enraged me that I struck them away. "Tell me you will not have a ball! Do not toy with me! I am not a child!"

My husband heard me name the ball and he thought me only dismayed by its loss. He smiled to know my rage was a little thing. He said, "I have a thought that a ball right now might not be very seemly. A blow at us here begins to seem likely. Page believes that word of a Governor's ball will make the people doubt their danger."

Thomas is so boxed by Mr. Mason's Constitution that he cannot take a breath without the Council's permission. This ends the abuses we anciently suffered by whim of the Royal Governors, but it frustrates my husband at every turn. He bears but the title; he has not the power. It may have been my sympathy for his frustration with his Governor's role that made me say, "Bother the great Mr. Page! He so much envies you your success that he is bent upon denying you any pleasure!"

My Thomas was profoundly shocked by the fact of my suggestion and by its substance. He imagines the best of every one; he could not now think ill of Page. "I agree with him," he said like a breath of cold. "Oh my dear, this war cannot last much longer. We shall give our ball to celebrate the peace. Keep your gown at the ready. It cannot last long." Thus he coaxed me like a child with a pretty promise.

"Bother the ball!" I said furiously. I sat up further against my pillows. "I am not a child!"

"Indeed you are not a child."

"And I mean this most devoutly, sir. I will not again spill the seeds of my children. You may find your mistress. That I will not do."

My husband feels a near physical pain if ever he denies me any thing, and now his pain that he denied me the ball gave a perfect opportunity to beg for my son. I had this shameful thought once my words were out, but I put it fast away.

"I would never take a mistress!" He seized the edge of my speech that he need not touch its center.

"Then live you celibate." Recklessly I said, "For my own part, I shall have a son."

"We do not need a son!" He stood from the bed, quite vexed that I called up our ancient quarrel. "You cannot bear children! Each one nearly kills you! How might I ever live with myself if you bore me a son and then you died?"

"But I am not a child! If any decision is one that I must be allowed to make for myself, it is this decision. This is my life. I have my right to use my own life."

He looked at me for interest in this new thought. "You have not the right to cause me so much pain."

"My right to use my life is far beyond your right to be spared a little pain."

"But I prefer your life to a hundred sons!" he said from his rising exasperation. "I cannot live content for one day without you. I grieve if we must be apart the morning. I have made my peace that I shall not have a son. Why is that not the end of it?"

"Because I must have a son. The need is my own."

I said this, and then of a sudden light as if angels revealed the face of God I knew that what I said was a deepest truth which my soul had not said even unto itself. "I will have my son. I am a female, but my son will be of me and he will be a male."

The angels may have spoken to him as well. He stood for a moment perfectly still. Much as he does most completely love me, I do not believe that before that moment he ever saw me whole as a separate person with needs and desires other than his own.

"I am well," I said when our long silence came to vibrate on the air between. "I have not been ill these six months past. I do feel in truth most completely well. If I will keep to my cooling foods and drink my Gabbler's potion, I know that I can have my son. I deserve the right to try."

"But the child is of the father," Thomas said in a voice gone bright with interest. He said this, for we have wondered together how the child can be entirely of the father when Betty's children are born of a hue which is between the father's and her own. It is this that comforts me with the thought that my son will have some tint of myself, although it is true that his greater part must be the male homunculus.

"If my son is of you I shall rest content. But Thomas, he will be my son! He will have no limit upon his life. Oh, my dear, if you would deny me nothing how can you deny me this?"

My Thomas sighed the dear small sigh which means that he keeps his former opinion but I have managed to turn him around so he is forced to yield. He bent to the table and blew out the candle. He came onto his own side of the bed and drew me tenderly into his arms so the length of my person was against his own. We had naught but shirt and shift between.

"You must be attentive to your own health, Patty. I never shall forgive you if you die."

"What care I then if you forgive me, Husband? I shall be dead. I shall but laugh."

This I said with perfect gaiety. Despite my words Thomas caught my mood, that gaily I risk my life for my son, and if I have no fear then neither must he fear. We felt ourselves altogether removed, so danger and death were far away. And we had in the night most tenderly a perfect communion of the marital bed from which I am certain a son must arise, and not just a son but a great son worthy to carry the name of so great a father.

We said then no further words of the ball, but before my husband left me this morning he gave me from his pocket seventy pounds. He counted the money out carefully, for some was in Continental bills and these we style dollars for a greater confusion. He said, "You may have more when you need it, Patty. Give to them the very grandest ball, for only heaven knows when we shall have another."

WILLIAMSBURG FEBRUARY 4, 1780

*N*ow at the last I may write of my ball. Its fate has been decided. For long it has balanced upon an edge, so it might have been a triumph or it might have been a shame and I could not bear to write of it. Each person creates her own history in a manner most comforting to herself, and long for beyond a month gone by I believed that ball would be no part of my own.

Never was a ball so plagued by Fate. We were at its planning for the month of December, myself and many ladies of the Assembly who have missed the gay life as I have missed it. Fanny Page would have given the grandest ball to surpass that famous Philadelphia Meschianza which was given by the British for their five hundred guests while our poor soldiers starved in the Forge Valley. They had a whole army for its preparation and every entertainment to please the eye from parades and mock-jousting to fire-works and plays and halls rich with mirrors and ribbons and flowers. Many Whigs forgot themselves to attend this ball given shamefully by their conquerors, and it is said that every belle of the town thus made herself detestable to Patriot beaux. I pity those belles such a complication; glad am I to have lived my youth before ladies must face their political test. But we could not match the British grandeur. Liddy Burwell declared it a benefit that we would be able to do no more than to give a cool and dignified frolic to elevate the spirits of a town at war.

"Let us have the militiamen and their wives. We might invent a military reel! Let us have for decoration the blue and red of the flag and for dishes the very food of the soldiers."

"Please, madam," said my Fanny Page. "Soldiers dine on corn-meal seethed with its maggots. Let us at least spare our husbands that."

Our committee thus began its work divided, with some ladies ardent for a gaudy ball and others as ardent that we must suit the war but all agreed that a ball must be given. Our dear General Washington gives his balls if ever he finds but the least excuse, and the British give their balls. If we give our own ball, we say out aloud that we are free.

Our Virginia militiamen wear hunting-shirts with trousers or breeches of wild-caught skins, and they have their knives and their muskets or rifles and they are so greatly fierce of look. We have few soldiers of the Continental Army, but we have some many militiamen who gather to defend the Capital. Six of these made our orchestra who played fair at the horn and fiddle, and very many more we prevailed upon to invent my Liddy's military reel. We said they must also bring their wives, but most said their wives were miles away. Then one man who would speak out plain told Sukey Brewer that all such women are fearful to show themselves among ladies, for they have no gown which approaches fashion and they know not the proper way to dance.

I heard this after the ball was past or I would have found some remedy. Poor women! That they avoided our ball while their husbands who defend us danced with ladies seems by far its most appalling aspect. They must toil alone to tend their farms like Cinderellas upon the hearth, and their Princes went without them to the ball and never fairy rescued them.

Before I knew their pain, I thought we did well to give honor to the common people by having for guests more than fifty militia and few of these were officers. We sent letters to Members of the House and Senate and very many other of the usual families, and to Admiral Vaudreuil and his officers of the French ships that winter in the Chesapeake Bay. Even with the advent of the winter season, we had for our guests almost two hundred people.

Some ladies had a fear of the militiamen. They worried that they would swill and fight and spit tobacco-juice upon the floor. True it is that soldiers must have their tobacco, but this we could manage with many spittoons, and we thought to enlist the help of the officers if ever a man gave the least offense. We must learn to make our society across every border from class to class, and I had a fond conviction that the common men would raise their behavior to suit the event. For the Palace ballroom is very grand, with its blue walls edged in gilded leather and its great carved moldings and elegant lustres ranged along the ceiling to give it light. I little was aware until I saw that ballroom how shamed I ever was by my Pappa's ballroom which had not even finished walls. My Pappa made a sport of it, that he lived with the gentry and gave his balls but ever he was that immigrant boy so he gave his balls within a barn. No man but my Pappa could so mock the gentry and have them love him all the more.

The fashion when balls are given in town is to have the greatest supper when the dancing ends. Thus it was that we had our small pre-ball for the children of Patsy's dancing-class, and they danced fine together their minuet while every proud parent watched and smiled. My little Patsy danced like a lady most gracefully with young James Smythe, and at seven she approaches unto half the age she will be when first she is a belle.

I am diverted. Here I begin my ball, and I have not told how it nearly was lost.

My Thomas is so much occupied that seldom we ever discussed our ball. He meets with his Council every morning and labors at his papers in the afternoons and he meets it may be long into the evenings with various political dinner guests. He tells me little of all that transpires for he knows I little care for it, so it was from the ladies and not from my husband that I learned of the sailing of the British fleet. This had been our great rumor for all of the fall, for the British have met with such success in their conquest of the Georgia that all know for certain their next campaign will be a great attack upon the south. To the north, they can but hold New York and General Washington has them boxed, but far to the south they have no opposition. All know this, and all have known it so long that it comes to be but a fact of our life that the sun has risen and the sky is blue and the British soon will attack to the south.

In the fall we had many rumors that the British had sailed from out of New York, and then we heard that they had not sailed and then that they had sailed again. This contradicting intelligence had a great effect upon my husband, for he labored to make return of our militias and to gather stores of food and supplies and to form his plans for our defense if ever the British should strike us here. Yet ever he remained so mild and cheerful, never he showed any least alarm, so I thought he but did what he ever does, that he carries all his work beyond an end of perfection. And all of the town was thrilled by its ball as nearer we came to our Christmas Eve. The only certain topic in every shop in Williamsburg was the Governor's Ball, and this not alone my observation but every lady said it so. Then but a week before our ball came a letter from General Washington to inform that a very great British fleet had sailed from New York upon the tenth instant. Likely they meant to attack the French squadron that winters in the Chesapeake Bay, and likely they were bent upon attacking the Barracks to free the prisoner soldiers there.

Upon receipt of this intelligence, my poor dear husband must put to execution his battle-plans. The militias at the Capital marched to move all provisions to farther up the York and the James, and artillery was set and men emplaced to make defense of Norfolk and Princess Anne. Great care did my so dear husband take that he not alarm the people, but within a day our Capital gay for Christmas was become a city horrid with the fear of war. Those upon the street who had gaily said that their Governor's lady was brave for her ball now said that never has there lived such a frivolous and greatly foolish creature who would give a ball in the midst of a war. What had been my triumph was become my shame.

I knew not what to do. I did feel shamed, yet I felt some little indignant, too. Can the character of any event be so transformed within one single day? I think it not. Yet when my husband returned at dinner-time of the day before our ball he found his wife distraught unto despair.

"Oh, my sweet dear." He asked not the cause of my pain, for his Council had discussed it the morning long. He folded his arms about his wife as she laid her head against his breast and he set his chin upon her cap so she felt his jaw move when he spoke. "I am certain the fleet will land to the south. They mean to subdue us from south to north, so Charles Town is their most likely target."

"We shall cancel the ball. We shall assign it to me so it cannot bring any harm to you."

"I have assigned it to me. I have told the Council the ball was all my own idea and my poor patient lady has made for her husband the grandest war-ball ever seen."

At this I looked up in disbelief. His smile was so tender that I almost smiled, so I ducked that he not see my smile and think me cheaply comforted.

"Do you think it wrong or out of taste that we live our lives while the war goes on?"

"No," I said, for I did not.

"Do you not believe that the greatest effort the Governor's lady can ever make is to show forth the very gayest life so all will remember why we fight?"

"Well, that, and also to care for the poor." This I said, for the way he said it out did make it seem to be quite foolish.

"So have your ball! Dear Patty, you never must let a public clamor direct your speech. This ball is your speech. It is what you believe, and you have your right to say it."

"I wish I never had begun it."

"That I do not wish. I shall have such a wish only if your gown is not perfectly lovely and your smile is less than completely bright."

I could not disappoint a man so good that he made of my shame a Patriot virtue. I struggled to amend my mind as I worked in concert with my so dear servants, who thrilled as if they were hosts themselves so their joy in the ball greatly raised my own. Briefly I worried that no guests would come, but the next morning we had notes of acceptance from some who previously had declined. It seemed not support, but a curiosity to see how the lady might manage her shame. Yet I did what my husband commanded of me, and I made myself completely lovely. My Bett and Betty craped up my hair with false-curls beneath Margareta's hat which bears plumes and lace upon yellow satin with small bright beads to catch the light. Cosmetics I have never worn for I wear a constant natural blush, but Betty powdered all my face and she made the red cheek-dots which are the fashion. She said it was a camouflage, for likely I would blush the whole night through and this made it deliberate.

I wear little jewelry, for I have not thought that I can wear it well. I wear my mother's miniature upon my wrist and my Pappa's upon my other wrist, and her pearls I may wear for a gaudy dinner if ever they come into my mind. Such poor dignified decoration was not enough for the grand ball-gown which Mr. Miike has made of my wedding-gown, yet for my need there was a remedy as perfect as if it had been ordained. My husband's mother had a suit of diamonds which she deemed such a grand possession that never she would wear them for all of her life, and these have come down to my sister Carr. My so dear sister never wore them either, for she deems them improper for a widowed lady. And Thomas has long assisted her, so a year gone by she begged of him that he take for his payment her Randolph jewels. This he did, but only to keep them safe that she never feel compelled to sell what are for the family a legacy and by rights should go down to our farthest children. So we have the jewels. They are a necklace of filigreed squares of gold and diamonds, quaint and old, with a drop-pearl at center near the size of an egg and ear-rings the like with like their drops. They do not approach any modern fashion, but when put together with my gown they made a perfection so complete that they might have been designed for that single night.

My Thomas was speechless when first he saw my yellow gown upon that ancient day. When he saw it again on the night of the ball with my Hessian hat and his mother's jewels he was again speechless, but his eyes went bright and his mouth moved as if he meant to speak. He was dressed most fine for the ball himself in green brocade with buff breeches and waistcoat and a velvet ribbon on his queue. "Oh my dear," he said, but it sounded a croak. He cleared his throat and said, "You do me so proud. Oh, Patty, never in all the world has there ever lived such a beautiful lady!"

This speech I well liked, but it frustrated him for he thought it inadequate to his emotion. For very joy he threw up his arms, His Excellency the Governor of Virginia. He threw up his arms, this dignified man who little says in the presence of servants, and while my maids watched he danced his jig and he laughed and said, "I love her!" to the walls.

The ball itself was anti-climactical. We moved through it fixed upon one another, my husband enraptured by his wife and I so deep in love with him that it seemed that never before that night had I completely known him. Yet I think of it, and I am aware of the tensions we were too deep in love to feel. We opened together the first minuet and then we must dance with other partners, my husband with every prominent lady and I with the Marquis de Vaudreuil and Page and Madison and some many others. But ever my eyes were upon my husband. Ever his eyes must follow his wife.

There was lag of response when we opened the ball as if none had expected that we might dance, and every face was upon me in what must be more than respect of my beauty. Only those can be shamed who are aware of shame. I never could have feigned a prideful conviction, but my joy in that moment was so complete and my husband's delight in his wife was so plain that we had no thought beyond ourselves. The world must be wrong, for we were right. In the face of such a Governor and his lady most guests very soon put away their scandal, and then it seemed but an usual ball with the difference that many guests wore skins and they never danced at the minuets but they danced fair and fancy at the reels. We even had our Christmas fire-works which we have longed for now these four years past, for we never had enough of powder to spare but all was for the army. We had some fire-works viewed from the windows to culminate Liddy's military reel, some wheels of colors with hiss and report which brought to us tranquil Christmasses past and settled upon us a mood of gaiety before we went in to have our supper.

Yet still we talk of that military reel, which came to be a gay drill to music of two dozen armed militiamen so rapidly danced and so sharp of gesture that a cry of "Huzzah!" went up from the gentry. For that few minutes we shared one class, all together of a perfect Patriot feeling, and now when any one mentions my ball that military reel is what they praise.

I am proud of some elements of my ball, that I said my piece and I gave to the town its evening of pleasure away from the war. Late word has come that the British sail south and they never were bent for the Chesapeake Bay, so history has proven my ball quite brave. Never does any one style me foolish now. I am justified, yet I am so ashamed that I nearly refused to write of my ball. What shames me is the thought of those common women who thought themselves unworthy of the presence of ladies, and the fact that I was so unaware that not until Sukey confided their story did I give any thought to what their lives must be.

I am so blind! I knew that every poorest woman must be fed and clothed, that I very well knew, but what I had forgotten is that they are women. Their minds must be very like my own. When ever I give a gaudy ball or wear upon the street what they cannot wear, I shame them as I would myself be shamed. Now I see that there can be no pride in holding any greater possession, for every such possession disheartens those others who never might aspire to it. Where will this end? It seems an awareness like my first awareness of the pain of the slaves and it adds to it, for if I think of my servants and how they might also have wished to dance I am pained the more. I can see no end. Now I take upon myself for every wronged person not alone his physical pains, but I suffer at his every disappointment, at each least denial and every strife.

My dear husband is right. He long has said that all must be equal before the law, and now I see his words no longer as words but their wisdom is graven upon my soul. Each smallest farmer must be lifted up and gentlemen all must humble themselves, and well it may be that we shall meet at a level which brings a perfect happiness to us all. No man can live content who is less than his neighbor and lacks any means to better himself, and certain it is that the greater man can know no peace in his deepest heart while his neighbor yet suffers any least despair. For my part, verily I do believe that never I shall ever give another ball.

RICHMOND AUGUST 21, 1780

I had thought to put away this book. It seemed most self-indulgent for a lady to sit and write in a book when her sisters of different class and race may not do like the same. It seemed a mere addictive vice, as a man may strive to quit of tobacco, and well the like I strove to quit but all to no avail. My journal is my friend like no other friend, for while all others might judge my opinions or disparage my fears or tell me fears of their own, my dear patient journal but takes every word and gives in its place a welcome peace.

We removed in April last to Colonel Turpin's house in Richmond, which dear small house upon Shockoe Hill must likely be our home for these two years to come. They limit my husband to three one-year terms, the which but condemns him to three years' service as certainly as if he is bound for a crime. It is a pretty house, but small so we must build onto it rooms for our servants, and this Great George has cleverly done. We can hear from our house the sound of the falls where the water rushes among the rocks, and this small sound in the night is so pleasing that I forgive my Richmond her poor plain face when the song that she sings is so clear and sweet.

I am glad for every small distraction of making for us another home, for the war in this summer has turned so ill. Charles Town has fallen to the British. The greatest city of the south is lost, and with it the southern Continental Army to a number of some two thousand men and many the like of militiamen. Indeed, the whole of South Carolina is lost for there rose in the state a Tory army which had quiet lain against this event. It is said that the state is at full civil war, and with the British army to support the Tories our patriot Whigs cannot prevail.

We hear again the stories that ever we hear of the terrible raiding and plunder, the farms and plantations all burnt to cinders and the families in carts upon the road. All the worst predations are by the Tories against what late had been their neighbors: neighbor murders neighbor and burns his farm for naught but a preference of his government. One British commander has made his name with a lethal Tory cavalry, that he attacks of a sudden and he gives no quarter but he kills his prisoners every one. His name comes to strike such a blow of terror that mothers now use it to admonish their children, that Bloody Ban Tarleton will have them away unless they mind their elders well.

So Georgia is lost, and now South Carolina. But one state between and they are at our door. All know what surely the British must know, that Virginia is the heart of these United States and if she were taken our cause would be lost. Thus we fight in Virginia not just for ourselves, but we fight for the survival of the Continent. My dear dear husband has worked both day and night without cease this summer long, that he raise up the soldiers and the food and muskets to build again the southern Continental Army.

General Lincoln was captured away at Charles Town so General Gates was put up in his room, the same most proud fine general who captured Burgoyne at Saratoga. He paused in Richmond on his journey south so we had some brief acquaintance of him, at which I came to rest uneasy despite my little experience of generals. I said to my Thomas, "If I were a private soldier I would hope for a general with fewer finger-rings and a lesser resort to his perfumed oils and his rum and his snuff. But that is just my opinion."

"If you were a private I would pity the British! Oh Patty, never judge a man by his look. He can fight well enough despite his finger-rings."

That he could not do. The British had placed their supplies at Camden in South Carolina, which town the general determined to take what ever be its cost. My husband sent a thousand militiamen, all that he could quickly raise, and these poor men were put to the battle directly they arrived at the Patriot camp. So weary as they were and unused to war, they could not lead the fighting. They broke and ran like a very torrent, and after them ran near all of our army and General Gates ran the farthest of all, a full fifty miles in one day's time.

I have said it light to make a sport of it. They ran all tumbled over themselves, so foolish the thought of an attacking army which sees a first defense so it turns and runs. But the reality was a ghastly thing. They plundered their baggage-wagons as they ran, they abandoned their own poor women and children, they cut down their officers who tried to turn them. Nothing so dreadful as an army in flight. And after them the British cavalry came with Bloody Ban Tarleton in the van, his Tories slashing to right and left and killing all the wounded as they fell.

I knew some few of those militiamen. They danced very gay at my holiday ball. Now I want to be as many others are, full of a rage that they so betray us, but ever my mind supplies their faces. Why they turned coward I cannot guess, but we who sit at peace in our parlors must not presume to judge these others. I grieve for them, both for those who fell and for those less lucky who survive in shame.

At peace we may sit within our parlors, but still the pains of war are at our doors. The money has become without a value; we trade more often than we buy or sell. We have not a where to sell our tobacco, we plead for help abroad to no avail, and the crops have failed these two years past so food has come to be quite scarce. It is a peculiar scarcity. We shall not starve, but food has been in plenty our whole lives long so its scarcity is a terrible lack. Few pigs now run upon the street. Every rib of every horse is plain to see. The gentry eat so much of food that many have become most greatly fat, and these now decline so their clothes hang loose while they yet remain in passing health. Even the poor do not starve in the town, but I come to worry for the far small-planters who live every year from crop to crop so the famine must serve them very ill.

And it ill serves General Washington's army. He does very little these two years past but to suffer and starve from place to place as he counters an enemy fat and gay which little cares to fight. He wintered at Morristown in the Jerseys and lately he has fought what he ever has fought, just a movement of the British out from New York and a careless movement back again. His northern army greatly declines for none will re-enlist to it. They receive food every second day and at times no food for more than a week, and they are paid in Continental bills so poor that the Congress takes them back in payment at forty bills in place of one.

My dear Mrs. Washington has sent to me a broadside of Pennsylvania ladies who canvass their neighbors door by door. Very much of specie have they raised and dispatched to General Washington, and now the good brave general's lady sends their broadsides to every governor's lady that we each within our various states might collect our monies like the same. Never mind that Virginia has become so poor that starved horses fall and die in the streets, and the Governor's lady served one such horse to a table of guests and swore it beef. Never mind that every farthing we can gather must go to the defense of North Carolina. This Mrs. Bache and Mrs. Reed of Pennsylvania will brook no denial for any cause, and every poor mother with pence saved out to buy her children's winter shoes must put her pence into the common cause or think herself no Patriot.

My feeling upon receiving this broadside was very like my ancient rage when my Betsy's Patriot friends called my mind into question because I wore my silks. Yet I must within my official role do something with the document, so I sent it on to Mrs. Tucker. She is a most ardent Patriot lady, and if I can think of any lady going house to house to beg for the army my dear friend Frances would be that one. She may do as she likes. I wish her well, but I have not the face to beg of poor women who hardly can afford to feed their children. At any event, I am become too ill. The war for the nonce must carry on without me.

See how at last I have learned to place my country's pains above my own. I am grievously sick for the whole of August of a terrible kidney-fever, and this fact I have forborne to mention through three pages written over two days of time while I alternately writ and slept and labored upon my chamber-pot. I put my country's trials above my own. If my poor pains could ease my country's pains I would suffer content for evermore.

My babe will be born at the end of November. My dear husband is so alarmed for my health that again he insists this will be the last, the which it very well might be. I doubt that I can weather these pains again. But my dear Betty has just lately arrived and she will not swear that I carry a son so I fear that again I shall bear a girl. If I bear a girl and recover my health, I have no doubt that I shall bear again. My Betty has come to care for me. We could not keep her youngest in Richmond so she had returned to Monticello, but the pleasure of having her here with me now makes me wish for some way that I might keep her here.

RICHMOND AUGUST 31, 1780

I must write an amazing conversation. I have not the time, but the words may leave me so here in haste I sit and write. We plan a great party to dine so I should be at the kitchen to see to the cooking, and that all the more since my husband as yet will not believe that I have my health. I must show him forth a most exhausting vigor; to sit and write the day will not look well. Yet to lose my conversation with my so dear Betty is a risk withal that I cannot take, for I have a thought that if I write it out and read it again and over again I shall come to a perfect understanding. I must write. They will manage how ever they may.

My so dear Betty has restored my health. None other but my husband could so well attend me, and he is so immersed in his grievous duties that he had not the time to sit by my bed. But Betty commanded that I be well. She made my cooling foods with her own dear hands and forced me to eat if I would or no, she forced my draughts of water and Gabbler's potion, and ever by day and even by night she sat here fast beside me. I had no choice but to improve or to face her wrath, and that no mortal would dare to do.

I find a comfort in my Betty's presence which I think is like the comfort of a little child held very safe in its mother's arms. With her, all is usual. She is above war and every such-like human crisis. With her is food enough and all in health and the sun and the rain safe within their seasons. I feel with her a comfort I need so desperately that I said this morning when she brought me my breakfast that I might tarry longer in my bed, "Betty? Would you very much object if I kept you here longer away from your children?"

"No, mistress. Only send away your children, too."

"You need not be sharp! I but asked you the question. Or perhaps we can bring your youngest here."

"I do not want them here. This is a foul place. Monticello is their home and all they know."

I ate of my dish of peaches and plums seethed together with raisins and such-like things which I did not always recognize. Betty puts in my food very many herbs and what else the slaves may find in the woods, and our guests this day will eat the like and think me clever to feed them so well. I press my servants to find more food and little ask from whence it comes. While my husband is the Governor of Virginia, I vow that his table shall not shame him. But I ate, and I considered my Betty's words. At length I said, "Why are you so sharp? You need but say that indeed you would mind. You need not shame me for it."

"I fear that you will keep me here. I must turn you the table very plain." She stood by the window so the morning light was full upon her face. I knew from the sounds that a carter was driving his beaten animals up the hill with a load of stones beyond their strength. I could not think of the pain of the horses, for I had not the power to improve their fate; I have run out of doors to plead with carters and seen them abuse their beasts the more. These are desperate times and they must eat: their horses must bear it how ever they may. I could not help the horses, so all I could do was to focus very hard on my Betty's words. I had not thought of Monticello as her children's home, but indeed it is theirs as it is my own. I had not thought of my power to keep her, but indeed I have the power and I may keep her. These thoughts were tumbled fast in my mind with the shouts of the carter and the slip of hoof on gravel and the harness-sounds.

"Betty? Will you tell me one plain thing and not be angry for it? Why do you consent to my power over you? No anger! I am ill!" I said out quickly, for her face when she turned was gone dark with rage. "Forgive me! I only beg to understand. There is some thought in the mind of the slave which makes him willing to be enslaved, and I cannot know it. I am very much plagued. Oh Betty, you know how much I love you. Only tell me this once. Make me understand."

"Can you tell me the thought in the mind of the master which makes him willing to own his slave? If you know the one, you will know the other." So she said, and her words struck my mind like rocks for my husband is distressed by this very question. He bears a very great aversion to the holding of any power over another man, and he is dismayed to see how greatly some love that wielding of power for the sake of power.

"I know not why the master wants his slave. That is, beyond his wish to get the plowing done," I said while my mind was stuck fast upon that terrible, greatly inexplicable fact that some love their power for the power itself. I have friends among ladies who delight to say that a maid cannot embroider or pour their tea so they must chastise or even beat their slave for a prick out of place or a spotted cloth. Fine gentlemen I have known to require that a coachman grovel if a horse is lamed, or a butler clean up the floor with his tongue that he never trip again. Not all are like my own dear husband, who hates this power of one over another. Some people find in the owning of slaves a greatly obscene delight.

"You reason outward from yourself," my Betty said with her voice more gentle. "Leave off your own mind. Think beyond what you are."

"That no one can do." I smiled to think that she would expect so much of me. "Will you tell me, Betty? Why do you not run? I nearly am afraid to say it out for fear I put the thought in your head, but the thought is there every day of your life and yet you do not run. Will you tell me why?"

"Why do you not run? Why does your husband not run?"

"But we have no need to run."

"You have no need? Oh, mistress, you risk your life that you might give your husband a son. You must run instead! Run!"

"But he does not force me. It is I who crave to bear him a son."

"Then run from your craving! You must leave it off! A son can never be worth your life!"

"Now you sound like my husband." I spooned another bite which tasted sharply of some wild flavor.

"Does he truly insist that you must leave off bearing? Then obey him, for the love of God! You so glad obey him in everything else!"

"We talk of you, Betty. We do not talk of me."

She blew out a sigh with a very great force. "I do talk of me. We are each of us slaves." She looked again out the window, where the noise was less. I tried to convert it to the music of the falls. I would hear only water, which never must suffer. "We are all of us slaves," she said again. "If I am to make any sense of my life and forgive where ever I must forgive, I must step farther and farther back until with the eyes of God I see. Through His eyes there are only slaves. Some live rather better than the others."

"Through His eyes, that may be true enough."

"Then what right has one slave to judge another?" my Betty said most ardently. "Each slave must adapt to her own chains. You ever are at pains to make judgment, mistress, and although you judge with the kindest motive, still you judge. Do you recall those women who pained you? The wives of the militiamen? Mistress, have you ever once thought that they might disdain to attend your ball? That they laugh behind their hands to see the ladies pass? That each when she looks upon the world must look from the center of her own self?"

My cheeks then grew most greatly hot. I bent to my bowl that she not see. I am glad to believe they suffer less than I had imagined they might suffer, but the thought that they might disdain their betters is a shame of the world stood upon its head.

"I also see from my own self, mistress. If I do not run, it is only that I am best served if I do not run. And I love you, mistress, but I tell you this: if ever your husband should die in the night you will find every Hemings has run by the morning. We refuse to be sold. And you know our risk so you will never hunt for us."

"But I would free you! Never need you run away!"

"We will run. You have not the power to free us."

For this I had no answer. I dipped my spoon, although I no longer had the heart to eat.

"How can you presume to judge your slaves? That their minds are greater or lesser than yours or they have a greater or a lesser will to run or not to run or submit or not submit? What gives you the right to be our judge?"

This she said so fiercely that I looked away, that her eyes not burn very holes into mine. As my husband is composed of innocence and wisdom, so my Betty is all of love and anger and the one fiercely feeds upon the other.

"There is no common mind of a slave! Each makes his separate choice to submit, and that choice is freshly made every day so if the day ever comes when the world has changed we each in a moment can choose our freedom. Yet not freedom, mistress, for God can see that we but choose a different set of chains. You only have slaves in Virginia now because we choose for the time those chains we know."

I wanted to say, "That is sensible," but my Betty would greatly scorn my approval.

"Will it turn your world too much on its ear to know that some slaves are glad of their lives? To have but a simple right and wrong and be fed and spared the care of oneself makes a satisfying shape for many lives, mistress. Even the hands in the fields have pleasures. And each finds a way to mock those others who think them better than himself, so the meanest hand disdains his overseer and his master in the house upon the hill. All see out from that precious center. Each slave is the center of his own life."

This seemed to me so profound a thought that I must make pause to find its shape.

"Perhaps I am too hasty to free the slaves. Perhaps some would prefer the life they know."

"Of course you must free us!" she said near a shout. "Our slavery is a stain upon this earth! Free us! Make to us a thousand amends, and that will yet not be enough! But more than that, mistress, never judge us. Never presume to know what is right or good or to render any judgment at all. Your way is no better than is our own. We may carry our chains how ever we like."

"Yes. True. You are right. You are always right." That sounded as if I had carelessly said it out to put her words away, when I find in them the deepest truth. Yet to tell her so seemed to make them less. I bent to my bowl as if I meant to eat.

My Betty folded my husband's night-shirt and cap and fell to setting our chamber to right, well pleased, I thought, by what she had said. My Betty ever loves to hear her own words. I watched her askance while I contrived to eat, but I had so little wish for the food that I could not bear its sight or its smell. And one thought there was that so greatly pained me that I could not forbear to say it out.

"Betty? Would you truly run if my husband ever died in the night? Would you run from me when I would most need you? Can I mean so little to you as that?"

"Eat your breakfast, mistress," she said with impatience. "But look! You scarcely have begun to eat. Must I spoon it into your mouth myself?"

RICHMOND NOVEMBER 24, 1780

*T*his poor journal starves for a bit of joy. I must give it now a surfeit. Today when I thought to sit and write I read first some parts of entries past, and I think now that if I were mine own journal I would run off to find a better mistress. I live every day such a joyous life! Where is my joy here? Where are all my pleasures? My husband must ever be spared my journal. Our married life is so completely gay and so little of gaiety is recorded here that he would think me less happy to be his wife if ever he should read it. Upon some distant day when the war is past I shall buy a new book and create a new journal which finds its facts from this my first but carries throughout a more perfect joy. My glad gay journal I shall share with him. My first, with its pains, I shall consign to the fire.

Our two months past have carried such excitement that all I can do is to write it out, the family and the nation all intermixed, for such indeed is the way it comes. Our awareness of events makes no distinction, but all events seem alike our own.

At the first of October there came to us word that our General Arnold has defected to the British. And not just defected, but he very nearly surrendered up our fortress at West Point and our dear great General Washington and his aide the young General Lafayette. All that has spared us this grievous disaster which surely would have doomed our entire cause was the fortunate capture of a British Major with the plan of the fort within his shoe. General Arnold escaped to the British lines and he left his children and his poor young wife, who then was driven mad to learn of his treason. Ever the women must suffer in war, and how she will survive I cannot say. But consider this: near our greatest hero has become in a moment our greatest shame. Every child in the streets hoots out his name, and this with his defection but two months gone. Yet still I cannot believe it true. No gentleman could spurn his country so.

Then while we yet wondered at the news of Arnold, in October came a fine turn of the war at Kings Mountain in the North Carolina. Our militias there fought a Tory army and killed or captured a thousand men, the which we hope may dispirit the Tories so those who can be swayed may return to us. Many planters little care for the politics but they go to the side which best gives its protection, and lately with the strength of the British army they have many gone over to the Tory side. Still, many lie out in the woods that they need not swear allegiance to the British King, and these we may lure if we can show them strength. How greatly we have hungered for a victory! Some Virginia militiamen fought at Kings Mountain, and they fought so fiercely with all their hurts that some gave what is styled "Tarleton's quarter" and they killed every Tory who tried to yield. Still, it was a noble victory and it was food for spirits starved by war and driven to despair by our Camden rout.

Then while we thrilled at this news of Kings Mountain, British sails were seen in the Chesapeake Bay. A fleet of fifty ships of war sailed into Hampton Roads as if they sailed up the Thames. They took off Newport's News and Portsmouth. We had there no effective militias, and any opposition the local planters might give to an army of five thousand men was less to them than the stinging of flies. We had no hope beyond delay.

We long had been dreading this very invasion all day and night these five years past, so the fact of it brought a surprising calm. The British have come and we must fight. Indeed, it came at a positive moment. We find such success in the South Carolina that General Cornwallis, the British commander, is said to be in rapid full retreat. Yet our own south counties are turning Tory by the very nearness of the British army, and some in Pittsylvania even plan a revolt that they may yield up Virginia without a fight. So we had in October a great agitation of Arnold and Cornwallis and Pittsylvania and Kings Mountain, a giddy surfeit of immediate events when for long no event had occurred at all. After such a month, the British sails of invasion were a greatly suitable final sight.

My husband had early word of the fleet, although he thought its sailing unlikely since the sailing of the French from out of their Indies must keep the British at New York. But there was risk of a fleet, so he took some precautions of the moving of supplies and such-like acts. In truth, he had little more he could do of early preparation for our defense, for every man and musket and bit of food was claimed for the building of the Southern Army. He dared not short the Continent, for if we lose the Carolinas our cause is lost.

But then the sails were seen. Then the Carolinas' needs must give way in favor of our own. My husband moved at once to call up militias, he called up ordnance and wagons and food, and he worked from our parlor the clock around. There was such a hurried to and fro of officers and Express-riders into the night that I could not sleep, but I lay in my bed greatly round and miserable with my child and listened while her father worked to save her country. Curious it seems that I was not afraid when ever I am fearful of each least thing, but a woman just days from her lying-in is so steadily fixed on her own event that she has no care beyond it.

While my husband yet labored to counter the fleet, I suffered the renewal of my kidney-fever which signals when I shall deliver. Whether birth brings the illness or illness the birth is a question I have not the wit to untangle. But I fell greatly ill of a kidney-fever when I thought the birth must be a month to come, yet my count was wrong. My Lucy came forth a giant infant lusty of voice and so greatly fat that Thomas must weigh her. She weighed a full ten and a half pounds heavy!

I had made my peace that she is a girl much before my Lucy was ever born. Betty said it plainly from her rage at me that I have so foolishly risked my life, she said right out that it is a girl so my risk of my life is all for naught. For my comfort, I must give to this child a purpose. She is not a son, but she seals for me a promise to our slaves that they shall be free. Naught can I do for my so dear slaves but to make my feeble hopeful promise, but I seal my promise with the life of my child. For my slaves I name her my Lucy Elizabeth. Dear Thomas may for the nonce believe she is named for his sister Lewis and my sister Eppes, but Lucy is for my Betty's babe and Elizabeth is after my Betty's name. This secret pact known but to myself still makes for me a great satisfaction. My husband in his wisdom shall free the slaves and this is my sign of our covenant, that we dedicate to them our precious child who is born as robust as our promise.

I had not my Betty when Lucy was born but a woman of the town well attended me, and I had my dear fat Ursula too who yet remains as fat as ever she was. Her Isaac approaches unto five years of age but she never has since borne another child, and now she is aged beyond forty years so Isaac will likely be her last. Where we live all together in so small a house I see very much of my George and Ursula. Seldom had I seen them together before when they had by day their different roles, but here about the rooms I hear their words as soft and warm as a lovers' kiss. They are by one another styled Queen and King. This was my revelation.

"Queen? Girl? Have you any more eggs to spare? Mr. Cory's John has a slab of bacon. He will take for it two dozen eggs."

"He shall not have my eggs! His bacon is spoilt!"

"That it is not."

"Just put your nose to it, man!"

"All bacon smells alike."

"To a field hand like you."

Then comes a laughter as sweet and gay as if from a chamber, hers and then his, and I bend to my mending that I not listen. Yet sweet it is, and much sweeter still, for few of any station may share such bliss.

I am diverted. I must resume my tale.

With General Gates disgraced at Camden, the Congress put up General Greene in his room to build again the southern Continental Army. We had the company of this fine gentleman when he came through Richmond a week gone by, and I found him a cool distracted man with concern for naught but the army's needs. A general he is in every bone, but I better like the General Baron von Steuben who takes now military command of Virginia in the face of our entry to the field of the war. This Baron comes to people prepared to love him for their friendship with other Germans, and he is in the pattern a gay plump gentleman amiable of face and manner and ready with delight to mock the British. Upon his first encounter with my sweet Polly who grows beyond two years of her age, he dandled her laughing on his knee while he sang to her a German tavern-song which he said was a description of King George's personal powers and his lack of them. Well it is that Polly's language is English! The good Baron claims to have forgotten every song that is fit for the ears of ladies, so long has he labored at this war.

From the Generals we learned most amazing details of the late defection of General Arnold, for the Baron had sat upon the military board which condemned the poor young British Major whose capture foiled Arnold's terrible plan and prompted his escape. And General Greene said that at Washington's behest he had tried to exchange the Major for Arnold, the which was a proposal so greatly shameful that our enemy rejected it out of hand. Wrong it may have been, yet I have a thought that honor may lie above etiquette. Young Major André was good and noble, a gentleman worthy of the name, while General Arnold is a ruthless devil. For a good man to die in the room of a monster cannot in any way be right.

Here is their story. It seems that the Major André dealt with General Arnold quite honorably, and he wore his uniform on neutral ground as befits the custom for dealing with traitors. At worst, he should have been caught and exchanged, a prisoner of war and not a spy. But Arnold lured André behind our lines and forced him to don a civilian coat, and thus arrayed when he was apprehended the poor Major must be hanged as a spy. There was none up to Washington himself could save him, although gentlemen wept to see him die and they swore a yet more terrible vengeance upon the agent of his destruction.

Arnold nearly took all our hopes as well. He betrayed to the

British our General Washington's travels with only his staff for guard, and had he not been exposed in time it is likely that our dear friend would have been lost. That we could not have borne, for he is so much loved that some put him up now for Dictator-King in the room of the foolish ineffectual Congress. No man of value could support such a thing when we struggle so hard for our liberty, but the fact that it is proposed at all shows how very greatly he is loved.

So we passed a single pleasant dinner in making our acquaintance of the Generals, and then they passed two further days tight-closeted within our parlor to assist my husband with our defense. Our military state was alarming to them. We suffer a lack of muskets and a shortage of food still despite this better harvest gone, and a shortage of leather and cartridge-paper so no least thing is in supply. Yet my husband must ever make them aware that he can give the British fleet just his least response, lest in striving to repel what is a weak attack he leave exposed our south and west from whence he is convinced our defeat would come. Indeed, the odd dallying of Leslie's fleet for what had been nearly a month gone by made my husband believe it awaited conjunction with the army of Cornwallis from the Carolinas. This conjunction now could never be since Lord Cornwallis has been driven east, the which must prove my husband's wisdom in supporting the Continentals on our southern front.

I heard bits of such perplexing talk as I served them where they worked in our parlor. They had for service Bob and Jim and what help I could give them fresh up from my childbed, for the generals greatly mistrust the slaves. General Greene would have put the boys away, too, but Thomas swore to him that they are honest, and their pale skins made them seem nearly white so with reluctance he allowed their service. But not Martin's. Martin is too greatly dark and no word of my husband swayed the general's mind, for when ever the British take any place every slave within it deserts to them. I comforted Martin's dignity by saying the general is too low-born to have the manners of a gentleman. This consolation he was glad to hear, but he passed their visit in a perfect rage.

The worry of insurrection in the Pittsylvania and then the invasion of the British fleet bade my husband do what he has forborne to do, and send away to Maryland our enemy friends who sojourn at the Barracks. In truth, we have been at pains to feed them. We could not short their food for decency's sake, and indeed we feared we must feed them well lest they send off word that Virginia is starving and she must soon submit. He is right, I know. No consideration of friendship must intrude upon the needs of the Continent. Yet I think it a hard and grievous thing that women and children must be set to march when they have no thought to carry a gun and the winter is rapidly coming on.

While my husband yet labored to create our defense, the British pulled their anchors and beat a retreat. Leslie's fleet left Portsmouth on the sixteenth instant and seemed at first to venture up the James, but we have late word they have put out to sea and likely they are headed farther south. So what might have been a cry of pain to my journal has become a shout of joy. Indeed, God's mind can only be glimpsed from these, His unexpected acts, that when we cannot make sufficient defense He comes on our side and gives us aid.

TUCKAHOE JANUARY 4–5, 1781

*W*e are invaded. I sit in the frozen dark in what was my husband's boyhood home, and I know not whether he lives or he dies. I listen for distant musket-fire and hear but the hiss and crack of the hearth and a heavy breath from my dear dear Patsy who stirs now troubled in her sleep. This plantation is meant as a rally-point for militias come from farther west. None has come, so as yet our only defense is the Tuckahoe servants who patrol to guard us with harvest-scythes and fowling-guns. Twice since the early darkness came one slave or another has foolishly fired, and dear Mr. Randolph has come to tell me the boy was mistaken. We are yet safe.

I shall not sleep this night. My three babies sleep, dear Polly and Patsy curled one inside the other and Lucy safe within my little Bett's arms. We have the boys, too, but we had not the space to carry all our servants in my chaise. Great George and Ursula and Mary and their babes must all be left behind. I could not bear so to leave my slaves, but Thomas begged of me in his frantic haste that he have us safely away from Richmond. Then my George begged. "Please, mistress," he said. "I must remain to protect your goods, and this stubborn wench will not leave without me. You go along. We shall be quite safe."

My Great George smiled his ugly good smile. My husband was so desperate to have us away that he checked again the harness and instructed our Bob and again and again he returned to plead. So I had no choice but to enter my chaise while Ursula held fast my tiny babe scarce two months of age and already in flight before her advancing enemy. My Ursula's face when she leant her great body into the chaise to hand up my child was set in a silent wail of pain, her mouth and her eyes most round and wide. She feared for herself, but in her kindness she also greatly feared for these my children and especially for the two she had put to her breast.

"I am sorry. Oh, I am so sorry." No more than that was I able to say before my Ursula was gone away from the door and replaced there by my dear dear husband.

"I shall catch you up at Tuckahoe. Only look at your face! My dear, will you please try to leave me a smile?"

It approaches close to midnight now. The cold is a living, sinking thing which cramps in my fingers and pierces my lungs and I tremble in Mr. Randolph's greatcoat and above that my cloak, and this with the fire that Bob yet tends in the fireplace. He also cannot sleep. He would be with his master. What shall I write? I think to write of the ball. I must write of my husband alive and at peace or I know that I shall not survive this night.

My Thomas took it as a thing foregone that we would again give a Christmas ball. I tried to say him nay. When he first raised the ball, Leslie's British fleet was a fortnight gone and I could not by any power of mind imagine that we might give a ball. "Then you let them win," my husband said. "Is that not what you always say? If we yield up our pleasures then they have won?"

"Well, but if we were to give a ball we would have to invite every soul in Richmond. We have not a where to entertain so many."

At this, my husband looked at me from where he yet wrote at our chamber-table. Late it was beyond ten o'clock. I had but taken to our bed while still he wrote out his endless lists of militias and ordnance and food and cloth that he have it for his Council in the morning. He said, "Patty? Why must we invite every soul in Richmond if we give our ball?"

"We are all equal beings. No longer may we prefer the gentry over common people."

At this he stood his quill back among its fellows with a gesture as if he all but said that little Patty has gained another misapprehension and His Excellency the Governor must set her right. He said, "But my dear, may we not have our friends? Do you think that to be all equal beings we may not prefer one over another?"

"You know my meaning!" I wished not a conversation that would show me up to be dim and foolish and trouble my mind so I could not sleep.

"I know not your meaning. You have said things of late that seemed odd, now that I think of them. Do you believe that people can be forced to be equal?"

"There is no forbidden thought! You have said so yourself!"

"Oh, Patty, listen." He made to rise, but if he rose from his chair he would comfort me. Tenderness would lead unto tenderness, with our babe new-born and I not well and our battle over the next child not yet fought. He sat again.

"My dear, we indeed are equal. We are equal in our rights and in the sight of God, but always there will be those of greater minds or greater or lesser skills and merit. People will always prefer their fellows with tastes and background which resemble their own. To force a perfect sameness cannot be liberty."

"But we must be alike! Unless we are all alike the common people can never advance. The slaves will never be more than slaves. Can you not just once make us all alike? May we not then carry on from there?"

He smiled at my notion. I saw his smile by the flicker of his table-candle. "If we did such a thing, within one generation you would see again a division by rank. And there is no need. If we but remove any barriers in the law or from a lack of learning we shall find the most able of every rank will soon come together at the top. Only look at your own good father, Patty. He was born a penniless Lancaster lad and he rose to be one of the greatest men. He did it by his character and the strength of his mind."

"He did it by head-rights and the selling of slaves!" I said before I could catch myself. I do ever love and respect my Pappa, but as I lose my recollections of the man alive I see him as he was in truth. I think him not a model for any thing.

"Oh, Patty."

"Indeed, do not make us alike. You are wiser than I, and if you see not the need then I am sure there will be no need. But my dear Husband, never can we live well together while we suffer fears and angers only based upon rank! Can we not give a ball, yes, give a ball, but use for it one of the tobacco-houses and have there every person of every rank and wear simple dress and dance but reels and make our new friends of every station?"

This was not the ball that my husband had envisioned. I think what cost him the greatest pain was the loss of his wife in her wedding-gown and her Hessian hat and his mother's jewels, a very Virginia queen. But once past that loss he admired my notion; and as he ever does he admired my mind. For all that it has not the strength of his, he finds in it a strength which is all its own. "Can you truly see a world where there is perfect sameness and not any difference of class or race? How does it look, Patty? What do you see?"

I cannot describe for him what I see. Indeed it is a most peculiar vision, every male and female of every shade all smiling alike, all bowing together, all greatly polite and very gay. I see them every one dressed alike in the kind of plain gown that gentlemen wear but wide enough that they all might ride as my Fritschen rode, with her legs astride. She greatly shocked the ladies so to part her legs but I vow that her seat was more secure. They would all labor at their various tasks best suited to their tastes and strengths, but all such work would be of equal weight so each would feel an equal pride if he tilled the fields or tatted lace or cooked or wrote or whatever he did. Each child of tender age would be put to learn and not required to earn his keep. There would be no slaves nor masters. The greatest crime would be the causing of another any least distress. I had not envisioned my perfect world until my husband sought a view of it, but once I began all my thoughts came at once; I saw my vision whole and true. Yet I could not describe it to him. I could not bear to have him need to shatter it as surely he could shatter it very well by telling me the thousand thousand reasons why no such perfection could ever be.

My ball could not approach my vision, yet still I liked it very well. We used for it a tobacco-warehouse near by the edge of the Shockoe Valley which smelled as our Forest ballroom smelled of tobacco and foods and the ladies' gowns. Many members of the Assembly had fled to their counties so our guests numbered only a hundred people and of these far the most were the common people that my dear friends Sukey and Liddy and I must patiently lure to attend our ball upon promise of reels and abundant food and the friendship of all the ladies there.

I also would have had our dear house-servants, but we could not have slaves to attend our ball. As Sukey said, we would lose the masters. So I comfort myself to think of a ball in three years' time, or five, or ten, when we shall dance together all alike once the war is over and the slaves are free. As our memory fades of this grievous time we shall come to see slavery as I see my Pappa. Ever we shall keep our fond good thoughts of the gay life we shared before the war, but greatly stronger will be our revulsion to think that one man has ever owned another. Former master will gladly dance with former slave that they put this horror far behind and never see it more.

So we had but one color of guest at our ball and the men all wore their breeches, yet still it was such a gay odd thing that it had some flavor of my private vision. All felt merry to step for a moment to another odd inverted world, and in this world since the Governor willed it and the Governor's lady did like the same the most delicate lady could give her hand to dance with a blacksmith from off the street. I chose out baker and carter and many whose work I did not know, and I soon learned not to ask their work for to say it reminded them of their station. But I found in my ball the gayest delight, as if in a moment all was changed and I had made one class of men to continue past my ball for evermore.

My husband ever wears a grave cold look beyond his circle of friends. He is tender of the critical words which gentlemen in politics must learn to bear, so his look when he ventures out of doors is of one who ever expects a blow so his face is his armor to counter it. On occasion I will say, "My dear, will you smile?" when I can say it privately, and my jest will force his usual smile as fleeting and sweet as a hummingbird's wing. But his shy cool manner when out of doors has brought to him a public character so greatly at odds with the man himself that I despair of a way to counter it. Yet he so enjoyed our universal ball that his armor slipped and fell away. He gaily danced with the common women as if they were far the greatest belles and

*M*y husband is alive! He comes to us smelling of cold and horse and a most alarming scent of guns. He has been at the Foundry and the moving of arms and powder out of the way of the British. He has no news of Richmond. He has heard no firing. Now he laughs that I have run to kiss him and run again to tell my journal. I have not time to write. It is past one o'clock. I shall lie with my husband and to sleep.

FINE CREEK JANUARY 7, 1781

*T*his cabin was built by my husband's father. It has but four rooms, and its single virtue is a humility so abject and so complete that were the British to arrive at the door today they would have no thought to find the Governor's lady. My Thomas sent us here on Friday morning, eight miles more above Tuckahoe and safer for being across the James which we think the British unlikely to cross. He joined us again on yesterday evening after we had suffered two days of such fear that my heart ticked loud within my breast and each next tick must be its last. The British are in Richmond. They took the town upon Friday last while my husband watched from across the James. Every man had already fled the town but some few militiamen bold to fight, and these few fled at the alarming sight of British Regulars upon the road.

"But what of Ursula? What of Great George? What has become of all our people?"

I was frantic that we must know their fate but my husband just said, "They will likely hide." This said, he fell desperately onto his bed although it lacked any pillow or even a sheet and he lay full-clothed curled like a child and slept like the blessed dead. He rose before the dawn and before his wife. I woke alone then and believed him gone. I ran out in a very panic to find him standing by the militiamen's fire, whose glow of orange was the only color.

"Thomas!" I had slept in my gown. The rain had come hard for much of the night and the morning air was so cold and wet that mist froze with tears upon my cheeks. Our Bob and Jim had the horses by, and my dear Bob came to his mistress then and put his own coat about my shoulders, warm of the comfort of his body.

"Come and have breakfast," my husband said. "Mind the ash. It gives a flavor. Only look at your face! No calamity can merit such a desperate face." He was merry to share the militiamen's breakfast of ash-cake and coffee by their warming fire. Only seeing the Andersons there to guard him made me fear for his safety all the more.

"You cannot leave us! That you cannot!"

At this, my Thomas looked away from me. He would not shame us both so to argue in public.

"We must go now, madam," Mat said plain when our silence hung too long between. "We must try for Arnold. If we go right now, we yet may catch him unawares."

He looked at me from where they rolled their blankets to hold their mugs and spoons within. This Bob and Mat Anderson are constant friends, a former master and his former slave, and Bob is a fifer and Mat a drummer and they play when the militiamen march and train. Mat has begun to court our Mary so we see them often about our kitchen. I was briefly distracted by these thoughts, for the name Mat said was as passing odd as if he had said they hunted Beowulf's Grendel.

"Arnold? You go for the traitor Arnold?"

"He leads them, Patty," my husband said most grim and angrily through his teeth. "He seeks plunder. The fool tried to sell me Richmond. Now he has left it any way."

"Why did you not tell me their leader was Arnold?" So I said, although I knew his answer. My husband has grown so enraged by Arnold that he styles him a craven parricide and assigns to him the role of the blackest traitor of all of human history. He so very seldom harbors such angers that they are for him a point of great distress. Had I known that Arnold himself was in Richmond, I would have very greatly feared that alone and armed with naught but his rage my Thomas might confront him. He would duel with him; he would offer himself if the British yield Arnold in his place. I knew not what mad thing he might do to soothe his so unnatural rage. "You go to fight him? But you cannot fight! You are not a soldier! You cannot fight!"

"Oh, Patty, the British are gone from Richmond. Will you show a better courage than this?"

It shamed him for his wife so to weep and complain and very well it shamed me, too, but I could not stop. I was near to hysterical. I must make some feeble explanation. "But the horse is not a war-horse! He will throw you off if you come near any firing."

Thomas makes Caractacus his riding-horse. The beast is

splendid, near eighteen hands tall, a red-bay devoid of any white. He looks well the part of a gentleman's horse, but he is in truth a bold young stallion at times near-demented in his capers.

"My dear, I rode him to death on Friday. A cannon at his feet could not have roused him. We have found your limit, well enough!" he said as he gaily slapped the horse's neck. "Now will you kindly promise your mistress that you will take a perfect care of me?"

"No sir!" I said with my voice made high. "I shall pitch you, sir! You had best remain here!"

"If you pitch me you shall never see another filly," my Thomas said sternly to the horse.

"Then mount up, sir! I will carry you well!"

At this sportive talk between husband and wife the Andersons gaily laughed aloud. My husband gazed so warm upon me that I must smile at him despite my tears. "Never fear," he said so softly that the others were not aware that he spoke. "All I know of death is there would be no Patty, so I shall be careful to preserve my life."

"I shall pray." I know not from whence that came, for never I pray beyond the doors of the church. God indeed knows very well what He means to do and not to do, and for Patty to plead for her husband's life will little serve to sway Him. But Thomas thought it a splendid answer. He kissed me there upon my forehead and left a little spot of cold while I watched him step to mount his horse. Tall red-haired man and tall red-haired horse: they made bits of color in the rising light, both champing the bit to be away.

It is near after dawn. I have watched for long that place on the road where he dipped from sight. I bade him promise to return before dark or send me a note that I might sleep, but still I must somehow pass this day. It is time I must write of our great invasion.

Twice within eighteen months of time the British had come and gone away, so it seemed to my husband and his Government likely that the swamps and rivers of the Tidewater region where Patriots lurk behind every tree must give pause to any British fleet intent upon invasion. If an enemy comes it will be from the south or likely from out of the western forest. Tories and Indians have amassed to the west an army of two thousand savage men, so my husband gathers men for Colonel Clark that they march upon Detroit when comes the spring. And not just the spring, but to be precise they intend to march at that single moment when the rivers melt enough to navigate but the ships remain frozen upon the lakes. This seems an odd detail, this need to fight at the moment when the ice is but a half-way gone. My husband is delighted to figure the date to be at the middle of the month of March, but I can only think that war is such trouble that were I made the general I would sue for peace.

But all of our defense these two years past has been against attack from the south and west. The shore for the nonce is little guarded, for the shore seems to be our safest edge. Then upon the last day of the year just gone came an Express-rider knocking at our door while we gaily partook of a Sunday breakfast and shared our Patsy's company. My Thomas had only that moment told her that tomorrow we shall mark our nine years wed.

"I highly commend to you the state of marriage. Your mother, however, has another view and she will tell you to choose a nonpolitical husband and one, I imagine, who builds in wood. What other good advice will you have, my dear?"

I was but composing an answer sufficient to bring a round of laughter from husband and child when came the loud knock and then came Mary, alarmed to carry the rider's pouch. That was our last gay moment. A Mr. Wray had seen twenty-seven sail of ships in the Bay all making in a fleet for Hampton Roads. He knew not what might be their flag.

My husband could not carelessly call out militias when already so many had been called, for indeed the fleet might not be British. Or if British, it could but stop at Portsmouth. If it went beyond Portsmouth it might be to forage. It likely was not an invasion-fleet. With Lord Cornwallis building his force to the south and his hold so unsure upon the Carolinas, a full sea-invasion of Virginia now seemed so altogether mad and unlikely that my husband must discredit it. Then upon Tuesday last came the alarming news that a body of the fleet had entered the James. They were likely bent for Petersburg, for there are gathered our military stores in readiness for General Greene. My husband called up reserve militias to a number of beyond four thousand men that they rush to the defense of Petersburg.

Then it was that we began to carry to Westham the army's goods and the Government records, and for this we committed our wagon and phaeton and every horse we maintain in Richmond beyond Caractacus and the four to my chaise. I was careless to commit our wagon which should have been kept to move our slaves, for not having been so near a war I never once had the obvious thought that if we move the papers we should move the people.

The British sailed rapidly up the James with the wind direct behind them. They anchored at Jamestown, from which event we thought they might make for Williamsburg, but the wind continued strong so they came up higher. Expresses arrived nearly every hour and were sent as often as they came, the militias as reluctant as ever they are so my husband must press them ever more desperately to come together and to arms. Then on Thursday last at five in the morning before the least sign of any dawn came that knock again to sit us awake and have us rapidly down the stairs. It was our dear sister and brother Eppes, come in flight before the British with their four sweet children.

"They have fought past Hood's!" my Betsy said as she pressed in through the door. The river at Hood's must pass through narrows, the which we have made to fortify, but that was against but a ship or two. It could not hold an army.

"They took Hood's last night," Francis said to Thomas as he had off his gloves and removed his hat. "They are anchored at Kennon's til the tide turns again. Only give them a wind and they are at your door."

I must kiss and comfort my sister and children while the candles were lit and the parlor-fire laid and my husband learned from Francis what he must learn before he called for clerk and rider. This has become his whole round of life, this work and work and little sleep and food when we put it beneath his hand. While Betsy saw to her older children I rocked her weary frightened Patty, but soon I must go and nurse my Lucy and pass her to Mary that she might be fed.

My Mary has become a most excellent nursemaid. For all that at first she refused the role, she takes in it now a very great pride when I praise her that my Lucy and her little Joe have become together so greatly fat that she might well nurse two more besides if ever we could find them. That we have had to leave our Mary behind when lately we escaped from Richmond town has meant that I must nurse for hour upon hour and my Bett gives my Lucy cow's-milk, too, and still she never gets enough. My Bett is six months gone with child, and the birth will greatly lighten her heart for she grieves her first which died in her arms. I know not the father of her child but my Lucy will be glad to share its milk.

When down I came again it was nearly dawn. My Betsy and children were standing to eat of cold bread and jam and potted beef. My little Bett urged that they take yet more as she went from mother to child to child, and she stopped and set her platter down to help little Betsy raise her hood.

"You go right now? Where do you go?"

"We make for Monticello," my Francis said. "Do you come with us, Patty. You must rouse your children."

My husband and brother had made my decision while I lay abed to nurse my child. But I would not go. Not even when my Francis demanded and Betsy pleaded and Thomas begged would I leave my husband at such a time and go so far away. I must know his fate from moment to moment. I will stay by his side if I die for it. And Francis could brook no least delay for a fear that the British were right behind, so before the windows were fully light he bade his family return to their carriage that they might be away. Then was I amazed!

I had heard a distant sound like the river-falls but louder, yet near enough like the falls that it had no effect upon my mind. Yet we stepped from the house to my brother's carriage to find a torrent in the street of wagons and horses and people walking with bundles and baskets upon their backs. They flowed up-river by every road. They even flowed there up our Hillside Street to find their way higher up Shockoe Creek, that they might make the ford where the water is shallow before they turn back to the James again. They must follow the James, for none could know if the troops were bent for Richmond or for Petersburg, and ever which landing the British chose these refugees must make for the opposite bank.

I had heard so many tales of the flights of whole populations when armies come that to see it there by my own house-door was a thing of passing wonder. There were not so many people. They did not cover the road, although down by the river where wagons waited to make their crossing of the Shockoe Creek the road was covered to both house-doors and back beyond what my eye could see. They were silent. I would have thought that flight would involve much of weeping and crying out, but we heard only harness and wood upon wood and the footfalls constant on the road.

Yet was Francis not silent. "Get in! You may not ride upon the box!" he said to Richy and Jack, who are grown to ten and eight years of age and eager to see what might be seen. "Ben! You fool! You should have turned the carriage!"

"Wait, Frank. You are pointed to the upper ford. If you try to cross below it might take you the morning."

So said my husband very calm. He had his pencil and paper in hand where he had been writing what Francis said, and he put up a scrap against the carriage and drew out the forest roads to the north. His dear hand trembled on the paper. Only then did I know how alarmed he was, and seeing that little fear in him was a terror too deep for me to speak. If my husband was at last afraid, it certainly was the very end of the world. He had sent Bob and Jim to fetch my chariot so it came to our door as the carriage left, and naught could I do but to look at it while my dear boys calmed the horses down made restive by the people in the street. "You might go to Tuckahoe," Thomas said. "I cannot believe they will go above Richmond."

So I woke my children and fed them quickly while Mary and Martin packed our box. They thought much of coats and cloaks and shoes but they cared not for gowns or shifts or breeches so we wear our clothes now for the fourth day straight and we wash and wash again my Lucy's three diapers which luckily Bett had pinned her on. The worst of our flight is this lack of clothes. A city would I give if I could just be clean.

Our horses were restive to see and smell that odd calm panic in the street. Remus cantered in place on the road and Gustavus bit for to grab Jim's hand. Great George and Martin carried out our box to place it to its hinges at the chariot-back, and Bett carried Polly and Ursula Lucy and I held fast to my Patsy's hand. Only then did I wonder how we all could ride. "But what of our people? Thomas! Wait! How can we all fit in this one chariot?"

"We must leave some behind. They are safe enough." I heard in his voice as if he said it out that he had been awaiting my sudden awareness, and now he was desperate and near to panic for he had not a way to counter it.

"We cannot leave any! That I will not do!"

But I did understand my husband's plight. The Governor's first duty is to his Virginia, and with so much of papers and goods to move he could not keep back his wagon upon the thought that he might later need it to move his slaves. He felt a guilt even that he kept back his chariot. He must bear his loss how ever he might.

"Thomas! Our people! We must save our people!"

He was lifting our daughters in through the door while Martin held Otter for his brother to mount. This having a postilion in his saddle was a further signal that soon we would go, and Otter threw a fit like a thwarted child. Little Jim was shaken upon his back. "Mind yourself, sir!" He calmly stroked the horse, a boy but fifteen years of his age. "Watch his feet! Master! Keep you free of his feet!"

"You must go, Patty. They will tear up their harness." This Thomas said, and then he had a thought to see that the traces were well in place. He spoke up to Bob where he sat on the box and he came back again to me nearly frantic. "Get in now, Patty! You cannot wait!"

"Some can ride the horses. Some can ride up behind."

"Oh no, mistress! That I cannot do!" my poor dear Ursula said right out. And certainly she could not fit within. I looked alarmed from face to face.

Then it was that my so very dear Great George came gently to say that we now must go, and he and the others must care for our goods and they would be certainly very safe. My Martin could go. He could ride up with Bob, and Bett was small enough to ride within. I must at least bring all my Betty's children, but Mary flat refused to leave Ursula and the more we pleaded the more she refused. So we allowed her to remain, but I repent of it now. My Betty would not forgive me the loss of her Mary; she surely would not forgive the loss of Mary's children. She has begged that I send them to Monticello but Mary refused to yield them up, and never would she go from Richmond herself for she and Mat Anderson are greatly in love. Mary begged to remain, and we granted her wish. Oh, if I were able to beat a slave I fain would beat my Mary, who ever only thinks of her foolish self and she thus puts at risk all her mother's peace.

RICHMOND JANUARY 11, 1781

The British army have stolen my slaves! They have taken even the children! Even Mary's little Joe, but a new-born babe, and dear little Molly so bright and sweet that she played with my Polly like an older sister and scolded her to mind her manners. We had come to saying their names together, that Polly and Molly do this and that. Oh, what shall I tell my Polly? What ever in this life shall I tell my Betty? To sit and write my pain is my greatest comfort so now in desperation I sit and write, but the pain of the loss of my so dear slaves and the anguish of fearing their terrible fates is beyond the reach of quill and journal. Never shall I ever know joy again.

My husband had kept us away from Richmond. At the time I thought he meant to keep us safe, but now I think he also meant to spare me awareness of the loss of our slaves in the hope that some might be lying out and they might yet return. He brought us to Manchester three days gone and lodged us across the river, but he would not let us cross to Richmond while the British army tarried near by. Westover is twenty-six miles below Richmond and eight miles below my Pappa's Forest. There it was that the British had landed, and there they waited for the wind to change, and while they remained so near to Richmond I must remain safe on the opposite side. Dear Mrs. Byrd of Westover is a cousin of General Arnold's poor wife betrayed. Only think of her anger that she must entertain him! An odd thing indeed is a civil war.

The British embarked on yesterday when the wind turned favorable from the west and they have fallen down the river again. They may strike below, but now Richmond is safe so when I had no word from my husband this morning I put myself and family in a Government boat which was taking back goods across the James. My Bob carried Polly and Bett carried Lucy and Martin made haste to take my arm since the rain had come heavy and we had in spots a mud so deep it might swallow a horse. The town was ravaged. Papers blew like snow, and furniture and trash lay upon the street and dead beasts lay around in heaps and some had been butchered where they lay. The smell of wet ash was on the air; they had meant to burn the town but the rain intervened. Yet the mess of the streets and the lack of people made such a hideous violation that I felt myself ill of it. Scarce I could walk.

"You must sit, mistress! Here, I have found a chair." What Martin had found was a dining-chair half-submerged it seemed within the mud, but when he lifted it clear he found it lacking the parts that should have been beneath the ground. We looked around, both he and I, to find a better chair, and then it was that I saw the hand.

It lay upon the road with its fingers gracefully curled as if it might hold a rod. It was an usual hand, the nails neat-trimmed and no blood or wound that I could see, but it had not a body. The wrist was severed neatly at the end of the palm. "Oh, Martin. Look at that!" I could not tell its race. It was passing dark, but the palm was not a lighter shade. It might be either race or sex, and it lay forgotten upon the road as so many things lay upon the road. "Oh my God!" Had they maimed a soldier for stealing? Had they fought with swords upon the streets? Had some master cruelly punished his slave? From whence had ever come that hand?

"Come, mistress. Do not sully your mind with that."

Yet I must stand longer, transfixed by that hand. It seemed like that moment when I first killed a hog and found my fear worse than the act itself, for every horror of every war was concentrated in that one hand. But to look at it made my back come straight. I could face any thing if I could face that hand. "I am better now. Let us walk right on."

So we walked all the way to the Hillside Street and then up the hill to our dear small Palace. It stood so quiet, like every house. I was calling before I was in the door. "George! Ursula! Are you here? Mary! Martin, do you run and find the children!"

But they are not here. Every slave who did not lie out when the British came is stolen away from the town and gone. When the British steal slaves they sell them in the Indies or they leave them to die in slave-stockades which have some been found on the barrier-islands, the slaves all starved and dead in heaps. I had rather they had simply killed them quickly! Will they separate them? But to think of that moment when they tear my George and Ursula from each other's arms and snatch from my Mary her three small babes makes me weep. I have wept for the afternoon. My Thomas at last said that I must write or I shall never sleep this night.

So I have written while he finished his final letters and sent them away with his final Express. Our worry tonight is for Williamsburg, for we wait to hear that the fleet passes Burwell's and then if it does not pass that point we know that it makes for Williamsburg. Yet now I care nothing for Williamsburg. The Forest is spared, and it matters not. All the damage they have done to us beyond our slaves is the stealing away of our corn and meat and the smashing of all of our cellar of wine so the house reeks of wine right to the roof. Yet the wine matters not. All the wine in the world is not worth one single human life.

My servants, before they were stolen away, put all of our silver and money and gold in a bed-tick beneath Mary's kitchen-bed. I found them there when I thought it odd to see that bundle where it should not be, and I pulled it out. It seemed a message from my so dear slaves, that they love us still and they will not blame us. I see the scene as if it happens now, my Great George bidding my Mary and Ursula to hurry quick and look around for the enemy bangs upon the door. They run to the kitchen. They hide the bundle. Then the three stand brave all in a row with skirts held to better shield the bed, with Joe in Mary's arms and the three bigger children peeking to see what might be seen. Ever when I see that terrible moment when the British army stole away my slaves, I see them standing brave in my kitchen with their only thought the hiding of my worthless treasure.

*T*here has been a break of time. We have had our dinner cooked up by Bett with the help of the boys, and they are in truth the most terrible cooks that all the world has ever seen. We had beef she had bought with the trade of a coat, and all of her burning and dousing with sauce could not hide the fact that the beef was spoilt. We had a fruit-compote as dry as leather. A soup thick as mud, with its strongest taste not peas but a flavor like a good brown soap. Poor Bett wept to serve it for she knew it was bad, and she wept any way for the loss of her sister, but my dear Thomas praised what he was able to praise, the shade of the soup and the flavor of the sauce she had made from what little spoilt wine remains. Now we come to our chamber. My Thomas makes his lists. I am greatly weary and would take to our bed, but he insists that I am not sufficiently cheered so I must write on yet more.

Francis rode back today from Monticello. He swears that a horse died under him, so fast and recklessly did he ride to come to the defense of his country now that he has his family safe. He seems to have had some desperate thought that alone he would drive Arnold out of Richmond, for he was crestfallen to arrive today and find the British already gone. Then at dinner he discussed with Thomas his thought that he will raise a troop of Horse. "Jack Hylton is eager to join me, Tom," he said while he took from the bowl Jim held. My husband and I like to serve ourselves, the which my Francis never would do, but our servants seem glad to be near us this night for the shock of their loss is very great. "Hylton has six or eight in mind to help us begin a troop of Horse. We shall set out tomorrow. Arnold will not escape."

"Oh Francis," I said, "you are not a cavalryman!"

Francis is a major of the militia, but very little he has fought and the training of farmers as militiamen is not a preparation for a cavalry fight. He has a reckless bravery which pays no regard to his limitations, but for me so to speak was so shameful that I blushed and bent earnestly to my soup. Were my husband not there, Francis would have made me some indignant reply that he might save his dignity and show me my place. My words had greatly belittled him.

"We have a great need for cavalry," my husband said to help us both. "The militias need Horse if they will fight. Without it, the British Horse panics them. I do believe that our greatest strength is the quality of our horses and our horsemanship." So he said, this profoundly gentle man who nothing knows of Horse or war. He begs to learn from officers, he studies what war-books he can find, and still when ever he speaks of war he speaks as a man who has learned a lesson and not as a man who knows the way to fight.

"I need a better horse, Tom. Where can I buy one? I hear they have stolen all my slaves and horses. I know not what ever I shall find at home."

"You may find your horses at Charles City Court-House. Hockaday's militia have taken for themselves all the horses the British stole and left at Westover. What ever can have been in their minds, Frank? How can they steal from their own countrymen?"

To hear my husband say this off-hand thing put fast in my mind two alarming thoughts. Might some Virginian have stolen my slaves? Or might they have plain been left behind?

"Did the British leave slaves at Westover? Any?"

"Not one. Oh, Patty, first they loaded the slaves and that was why they had to leave the horses."

"But why take the slaves?" Yet I knew why. Slaves will stand the voyage better, and they can be sold for more when the journey ends.

"Will you give us an introduction to General Nelson?" Francis said, and broke my thought. "He does mean to make some sort of stand?"

"He only means to protect the towns. We have not the strength to take Arnold's whole army, and the last thing Nelson means to do is to bottle them so they cannot leave the James," my husband said to Francis while he looked at me.

I was weeping again. That vision of my Mary and her little children and my Ursula and her Isaac and my dear Great George being driven up the plank to a British slave-ship was a pain that I had not the strength to bear. And now I weep again. I turn, that my husband not see my face.

His pain in this is no less than my own and indeed it may be greater, for he knows as I blessedly cannot know the details of what will be their fate. He swears we are likely to get them back. He jests that he pities who ever buys Mary if he thinks to require of her any thing, but I know he says the like to express his pain that Mary will be stripped of her three little children and beaten until very well she submits. I sometimes think it is harder for men that they have not the right to sit and weep. Just now, my husband is so pained by my tears that he says out with a forced good cheer, "Aha! The famous Patty's famous emotional journal has finally been filled beyond what it can carry."

This jest of "famous" I have not explained, but lately I have teased my husband that since he now has a brig named Jefferson and a fort named Jefferson at the Mississippi and a county named Jefferson within the Kentucky he has become very greatly famous.

Now he says, "Have you written what I just said?"

He sees me smile despite my tears.

"And did you just write that?"

My smile is greater.

He says, "You must not write what I say! What if some stranger should read your journal?"

He is standing. Good-night!

RICHMOND APRIL 16, 1781

*M*y baby Lucy will lie alone within this foreign ground. I have yielded up another child to this war. I cannot bear it. If death will mean that I shall hold again my Lucy and my Janey and Jack, then I yield myself to death as a bride to her husband. Welcome death! I cannot bear this sorrow more.

My husband would be alarmed to read this now. I have said to him that I am glad to die but he only ever pleads that I must write in my journal. "Come and write, Patty. It is ever your comfort," he has said to me patiently all of the morning while he sits at his table and contrives to work. When ever he holds me in his arms I weep yet greater and greater tears, so he left off the holding at the early morning. He began to say then that I must write.

I have set my journal on his drafting-table that I might stand and walk and write and walk and stop to write and walk again. I find in this writing no comfort at all. I please him, but I bring myself no peace. It storms to a gale. My Thomas should be with his Council but he swears that for the weather they will not have a quorum, and this when very well I know that his reason to remain is his worry for me. So worthless I feel. I demand all his care, and this when I am the most worthless wife who bears him but girls and even at that I cannot keep them living.

The Governor of Virginia takes a leave this morning with Virginia in such a terrible strait that even though he will not admit it yet the war for our liberty is nearly lost. We begin now to see what the end will be. I find a perverse kind of comfort in that, to know at last our ending. Georgia and South Carolina are safe for the British and North Carolina is soon the same, and once the British can draft their militias to fight for the King we shall be overrun. We may hold off the British Regulars, but the Carolina militiamen are very fierce. Even my dear brave Thomas says that when they side with the British we cannot win.

Now the only remaining question is where they will cut the north from the south. The Carolinas are lost, the north is safe, and Virginia has become the battleground, so the northern Confederacy may fight for Virginia or else it may choose to yield us up. We beg for its help! Our members plead at the Congress and Thomas writes north the most desperate letters, yet still little more do we ever hear than a most artificial sympathy. Those weary of war who now feel themselves free may think our Virginia a tiny price if to yield us up will buy their peace. But if the British take Virginia then we must leave it. My husband is their greatest criminal. My terrible fear is that he may refuse to leave his own dear country and all that he loves so if the British take Virginia we must die. I never would submit to British rule. They must not capture and try my husband.

When the British stole my Mary they killed my Lucy as sure as if they shot her through the breast. We could find no other nurse-maid at any price. Week upon week I watched my child decline how ever desperately I sat and nursed and the cow's-milk little bettered her. She did not like it so she little took it, my poor sorry stubborn willful babe. Hour upon hour I must sit and nurse while my Lucy wept for a breast of milk, my only great hope that I could keep her alive until my Bett delivered her child. Bett delivered up a most strapping boy. She has named it Wormley for a fancy of hers, that Wormley seems to her the most elegant name, but Wormley was born just two weeks gone. Bett nursed them together, and well enough my Lucy began to improve her strength, but three days past she was taken with a cold. I can write of it no more. She declined with her cold until she has died on yesterday morning.

My dear husband speaks to me now and again most soft and warm to distract my mind. Now he says, "I cannot tell you how glad I am to be leaving this office in May. I am not a war-governor. They should have a general. Now they will, and we shall be the better for it."

"You have done all that any man could do!" I say to him with indignation. I cannot bear to hear him criticized, not even if it is by the man himself. Some are angry that General Arnold took Richmond and now he cannot be driven from Portsmouth, and General Phillips, who two years past was our prisoner-friend when we dined at Blenheim, has joined him there with additional troops. Cornwallis marches northward now so they might crush our remnant of an army between, and all of this disaster is assigned to my husband. Upon him, too, fall the many faults of the spring-time raids up the Chesapeake Bay and the depredations of the Cherokees who have very nearly emptied Kentucky. Those planters not captured or cruelly murdered are coming back eastward in a very panic.

And all of this is my husband's fault. Because he is styled the Governor, to him alone is assigned the blame. And this, when they refused his good constitution and enacted instead the one of Mr. Mason which makes of the Governor but the head of the Council and assigns to him no separate powers. This, when he has not the right to draft soldiers and not guns enough and no money at all, for a full three hundred of the Continent's old dollars will buy but one dollar of the new. This, when he strives to oppose the foe while common men demand that he surrender us up and they swear out their loyalty to the British King and refuse to report when militias are called. They stand in their fields and plant instead and curse my poor husband as if he had willed it that the British should strike us at planting-time.

All of this blame is his in spite of the fact that the Continent abandons us! For six years gone of this wretched war we have spent all we had for these United States, we have sent our soldiers north and south and given our food and powder and guns so now the whole of the north is free. The British hold New York as a kind of Gibraltar but elsewhere the north enjoys an absolute peace. The north has its liberty, bought in great measure with Virginia's fortune and Virginia's blood, and now that we have spent ourselves for her and the enemy is at our very door she will not defend us.

"Are you better, Patty?" my husband says, for I have stood and written awhile. "Only think, my dear, of the life that we shall enjoy beyond the end of May. I intend to spend whole days of time just reading beneath some leafy tree. You will scold me if I dare to mention the war. Patty? Are you feeling better now?"

I try for a smile. He sees me yet grim. Again I must bend to my table and write. I am of two minds that he leaves the Governorship when two years are served but not yet three. He is desperately weary and spent of this work which consumes up to twenty hours of his day. He is miserable to be in the public eye where naught that he does is seen as right, and oh, beyond even all these pains he is driven by his mind which demands to be fed. But he leaves his office before the war is won. It cannot but bring to him a public shame that he is too sanguine to imagine now; he thinks too well of people. If he left his office when Virginia was free they would forget every pain we have ever suffered and he would be styled a very saint. But if he leaves it now, with the foe at our door, every failure of Virginia will become his fault. He cannot imagine what will be his shame, and I have not the heart to point it out. I will give to Virginia not one more child nor one further day of my husband's life.

POPLAR FOREST JUNE 28, 1781

*D*uring all the years I have known my Thomas, I have felt for him so many fears. It seems to me now that my fears for my husband have been as constant as my love: that he might fall to the British or fall from his horse or fall from the affections of political men seemed so greatly likely that at every hour I have suffered such desperate fears for him. And now my every fear has all come real, and I survive it. The world ends, and I survive.

A week beyond my Lucy's death we again were in flight before the enemy. General Phillips led a fleet standing back up the river, and rather than wait until it made for Richmond I took away my children and all my servants and went up to Elk-hill on the James and then to my sister at Hors du Monde. I would not again make a panicked departure with clothing and food all left behind, and people left behind, beyond my so dear husband. In truth I thought him very safe, for the dear young General Lafayette had only just arrived with a thousand Continentals to take his military command of Virginia.

I pause to remark upon Lafayette, who arrived with his staff as we made to depart. He is a bold young gentleman of twenty-three years with far the most engaging face and manner who speaks English well, but in his great excitement he mixes it together with the French. My Thomas swears that he is not always frantic; he bears just some briskness of the northern folk. Yet ever I shall see him as I saw him that evening, all talk and gestures and bright with emotion. My husband bowed to greet him, perplexed and charmed, amazed that they had sent to us a whole army of energy in one young man.

The fortnight which followed our departure from Richmond was a greatly sorry and desperate time. General Phillips and his army burned our navy at anchor and burned very much of supplies and tobacco and killed hogs and cattle and did great harm on all the south bank of the James River from Petersburg to Manchester across from Richmond. We had no army fit to challenge them and militias that were called came in too slow so my husband and General Lafayette must watch from Richmond while the British burned Manchester. Soon after that the General died. They said it was of a bilious fever, but he may have been stricken by almighty God that he so ill repaid all our former kindness.

While General Phillips lay ill and dying, I myself lay very ill. It was far the worst time for my poor dear husband to be summoned to the sickbed of his wife, and once again I must certainly say that I make my dear Thomas a most sorry companion. Having traveled for days when I drank too little and ate too much of what ever was offered, I was stricken with a bladder-fever soon after we arrived at Hors du Monde. I have learned to manage my illnesses so I suffered but little at my last confinement and recovered as soon as my baby was born. But then came my moment of inattention when I drank too little and ate too well. Foolish lady! In payment for all my folly I must suffer upon my chamber-pot.

My Nancy was so distressed by my pains that she sent Jim on Otter to ride to Richmond. My husband rode back with him all that night, and when he found me breeding a kidney-fever he sent Bob on Remus for Dr. Gilmer. I suffered a most terrible kidney-fever, but Thomas sat and nursed me with Gabbler's and water and it might have been his care or it might have been random but my fever came to lessen as a storm will abate. By the time we had the benefit of Dr. Gilmer I was begging for my husband to return to Richmond. He could not afford so to give me his time when his country greatly needed him, so I contrived with Dr. Gilmer to prove myself improved and convince my dear husband he must be away.

Virginia was without a Government. The Members of the Council and the whole Assembly had fled in a panic before General Phillips, each Member most concerned for his life and his lands and careless for the nonce of his country's life. My husband tried daily to convene his Council but never since April could he make a quorum, until at the last upon the tenth day of May he gained sufficient Members to make his Council. Then late on that day came Jim in haste to summon him to Hors du Monde. Our fear was that unless he hurried back his Members again would fly away. And this they did. They were most of them gone from Richmond in the three days he took out to be with his wife, so he had but one single day of his Council for all of that desperate month of May. This, when their sorry Constitution insists that without his Council he is forbidden to govern!

So my husband made haste to return to Richmond and dear Dr. Gilmer attended to me. I had not for all of these nine years past consulted him for my bladder-fevers, and it came to me now that my forbearance had served to spare me a deal of needless pain. He gave great attention to the classification of my miseries upon the chamber-pot, whether dysury with a normal draining or strangury with draining out by drops or ischury with draining stopped alto-gether, and all three alike have like their pains so I cannot see it matters. He insisted I must be bled out well and I must puke the bile to have my fevers pass, and I must drink but little despite my thirst and I must have meat and forgo slave-potions, and all of this he said with the kindest heart so I could not say him nay. He tasted my water and found it sweet, the which most greatly dismayed him, for a sweetness of the water is a sign of diabetes. I assured him my water is never sweet but only I had eaten too well of sweetmeats. I would have assured him of any thing, for my one great wish was to be rid of his kindness that I might have my Gabbler's and water again so I might again be well. At length Dr. Gilmer carried us to Tuckahoe. There we remained but two days more before Thomas came from Richmond to carry us home.

My husband is ever so hopeful and cheerful that he thought that our Capital must be safe, but in this opinion he was quite alone. While he spent that single day with his Council and then rode by night to attend his wife, the Assembly managed a quorum sufficient to adjourn the whole Government to Charlottesville. This my husband at first opposed despite his joy to think of a return to our Seat, for he feared that a flight of the Government now would greatly dishearten all the people. Then events took a turn so even my husband must say that we must be away. Lord Cornwallis crossed the Roanoke on the twentieth of May with all of his army to invade Virginia. He met up with Arnold at Petersburg. Thus were the two British armies joined to a number of seven thousand men.

There could be no alternative but rapid flight. No force of ours could stand against them. They stood very rapidly up the James and took back Richmond and took back Westham, and they came up as far as our own Elk-hill which never we had dreamed might not be safe. They burned every barn and every fence, they carried off every horse fit for work and slit the throats of yearlings and suckling foals, and they carried off every Elk-hill slave not quick to lie out and thus escape.

But we still knew nothing of Elk-hill's fate when we came to Monticello near the end of May. I was greatly joyous to see our Seat, for we had been away these two years past and now we were back for evermore and the joy of that was as if for ever the clouds had broken and dawned the light. The trim of the house was in need of paint and a leak or two had sprung in the roof, but if ever any haven on the earth was safe our great brick house on its hill was safe. It was so safe indeed that we took in to lodge the Speakers of both the House and the Senate and some few other Members besides, with beds and pallets in every room. This made for us a constant work, but even all our work was a very pleasure in my own dear kitchen and with food enough and all my dear servants but my Ursula and Mary.

Of them and Great George we have never had word. My Betty is certain they have made their escape, and this shows the very great strength of her mind for if events turn against her she can but demand that they turn about again and run her way. I cling for comfort to my Betty's conviction, yet still on some nights I mourn and weep to lie in my bed and think of my slaves made to suffer and starve so far away.

Each morning the gentlemen descended to the town to work at resuming their Government, and they came home for dinner at four o'clock and talked over wine long into the night while I played for them my so dear spinet to soothe their minds that they might rest.

Upon the hot evening of the first day of June we even had a band of Indians to dine, their leader a chief of the Kaskaskia tribe who lately has rendered much aid to Virginia. I witnessed then some bit of Government pomp, for the chief made a speech in passing English and he gave to my husband four deerskins painted with Indian figures enacting their stories. Then they sat in their circle upon our west lawn while they passed their pipe of peace from hand to hand, ten fierce-dressed Indians with their fiercer chief and beside him our chief who is my own dear husband. Even my Thomas smoked their pipe, whom never I have seen to smoke at all. The other gentlemen stood and watched. They would not sit, nor would they smoke.

These gentlemen well understood that my Thomas would refuse a third term as their Governor. I heard them discussing it over wine, they urging him to serve and he declining, so it must be assigned to their fault alone that Virginia went for days without a Governor. His term expired on the second day of June, and then on the fourth as the first light dawned there came a great pounding on the door below. I took up a pillow to cover my head. From the edge of it I saw my husband's dear legs as he hurried fast to don his breeches. I said, "Oh, please just let them win. Let us give it up and say they may win if only they will let us sleep." I heard a great commotion below but I shut my eyes that I might sleep on until my Bett came running to say that Bloody Ban Tarleton has come for her master. Then did I rise!

There was such a great confusion below that it took me some time to hear the story true, but a Captain of militia named Jack Jouett indeed had arrived to warn my husband. At dusk upon the night just gone, this man had been at Louisa Court-House drinking for his pleasure at the Cuckoo Tavern when Tarleton's whole Legion passed by the door. He knew them as Tarleton's for their green and white coats. Every child in its bed knows the shade of those coats. So he ran out by a hidden door and rode through the night beyond forty miles, and now here he stood, a great dirty giant with his face and hands scratched and his red coat in rags and all his body weary. He was certain as ever a man can be certain that Tarleton's whole Legion was directly behind.

"You may be right," said my Thomas very calm. "I am indeed grateful for all your trouble. Now sit you down. I must insist that you sit with us and share our breakfast."

The Captain for all of his weariness was too greatly fearful to sit and rest. He drained to the dregs a glass of Madeira and begged a fresh horse and was out the door. Yet my husband cannot fear. He calmly bade my Jim run to harness my horses and send Caractacus below that he might be shod, and he bade Bett pack the box we had just unpacked so we might be safe away. The other gentlemen were calm as well, and they sent off their servants to harness their horses and pack up their boxes and find their books. Thomas sent some boys to watch the road and especially to watch the town below, some parts of which we can see like a map from the carriage-turn and the edge of the lawn. My husband was so greatly calm with a vast and quiet deliberate calm that all within the house were calm as well. It was for the others a brittle calm, as if all but my husband harbored the fear that the least alarmed word on any account would have Bloody Ban Tarleton find our door. They discussed it over breakfast, all very calm, while I sat near to quaking. I was the only lady at table so I could not speak fearfully and shame my husband, but I fancied each moment must be the moment of knocks or shouts or musket-fire. Would they knock or simply break in the windows? Would they take all the gentlemen or only my husband? Very many such irrational thoughts distracted my mind while I contrived to eat so I would not consider my central fear. Colonel Tarleton is ruthless and he takes no prisoners. He kills his captives every one.

They decided after talk and after much breakfast that indeed such a movement by Tarleton was likely. The whole Assembly should be safe away. They thought to move beyond the mountains and they named there Staunton as the likely town, and then when all of this was decided and the gentlemen's servants held the gentlemen's coats my husband turned and said to me, "I shall catch you up at Blenheim."

He hoped to hurry us out with the gentlemen, believing that I would not shame us both to dispute with him in public. He feared that I would not leave without him, and indeed upon my life I would not leave. My face glowed to say it. I bowed my head. But I said, "I have forgotten the way to Blenheim. I fear you will have to come as well."

"Bob remembers the way!"

"He has forgotten. We have been away for these two years."

Each effort to persuade me I mildly countered. It was not precisely shameful, but my will was plain so he pulled my chariot out of the line that it not delay the others. It was then full morning and coming so hot that the gentlemen sweated and the horses' heads drooped. It seemed an ordeal, but at last all were seated and three carriages and two chairs were away and gone.

"Now get you into that chariot!" my husband said to me near instantly. This very rare anger had been building in him during all the time it took the others to go.

"No, sir," I said. "I shall remain if you remain."

"I do not intend to remain! I must pack up my books. I cannot leave the Government papers behind."

"Very well. We shall pack up your books together."

In the year before I first met my husband, his mother's house at Shadwell burned and he lost therein every book that he owned. When Colonel Tarleton found him gone he would burn the house and three thousands of books, and this loss my husband would not sustain even if it were at the risk of his life.

"They will come up the road. They will block your escape. I can ride through the forest. You must go now, Patty!"

"The boys will warn us," I said. But the look of his face, most vexed at me but devoid of fear made me fiercely say, "They will kill you, Thomas! Oh, bother all your foolish books. If they burn the house we shall build it again. Do you think I wish to live if it is not with you?"

"Think of the children!"

"I do think of them. If a risk to their lives will make you save your own then they are very glad to take that risk."

"You are vexing me, Patty! Obey me now!" and such-like angry things he said. But he could not stand and dispute with me while

Tarleton rode nearer to our door, so he went away angrily into the house. I very meekly followed him.

We set in then to pack his books, not all of his books but only his best which he could not bear to lose. The burning of Shadwell had bade him design his library shelves as boxes stacked, and these could be well carried out. For all of his anger at his willful wife, my husband came to feel some little joy for indeed he had known that I would not leave him. Soon he began our familiar play of jesting words spoken, his and then mine, less for laughter than for comfort of one another. Each word is a very most gentle touch. At length he said, "What think you, Patty? Ought we to be making Colonel Tarleton's breakfast? What might he prefer, do you suppose?"

I was panicked by my fear for my husband. My very skin trembled for my terrible fear. But I said, "The English love their tea. I shall have to send Jim to buy some tea in town."

"You remind me," Thomas said. "Jim, will you go and make certain your mother has warned the hired men and the people to lie out in the woods? If they lie out they will be quite safe. Run and tell her now."

This shows forth my very great fear for my husband, that I had not given any thought to my slaves. I was up and out before Jim could rise, and down the stairs and out to the kitchen to find my Betty and Nance and Suck where they washed up the breakfast-dishes. The kitchen with its fire was greatly hot so my servants stood out beneath a tree, and they worked there together in such a heat that the sweat ran warm upon their cheeks. Nance's infant Billy sat on a blanket with a spoon in his fist, spooning spots of light and seeming dismayed that they could not be caught. Only then, in the terrible light of the sun, did I recall my need for a hat and mitts. I said, "You must run! The British are coming!"

"I know that, mistress," my Betty said as if I had insulted her. "I have sent word to the quarters. Those who would remain are making for the safety of the woods. Those who would be free are packing their goods to be ready to go."

"They will not free them! They will sell them in the Indies! You must tell the people they will not be free!"

"My Mary is free. All her children are free."

"That they are not. I want to believe it, too, but the truth is the truth. The British will not free them."

"I shall tell them in the quarters what you say. Why any one would believe a mistress who is desperate to keep her property, I know not. Nevertheless, I shall tell them."

This odd speech from Betty gave me great alarm. She was altogether not herself, but she seemed some cold and willful stranger. I had a thought that this was my true Betty and all her kindness to me had been only sham, but fast behind that thought came my awareness that she had set her mind against me because she greatly loved me. So she meant to run. "You must not run to the British! Listen to me! If they take you they will sell you in the Indies! Listen! Please listen!" I said on louder, for she bent to take up a handful of sand to better clean her pot. She worked on a stubborn piece of crust as if my pleas were naught but a fly on the air.

Then came my husband running from the house as never in my life I have seen him run. "Come, Patty! They are climbing the mountain!" A tinker had ridden up to the house to say there were dragoons upon the road. He thought there were not more than fifty dragoons but they were mounted up and they came on quick.

"Betty, promise!" I said to her desperately. She would not look at me so I could only hug her, the pot and the sweat and the heat and all. "I love you! Save yourselves!" was all I could say while my husband hurried me up the lawn to where Bett and our children rushed to enter my chariot.

It was only at the very chariot-door that I knew that my husband still would not go. I was beyond any sense with my fear for my Betty and all the other slaves she might lead to the British, and there as a cap for all my pains I saw myself about to lose my husband, too. "I will not go alone!" I said with my very foot upon the step.

"They are bringing up Caractacus. I promise you, Patty." Here he paused, for he must make his promise right. "I promise that as I completely love you I will not let them take me." I would have preferred a more entire promise against the risk that he might defend his house, but he kissed me and I was into my chariot. We took a farm-road dreadful with ruts that the slaves use for their heaviest wagons; it went almost directly down the hill and it twice crossed the better carriage-road but never we saw the least sign of the British.

My husband did see them. He went into his house, my cheerful and ever sanguine husband, but Martin was superintending some of the hands to carry his books to a shed in the woods and Martin ordered him out. He said, "Master, get you gone. We can see to this." Thomas but stood and looked at him so Martin said, "We are lost if you are taken! Have sense and get you out of here!"

My husband was charmed by these words of Martin's. The boy does greatly love him. He gathered some few more Government papers and picked up for weapon his old sword-cane, and he tells me he walked in our parlor a moment and looked at my spinet and his some few paintings. That house has been the center of all our life since long before it even wore its wood and bricks. To leave it to burn was very hard.

Indeed, he nearly did not leave it. He rode down to a lookout spot upon an edge of the hill, and he looked from there with his long spy's glass. Nary a soldier did he see. He thought the tinker must be mistaken so he mounted to ride back up to the house, but his sword dropped from the cane so he must turn and find it. He had a final look once the sword was found, and now with a very great amazement he saw the poor invaded Charlottesville all teeming with bright-coated mounted dragoons. Naught could he do but to ride away. Our house and all we had must suffer their fates.

Thomas caught us up at Enniscorthy, to which farther place he had sent us on from Blenheim, and then on the next day we traveled together to Geddes in Amherst on the River Tye. We stayed with Mr. Rose for nearly a week, until we could learn our Monticello's fate.

They did not burn the house, nor did they steal from us aught but one unfortunate slave. That slave was Barnaby, who works in iron, and since he has a trade I shall fear for him less. My Betty did not run, nor did the others run. Indeed, to the last they were hiding our goods, the books in the woods and then the silver. They hid the silver beneath the portico floor, and the first dragoons came up so suddenly that Martin must drop the boards in place and trap poor Caesar there. Caesar could not escape without risking our silver, so he lay in the dark for the whole three days the dragoons were encamped about our Seat.

Bloody Ban had sent up a Captain of his with command to find the Governor. Martin told him his master was no longer the Governor, which made no impression on the Captain's mind. When Martin refused to say where Thomas was, the Captain set his gun against Martin's breast. "Tell me where he has gone or I shall fire!"

"Fire away, then, for I shall never tell," my dear brave Martin said out quick.

That the Captain never did. He would not shame himself so to murder a loyal innocent boy. They but searched for my husband a day or two and thereby drove our people deeper into the woods, after which they rejoined Lord Cornwallis's army where it camped to destroy our Elk-hill plantation. After this sorry feat they fell back down the James.

We thought to come to Bedford. Our Poplar Forest has a plain frame house which sets on a rise to catch the smallest wind. It is ninety miles more beyond Charlottesville and far enough from every scene of the war for us to feel here very safe.

But then only several days gone by we had a letter from our good friend Mr. Cary, who sits with the Assembly where it meets at Staunton. General Nelson is elected the Governor there, which happy election of a military Governor has greatly relieved my husband's mind. But then came Mr. Cary's letter to inform that when the Assembly meets in the fall it will inquire into my husband's Governorship. His fellows mean to try my Thomas as a criminal derelict of his duty, and nothing they could do even up to his murder could bring to him such a great distress.

We had passed a fortnight of the gayest pleasures in glad retreat and perfect rest, the war and the work all far behind. Naught did we do for that fortnight of pleasure but to ride out for hours and to read for more hours beneath a leafy tree. What I read beneath the tree I shall mention in its turn, for it makes a different story. But then came the letter. We sat beneath our tree when Bob came to carry us some few letters, and these my husband idly read. He handed one to me. It was passing long, so when he saw me carefully read the innocent part of it he showed me the dreadful part at once. Very little did I understand. "What does this mean? Catalogue of omissions? Misconduct?"

"They mean to try me, Patty." He stood to his feet with his head high among the fluttering leaves. I thought of that dear so ancient day upon the Forest mill-pond hill when he begged me to consider that we might be wed.

"They accuse you of a crime?" I could not believe it. The gentlemen are most of them very good friends.

"Virginia is invaded. Richmond is twice taken. It must be some one's fault. Well I can see the way they think, and it takes but one

Member to make the motion. Then all must vote to seek inquiry as the only way to clear my name." This my Thomas said as if he spoke his thoughts to push them out of his mind. Such thoughts would burn and fester there and poison what is his only haven. He did not deserve to suffer this!

"But you have done nothing wrong!"

"Now I must prove that." He dropped his book from his hand to the grass. "Please excuse me, my dear."

He meant to ride. I yearned to be with him then, but if I were along he must ride on slowly when what he needed was to gallop fast that he might outrun his thoughts. The greatest wifely skill is to know when she is needed and to know when she can offer no help. We would talk much that evening, but for the nonce my husband was glad to be alone. I tried again to read when my husband was gone, but I had come to the point of leaving my hill when I saw Jim bring up the horse to the door.

Caractacus has recovered from his war-exertions. He capered and danced and pulled at his reins while brave little Jim but stroked his neck and kept by his shoulder to be free of his feet. My husband came out and down the steps, and Jim held the horse that he might mount. They moved off then across the lawn while Caractacus capered and Thomas found stirrups and leant to test his girth. Our Caractacus little stands at stud this year since we have no mares at Poplar Forest, but we have only a few fine colts and fillies which Thomas had led down from Monticello for a fear that the British might return to our Seat. That they murdered colts at Elk-hill is greatly alarming, and he would not lose the best of what remained. These horses had only just arrived, and one is a beautiful three-year-old filly which must on that day have been coming to her heat. She had screamed for the stallion the morning long. I heard her scream again, and I thought I knew why Caractacus was so aroused. I looked at them alarmed where they trotted a distant copse that edged a new-mown field. They had just begun a sprightly canter when Caractacus again heard the filly scream, and he jumped in the air and whirled in place and had my husband off.

Caractacus came running back toward the house, his loose stirrup-leathers like pounding wings, while I shouted out for Bob and Jim and tried to run all of that great long field. I could not run. The heat was very fierce and my stays were so tight that my vision went to black. I fell in a swoon so the stubble of the hay-field stabbed me on my hands and face and the sun baked me hot like a very fire and I wept in a delirium of heat. I had run to try to rescue my husband but my husband instead must rescue me. First Bett and then Dinah found me there in the field. This Dinah, whom I saved, is a fair enough cook, and Thomas praises her cheerful manner for she sings now as ever she sang when a child. Only once he has styled it passing odd that he cannot recall this particular slave.

"She was a child when you counted in '74. You know we feared then you had not counted all."

"True enough," he said. He never mentioned it more.

Dinah now carries her second child, but she remains so grateful to her mistress who saved her that she wept over me and cradled my head and bent to give me shelter from the sun.

Jim and Bob had run on to Thomas. He was severely injured, for his head was banged and his right arm was so badly broken that the point of the bone nearly pierced the skin. But he sat up and saw that his wife was down and her servants there attending her, and naught that they said could dissuade him from standing with his hurt arm cradled against his breast and coming up the field to give her aid.

Dr. Brown came that evening and pronounced me well recovered from my stroke of heat, and he bade my husband drink a great draught of rum for the setting of his arm would be very painful. Thomas would not have the rum. He said that no pain could be greater than what he had endured that day. He sat while Martin held him about the breast and Jim and Bob drew upon his wrist and the doctor poked his arm to guide the bone. I held his other hand until he came to fear that he might crush my fingers, so he held instead fast to the arm of the chair. He grunted softly for his very great pain, but he would not cry out and he would not weep.

When we rose this morning I bathed the bang of his head and I bathed his bruises and bathed his arm before I bound it up again. While I bathed his body I bathed his mind, for he talks very much about the charges against him. He is wounded to his soul, but he is calm enough now to say that he can think of no alleged fault to which he cannot make a strong defense. "I have copies of most of my correspondence. Be careful, my dear! If you bind too tight I shall lose my arm and be unable to hold you."

I said, "Dear Husband, on every day of our marriage I have had three very terrible fears. I feared the British might hunt for you. I feared you might meet with some injury. I feared your fellows might give you a rejection and trouble your peace for evermore.

And now every fear has come to pass, and we survive it! Are you not amazed? If we can weather this terrible June I know we can weather any thing."

Thomas stroked my head with his good left hand while I bound up the right to lie against his breast. He said, "I ever have just one fear. If it comes to pass I know I shall not survive."

MONTICELLO SEPTEMBER 30, 1781

*T*he only book I carried in my box when we fled to Poplar Forest was my Pappa's alarming St. Augustine's *Confessions* that I never read more than a page or two for my most peculiar fear of it. But having survived even Bloody Ban Tarleton, no longer was I willing to fear a book. I sat me down and read it through beneath my leafy tree, and the book was so delightful to me that I turned about and read it through once more.

My Pappa never apprehended this book! He saw but the early struggles of the saint and he found therein a most sadistical pleasure, as if he saw himself in the room of God and above every struggle of the man. Yet this saintly struggle no man can escape. The saint does struggle to save himself as we all struggle greatly to preserve our wills against that greater will of God. But once the saint surrenders in his great despair and he falls at the last to the arms of God he finds a joy greater than all his joys in every former pleasure. Then he sees in all his life but the workings of God, so each former pain brings him greater bliss as it shows him the workings of the mind of God to bring him at last into God's own arms. Over fourteen centuries, his delight in God's will is yet so fresh and plain to me that to read the saint's words makes me feel it, too.

God has ever had me pinned, and I have not known it. Now I feel at once both the pin and the joy. His will for me is perfect, how ever I see it, His vision vastly greater than can be my own, so to fear any thing is but an idle waste. Now I feel myself safe upon the pin of God.

I have tried to say the like to my husband. He finds my thought of pinning to be odd indeed although I tell him the notion is from my Pappa, and he finds an unease in my vision that events are the product of a great overriding will. "Think you then that we have no free will? I may not choose if I shall lift this pen?" he said to me once at the start of July when I said to him in my flush of joy that our war will be won if ever God should will it.

He sat at his table piled with books and papers to make clumsy notes with his good left hand that he might answer some questions which were sent to him by Monsieur Marbois of the French delegation. These questions give a shape to the intelligence he has gathered now these many years past, for they request every manner of information on the people and the land and the life of Virginia. To occupy his mind in this terrible summer while he waits for his inquiry before the Assembly and he waits to learn his country's fate, he has applied himself to this list of questions. That he must write with his inept left hand or bear the pain of straining his healing right shows his mind's great hunger for this work.

For answer I said, "Of course you may choose if you will hold a pen." I did not wish to argue. I only meant to share my saint-created joy, but I saw us so far apart in this that I dared not say more and make the gap yet wider.

"I have read the *Confessions,* but many years past. I recall that Saint Augustine is wise and engaging but he feels in his religion far too much emotion. Read the Gospels, Patty. They will calm your mind."

"I do not wish to be calm! Oh, Thomas, I had never imagined that God might be real. Real beyond the church! Can you not see the difference? The Bible says He marks each sparrow's fall, and ever I have thought those were pretty words. But they are not just words! My dear, can you see?"

"We have our free will. God may mourn the sparrow, but He wills neither its moment of flight from the branch nor the shot from the farmer that brings it down."

"But He wills the sparrow. He wills it to be. He wills that the farmer must kill to eat. And yes, you may choose your pen, dear Husband, and the moment of taking it from its pot, but from somewhere came the thought to send you those questions. If God ever knows you, He knows nothing surer than that you will sit this summer through and write out your answers."

My husband set his quill back into its pot as if of a sudden it burned his fingers. "Then what is God's will?" he said to me mildly. "Tell me, my dear. What do you see?"

I knew not what I saw. If it is God's great will, then little Patty cannot apprehend it. I had but the smallest glimpse of it, as the lightning will illumine a bit of the night and hint at a very much greater world which cannot be seen until dawns the morning.

I said, "It is nothing so simple as our free will or no. It is more that all of life is one grand design and we only ever glimpse but the smallest bit so we make ourselves foolish if we argue together over only that little bit we see. But I do believe that God has a plan for us." I looked at my husband, then looked away. "We can follow it or no, but He has His plan. He has a plan as well for the course of the world, and we follow it or we follow it not, but ever when we stray we shall have our pains. This war we suffer now is one such pain. We may follow Him, or else we may suffer. The earth is the Lord's. He will have His way."

My Thomas gazed so intently at me that when I saw his eyes I must avert my own. "How might we then have prevented this war? And what do you believe He means to happen now?"

"Perhaps it was the British who thwarted God's will. Perhaps He always meant that we must be free. But if indeed it is otherwise and He means for us to submit to their rule, then submit we must and with a very great joy. I believe this now with all my heart."

Thomas sighed and sat back against his chair. I made myself to look at him. Dear Husband! He has the wit to show me foolish, but this he never will ever do. He gazed at me warmly to coax me to talk that he might ever better apprehend his wife. "How then may we know? How are we to know if we should win or lose?"

"We never must pray that we shall win. Always our constant prayer must be that God's will be done and we not thwart it."

"Oh, my dear. But what of all those who suffer? What of the innocents hurt by this war which was caused, now you say, by the willful British or indeed by the willfulness of your own husband? Why does God will they suffer?"

"None can know if He wills it or He does not will it. Dear Husband, I have never much thought of heaven but if indeed there be a heaven, too, then our earthly pain matters not at all if we shall sing with the Lord for evermore."

At this my husband opened his arms and I went to sit upon his lap. He gazed at my face and stroked with his fingers the hair at my temple where it enters my cap and he said, "You do astound me, Patty. You seem but a mild and gentle lady and then you say a thing so profoundly wise. Each person has his own individual mind so each sees God in a different way, and your view is as lovely as you are lovely."

So my husband at once both praised and dismissed what for me is the greatest revelation. My glimpse of God from the saint's *Confessions* is far too immense to be just my own. And it bears in my heart a remarkable fruit which shows forth the very great worth of the tree, for I cease to worry. Since I read that book every fear of my life is forever gone.

The nations make ready now to talk their peace, by which we likely shall lose the Georgia and one or both of the Carolinas which yet remain under British rule. This prospect that our confederacy might be divided brings to my husband such an agitation that when the Congress appointed him in July to depart for France and discuss the peace he gave to this appointment a fortnight's thought before he must decline it. I knew all along that he must decline. He must remain here to win back his honor and the Assembly will not sit until the late fall, if it sits even then. We are still deep at war.

Lord Cornwallis has gone into camp at York, which intelligence would give to us a greater distress were it not for the march of our dear General Washington come south at last to give us aid. I have forborne to think ill of such a goodly gentleman, for all that he has kept his army north while his own country suffered and was overrun and naught did he do to give us aid. Yet he comes south now. We have late had word that he is in Williamsburg with all of his army of something beyond ten thousand men, Continentals and French all intermixed. They mean to lay siege to the town of York to catch Lord Cornwallis in a pudding-bag and capture all his army there. The French fleet, which little has ever done but to lend us its officers to dance at our balls, has just driven off the British fleet. Now Lord Cornwallis may be trapped. Now we shall see.

Yet I feel in all of this no agitation of fear or delight over what may be. I believe I catch a glimpse of God's great will, but if it is His will then I shall not improve it by fretting over just this bit I see. Thomas comes to find a pleasure in my new religion, that his lady even has a religion at all, and he gaily says that if God intends we win He has arranged a perfect concluding scene. If we manage to trap Lord Cornwallis's army, we shall have back the south when we make our peace.

So we talked very much in the month of July of events of the war and of my husband's defense. He read to me his notes for Monsieur Marbois's questions and I read to him parts of the saint's

Confessions. Indeed it was a grievous uncertain time, but we lived in such a perfect communion that never have we ever been gayer together, despite all the troubles we must share. Then upon an evening late in July there came to me again that certain conviction that I must conceive another child. I had held the thought since Lucy's death that I must have a baby in my arms again, but in May had come my fevers. It was not until July that my health returning fully to body and mind demanded that I must bear another child. Never have I felt this craving more.

Yet I had used every trick to make my husband yield. Never again could I charm him or shame him or divert his attention at a certain moment and gain thereby the gift of his seed. We long have established our marital comforts which exclude the procreative act, and so well indeed do we have our pleasures that the sight of a babe makes me marvel to know that some yet choose the basic act when there are so many greater pleasures. But if I argued with my husband I never could win. I tried to think of one new strategy, one slant of an argument not yet tried.

"I have made my decision," I said to him upon that evening late in July as we removed our clothing and readied for bed. The night was hot, so for the nonce we had the windows open, and a faint black breeze blew through the room only little cooler than the stagnant heat. It brought a scent of hay and a distant singing, for the Negroes on Saturdays dance their jigs, and it stirred to a dance the flames of our candles set one beside the other upon our table.

"You have decided that we must defect to the British," my husband said as he doffed his shirt. "You wish to see London in the fall. Or perhaps you wish to sleep with windows open so we may catch together some vile disease and share all the pleasures of getting well. Am I right? Am I close?"

"You are wrong and distant."

"Well then, you must have decided that you shall kiss your husband at the earliest moment."

He came and kissed me where I labored to release my stays. Bett still must draw them, but I have learnt to release them. Once he had kissed me I said to his face, "I have decided that we shall have another child."

"I would have said that next," he said by rote. This guessing-game we long have played. "Oh Patty, do not talk of a baby now!" he said plaintively on the end of the game. I knew by his tone that he had dreaded this moment and he thought his position rather weak, but I could not see which attack he feared. I must for the nonce keep my former plan.

"I must conceive it this summer, that it be born in the spring. Babies do better when they have the summer."

"I will not again let you risk your life!"

"That was Lucy's misfortune, that she was born in the fall and she was moved so often in the winter cold."

"I will not allow it!"

"So I must conceive it now. If we delay we shall put at risk our baby's life."

So we spoke our two different conversations until my husband said, "You do not listen to me!"

"I listen very well. It is you who do not hear me."

"Is this God talking, Patty? Is this down from God?"

"I know not what God wills, but I know that we must not thwart Him by refusing to come together. If we try for our child He may grant it or not, but it must be His decision."

"But the act will give you fevers."

"I shall drink my Gabbler's."

"Oh, Patty." He turned away from me to find his night-shirt and his cap. Then it was that I guessed which attack he feared. He worried that I might claim my right to bear a child as one of my natural human rights, for we have talked some this summer of the rights of men and he has sworn that women have our rights as well. We are weaker and therefore we must be protected, but nevertheless we have our human rights and these are fully equal with the rights of men.

When first I heard him say this I felt a relief like the release of my stays for evermore, as if for all my life I had not dared to breathe and now I take a breath and the air is sweet. We have fought for so long to claim the rights of men, and I know that if men are secure in their rights their wives and their daughters will be protected. Truly for me that has been enough. But, oh! to hear him say that women have our rights and they are fully equal with the rights of men is a joy in my heart which makes my head come straight and my feet step firm upon the ground.

I said, "This is my own life, Thomas. This is my own body. I have my right to choose if I will bear a child. You may not forbid me to claim my right."

His night-shirt was a ghost by the candle's light. It froze and then moved, and so it proved me right. He said with back turned,

"Indeed you have your rights, but if you love me you will not risk your life."

"Then I have not my rights. You only speak the words. You do not truly believe them."

I thought he might make me some impatient reply but instead he turned and said, "I am your husband. If you bear a child and die that will be my fault."

"It will be my own fault. I have a right to my fault. If I have any right, I have a right to that."

He smiled but the faintest smile. The candle-light flickered on his face. He said, "You do indeed have your right to be wrong."

"Only think, dear Husband, that nothing is certain. A year gone by you had your famous county and your famous fort and your famous brig, and now your fort is taken and your brig is sunk and your county has naught but Indians in it."

"But I still have my inquiry before the Assembly. I continue to be famous, if only for that."

"Just until the fall sitting."

"My dear, why are you still so determined to keep on bearing? We have our two children. Why is that not enough?"

I laid my stays aside. Now I wore but my shift. After pause, I had that off as well. Only very lately have I acquired an ease to let my husband see me thus unclothed and he blinked to see me do it, as if by the act I asserted my right to mine own life. I went to my husband and kissed him the kiss of a wife who craves to bear him another child. And he would not put me away. His sanguine belief that all will be well and his love that bade him grant my every wish combined very well upon that night with his desire that we should come together. He only resisted while he said again, "Why? Only tell me this. Please tell me why."

I knew not why. I still know it not, as I sit here nursing my bladder-fever which I have suffered intermittently since that night. I hide from my husband the worst of these pains to keep him willing upon night after night to leave it up to God if we conceive our child. But I said on that night, "I will master my life. Just as you shall beat the British if it costs your life, so I will bear my son or I will die."

God indeed has His will. I shall try to obey it, but still I retain some little will of my own.

MONTICELLO OCTOBER 25, 1781

I have back my Great George and my Ursula and Mary and all their children safe to me. That they were recaptured at the fall of York when Lord Cornwallis surrendered his army up makes of that, which is likely the end of our war, now the ending as well of all my fears. There were held at York very many slaves, and many of these were sick with the small-pox and putrid-fever and such like ills. Great George kept our people apart from them and thereby he preserved to us all their lives where very many died. The British had no wish for the slaves' disease. They drove out the stricken beyond the town, and these wandered helpless and died in the woods and never any tended them. We had heard these stories while the siege went on, of the hundreds of slaves all diseased and dying, and we feared very much that ours might have lived thus long just to sicken and die as well. Our Great George made himself known to General Washington so he and those with him were quickly safe, but of Barnaby and the poor slaves stolen from Elk-hill we never have heard the smallest word.

My slaves are at home these two days gone. I am mildly ill with my pregnancy, and I was retching into my chamber-pot after having had a passing thought of dinner when I heard the wagon-sounds upon the road and the joyful people calling. I could not do as I wished to do, just run and hug them every one, but I calmed my stomach and went out to greet my people with a proper dignity. I took Mary's babe from her arms for a token, as if in holding him I held them all. He is fatter than any I have ever seen since he got my Lucy's milk as well as his own, and he sat in my arms a year-old child as gay as if York had been a happy home.

Oh, I do so greatly love my slaves that I grieve now to know that we must free them, for all that I have yearned for their free-dom as if their dear freedom would be my own. Yet I shall miss them! If any go away from me I shall fret as I have fretted this summer long that they might be ill or badly treated and I not able to give them aid. I fain would style them free and yet keep them with me, but that I have not the right to do. I must free them now from my deepest heart. If York ends the war, then it ends their bondage.

My husband readies for Monsieur Marbois his answers to that worthy gentleman's questions. Monsieur never contemplated such answers as these! There lies on the table in the library now a stack of beyond a hundred close-written pages with charts and maps and all such things, for my husband has written a very book. He includes for Monsieur a description of his method for ending the Negroes' slavery, with the teaching of the children until they are grown and their settlement at some far distant place.

"Why can they not remain here?" I dared to ask upon reading again this freedom plan. I have held it in my mind for some little time that we and they are better served if they remain with us here.

My Thomas said, "We do not yet know if white and black can even live together at all. We know not what differences there may be which go beyond the colors of our skin."

"But may we not try?"

"We cannot afford to try. Right now, while we claim our infant freedom and try to make a government worthy of it, we cannot risk an experiment whose failure would mean civil strife or even civil war. My dear, if your hopes are realized and the black and the white are much alike, they will come together by natural migration as all other peoples come together. We must not force it. That the slaves were brought here was wrong, and to abandon them to freedom in a stronger white culture would only compound that grievous wrong."

All of this I could see. But he thought me not persuaded so he said, "Emancipation is not an easy thing! We must first win over the minds of the masters, and that I am finding quite hard to do with their minds so taken up with other things. I cannot lead where no one else will follow. If I press it too hard, I shall make myself obnoxious and ruin my usefulness to my country."

"But now you plan to leave your country's service. Will that not free you to speak for the slaves?"

My husband sat at ease at his writing-table in the library that he so greatly loves and where he means to be for evermore. We have talked much of late of his decision to retire from out of the public service, which he means to do with all his heart once he stands before the Assembly and recovers his name. To have him retiring to his farms and his books is a joy for his wife past my words to describe it, yet I find myself some troubled too. He is a man so good and great that he deserves to retire in the greatest honor, but instead he retires in a near disgrace. To recover his name is not to gain his glory.

"I shall share with you an idea of mine," dear Thomas said as if he spoke through his window to the trees beyond and to the hazy mountains. "I had meant to wait to tell you this until I was certain of my plan, for I know that now you will hold me to it. But Patty, what would you say if we took perhaps two thousand acres of land and divided it to fifty-acre squares and settled it as a chessboard? We might invite Germans, who are good strong people and never yet tainted by the owning of slaves, and for the dark squares we might settle our own families. The Assembly likely would give its permission, for if they allow me to experiment here they are quit of my talk about freeing the slaves and ready to show me wrong if I should fail."

"But you will not fail! We shall work with them and teach them! We shall prove the blacks entirely worthy and the whites quite willing to live with blacks upon the next-door farm. Oh, Thomas! We shall succeed so well that the Assembly will be shamed into freeing the slaves!"

So I have this for comfort in all my pains, that I see ahead clear to our shining future. We are poor from this war, with the money so depressed that six pounds will buy but a single chicken, but we are upon our mountain very near self-sufficient. We shall pay off our debts and begin again. My dear sister Carr is indeed so poor that late in the summer she has joined us here, with her six lovely children and the two wild boys my Thomas loves as well as if they are his own. Dear Peter and Sam are nearly his sons for their mother is his sister, and their father is his Dabney who is dead to us now and buried down the hill these eight years gone. Thomas teaches all the children, and with special zeal he teaches those beautiful willful boys. He professes to see in them very great gifts beneath their rough wildness of having no father, and they gentle a little beneath his hands. Perhaps they will be for him sons enough.

So we have much to do to build again what the war has cost us in time and treasure, but build it we shall. Through my window I can see my own dear children, my Patsy and Polly with their Sally and Molly all bent to collect the gaily colored leaves which they will weave into leaf-baskets that soon will fade. They know not how brief will be the use of those baskets for children little notice the passage of time, but just the satisfaction of building them and the beauty of the baskets and their pride of creation will make them believe those baskets worth all their effort if they last for just one day.

In all our new pleasures of our fine new life, I hold one remaining painful thought. I fear that my husband will be shamed to posterity as the Governor who nearly lost this war. If he regains his name or no, he will have this shame. And now when he works to free the slaves if he fails he may gain thereby another shame, and his name will be sullied for all of time beyond any power to cleanse it. Yet my husband is a leader of this war! He did very much to bring Virginia through it, and he wrote for the Continent our Declaration of Independence which surely must bring to him some little honor. The people cannot know him as I have known him, for if they knew him truly they would love him well.

Yet he is quit of the people. He has given all he can to the struggle to gain our liberty, and now he says that his great reward will be his own good freedom. He retires to his family and his farms and his books with a joy as if his years of the government service have been his life's quota of work and worry and now he will play for evermore. He talks of his scientifical projects which he carries on now by the dozens and dozens, and he talks of the harvest and Monsieur Marbois's questions but he never once mentions his coming inquiry.

This inquiry to his Governorship before the Assembly is his final unmerited public wound. It pains him, but beneath the pain he finds in it relief of a clean-cut ending. He puts me in mind of a lady who is pained by the rejection of her ugly suitor whom she has treated well but she has not loved and she meant to quit him any way. "The truth is the truth, Patty. Distant posterity will judge me more kindly than do my rivals, but nevertheless the truth is the truth. I cannot waste my life trying to better my name. I intend instead to live it."

So he says to me when I manage to suggest that retiring directly may not be wise. Yet I see now a way that I might defend him. I find a most perfect use for my journal which makes the time and the pain of it all worth while. I shall write a book. I shall take what I have written here of all the great things that my husband has done and I shall write a fine book to show him forth as the very greatest gentleman. If Odysseus never had his Homer, no man today would even know his name. So I shall play the Homer for my so dear Thomas. I shall write all the great things he has done and describe his many services to his country, but all of that will only bring him honor. What will make him loved as he deserves to be loved will be what I shall write of the man himself, that there never has lived so kindly a man, so gentle and so completely good.

Words of Betty Hemings, Slave   *End of Summer 1782*

I am asked to do what I cannot do but a death-bed request cannot be denied so I shall do what I can. I have told this girl to write my words but she say to speak slow. That I cannot do. The Master will tear up the house tonight and never find this writing-book, and by the morning he will know who has it. I must write quick and hide it where even I will not remember where it is.

My Mistress ask of me so many things. She lay dying and right to the end she ask me, knowing both that I cannot do them and I will find a way to get them done. She ask me to write of her death, which is come down just this morning. She always so sick when she bring a child, poor foolish lady, she will keep on bringing. She come down so sick near her time in the spring we think she die of the childbed-fever, and that poor man out of his mind but she come back a little and linger on. She bring a fine girl and name it Lucy Elizabeth like the Lucy Elizabeth that die before. I think she be sad to have a girl, but she look at the baby and smile and say, "This is our child, Betty. Now we have back our covenant." She always saying things like that. She got no power so she make up her power all inside her head.

She come back a little when the baby born but still she desperate sick. The Master tend her day and night with Mrs. Carr that live here. They always in that room, the one or the other, until one day Mistress bid Mrs. Carr go out and find the Master. When Mrs. Carr gone, my Mistress give me this book with all the letters stuck inside that she always be writing and reading in. "You must hide this, Betty. Your Master will demand it but you must swear to him you do not have it."

(You see by these words that very well I know how to talk the way they talk. But I never will do it. I will kill myself first.)

My Mistress so sick, these words she say make quite a lot of words. She start in puking. I say she got to stop, but she scared they come back. She say, "I meant to take the private things out and publish what would show him to the best advantage but there is no time. You must wait until his death, and after his death you must have this published."

Far too many words. I put the book in my pocket to show I can hide it very well, and I help her drink and help her puke and then they come back so I hurry out. But did we have trouble! The Master spend the whole summer so sure his wife is going to get well. She know she be dying the summer long, but Master think he got all the power in the world so he think he can even keep his wife alive. But near about a month before her end she so thin and sick and she eat no more and he get his first little bit of a doubt. Then he want this book. She say she have it hid. He not want to upset her so near her end, but day upon day he bring up this book.

"I will not read it if that is your wish. I will burn it right here where you can see it done," the Master say to his dying wife while he sit and hold her hand in two of his. He sit like that the whole day long, just sit and talk and hold her hand. But that day he start to be near about frantic. He even lay the fire all by himself, right then on the hottest summer day.

That fireplace so near by the bed that Mistress say he must not light the fire. But he love that lady like no other man ever love any woman of any color, and he so gone crazy with his grief for her that he see her dying the way she is. He fix his crazy grief on her book and letters. It like he have the thought if he burn them all she might turn around and come back well. So she let him light the fire. She bid me find a box that have some letters in it and she let him burn that. He content for a day, but what he really want is to get this book. She say it safe, she say to put it out of his mind, and then she get so low she never talk at all but she never yield it up. Now give him a night to take that house apart and I know whose house he be searching next.

I must speak of her death. She fall to sleep a day and a half before she die in truth, but she rally some little before that time and she say now she going to say good-bye. So the Master let her have all the people in that work here near about the house, and she speak to them and thank them and say God love them and they go out the house all weeping and wailing. Mrs. Carr and Mrs. Eppes bring their children in and she lay a hand on each their heads and then they bring her own. Miss Patsy is near about the age of ten so she know her mother is grievous sick, but Polly just four. She talk and laugh to her mother, and the baby Lucy know not who her mother is. She fuss when the Master put her down with the Mistress to hold on her arm that one more time. Then the Mistress say she saying her final words. She say it like that, just as calm as you please. She weary from saying so many good-byes. She say, "Thomas, let my sister raise my children. I would not have them suffer under a step-mother."

"They will have no step-mother," the poor man say, still holding her hand in two of his.

"Indeed they will. I am sure you will remarry."

"That I will not do!" I think he mean to say more, but there be many people in that room.

"Never make me such a promise," my Mistress say. "I want your happiness above all else." I expect him to say he never happy without her but he will not say that and so trouble her dying. She say, "Now you will go back to the politics. You are free of any worries for your wife."

He say nothing more. I never saw such grief, for his poor face is all of long gray lines. He grieve so to look at her frail and dying but he look at her constant as if she will die at the moment when he first look away. He hold her like that until she fall asleep to a sleep so deep she never can wake.

This girl, Hanah, say she is weary of writing. Her Mistress teach her to read, and now she has not the patience to sit and write when her Mistress die. She is afraid. Are you not afraid? None can know what the Master now may do.

I would say here who my Mistress was. For that I must tell a story. I been lady's-maid to both her step-mothers. Poor child, they use her very hard but she stay through it all so meek and kind. Then the last one die and my Master say I got to go and lie with him. I hate the white. I would cut out that half from myself if I had the knife to do it. I tell him go ahead and beat me to death for I never in this life will lie with him. So he say then he sell me and he sell all my children. I got such an anger I go out and walk and leave the work at the middle of the day. Little Mistress come and find me. She say, am I all right? I tell her I enter a fight with my Master and one will die or the other will die but I will never yield.

She say, "Oh Betty, there is nothing to be gained from fighting. No issue can be worth all this distress." I tell her she is just a child and she know not the least thing of this world. She say, "But one thing I know very well. There are no bad people, Betty. The worse they seem to you, the more wonderful it is when you find their good traits here and there. And then when you find them the traits you once hated begin to seem rather charming, too, until you love the whole, both the bad and the good."

I say she just a foolish child but those words of hers stick in my mind forever. And that was my Mistress.

AFTERWORD

by Sarah Eston Hemings
August 14, 1946

LITTLE PATSY WROTE ABOUT HER MOTHER'S DEATH some fifty years beyond the event. It turns out Betty didn't need to worry. Jefferson was hoping to protect his secrets, but he sure didn't spend that night looking for a book:

> [My father] nursed my poor mother in turn with aunt Carr and her own sister—sitting up with her and administering her medicines and drink to the last. For four months that she lingered, he was never out of calling; when not at her bedside, he was writing in a small room which opened immediately at the head of her bed. A moment before the closing scene, he was led from the room almost in a state of insensibility by his sister Mrs. Carr, who, with great difficulty, got him into his library, where he fainted, and remained so long insensible that they feared he never would revive. The scene that followed I did not witness; but the violence of his emotion, when almost by stealth I entered his room at night, to this day I dare not trust myself to describe. He kept his room three weeks, and I was never a

moment from his side. He walked almost incessantly night and day, only lying down occasionally, when nature was completely exhausted, on a pallet that had been brought in during his long fainting-fit. My aunts remained constantly with him for some weeks, I do not remember how many. When at last he left his room, he rode out, and from that time he was incessantly on horseback, rambling about the mountain, in the least frequented roads, and just as often through the woods. In those melancholy rambles, I was his constant companion, a solitary witness to many a violent burst of grief, the remembrance of which has consecrated particular scenes of that lost home beyond the power of time to obliterate.

Martha's death was almost the death of Jefferson. He was so optimistic and so full of emotion that he loved her with nothing held back at all, so her dying that way was a permanent pain for the forty-odd years he had left of life. And think of his guilt! He let her keep on bearing and eventually all those babies killed her. You can see him slamming his head against a wall or slapping his forehead or pounding the table every time in all those forty years he remembered again how those babies killed her. In later life he was a stubborn man so certain he was always right that he would trust in nobody's ideas but his own, and you can see pretty well what hardened him up. This woman he loved had died so young after he had let her bear six children against his nagging better judgment. After that, a really sensitive man is going to trust in nobody else's opinions.

Martha's death cost Jefferson not just his wife, but it cost him his home and his planned-out future. He couldn't stand the sight of Monticello, and in fact when he came back ten years later the first thing he did was to make it so different that Martha wouldn't know the house that stands today. He spent those two months after her death working up to the point where he could be with people, and then in November Congress named him again to negotiate the peace in France. This time he accepted. He had to get himself as far as he could from Martha's grave. So he went to France, where he served until they had their own Revolution in 1789, when he came home to become the first Secretary of State. Then he served out a term as the second Vice President, and in 1801 Thomas Jefferson became the third President of the United States. As

Martha had predicted he went back into politics, but it was a consolation life and not the one he had wanted.

Jefferson grieved for Martha all the rest of his life. People have
found this so hard to believe since they never had the chance to
read this book that from that day to this they have made up stories
to link him with one woman or another. Maria Cosway? Sally Hemings? All just lies. Some people prefer lies to the plain sweet truth.

I don't think he meant not to marry again. He tried to do a
little flirting in Paris as he put behind him the worst of his grief, but
he was careful to flirt just with married women like Maria Cosway
and Angelica Church. The letters he wrote to them read like letters
of yearning for his poor lost wife, and you get the sense that what
he really was doing was looking for another Martha. But there was
no other Martha. He learned that in Paris, and after that he never
tried to love again.

The Sally Hemings story is the one that gets me. Nothing in
this world could be more foolish. A bum named Callender bore him
a grudge so he published a batch of vicious lies and the Sally Hemings story was the one that stuck. People like to think a man so
moral was just another varmint deep inside so all down the years
they've loved that lie. Even I loved it, which is peculiar since it
came very near to killing me off fifty years before I was even born.

My real grandfather was Samuel Carr. He was every bit as wild
as Martha says he was, and the story my mother got down from
Eston was that those two fell in love like a house afire at the time
they were just coming out of their teens. They carried on that way
through both his marriages. Everyone at Monticello knew it. Even
Jefferson himself likely knew it, but Sally was willing so he wouldn't
meddle. Then in 1802 the story came out of the near-white children on Jefferson's hill that he had supposedly fathered, and Sam
dropped Sally like a ton of bricks. There were two more babies to
come, and Eston was the last, so that was when my life came to
hang in the balance, but fortunately Sam's love or just his lust let
him overcome his scruples. In a couple of years he was back with
Sally. And that was just the way it was.

Only after Sam dropped Sally for good did she start to tell her
children the lies were true and their master was their father. Eston
said she was a proud, vain woman, and bitter because she was
almost a lady, being raised as she was in the master's house right
with the master's children. She seized on that lie until she believed
it herself and some of her children believed it, too, since a Presi-

dent makes a better father than a rake coming slyly to cheat on his wife. To his credit, Eston never believed it. I believed it, though. I came to love that story until the first time I read this book. It's clear to me this Jefferson here could never have used a slave that way, and what's worse, poor Martha is spinning in her grave to think anybody would believe such a thing. I say she's been spinning long enough. I'm sorry if you're disappointed.

So Jefferson went from planning his perfect life to making his plans for the perfect country, and he did more than any other man to shape the final country we became. He made the Louisiana Purchase to double the size of the United States and he pushed exploration to the farthest coast to try to claim the continent. And he claimed our rights. From freedom of religion and the press through every other freedom you can name, all those rights we hold so dear today were pretty much formed in that one man's head. He thought common men should have the power because politicians are selfish and corrupt so he believed in universal education and limits on political terms of office. He fought to keep the government small and the power square in the hands of the people. But he had to drop slavery. As he said to Martha, human nature was progressing so the problem likely would solve itself and if he tried to force it before its time he would ruin his usefulness to his country.

He was useful, all right. Thomas Jefferson was the most useful man who ever lived. And since that's true, Martha's death must have been the most important event in American history between the Revolution and the Civil War.

Think about it. If Martha had lived, Jefferson would have retired in 1781. He'd have kept slavery as his one big cause and likely solved the problem around 1800 in a way that really solved the problem. As he said, abolition was just half the battle. If Martha had lived, there would have been no Civil War, no segregation eighty years after the fact, and this old woman wouldn't be worrying now they're going to come and throw her out of her room if they find out she isn't entirely white.

On the other hand, there would be two or three countries where the one United States stands today. Nobody else but Jefferson would have grabbed up territory and pushed for expansion the way he did. And without the one big United States we'd likely have lost the Second World War so we'd all be living under Hitler now. On balance, I guess we're better off. Even Martha herself would say so. I know she'd be thrilled to see how high the name of her Thomas stands today. But history is a funny thing. It tells one certain story, when there were lots of unsung people who were just as important as the famous ones. It does give you something to think about.

AUTHOR'S ENDNOTE

Thomas Jefferson and Sally Hemings

THE SALLY HEMINGS STORY IS LITTLE MORE THAN the fruit of one defamatory article by a journalist bearing a personal grudge. No proof was offered at the time, and despite heavy research no proof of the relationship has turned up since. That the Sally Hemings story has recently changed from a discredited rumor to a popular truth says more about us than it says about Jefferson, but no amount of belief can alter fact.

The dead can't defend themselves. They rely upon us to study their lives and to err, if at all, on the side of believing the best of them and not the worst. The burden of proof rests heavily on those who would advance the Sally Hemings story, and the plain fact is that what evidence there is tends to prove instead that it never happened.

If you have trouble giving up the Sally Hemings story, please read Virginius Dabney's brief and excellent book, *The Jefferson Scandals*. The story is not harmless. It is so at variance with Jefferson's character that it's impossible to believe it and have any understanding of who he was.

SELECTED
BIBLIOGRAPHY

What follows is a partial list of the sources consulted in researching *My Thomas*. Not included are numerous periodical articles and conversations with Jefferson scholars which immeasurably aided my understanding. I am grateful to the authors listed below and to their publishers. Without their excellent work and their great generosity in sharing it, I would have found this novel impossible to write.

ADAMS, WILLIAM HOWARD. *Jefferson's Monticello*. New York, Abbeville Press, 1983.

BAILYN, BERNARD. *Faces of Revolution*. New York, Alfred A. Knopf, 1990.

BAUMGARTEN, LINDA. *Eighteenth-Century Clothing at Williamsburg*. Williamsburg, The Colonial Williamsburg Foundation, 1986.

BEAR, JAMES A., JR., ED. *Jefferson at Monticello*. Charlottesville, University Press of Virginia, 1967.

BECKER, CARL. *The Declaration of Independence: A Study in the History of Political Ideas*. New York, Vintage Books, 1958.

BEDINI, SILVIO A. *Thomas Jefferson: Statesman of Science*. New York, Macmillan Publishing Company, 1990.

BENNETT, LERONE, JR. *Before the Mayflower: A History of Black America.* New York, Penguin Books, 1984.

BLUMENTHAL, WALTER HART. *Women Camp Followers of the American Revolution.* New York, Arno Press, 1974.

BOORSTIN, DANIEL J. *The Lost World of Thomas Jefferson.* Boston, Beacon Press, 1948.

BOOTH, SALLY SMITH. *The Women of '76.* New York, Hastings House Publishers, 1973.

BOWERS, CLAUDE G. *The Young Jefferson 1743–1789.* Boston, Houghton Mifflin Company, 1945.

BREEN, T.H. *Tobacco Culture: The Mentality of the Great Tidewater Planters on the Eve of the Revolution.* Princeton, Princeton University Press, 1985.

BROOKES, R., M.D. *The General Practice of Physic.* London, T. Carnan and F. Newbery, Jr., 1777.

BULLOCK, HELEN. *The Williamsburg Art of Cookery or, Accomplish'd Gentlewoman's Companion.* Williamsburg, The Colonial Williamsburg Foundation, 1966.

CAMPBELL, NORINE DICKSON. *Patrick Henry: Patriot & Statesman.* Old Greenwich, Connecticut, The Devin-Adair Company, 1969.

CAREY, JOHN, ED. *Eyewitness to History.* Cambridge, Harvard University Press, 1987.

CARSON, BARBARA. *The Governor's Palace.* Williamsburg, The Colonial Williamsburg Foundation, 1987.

CARSON, JANE. *Colonial Virginia Cookery.* Williamsburg, The Colonial Williamsburg Foundation, 1985.

CARSON, JANE. *Colonial Virginians at Play.* Williamsburg, The Colonial Williamsburg Foundation, 1989.

CHILD, MRS. *The American Frugal Housewife.* Boston, Carter, Hendee, and Co., 1833.

CLINTON, CATHERINE. *The Plantation Mistress.* New York, Pantheon Books, 1982.

CRIPE, HELEN. *Thomas Jefferson and Music.* Charlottesville, University Press of Virginia, 1974.

CULLEN, WILLIAM. *Practice of Physic.* London, 1784.

CUNNINGHAM, NOBLE E., JR. *In Pursuit of Reason: The Life of Thomas Jefferson.* New York, Ballantine Books, 1987.

DABNEY, VIRGINIUS. *The Jefferson Scandals.* Lanham, Maryland, Madison Books, 1991.

DAVIS, DAVID BRION. *Slavery in the Colonial Chesapeake.* Williamsburg, The Colonial Williamsburg Foundation, 1986.

DEPAUW, LINDA GRANT AND CONOVER HUNT. *"Remember the Ladies": Women in America 1750–1815.* New York, The Viking Press, 1976.

DEWEY, FRANK L. *Thomas Jefferson: Lawyer.* Charlottesville, University Press of Virginia, 1986.

DUMBAULD, EDWARD. *Thomas Jefferson, American Tourist.* Norman, Oklahoma, University of Oklahoma Press, 1946.

DURRELL, GERALD. *A Practical Guide for the Amateur Naturalist.* New York, Alfred A. Knopf, 1988.

EARLE, ALICE MORSE. *Child Life in Colonial Days.* Williamstown, Massachusetts, Corner House Publishers, 1975.

EARLE, ALICE MORSE. *Home Life in Colonial Days.* Middle Village, New York, Jonathan David Publishers, Inc., 1975.

FITHIAN, PHILIP VICKERS (HUNTER DICKINSON FARISH, ED.). *Journal and Letters of Philip Vickers Fithian.* Charlottesville, The University Press of Virginia, 1957.

Fox-Genovese, Elizabeth. *Within the Plantation Household: Black and White Women of the Old South.* Chapel Hill and London, The University of North Carolina Press, 1988.

Galenson, David. *White Servitude in Colonial America.* Cambridge, Cambridge University Press, 1981.

Garrett, Elisabeth Donaghy. *At Home: The American Family 1750–1870.* New York, Harry N. Abrams, Inc., 1990.

Glasscheib, H.S., M.D. *The March of Medicine.* New York, G.P. Putnam's Sons, 1964.

Greene, Jack P. *Landon Carter: An Inquiry into the Personal Values and Social Imperatives of the Eighteenth-Century Virginia Gentry.* Charlottesville, The University Press of Virginia, 1967.

Hazelton, John H. *The Declaration of Independence: Its History.* New York, Da Capo Press, 1970.

Hoffman, Ronald, and Peter J. Albert, eds. *Women in the Age of the American Revolution.* Charlottesville, University Press of Virginia, 1989.

Isaac, Rhys. *Worlds of Experience: Communities in Colonial Virginia.* Williamsburg, The Colonial Williamsburg Foundation, 1987.

Jameson, J. Franklin, ed. *Letters of Members of the Continental Congress* (vols. I–III). Washington, D.C., The Carnegie Institution of Washington, 1921.

Jefferson, Thomas. *Thomas Jefferson: Writings.* New York, The Library of America, 1984.

Jefferson, Thomas (Robert C. Baron, ed.). *The Garden and Farm Books of Thomas Jefferson.* Golden, Colorado, Fulcrum, 1987.

Jefferson, Thomas (James A. Bear, Jr. and Lucia C. Stanton, eds.). *Jefferson's Memorandum Books.* Princeton, Princeton University Press (manuscript).

Jefferson, Thomas (Julian P. Boyd, ed.). *The Papers of Thomas Jefferson* (vols. I–VI). Princeton, Princeton University Press, 1950.

Jefferson, Thomas (Erik Holden). *An American Christian Bible Extracted by Thomas Jefferson.* Rochester, Washington, Sovereign Press, 1982.

Jefferson, Thomas (R. de Treville Lawrence III, ed.). *Jefferson and Wine: Model of Moderation.* The Plains, Virginia, The Vinifera Wine Growers Association, Inc., 1989.

Jefferson, Thomas (Bernard Mayo, ed.). *Jefferson Himself.* Charlottesville, The University Press of Virginia, 1970.

Jefferson, Thomas (Douglas L. Wilson, ed.). *Jefferson's Literary Commonplace Book.* Princeton, New Jersey, Princeton University Press, 1989.

Ketcham, Ralph. *James Madison.* Charlottesville, University Press of Virginia, 1971.

Kimball, Marie. *Thomas Jefferson's Cook Book.* Charlottesville, The University Press of Virginia, 1976.

Langguth, A.J. *Patriots: The Men Who Started the American Revolution.* New York, Simon & Schuster, Inc., 1988.

Lehmann, Karl. *Thomas Jefferson: American Humanist.* Charlottesville, University Press of Virginia, 1985.

Lemay, J.A. Leo, ed. *Robert Bolling Woos Anne Miller: Love and Courtship in Colonial Virginia.* Charlottesville, University of Virginia Press, 1990.

Lewis, Jan. *The Pursuit of Happiness: Family and Values in Jefferson's Virginia.* Cambridge, Cambridge University Press, 1983.

Malone, Dumas. *Jefferson: The Virginian.* Boston, Little, Brown & Co., 1948.

MAPP, ALF J., JR. *The Virginia Experiment*. Lanham, Maryland, Madison Books, 1957, 1985.

MAPP, ALF J., JR. *Thomas Jefferson: A Strange Case of Mistaken Identity*. Lanham, Maryland, Madison Books, 1987.

MAPP, ALF J., JR. *Thomas Jefferson: Passionate Pilgrim*. Lanham, Maryland, Madison Books, 1991.

MATTHEWS, RICHARD K. *The Radical Politics of Thomas Jefferson*. Lawrence, Kansas, The University Press of Kansas, 1984.

MAYO, BERNARD, ED. *Thomas Jefferson and His Unknown Brother*. Charlottesville, University Press of Virginia, 1981.

McLAUGHLIN, JACK. *Jefferson and Monticello: The Biography of a Builder*. New York, Henry Hold and Company, 1988.

MELLON, JAMES, ED. *Bullwhip Days: The Slaves Remember*. New York, Weidenfeld & Nicolson, 1988.

MEYER, CLARENCE. *American Folk Medicine*. Glenwood, Illinois, Meyerbooks, 1973.

MILLER, JOHN CHESTER. *The Wolf by the Ears: Thomas Jefferson and Slavery*. New York, The Free Press, 1977.

MONTGOMERY, FLORENCE M. *Textiles in America 1650–1870*. New York, W.W. Norton & Co., 1984.

MORGAN, EDMUND S. *Virginians at Home: Family Life in the Eighteenth Century*. Williamsburg, The Colonial Williamsburg Foundation, 1952.

NICHOLS, FREDERICK D. AND JAMES A. BEAR, JR. *Monticello: A Guidebook*. Monticello, Thomas Jefferson Memorial Foundation, 1982.

PETERSON, MERRILL D., ED. *Visitors to Monticello*. Charlottesville, University Press of Virginia, 1989.

POLE, J.R. *Equality, Status, and Power in Thomas Jefferson's Virginia*. Williamsburg, The Colonial Williamsburg Foundation, 1986.

PUSEY, EDWARD BOUVERIE, TRANS. *The Confessions of Saint Augustine*. New York, Quality Paperback Book Club, 1991.

RANDALL, HENRY S. *The Life of Thomas Jefferson* (three vols.). New York, Derby & Jackson, 1858.

RANDOLPH, SARAH N. *The Domestic Life of Thomas Jefferson*. Cambridge, Massachusetts, University Press, 1939.

ROUSE, PARKE, JR. *The James: Where a Nation Began*. Richmond, Dietz Press, 1990.

SANFORD, CHARLES B. *The Religious Life of Thomas Jefferson*. Charlottesville, University Press of Virginia, 1984.

SAVITT, TODD L. *Medicine and Slavery*. Chicago, University of Illinois Press, 1978.

SCHEER, GEORGE F. AND HUGH F. RANKIN. *Rebels and Redcoats*. Cleveland, The World Publishing Company, 1957.

SCOTT, ANNE FIROR AND SUZANNE LEBSOCK. *Virginia Women: The First Two Hundred Years*. Williamsburg, The Colonial Williamsburg Foundation, 1988.

SELBY, JOHN E. *The Revolution in Virginia 1775–1783*. Williamsburg, The Colonial Williamsburg Foundation, 1988.

SHEPHERD, JACK. *The Adams Chronicles*. Boston, Little, Brown & Co., 1975.

SMITH, PAGE. *A New Age Now Begins* (two vols.). New York, Penguin Books, 1976.

SOBEL, MECHAL. *The World They Made Together: Black and White Values in Eighteenth-Century Virginia*. Princeton, Princeton University Press, 1987.

SPRUILL, JULIA CHERRY. *Women's Life & Work in the Southern Colonies*. New York, W.W. Norton & Co., 1972.

STAMPP, KENNETH M. *The Peculiar Institution: Slavery in the Ante-Bellum South.* New York, Vintage Books, 1956.

STOKESBURY, JAMES L. *A Short History of the American Revolution.* New York, William Morrow & Co. Inc., 1991.

STONE, WILLIAM L., TRANS. *Letters and Journals Relating to the War of the American Revolution, and the Capture of the German Troops at Saratoga by Mrs. General Riedesel.* Albany, Joel Munsell, 1867.

STONE, WILLIAM L., TRANS. *Memoirs, Letters, and Journals of Major General Riedesel.* New York, The New York Times and Arno Press, 1969.

TATE, THAD W. *The Negro in Eighteenth-Century Williamsburg.* Williamsburg, The Colonial Williamsburg Foundation, 1965.

TUCHMAN, BARBARA W. *The First Salute.* New York, Ballantine Books, 1989.

WAGMAN, JOHN. *On This Day in America.* New York, Gallery Books, 1990.

WARD, HARRY M. AND HAROLD E. GREER, JR. *Richmond During the Revolution 1775–1783.* Charlottesville, The University Press of Virginia, 1977.

WEIL, ANDREW, M.D. *Natural Health, Natural Medicine.* Boston, Houghton Mifflin Company, 1990.

WEISS, GAEA AND SHANDOR. *Growing & Using the Healing Herbs.* Emmaus, Pennsylvania, Rodale Press, 1985.

WHIFFEN, MARCUS. *The Eighteenth-Century Houses of Williamsburg.* Williamsburg, The Colonial Williamsburg Foundation, 1984.

WILLIAMS, GUY. *The Age of Agony.* Chicago, Academy Chicago Publishers, 1986.

WRIGHT, LOUIS B. *Tradition and the Founding Fathers.* Charlottesville, University Press of Virginia, 1975.

ZAGARRI, ROSEMARIE, ED. *David Humphreys' "Life of General Washington" with George Washington's "Remarks."* Athens and London, The University of Georgia Press, 1991.

ZINN, HOWARD. *A People's History of the United States.* New York, Harper & Row Publishers, 1980.